"Mandragora is a welcome escape from the veiled confessions of your average first novel. . . . Emily Barton knows about the moments, sometimes thrilling, often sad, when the invented and the wished-for converge—or collide—with unbending actuality."

—*The New York Observer*

"Delightful. . . . The best aspect of this well-written book is that it lends itself to debate—what is progress? Is it so important? . . . Highly recommended."

—*Library Journal*

"If we've outgrown fable the way children outgrow swing sets and fairy tales, one hopes there's still room left for a writer like Emily Barton, whose first novel reclaims the form with wit and subtlety."

—*Newsday*

"Inventive. . . . Barton's novel isn't about postmodern gamesmanship; it's a heartfelt vision of a hardscrabble Shangri-La on the verge of being hauled into the shocking light of the present."

—*Los Angeles Times*

"Barton has managed to write a novel that is simultaneously antiquated and topical, obscure and familiar, a convoluted allegory and a submerged confessional narrative. . . . The characters are genuine, and their quests for knowledge—and their fears of losing their souls in the process—will spur readers on."

—*The Village Voice*

THE TESTAMENT OF
YVES GUNDRON

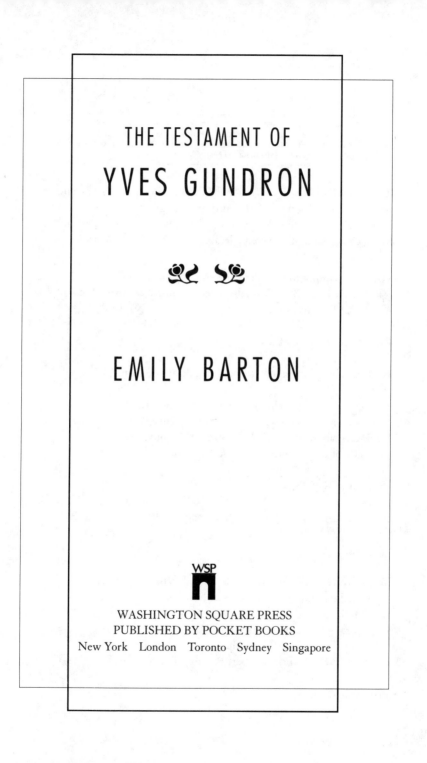

EMILY BARTON

WSP

WASHINGTON SQUARE PRESS
PUBLISHED BY POCKET BOOKS
New York   London   Toronto   Sydney   Singapore

WSP A Washington Square Press Publication of
POCKET BOOKS, a division of Simon & Schuster, Inc.
1230 Avenue of the Americas, New York, NY 10020

Copyright © 2000 by Emily Barton

Published by arrangement with Farrar, Straus & Giroux, LLC

ISBN: 0-7434-1148-X

First Washington Square Press trade paperback printing June 2001

10 9 8 7 6 5 4 3 2 1

WASHINGTON SQUARE PRESS and colophon are registered trademarks of Simon & Schuster, Inc.

Cover art by Simon Bennink (1483–1561),
"October—Ploughing," from the Salting Book of Hours,
courtesy of the Victoria & Albert Picture Library

Printed in the U.S.A.

For my father, and in memory of my mother

"Heavens! how they caught me as I left the room, the fangs of that old pain! the desire for some one not there. For whom? I did not know at first; then remembered Percival. I had not thought of him for months. Now to laugh with him, to laugh with him at Neville—that was what I wanted, to walk off arm-in-arm together laughing. But he was not there. The place was empty.

"It is strange how the dead leap out on us at street corners, or in dreams."

—Virginia Woolf, *The Waves*

THE TESTAMENT OF YVES GUNDRON,

YEOMAN FARMER OF MANDRAGORA VILLAGE,

BEING A TREATISE ON THE NATURE OF CHANGE AND ON THE COMING OF THE NEW WORLD

❧ ❧

EDITED BY RUTH BLUM

PART I

CHAPTER ONE

THE FIRST INVENTION [1]

magine the time of my grandfather's grandfather, when the darkness was newly separated from the light. Society was only a shadowy image of what it would soon become. This was Mandragora before my invention and all that it set in motion. People spoke to one another, but their habits of thought were coarse. People lived in fear. Our forefathers farmed, but with great difficulty; a man used a sharp stick to dig a hole for each seed, and furrowed his fields by dragging his fingernails through them and picking out each small stone. Often a whole spring passed in preparing the ground, and families went hungry or died come winter. They had fire, but they had no candles, nor did they have proper looms—when a woman made cloth for her household, she wound the woof through each strand of warp, and tamped down each row of weaving with her fingers. It took so long to make a bolt of cloth that growing children went about in tatters because their mothers could not keep pace. Men knew how to count and keep tally, but they had no numbers bigger than twenty. Twenty acres was the size of Mandragora's largest farm (my grandfather's, which I

---

[1] In editing this manuscript for the general readership, I have regularized Yves Gundron's spelling and punctuation—for example, by setting off reported speech in double quotation marks. In rare instances in which Gundron appeared to have misused a word, I have made the necessary corrections. All chapter and section divisions and footnotes are mine. (Ed.)

cultivate still), and twenty sheep the size of its largest flock; what need had they to reckon the infinite? Men's faculties may have been as well developed as ours, but they spent so much effort scratching their existence from the soil that they had no time for ideas or contemplation. What sufficed sufficed; and however much men might have profited from introspection, their days were full of drudgery that kept it at bay.

Such darkness persisted nigh unto the present day, and might nearly have persisted ever, had not a glimmering seed of an idea taken root in my mind and beckoned me out of the night. I wish it had been an idea of philosophical profundity, one that could explain to men where God resides or what happens to our essence after death, but it was only a workaday idea, the kind a farmer such as myself might have about his farming. Of all the events to set the process of history in motion, mine was a realization about my horse. Had I known then what terrors my invention would bring us along with its joys, perhaps I would have allowed the idea to drift off like a thousand other daydreams. I could not have envisioned myself, two winters later, spending these long nights writing in my barn, writing against what seems the inevitable outcome: that I, and all that I have wrought, will be forgotten utterly as the future gallops forth to devour us. At the time I knew nothing but the perfect beauty of what I imagined.

I have already gone ahead of myself, however, for you do not yet even know what I accomplished. Perhaps you will best come to understand the deed's magnitude by its first outward sign: because of my invention, I was able to name my horse. I called her Hammadi. My neighbor Ydlbert von Iggislau named his horse Thea. These names had weight for us beyond their intrinsic beauty, because these two work-weary horses were the first anyone had ever named. No horse before Hammadi lived long enough to need a name. It was enough that God had given us the beasts to serve us; we had never spent enough time with a single one to come to know its soul. We named our other animals—sheep and billy goats, for example, performed no labor and had fair chances of survival. My cow, who had provided me milk even before I married Adelaïda, had always been called Sophronia, and seemed worthy of such a name. We loved our horses nonetheless, as we loved our crops and loved the gentle spring. In their infancy we patted their soft ears and watched their first, faltering steps with the same fear and pride we felt in watching our own growing babes. We had little to spare, but the horses performed important duties, and we thanked them when we could with windfall apples or carrots that had gone early to rot. And in times of trouble, we prayed for our horses, sure.

But we could not risk giving a horse a name. They were subject to all manner of plagues, maladies of the tooth, hoof, and digestion, sometimes a dread illness that turned a healthy horse to a deranged beast, choking on its own frothy spittle, spewing blood from every orifice. Because God is merciful, such a horse rarely lived longer than a day. Horses died young, as all creatures die young—like hatchlings in the nest or children yet unable to speak, foals were delicate, without sense, and held always in a balance that desired to tip against them. Sometimes God spared a foal its childhood torments, and it grew to be a strong adult, suitable for work. The seasons could not turn round upon a workhorse, however; they often died in their first few months of service. Even the smallest human error could bring a horse to its knees. I hitched my third horse, a beautiful chestnut mare whose white socks I brushed down of mud each night, to a full cart of grain one August morning—a cart only slightly more full than that she had pulled the week before—and she strained too hard under the load. Before I could loose the choking strap from her neck, she stood quite dead at the edge of my farthest field, her eyes popping and her tongue aloll. Her pained and frozen visage struck terror into my heart, and I let much of the shocked wheat go to rot in the field because I dreaded to approach the dead horse. After a few days I enlisted the help of my closest companions—my brother, Mandrik le Chouchou, and my neighbor Ydlbert von Iggislau—to drag the stinking, stiffened carcass away. "Fear not," Mandrik told me, bowing his head of fine brown curls before the sight. "The multitudes depart our presence thus, but the few escape intact." Ydlbert set his hat on the ground, revealing his balding pate to the hot sun, spat in his two strong hands, and set to hacking off the edible sections and the horse's skin. I could neither think long on the commentary nor bear to watch the flaying, so I returned to our house, where we wintered in poverty and want, except for copious lots of salted horse meat.

I am not certain I have conveyed the direness of our situation. We could not produce horses fast enough to make use of them—the chances of bringing both a male and a female to healthy adulthood were few, and when they mated, the spirit often left the foal before it left its mother's womb. Horses—like even the bravest of women, my first wife, Elynour, among them, may she rest in peace—often died in giving birth, and a foal would languish on the diet of sugar and water it suckled in its mother's absence. A foal that persevered to its adulthood was prone to the aforementioned afflictions of the body; those beasts we acquired from Andras Drck, the dealer, were healthier, but often dearer than their short lives made worthwhile. Watching a horse in my barn at night, I sometimes saw in its trusting downcast eyes a premonition of the death that the weight of its suffering would surely and eventually bring. Our ancestors dreamed up a thousand spells to save them, but though a man might studiously recite his

> *Day be bright,*
> *Load be light,*
> *Bring this horse safely*
> *Back home tonight*

it only worked when the spirits were willing. When the horses did not die of their sundry natural maladies, they strangled pulling loads.

I and my countrymen desired the plight of the horses to be otherwise, but we knew no way to bring about the change except through ardent prayer, in which we engaged together each Sabbath, and in which many of us engaged alone in the dreary hours before sleep. It is by such meditation, as well as by luck, that eventually I came upon the solution, a solution so simple yet so unknown that we did not have a name by which to call it. Though human vanity convinced me that the invention was the product of my mind, I soon came to realize that I had received both a vision and a blessing; only much later did I begin to see the terrors such a blessing can wreak. That first night I gave the longest prayer of thanks I have ever found it within me to offer, and thus, with a heart full of devotion, did I learn the thing's Heaven-given name: Harness.

Before we had the harness, we would tie a piece of flaxen rope or leather thong around the neck of the beast, secure the two traces to the swingletree of the cart (which at that time had but one wheel, square in the center of the load), and hope for successful drayage. If the horse was strong and the cart half laden, the burden arrived with its bearer intact, but the more weight we placed on the cart, the more likely it would strangle the horse. God is merciful, but he does not remove weights from around the necks of beasts, and we lost many horses in this manner. We gambled accordingly on each load; if it arrived safely, then we could eat, and if ill befell it or the horse, we couldn't. The material loss was, however, only part of the grief when our horses died. Even before we dared name them, we grew accustomed to their wants and ways. When we saw their dear lips, black as night or pink as a newborn babe, grimace in pain, it cut our hearts, as it would cut your heart, in two.

One morning when the sun had not yet lifted his chin above the mountains to the east, I dreamed I was a horse dragging a cart heavy with sacks of flour. In the dream the hands of a black devil pulled the rope taut about my neck, and I knew the terrible truth of how cursed our horses felt. I awoke with a start and sat gasping for breath in my bed, holding my hand over my chest to see that my heart was still beating. I felt it working its miracle behind the bone. My wife, Adelaïda, quickly awoke beside me, her yellow braid brushing across my cheek.

"Yves," she asked, "what's wrong?"

"I dreamed the devil was choking me. I dreamed I couldn't breathe."

Adelaïda settled back into the bedclothes. "It'll be a bad season for goldenrod, then. We'll have to keep Elizaveta indoors."

But I knew in my aching heart that the dream had been a prophecy of a different kind, though none of my deceased kin had come to herald it in the usual fashion. Of a sudden it seemed quite natural that a rope should choke a horse's throat, just as the devil's hands choked mine. But, like me, the horse had a hard place above her heart, a shell to protect the most sacred part of her, and if I could bind her to the cart across that place, it would make use of that strength instead of aggravating a weakness.

The next morning, after briefly watering the near pasture and dumping the night's slops out besides, I brought my horse—nameless still—out into the yard, tethered her to the stake, and took strips of cured leather and pieces of flaxen rope from the barn. The chickens clucked in the yard, and my dog, Yoshu, bit fleas off her yellow backside, annoyed that I should pay more attention to the horse than to her. Elizaveta, a year-old infant then whose eyes had but recently gone

9

brown, rolled into the yard behind me. Adelaïda had tied the child's left ankle to the kitchen bench with a length of twine, so that she could roll only a short distance from the door. My wife stood in the doorway with her distaff, spinning and watching the child play with her doll. They were the picture of beauty in the early-morning light, both fair-haired and sturdy, Adelaïda's round face ruddy with health around her gap-toothed grin. Her long braid shone, and she rocked her round hips slightly as she spun; Elizaveta fixed her gaze on her doll with a grown woman's intensity. Thus to observe their morning activities—so different, yet so intimately tied—brought me great pleasure and renewed dedication to my project.

I watched the horse as I worked, wondering if she would give me a sign how my invention should progress. I had acquired her from the dealer three years since, and she was the best, most intelligent horse I had yet owned—not the most delicately featured, but a solid work beast, bay of hue, with a silky black mane, beautiful white feathering over her hooves, and a white star between her brown eyes that gave her a thoughtful air. She switched her tail, and wagged her head expectantly, but she could give me no advice.

With all the combined efforts of my intellect and soul, I could imagine no way to secure a strap around the horse's breastplate. Every position, it seemed, caused the thong to slip back up to her windpipe. In any position she would choke.

Adelaïda spun her flax into a long thread as fair as her heavy plait. "That doesn't seem to be working," she offered.

"I can see that."

"It's too bad the horse doesn't wear an apron, because you could tie the ends of the straps to it and that'd be that."

"A fine point, but one which I must qualify," I said, mindful that my wife's tutelage was among my duties upon this earth, "by reminding you that horses, who do no women's work, require no aprons."

"I was only remarking how much easier for you it would be if they did," she replied. "I've more wit about me than a suckling child."

I was chastened by her saying, for, either by accident or by God's grace, Adelaïda had solved the problem as she spun. The horse had no need for an apron, true, but if I provided her a tight-fitting girdle, then I could attach a strap to it across the breastbone; from this, in turn, would emanate the traces that bound it to the cart, thus distributing the weight of the load over a more solid area of the horse's body. I measured the horse's girth with a length of twine, and with another the distance about her breastplate, and retired to the barn to cut leather to those lengths. This leather I sewed to its own edge, so that it made a long, hollow shape, like entrails; and this I stuffed with straw, so that the straps could cushion the horse even further against the blow of labor. Elizaveta continued to roll about the front garden, gurgling her native song of praise. Although I shut the barn door to ensure the stillness necessary for work, I could faintly hear Adelaïda singing a song she oft sings as she works:

> *Well, I love Yves Gundron,*
> *Tell you, Lord, I do.*
> *Yes, I love my old man Yves,*
> *Yes, indeed, it's true.*
> *But the fact that he don't listen,*
> *Lord, it makes this woman sad and blue.*
>
> *Yves, he leaves me 'lone*
> *And plows his fields all day.*
> *Yes, he leaves me 'lone*
> *While he plows all day.*
> *But I wouldn't feel so lonesome*
> *If he'd just listen to what I say.*[2]

Though she intended her music as a reproach, it reminded me of my mother, who had ever a song upon her lips; it aided me in my thinking, and spurred me to complete my work. I stitched the breast strap firmly to the girding strap, so it would hold tight, and furnished the girding piece with an old iron buckle and multiple holes, so I could adjust it. The two ends of the breast strap I left long, that I might tie them to the

---

[2] Aficionados will recognize the structural similarity between some of Adelaïda's and Mandrik's songs and the blues, which otherwise do not exist in Mandragora. Many of the songs Mandrik and Adelaïda compose extemporaneously are simple ballads, as one might expect in such a community; but the blues aesthetic which marks some of the songs seems to have been brought to the village by Mandrik and Yves's grandmother (who was also Adelaïda's grandaunt), Iulia Gansevöort Gundron, the only stranger ever recorded as having visited the village before me, and widely believed to have been a silkie, or half-human spirit of the sea. All other music in Mandragora consists of devotional chants in the diatonic scale.

cart. Fashioning the device, a labor of love unlike any I had yet known, took the better part of the day, but the sun sped past in what seemed an hour.

He had not yet reached the western edge of the horizon when I brought my work out and showed it to the puzzled horse, who was nibbling the scant grass of the near pasture. The shyness of her usually forthright gaze told me that she knew her life was about to change irrevocably. When I slipped the strap around her breastbone she hung her head, anticipating the drudgery of all the many workdays that had come before. She kicked when I fastened the belt about her midsection, and again when I tightened it and adjusted the breast strap. The fit, even on that first attempt, was nearly perfect—evidence, it seemed, of God's desire for man to have this invention. Sophronia, the cow, kept chewing nonchalantly on her cud, but I knew she was watching with something more than her ordinary interest. I fitted the horse's lead about her head, and she burred in annoyance.

"Adelaïda!" I called. She appeared in the doorway, now in shadow, with the child on one hip and her distaff in the other hand. "Look at the horse!"

"What in Heaven's name have you done to her?"

"I've made an invention."

"It doesn't look kindly."

"Never mind its outward form—will you help me bring the cart?" It was not so heavy that I could not have moved it alone, but I wanted her nigh when the great event took place. She tied the child back up to the bench and rested her spindle against the door frame. Together we maneuvered the awkward cart out of the barn, and pulled it up behind the bewildered horse. I fastened the ends of the contraption to the cart, and tested their hold. The horse hung her head and looked at me askance, but when I clicked my tongue and urged her to follow me by tugging gently upon her lead, she knew the moment of reckoning had arrived, and began, hesitantly, to walk. For what seemed an eternity the traces pulled taut, and then the cart began to roll at a stately pace behind her. The horse, who still believed disaster was imminent, continued to regard me. But nothing went amiss. The cart's solid iron-clad wheel whined, bumped, and turned as it always had, but nothing pulled at the horse's throat. I put my hand upon the horse's neck to stop her.

"Adelaïda," I said. "Climb up on the cart."

She pursed her lips. "This much seems miracle enough."

"But another is about to unfold," I said, uncertain though I was. "Climb on." I prayed silently as Adelaïda hitched her skirt up, revealing her pale underskirt, and climbed up to the bed. I saw her lips moving, if not in prayer, then in a song of private devotion. Once more I clicked my tongue at the horse, and though she strained to set the cart in motion, she soon lifted her white feet high, and carried Adelaïda without apparent effort toward the southern fields. Adelaïda whooped with glee, for she had never before moved so quickly. No one had ever moved with such speed, and had I not known the cause of her rapid motion, I would surely have thought her an Arab upon a magic carpet or a witch in the Devil's thrall.

Adelaïda is by no means as heavy as a load of turnips, but she has weight enough, if not to strangle a horse, then to make her struggle in her labors. The horse, however, pulled my fair wife with ease. When at last she tired of her sport, I returned to the barn and brought forth a bale of last year's hay, Yoshu nipping at my heels. As I hoisted the hay and the dog onto the cart, both the horse and Adelaïda winced, but the added weight, nearly equal to my wife's, did not cause the horse more than a moment's pause. Finally I stopped the cart again and climbed aboard.

"Yves!" my wife cried. "You'll surely kill her." Yoshu, ready for adventure, voiced her approval of my scheme.

But I persevered. The horse looked round, wondering where her master had gone. I stood at the forward end of the cart and yelled at her to go, but she did not understand, as I was behind her. I had left her lead dangling before her, as it always had before, so I had no way to signal her to start. I reached over the edge of the cart and slapped her croup, shouting. She turned her head to recognize me, and showed by the gleam in her eye that she understood. She pulled all of us—myself, Adelaïda, the dog, and a dry bale of hay—until the sun went down. That evening I rewarded her with oats from my own provender, and with the previous year's dried apples, and scrubbed her down until she gleamed from crest to tail. Elizaveta, when we returned to the house, was completely bound up in her string, and lay with her arms pinned to her sides, blinking.

That was the night the device's Heaven-given name appeared to my inward ear. Harness would be its name henceforth until the generations expired. I was still speaking the name to myself when I rose before dawn to bring wood for Adelaïda's fire, and as I spoke it, I realized that this one simple word meant that our horse, with God's grace, would survive into her dotage. She would become a member of the family. She, too, would require a name. Again the voice spoke in my inward ear: Call the horse Hammadi. Its beautiful sound rang throughout my body and mind. Although the wood was heavy in my wood sling, I stopped at the barn. All the animals stood wide awake and expectant, and the horse looked at me skeptically, her white star shining, as she hoped for a breakfast as fine as last night's meal.

I said, "Hello, Hammadi."

She flared her nostrils and flattened her fine brown ears against her head. Perhaps this form of greeting had, in the intervening night, attained an almost human eloquence. I could practically hear her whisper, "Hello."

That day was a Saturday, one among the many. On Sundays God decreed a day of rest, but after we went dutifully to worship, and ate a solemn meal, we would return to our everyday work. We dared not tell our priest, Stanislaus, that we worked on the Sabbath—he was too young to have real experience of the world and its ways, and such an admission might have shaken his confidence. Our old priest, Father Icthyus, had fed us full up on the fear of God; but Stanislaus, thin as a reed in his dun-colored cassock, looked down his hooked nose at whatever he studied, his Adam's apple bobbing ever in confusion, and could not inspire us to the same frenzy of worship and dread. Though he was a young enough fellow, he held to his doctrines with an old man's fervor; and his unwillingness to grant pardon for our workaday follies made us hesitate to admit to him our real sins. The truth was that, whatever God had decreed, survival required a great deal of labor, and to take more than half a day of rest would have meant our demise. And as for spending one day in contemplation, for the multitudes there is nothing to contemplate beyond work; we think about it while we do it. Clerics or no, it is better to bring in the hay on a sunny Sunday than to meditate upon God's goodness and allow the hay to be ruined by an evening rain.

Sunday morning Adelaïda and I put on our good clothes, tied Elizaveta to a clean string to keep her from running wild in our lovely sanctuary of St. Perpetua, and walked to the village for services. The air was crisp and the sun bright, and I was humbled by the beauty of the mountains that lifted their heads to Heaven all around us. That day our church, with its jewel-hued murals, its clear morning light, and its great congregation of farmers, seemed truly the house of the Lord. Stanislaus's sermon was a dreary injunction against drunkenness and profanity, but all the same was I ardent in my devotions. Adelaïda looked especially beautiful that day, and when we joined together in silent prayer, I thanked God for her as well as for my new invention and my horse. My friend Ydlbert must have noticed the happiness on my face, for as we left the sanctuary he regarded me with a look of some curiosity. I held my silence as we began the walk home—Ydlbert and I together, followed by our strong wives carrying our infants, followed by four of Ydlbert's sons, who walked in a row, each holding the previous child's string. The frontmost son, whose name I could not recall, held to the back of their mother's apron, which she kept tied in a scrupulous knot. The eldest, Dirk and Bartholomew, scuffed at the dust behind them all, their dark hair hanging forward over their eyes as if they were brigands.

Ydlbert said, "Has something happened, Yves? You look different." His gray eyes were bright with expectation.

I believe I blushed from pride. I told him, "I think I invented something."

"I hope it's better than that damned thing you made with iron filings."[3]

"Indeed," Dirk said. "That was a foolish invention."

"Ydlbert," his pinch-faced Anya said, as her sons guffawed. "Not on the Sabbath."

"I call it the harness. It allows me to attach my cart to my horse without strangling her."

Ydlbert laughed, as he does, with all his soul, and with his great, firm belly heaving. "Oh, well, if that's it, congratulations."

"Ydlbert," I said, "I'm serious. When I used it to tether them together, the horse dragged me, Adelaïda, a bale of hay, and the dog without the slightest strain."

---

[3] A primitive compass Yves called a south-pointer.

"Yves," he said, poking me in my gut—which was only half so ample as his own—"save your fairy tales for bedtime."

"I'll bet you three guilders it works."

Ydlbert raised and drew together his brows. Three guilders was somewhat more money then than it is now—enough to buy a pound of fine sugar or all the cinnamon one's wife could bake with in a year. "In that case, my friend, I'll come see."

Bartholomew said, "Father, he's baiting you, sure," but without enough fire to offend.

Ydlbert lived half a mile closer to town than I did, and parted from his family at the rise that marked off his property from my own; Anya trudged down the gentle slope in the brilliant sunlight, her noisy children following behind like a family of rumple-headed ducks. Ydlbert accompanied us to our farm, and thought, no doubt, that I had prepared him an elaborate joke. Adelaïda took Elizaveta into the house, and as Ydlbert stood with his arms folded across his chest, I brought my horse, whom I could hardly grow accustomed to calling by her God-given name, Hammadi, outside. Since yesterday evening's exploits, she had begun to stand taller, and her eyes shone with knowledge of her accomplishment. The animals, out grazing in the near field, gathered round to bah and grunt with expectation. Ydlbert helped me drag the cart from the barn, and we pulled it in a wide circle to Hammadi's rear. I hitched her into her harness, which she accepted this time with joy, attached her to the cart, and repeated the previous day's successful experiment, this time with Ydlbert the skeptic in tow. When first he felt the forward motion of the cart, he crowed with joy at my invention. "You've done better than invent the wheel!" he yelled, tossing his cap into the air and revealing his comical bald spot. "What good was the wheel before we had your blessed harness to make it worthwhile!" Chornaya and Flick, the two black sheep, bahed in unison; God be praised.

My heart glowed with pride; I had brought a new, good thing into the world. I stopped Hammadi's circuit, and walked to where Ydlbert had hunkered down in the cart. With my hand on his broad shoulder I told him the dearest secret of all. "I named my horse."

He smiled, uncomprehending; his teeth were worn down from more than thirty years of good use. "What do you mean, you named her?"

I said, "She's not going to die now. I gave her a name, as we'd name any other thing."

"What name?"

"Hammadi." The name still rippled like the faint echo of bells over my ears.

Ydlbert nodded and looked at Hammadi, for the first time thinking of her by her own name. Knowing this gave me joy. "Yves," he said. "We've been friends since childhood."

"Yes."

"Please make me a harness, for my horse, also."

"With pleasure," I said.

Ydlbert continued to nod, and looked off toward his ancestors' land. "Then I name my horse Thea," he said.

"And my three guilders?"

He smiled broadly. "I'll pay you anon."

"I don't want it. Come," I said, steering him toward the barn to begin on the second harness.

By Monday morning, then, two horses in our village had names. I cannot overstate the importance of this development. In Mandragora, we do not even name our children when they first emerge from the womb; we call them "daughter" or "son" until they have lived a full year. On the first anniversary of a child's birth, we name it, for by then it has weathered the most difficult season of its life, and we can pray for the child once it has shown us the light of its soul. But in reality children, like horses, die all the time, for the strangest of reasons. Each morning as I wake, I wonder when Elizaveta will be taken from me.

What a mark of our faith, to name our horses as we would name a year-old child. Our neighbors thought we'd gone mad—except for my brother Mandrik, the one man in our village who understands more than the ordinary workings of machines and of God, the one man I defer to in judgment, however odd my countrymen think him. The villagers had not yet witnessed what the harness could do; how could we expect them to believe without any visible sign?

We grow what we need to survive—a crop of wheat, smaller crops of oats, rye, or barley in rotation, and a row of flax in the vegetable garden. My brother keeps an orchard of trees that produce many fruits of his own invention—strange, succulent things of rare colors, which require his constant gentle care and provide one of our chief pleasures. We preserve what we can for the dark days of the year. We give some to the Archduke's[4] household and bring the rest to market, where the townspeople buy the goods to feed their families.

When the horse could bear little weight, we loaded some of the fruits of the land onto our one-wheeled carts, carried the rest in our wood slings, and prayed each minute of the five-mile journey to town. Thankfully, we went to market only once a week, each of us bearing the choicest of his produce, peas, parsnips, or pears. If such a one as Gerald Desvres, who owned a great tract of meadow, had surplus hay, he would bring that to feed the town horses. Ydlbert, who is, after all, a sap, sometimes loaded his cart with wildflowers—then he could load it high, because they weigh almost nothing. His brother Yorik, who bordered the forest, sometimes brought a load of firewood. As the sun rose we began to lead our horses up the road. Mandrik has the best voice among us, clearer than the first birdsong of spring, and so he often accompanied us singing ballads of events in the times of our miraculous grandmother[5] sprung from the sea; and when we were lucky, he sang to us from the repertory of his many adventures in Indo-China.[6] Those tales, weird and fantastical, filled us with wonder and delight.

The journey to market was grueling, despite that the terrain was smooth and gently sloped. Many a man could be heard saying spells for safe drayage under his breath, especially at the crossroads. Horses always managed to slip free of their burdens—not my Hammadi, mind you, even before she had her name—or lose their shoes. And when finally we arrived at the city, we had to pass single-file through the gate and the fetid streets, which were closed to the sunlight, full of the odors of refuse and garlic. If a townswoman had hung her laundry in the street, the passing horses would knock it down, but it hardly mattered—even on the line, the linens were far from clean, and their descent to the gutter seemed, sadly, a return to their natural state. The younger sons, Ydlbert's and Desvres's especially, covered their noses in disgust. We wove between crumbling buildings until we arrived, quite

---

[4] Urbis of Nnms.

[5] The aforementioned Iulia.

[6] Mandrik reported to his countrymen that during a three-year absence he traveled to Indo-China via India and the great Silk Road.

abruptly, at the church steps, where we spread our wares. The horses and carts blocked off most access to the tight, oddly shaped apron of stone, even crammed as they were nearly atop one another, and the residents of the town always cursed us, spilling their slop buckets on us, kicking our horses in the shins as they struggled past.

The townspeople were niggardly with their pennies, but they needed everything we brought them; if we could have produced twice as much, they would gladly have bought it to feed their families. Still, in those days it might take six months before a farmer could save enough money for a new earthenware jug or a hundred well-made nails.

But that all happened in the past, which with impunity I can tell you ended on a spring Saturday, when I stumbled upon the miracle that changed our lives. On that April day the present as we know it began.

Can you imagine the changes this single innovation has already wrought? At first it merely staved off the death of my horse, which was in itself a miracle. But after I showed Ydlbert my invention that fateful Sabbath, we retired to the barn to make a harness for his Thea—a black horse, not as proud of stature as my Hammadi, but nearly her equal in intelligence, and with a similar spot upon the forehead. The next morning was Monday, and we hitched our horses to our carts, loaded them fuller than any carts had ever been loaded before, and began our walk to town on our way to the city. Before we had reached the shrine, all our countrymen were abuzz. Wido Jungfrau was shaking his balding head, his thin lips pursed in disapproval, as ever. Jude Dithyramb simply stood with his mouth agape. My brother Mandrik, who in his haste had forgotten his shoes, ran up beside Hammadi on the road and tried to look into her eyes. "Halt!" he commanded her. "I pray you, sister horse, halt!" Hammadi, who had always been obedient, quit walking. "Why do you not expire under your heavy load?"

"I made her a harness, Mandrik!" I shouted. "She bears the burden with ease!"

"Hush, my brother. I have asked your beast a question; I await her reply." Mandrik bowed his head respectfully while Hammadi flicked her face to the side twice, shooing off bugs, and worked her black lips together as if in speech. Then my brother, unshod but steady on his long, bare feet, made a slow circuit of inspection around the horse and cart, testing the strength of the harness at all its junctures. Mandrik smiled so wide he showed his strong yellow teeth down to the roots and turned up the corners of his soft blue eyes. "What a miraculous thing you have made, Yves. We must offer thanksgiving."

I bowed my head to him; since earliest childhood he had manifested his superiority in matters of the spirit. "I have offered it moment by moment since."

"But we must all thank Providence, for now that you and Brother von Iggislau have this wondrous—what did you call it?"

"A harness," I said.

"This harness is a boon, but may also sow the seeds of unrest in our midst. You must provide them for all your brethren, lest the fabric of the community be rent. And you must thank our grandmother, in case any of this was her influence."

"That old witch," said Wido Jungfrau.

"Hold, Wido," I warned him.

Ydlbert's Dirk, who hadn't eaten since breakfast and already was growing cranky, said, "Mandrik, why can't you go about shod, like other people?"

My brother, who had perhaps not yet remarked upon the nakedness of his toes, looked down.

Ydlbert swatted his son's arm. "You'll learn to respect visionaries and holy men."

He flicked his curly hair out of his eyes. "As you say, Father. I was but asking after his shoes."

Wido Jungfrau said, "I don't know why we need this thing. We always got on fine before."

"Then suit yourself," said tall Jepho Martin, nodding vigorously to his own elder brother, Heinrik, "because I want one."

Said Heinrik, with reverence, "It is one of the loveliest things I have ever beheld."

"We are all equals when we are born from our mothers' wombs and when we return to God's dark earth," said Mandrik, "and we must strive always to maintain our balance in between. To market with you, for the nonce, and Godspeed."

The two harnesses created quite a stir among the townsmen, who as a result were more willing to pay a fair price for our goods. We were all pleased with the outcome of the day. After market, then, I traveled to the edge of my northern fields with barley ale and a bunch of flowers to offer up at my grandmother's cairn. The story went that when she was a young woman, my grandmother Iulia washed up in the tide with sea vegetables and fish, naked as the day God made her, with her dark auburn hair in a salty tangle behind. Some fisherman, his name long since lost, brought her the long journey inland to our village—which I am told sits in the very center of our island, a single verdant dip in the surrounding mountains—during which time she would nor speak to him nor eat. As it happened she spoke English, but in a strange, harsh voice, which made everyone think her a changeling or at best a thing of the sea; yet old Matthias Gansevöort took pity upon the poor wretch, and accepted her into his crowded house as daughter. There she surprised him with her industrious weaving and her knack for concocting dishes more varied than porridge;[7] and soon enough, she began to compose music, bending the syntax of our tired old language to her will to make the sad, syncopated songs which eventually she passed on to my brother, and with which talent my wife was also blessed.[8] Iulia never lost her memory of the sea, nor quit telling tales of a great land beyond it, nor rid herself of the peculiar frankness of demeanor that marked her when she was first dredged up, and so was always somewhat feared among the villagers, who would not have her buried in the churchyard. There she was then, looming large above my land. I thought she would be glad for ale and flowers, though wildflowers grew all around; and I asked her to bless my invention. The next day Ydlbert and I brought our neighbors to my barn and instructed them in the manufacture of harnesses, and of long reins that we might stand in the carts behind the horses. Gerald Desvres brought a jug of fermented barley to share around the threshing floor, and recited the briefest blessing:

> *All saints! All saints! All saints, hear!*
> *Bless this measure of barley beer!*

---

[7] None of these alleged recipes has survived.

[8] *Man tell a woman lies,*
'Spect her kiss his feet.
Yes, a man tell a woman lies,
'Spect her kiss his feet.
But when Judgment Day acomin', man,
You be sorry you's so indiscreet.

It having thus been rendered safe, by nightfall our horses were all be-harnessed and our heads wobbly with liquor. We decided to meet thus every month on the new moon, if not to discuss inventions, then for the drink.

At next market, my whole village—even those I disliked—had har-nesses, and it became clear that our carts were now insufficient. Previously we had chosen among our weekly crops and loaded the carts tamely; now we loaded them to breaking with vegetables and fruits, and even then the horses, though tired, seemed little troubled by the journey. The carts needed to be different somehow, but every cart I had ever seen had been exactly like the one Hammadi now pulled; how was I to imagine a different way? One man cannot change everything in his lifetime.

My brother, however, has an ability I do not understand to see things anew; this is, he tells me, a result of his wide journeys and of his lapsing into his states, and also perhaps explains why he has such gifts in singing and in grafting new trees but no real ability to work the soil. Mandrik retreated to a high-up crook in an oak tree for a day, taking with him only a gourd full of water, a slate, and a chalk rock, and when he returned, he brought me a drawing of the new cart. It had, as no cart had before, *two* wheels, one on either side of the axle log in the middle of the cart. With two wheels for balance we could make the carts longer, wider, and able to bear more than twice as much weight. Mandrik's design, which he explained to me again and again as I cut wood and assembled the contraption with nails, also called for higher sides, to keep stray carrots from spilling over.

Mandrik and I loaded all my goods onto my new cart the next Market Day, and still it was not full; and when we drove Hammadi through our town, imagine the astonishment this new invention aroused. "Crikes," Jepho Martin said, the only man tall enough to peer well over the high sides and into the marvelous machine. "I'll give you five rounds of cheese if you'll help me and my brother make carts like this one. I can only imagine how happy it'd make old Heinrik. We could let the children sleep in them, in good weather." Within two weeks, every man in the village had a Two-Wheeled Cart to accompany his harness, and our meager incomes began to seem less bleak besides. The townspeople had surely been hungry all the years of their lives, because as much food as we brought them, they were able to eat.

But since Adam's fall it has been our lot for circumstances to try our intelligence and faith. And look you: we had been satisfied until that time, but as soon as the prospect of a better fortune became manifest, we pursued it with all our hearts and minds. Over the summer and fall we built larger, stronger carts, capable of increasing our material wealth; and their increased size did not make them unkind to our precious beasts, all of whom now bore names. When at last we perfected our new carts—when they were as big as we desired them, and as sturdy—we had had our fill of inventing. One Market Day that winter we arrived at the gates of the city as the Prime bells began to ring in the dark morning. Ydlbert was at the front of the line, leading the proud black Thea by her reins. We heard a thump, then Thea's whinnying complaint. She stamped her feet for punctuation.

"Ydlbert?" I called to him, leaving Hammadi's reins in Mandrik's idle hands. "Brother von Iggislau, what ails you?" My breath left me in a chill cloud.

Jungfrau said, "Bad news, I'll wager. It's about time the Devil caught up with us." I had lately noticed that small children kept their distance from him.

As I approached the gate, I could see only the rear of the cart, protruding. Ydlbert and his horse appeared to be already somewhere inside. The cart began to shake, and first Ydlbert's hands, then his whole head and torso appeared atop his carrots and turnips. "The blasted thing's stuck. It's stuck in the bloody gate."

Jungfrau let out a hoot, and good Ion Gansevöort hushed him. Some of the boys were giggling, though.

I said, "That can't be."

Ydlbert tumbled over the vegetables and landed solidly on the ground. "Look, then." He wiped himself clean, then blew into his hands, as he led me to the front of the cart. Indeed, the cart had caught both sides of the narrow gate. At least two hands' width of cart would not fit through.

We backed the horses up and led them to the side of the road while we conferred—the townsmen treated us bitterly when we left horses near the church, so we did not want to block their ingress and egress through the Great West Gate. It was a bitter chill, though thankfully without snow, and every moment's delay made us more impatient. We had brought our tarpaulins to cover the ground before the church; now each of us lay his on the hard ground, filled it with as many vegetables as he could hoist, and carried the load into town, just as it was in the days of our grandfathers' grandfathers, who knew not how horses could be made to do a man's labor. The Martin brothers, Heinrik and Jepho, were bent so far under the weight of their burdens that their spectacular height was reduced to that of ordinary men. The sun was well up when finally we set our goods out to market; the townsfolk quibbled over the freshness of the food, and we left with numb fingers, half our goods still in the carts, and light pockets.

A while past dark, I reached Ydlbert's home. The middle boys, who'd come with us, ran to the warm hearth; the smallest were strung up dreaming in their hammocks; and the elder two were not to be seen, though likely out lifting the skirts of Heinrik Martin's and Desvres's nubile daughters. Anya, weary-eyed, plunked bowls of porridge onto the table, then retired to her fireside chair, where she wound yarn from her distaff into a ball. At her feet an infant cat unwound yarn from another ball, but Anya worked more quickly, ensuring that the progress of the yarn was overall for the good.

"Was it a good day at market?" she asked. Her thin lips scarcely moved when she spoke, so tired was she from her days of rearing sons.

Ydlbert poured us milk from the bucket. "The new carts are too wide to fit through the city gates, and we had to carry the vegetables on our backs."

"Monkeys, all," Anya said, though we knew monkeys only from my brother's stories of abroad.

"It was dreadful, wife."

"Now you know what it's like to trudge about with seven bairns inside you," she said, and stood up to check the smaller children's placement in their hammocks.

Ydlbert ladled more porridge into our wooden bowls. "We have to do something about that gate, is all," he said.

"Cast a spell?"

"Talk to the Archduke."

When I arose the next morning at sunup, Ydlbert was crouched on my stoop, holding a baked potato, that miraculous and most nourishing food my brother so providentially brought back with him from the Beyond, for warmth. The dog eyed his provisions greedily. "For the sake of the Lord God," I said, "you can come in, man."

"No time," he said.

"We've got hot porridge, and some fine pickles."

"And no time to eat it. This matter cannot wait."

I wrapped myself up in my warmest garments, and we detoured up the side path to fetch my brother from his simple hut. We found him cutting back the dead vines in his winter arbor. Mandrik was the only man in the village besides myself and Father Stanislaus who could write, and had a fairer hand than I for drafting a petition. Besides, if nothing else, good luck followed him like the stink follows a stuffed cabbage; and he brought along his psaltery, and sang a song of his own devising to while away the walking time and to ease our restless spirits.

> *We can't fit our carts*
> *Through the city gates.*
> *No, we can't fit our carts*
> *Through the city gates.*
> *But we gone petition the Archduke*
> *Before it gets too late.*

> *Now, Ydlbert and Yves,*
> *They don't believe in what I write.*

"Yes, we do, brother," I interjected, to which Ydlbert appended, "Amen."

> *Yes, they doubt me like Thomas,*
> *They don't think I'm all right.*
> *Just wait until we reach the castle*
> *And everything's gonna be out of sight.*

Despite Mandrik's optimism, we knew we had no chance of being admitted to his Urbanity's presence. What was he to do—accept petitions from every bumpkin farmer who came urgently to seek his counsel? No, we would leave our letter, beautifully penned in fine black ink by my brother, with our humble entreaties for kindness and mercy.

The Archduke's castle stood sentinel over the southern half of the town. As we approached from the west, its crenellated towers loomed over the walls, theoretically protecting them from barbarian invaders, though, for one thing, Nnms had never been invaded, and, for another, if I were a barbarian, a place with good masonry would be my choicest choice for attack. None of us had ever been to the castle—the Archduke sent his red-liveried men around the village whenever he needed anything—though its towers were all we could see, except the steeple of the church, over the walls.

Once inside we did not turn, as was our custom, toward the sanctuary, but south, toward the Archduke's castle. As soon as we left our familiar path, however, we became disoriented. This was an ordinary occurrence in the city; the streets were so narrow and wound so tight that it was impossible to know where one stood, and since they shifted every time someone burnt down his forge or added a new room to his home, they were never the same two weeks in a row. At least in the winter the stench was less pronounced. Ordinarily I carried my south-pointer, but in the hurry to get to my brother and to town, I had forgotten it. At each turn we were thwarted by walls, laundry lines, slop piles, archways, and dark stairs rising toward invisible heights. Before long we were lost utterly. Mandrik handed Ydlbert the psaltery and turned in a slow, patient circle, snapping his middle fingers against his thumbs.

"What are you doing?" Ydlbert asked, stomping his feet in his worn shoes. Not having grown up in the same household, he had less tolerance, I suppose, for my brother's divining tricks.

> Long way to go,
> Can't see the towers from here.
> Lost our way, Lord,
> Can't see the towers from here.
> But one itty-bitty sign, Lord,
> Makes the True Pathway clear.

He stopped snapping and held his arms at his sides. Then he turned back the way we'd come, saying, "It's that way."

Ydlbert rolled his eyes. "How do you know?"

Mandrik shrugged. "Give me back my psaltery before I lose my temper."

Ydlbert handed it to him and cast me a sidelong glance.

Mandrik hummed to himself and led us down a few blind alleys, but before long brought us to the Archduke's gate, narrower than the town's, and the only opening in the sloping granite wall surrounding his demesne. The guards, identical in height and accent, and shivering in their silken livery of ruby hue, were surprisingly courteous once we showed them our petition, and they summoned us across the vast courtyard to the door.

As we had imagined, we were not to be admitted to the presence of the Archduke, but we were shown to the impatient attaché, who was clad in flowing black silks and stood tapping his narrow-toed shoes and fingering his shiny mustache. Mandrik smiled, bowed, and so charmed the attaché that, despite his nervousness, he allowed us to present the skeleton of our case aloud, and with feeling. Mandrik sang this petty functionary only a short snippet of song:

> We love the Archduke,
> He's our mainest man.
> Yes, we dig him deeply,
> He's the mainest, mainest, mainest man.
> (Skeet a deedly deedly doo doo doo-ah)
> And if he'd widen up the West Gate,
> We'd serve him the best we can.

By the end of the verse, the attaché had tears in his blue eyes, and daubed at them with a black lace-edged handkerchief before applauding my brother's song. Calling out, "Bravo! Bis! Bis!" he accepted the petition with a show of grace. I used my walking stick to draw a diagram for a wider gate on the ground, and I explained, in the best words I could muster, that, while in our interests, the new gate would also serve the town. "Oh, absolutely," said the attaché, really quite overcome with feeling. "I have never received a petition so worthy of the Archduke's attention. Rest assured that I will relay it to his Urbanity. Do take his and my warmest wishes back to your countrymen." He gave us a skin of wine to ease our journey home.

Ydlbert and I drank the wine on the road, and arrived at Mandrik's hut stone-drunk. All three of us slept around the fire on his bare dirt floor, but when Ydlbert and I returned to our families in the morning, we were more flush with the good news than with the morning chill and the previous night's debauchery.

The next Market Day, when we headed back with our awkward

carts and our tarpaulins, we saw hazy dark smoke on the horizon; it was clear, even from a distance, that something was afire. When we reached the city, we saw that the gate had been widened by twice the length of a man's arm. The squalid row of tenements which had previously intervened between the gate and the church square had fallen into heaps, razed. Two old men with buckets were dumping dirt on some of the smoldering remains, and three or four bands of children climbed and slid in the rubble, searching for spoons and bits of colored tile and glass. One woman picked dourly through the remains of what once had surely been her hovel, clutching a wailing infant to her breast. This part of the city had never before seen the full light of day, and suddenly it was flooded with light, as healthful and clean as one of our own fields; and yet to see this misery exposed seemed untoward, as if we should avert our eyes. But we could not avert them. "Looks like something's happened," said Ydlbert's brother, Yorik, who had perhaps never been the brightest star in Mandragora's firmament. Ydlbert slapped him, but it seemed in jest.

We processed through to the center of town, and there set up shop around the kettle fires the townsmen had lit. Around us they walked with their hands shielding their eyes, both from the smoke and from the uncustomary brightness in the square. Even the space before the church was clearer now—the Archduke had, without our prompting, razed the filthiest habitations, so that we could display our produce in better view. The next week, aware of how much space had gone unused, we brought even more of our goods to sell, and the week after that, some of the local tradesmen began bringing their wares, to take advantage of the milling people and the light. A potter sold jars and crockery; the tanner draped hides over a sawhorse; the smith stood at one corner of the empty space, calling for horses to be shod. Each week the market grew bigger, and each week more debris was removed, until finally, that spring, there was a fine, clear path to the sanctuary, a processional wide and grand enough for princes and kings. The road within the city gates was surfaced with broad, flat stones, smooth underfoot and to the carts' wheels. "It's Paving," Mandrik told me, the first time we drove our wary horses over them. "I have seen it in Indo-China, though there it was all of hammered brass, making the roads sparkle brighter than a courtesan's eyes." I had never seen a courtesan nor heard of paving—I knew only that what I saw was beautiful. But

Mandrik knew that something momentous had happened, even if I did not have the knowledge to understand his explanation fully.

Each week we brought more and more of our crop to market, until it seemed our land could no longer stand the burden of such production. That spring was balmy, with soft rains and a strong sun, but we dripped our sweat into the ground every hour of the daylight, and still could not sate the townspeople or exhaust our soil. One day as I worked on my farthest strip—near my grandmother's cairn—wishing I were my brother that I might have a song to sing, bathed in sweat, toiling in the heat of the midday sun, pulling a wooden plow so old and worn that I would soon need to replace its coulter and share, the next great thought insinuated itself into my mind like a whisper: *Hammadi could pull the plow for me, and I could simply walk behind, to guide it. Hammadi could pull a much bigger plow than can I.*

I gave up the rest of the day to tinkering, and by nightfall had constructed a new harness for plowing; the next day I attached handles to the plow so that I could guide it from behind. Ydlbert stopped over the next morning—from his adjacent strip he had seen me leave mine two days since, and wanted to make certain I had not taken ill. I led him to my barn, hitched up Hammadi, and set her to work. She performed the work of three farmers with only a fraction of the effort and none of the grumbling. Ydlbert shook his broad, balding head, and crouched down as if exhausted in the good dirt that marked the border between our two fields. "Yves," he said, "think of it. Think what you've done. The horses will do all the work—we'll finish at noon and lie about the rest of the day."

I followed Hammadi to the end of the row. She wasn't going straight, exactly, but she pulled the plow with ease; I could certainly make it larger. I then returned to my friend and sat down in the dirt beside him, and we talked of the idyllic life to come. Ydlbert was right— we would have time now to patch the holes in our roofs and our children's shoes, to dig wells, perhaps even to help our wives tend the herb gardens and spin wool. Ydlbert wanted to go to the glassmaker to learn to blow vessels. All my life Mandrik had pestered me to write down tales, but I had never the time nor the inclination, particularly as he was no help with quotidian labors. Now, who knew what I might find time for? I did not know then that I would find myself writing this history, but I knew that my world had changed such that something might get written. Hammadi stood gently munching the grass at the end of the row, for she did not know to turn around and work the next piece of land. It hardly mattered. She could be trained.

I admit that at this moment a small stone of doubt lodged in the bottom of my stomach, for I realized that this vast plot—these twenty acres, as big as any plot of land had ever needed to be—this land to which my father and his forebears had given their lives dutifully and without complaint, these strips of land they had leveled stone by stone and tended until they were among the finest in the valley, would no longer suffice.

The harness in its various forms has changed our lives in many ways for the better. We grow more food than our families can eat, more than we can sell to the town. Our soil is rich, and our farming advanced—each generation has made some improvement in the methods of husbandry, but none so remarkable as ours. We have money as we never did before, and our city, which was a stinking gutter, now glitters like the stars in the great dome of the sky. That first paved path was only the beginning—now the city has long, wide roads stretching toward the four cardinal points of the horizon, all paved in gray stones, so that even Andras Drck, the horse dealer at the far northern edge of town, is as easy to reach as my nearest neighbors. Suddenly, where there once was squalor, there is light, air, and free passage. The Archduke soon issued an edict to name these paved passageways as one would name a child or a place—they won't be knocked down, these paths, they won't shift with the rain. The roads will then be like our horses—once so temporary we hardly thought about them, they will now endure.

Finding our way in the city is different with these roads. In my youth we navigated as do, my brother says, the sailors at sea—we fixed the positions of the sun, towers, and steeple, and hoped to find our destination. Later we had my south-pointer, but it told only if one was facing south. Going anywhere in town was trouble—it made the breath come short and the eyes sting. Now everything is flooded with light, and we go straight from one place to another, knowing our location at all the places in between. The city is half as large as once I thought. It only took so long to get anywhere because one had to circumvent so many buildings, gardens, and walls.

I have built already a storeroom onto my home, and rethatched the roof, and I would like to buy a second cow next spring. I bought Adelaïda eight yards of pale blue linen, like a noblewoman's, and a vast array of spices. Because of one invention, the city, my city, is outgrowing its walls.

All of this change is wondrous, no doubt; and yet I must admit that when I invented the harness, I did not imagine that it would bring hardship along with all this bounty. I did not know that the whole world would change when I made Hammadi her first harness. I did not know that I might someday want the old world, or some of its ways, back.

If this one tiny bit of human ingenuity, the contribution of a man with no title, hardly a name—if so little can change so much, then I fear for our future. I fear the things our children will know, the things of which we can only dream. My prayer, my ardent prayer, is that we are moving forward, and toward the path of God.

CHAPTER TWO

THE ARRIVAL

 ur ancestors crossed the great body of water that lies between Scotland[1] and ourselves in paper boats sealed with pine sap and loaded nearly to sinking with "figs" and "pomegranates." They had not got these fruits in Scotland, but in the Great Land across the water they had left generations before. Lack of these fruits was one of our ancestors' greatest fears for this then-uncharted land, and with good reason: as their ballads record, our soil is too rocky and our winters too cold for anything so soft and sweet to grow here. I have seen drawings of their cherished fruits and of their boats. My brother, the only man among us who has braved the bare horizon and felt the salt lapping of the waves, made such a boat for his wanderings, and reports that he found it comfortable. Countless generations ago we crossed the cold water in order to escape persecution at the hands of in-

---

[1] I asked Yves how he knew of Scotland, when he had not only never left the island but never left the valley of Mandragora to see the sea. "Do you know the name of your grandmother's grandmother?" he asked me.

I shrugged my shoulders; I knew it vaguely.

"Exactly so do I know my people's origin."

"But don't you ever wonder," I asked, "what it's like there? Don't you dream of going back to see where they came from?"

His habitual good will lighted up his clear, gray, sun-wrinkled eyes. "To a land from which they barely escaped with their lives? You're crazy, woman. I'm glad they got out."

fidel prelates who denied the tripartite unity of God, and who murdered all who attested it. Our grandfathers' grandfathers found this country welcoming enough after the hardships they had suffered—neither too green nor too barren, excellent for the cultivation of grains and sheep, and secluded from the prying eyes of strangers. Here they settled into their old ways, and we have never found reason to wander hence. We know our mountains to the east, our mountains to the west, our mountains to the north, and our mountains to the south, and none of us, save Mandrik, has sought what lies beyond. Indeed, before he set off on his wanderings, the only contact anyone knew of with the world beyond Nnms was my grandmother's arrival from the depths of the far-distant sea.

Then, two years to the day after the advent of my wonderful invention, the stranger came up out of the east.

My harness had changed Mandragora, the appearance of our environs, and the lives of the people, so much for the better that Father Stanislaus (who seemed well-nigh young enough to tag after his mother on a string) had declared it a holiday, Di Hammadi, which we celebrated in the grove adjoining Desvres's meadow, from which we could see the distant towers of Nnms.

On that second Di Hammadi, the village children danced about a Maypole decorated with the binding straps of worn harnesses. We adults danced with abandon around the children, for we were intoxicated with the fermented fruits of our orchards and fields, and had been eating the foods beloved of our horses: sugar, carrots, and oats. In addition, of course, we had roasted two pigs and a dozen hens, and brought forth the last of the previous summer's pickled vegetables. Mandrik shared with the company his first fruits, hard green plums and peaches just begun to ripen, on which the children feasted. We were all dressed in our best clothes, the women with ribbons in their hair. We sang songs of great praise and of great ribaldry. (Dirk von Iggislau, too young yet to know his way with the hops, grabbed red-haired Prugne Martin's arm and burst into an impassioned rendition of "I'll Harness you, baby, if you'll pull my Plow." Her ripe breast heaved with laughter.) It was the first warm day of April. The crocuses had thrust their blue and yellow heads through the black earth, and the trees in the tepid sunshine were ablush with blossoms and new leaves. I had just finished shearing my sheep and sowing my rye and summer wheat, and was sufficiently spent with the labor to enjoy the festival air completely. My vision grew slow with young beer, but kept circling dazedly around the fair, plump figure of my wife. She was arrayed in her best dress of pale blue linen, which reflected both the heavens and her eyes, and wore the necklace of milky green jades Mandrik had brought back from the Orient and given to my first wife, God rest her soul. Each time Adelaïda smiled I fixed on the fetching gap between her front teeth, and my tongue desired to probe the space therebehind. After perhaps an hour of coveting her thus, I steered my woozy gait toward her and pulled her by the hand out of the dance. What matter if our neighbors saw us wander off? I had made them a holiday, and they, too, had imbibed the hops' succor. Furthermore, it had been three years since we'd had Elizaveta, and but one bairn had been born to the parish since Advent—a boy child, Tansy Gansevöort's—so none could fault us for our endeavor.

I led my wife out into the East Meadow, whose long grass lay parched and flattened under the clear, glistening remains of the snow. As we left the grove, we passed Wido Jungfrau lazily watering Desvres's field with his back to the crowd. "Hail, Yves," he called out, and I called back, laughing, "Hail." Just as we came clear of the villagers' view, we saw, clad all in black and stomping among the puddles, the strangest woman I had ever beheld.

"Oh, excuse me. Wow. Hello," she said, looking up and down my wife and myself. "Am I glad to see you." She was tall—a hand taller than I—with short black hair curling wanton and loose only to her shoulders. Her eyes also were black, and her pale skin ruddy from sun and wind. Her smile was broad and immodest, revealing a shock of teeth as white and regular as the pearls on the cover of Father Stanislaus's Missal. She wore a woolly black shirt unlike any I had ever seen, and some manner of men's black trousers so slender that I could see each curve of her hips, thighs, and calves, and promptly looked away from all three. Most peculiar of all was the tumor that grew from her back, all reds and purples like raucous spring flowers, and sprouting everywhere shiny protuberances and black tendrils. I tried also to avert my eyes from this abomination, but it drew them thither with its terrible countenance. Now I knew what the people of my grandfather's generation must have thought when my tall, curl-bedecked grandmother appeared among them. "You have no idea—I've been wandering, literally, for days now. I've been looking for a certain, for a village, but I lost my compass. I thought it would be the end of me." Though she spoke English, her accent was broad and flat, and cut through the air like the ploughshare through the sod.

I could think of nothing to say, and noticed that Adelaïda had pulled herself ever so slightly behind me.

"Thank you so much for finding me. Where are we?"

I realized that my grandmother might have excited similar disgust—and that the tones of her voice might have rankled so—and tried to keep down my temper and fear. "The Great East Meadow past Gerald Desvres's field. Everyone's in the grove for a celebration."

She looked about slowly. "And what town are we in?"

"This is the village of Mandragora."

She stopped still. "Mandragora?"

"That is this hamlet's name. Yes." I felt my wife disappear entirely behind me.

Her sharp eyes grew somewhat red. "And what's Mandragora near?"

"Only these mountains, and the city of Nnms."

"Neem?"

"Nnms," I repeated, exaggerating the friction between tongue and teeth.

The stranger turned in a patient, meditative circle, then cast her eye less greedily upon us. "I can't believe it."

"What?"

"I'm here. I found you."

Perhaps in her wandering she had fallen prey to sun madness, which would explain her wild countenance. "Where did you come from?"

"From Boston. I'm Ruth Blum, by the way." She extended her white, bony hand toward me.

Such intimacy had only ever been afforded me by my wife, and the sight of the hand approaching brought blood to my face. Still, the customs of her country were, as evidenced by her attire, quite different from ours, and her gesture of friendship, despite my native mistrust of strangers come out of the hills, struck my heart. "I'm Yves Gundron, of the third farm past the village." I could imagine what I looked like to this creature—a solid farmer, a hand shorter than she and bruised by decades of wind and rain, my brown locks in need of a trimming and my shy, buxom wife half hidden behind.

"A great inventor," Adelaïda, still behind me, stammered.

"And my wife, Adelaïda."

"What kinds of things do you invent, Mr. Gundron?"

My wife said, "Wonders, absolute miracles, all."

"I have improved upon our farm implements. You may call me Yves. Where is it you say you're from?"

Adelaïda whispered, "The sea, sure. Look how she resembles the paintings of your grandmother."

I held a finger up to her. Ruth's face was singularly elastic, and quickly recomposed itself into a half grin that, at its wavering edges, conveyed sadness or confusion. "Boston. I imagine you've never heard of it."

"My brother, Mandrik le Chouchou, is the only man among us who has left the village. He has traveled the world, and never mentioned such a place."

Her dread tumor creaked and shifted, despite which she let out a sweet, musical laugh. "People say it's not much of a city, anyway."

I asked, "What is it like there?" Because surely it wasn't like here, if she went about dressed that way.

She looked Heavenward for an answer, as if Boston were spread like the stars across the great sky. "I'm not sure what to tell you, or where to begin. I'm not sure what's the right thing to say."

"Tell us how things are, and don't fret about the consequences."

She nodded, never taking her eyes from us as she thought. "I'll see if I can explain. It's not like it is here. It's a large city, equipped with all the modern conveniences, and with a number of universities, which is how my family ended up there. There are lots of young people, though it's conservative in some ways, too." She stopped to regard us, and quieted her tone. "None of which means anything to you, does it?"

"Not a word," I solemnly agreed.

"I'm sorry. I'll try to think of a better way to explain."

Adelaïda, still from behind, whispered, "Does she speak English?"

"I think so, though I cannot follow all her meaning."

"I'm sorry," she said. "Will you stop me, when I'm not clear? I want to be clear."

"There's no need to be sorry. You are welcome here, even if we don't understand you." I fervently hoped that the emotion thus expressed would follow its expression. "The village is on holiday today, in celebration of one of my inventions. Will you come with us for sustenance and barley ale?"

I think her mood picked up at the mention of the ale, for she thrust her chest forward and resettled the gruesome tumor on her back. "Sounds great, thanks."

Our idyll trounced, my wife and I joined hands and led the stranger back to the clearing in the grove, wherein our neighbors made merry. Perhaps, I reasoned, her oddity was purely one of form, and once we grew used to it we would like her. I hoped this would be so, for I did not like the discomfort she then elicited. I also hoped that discovering her on the day of my festival might be an auspicious sign, despite the cold tremor which tickled my spine when I thought of her tall, strong body clomping through the field behind me.

"How many are you, in the village?" she asked.

"But a few score, counting beasts and babes."

"All born and raised here?"

"All, aye."

She walked silent a few paces, then added, "But you say your brother's been all over the world?"

"To the Orient."

Children were still dancing at the Maypole, but the elder boys, Ydlbert's among them, had wrested the straps from the tots, and were now jumping and spinning like heathens. Prugne, her freckled bosom half bared to the breezes, spun about like a top, calling joyfully to the skies. To appease the small ones, Mandrik had hitched a cart to Hammadi, who was festooned in garlands of white flowers and anointed with oils, and drove the children about like so many bushels of potatoes. Their small heads, russet- and flaxen-haired, peeked above the high walls of the cart, blissfully accepting the warmth of the April sunshine and the coolness of the breeze.

"They're having a Renaissance fair, only they're not," Ruth whispered, unintelligibly, behind me.

For a moment I hoped that our arrival would go as unnoticed in the general tumult as our departure surely had but a while before, but a dark, brooding hush soon spread about me like falling snow. The cart ground creaking to a halt, bumping up against Hammadi before it stopped, and my horse stood facing me, her brown head high, her star shining watchfully forward. Soon the whole square was silent but for the wailing of Tansy Gansevöort's new bairn and the humming of one lone locust, come up too soon from the thawing earth and destined to die.

Miller Freund, his hat perched all the way back on his head, muttered, "Leave it to Gundron to bring such a strange thing home."

"Friends," I addressed the assembly, "for the first time in two generations, we have a visitor in our midst. She calls herself Ruth Blum, and speaks English. Do not be frightened. She did wander days and nights in the wilderness before she appeared to me and my wife but a stone's throw from this grove."

"What were you doing over there, hm?" Dirk questioned, then stuck the tip of his tongue salaciously through his teeth.

Anya slapped him, and his brother Bartholomew cheered.

Father Stanislaus rubbed the back of his long neck nervously with one hand. "Looks like a sea-thing."

Wido Jungfrau, who had been known to see the doings of evil spirits in a measure of spoiled milk, took his pipe out of his mouth long enough to say, "Looks like the Devil's work to me."

Yorik said, "Nay, in the pictures devils have tails and claws."

"You never know what's beneath the clothes."

"On the contrary, I think I can see it right clear."

Bartholomew whistled and his younger brothers whooped their praise.

"She may, gentlemen, be no emissary of darkness, but an angel come to reside among us; or, as I think most likely, an ordinary person, come from far off. Who can say? Whatever her purpose, she is as solid of form as you and I." To demonstrate I leaned my hand against her arm, and she swayed slightly under the weight of her tumor.

Dirk, between two bites of bread sopped in ale, said, "Gundron, I can see everything about her legs." The boys erupted all around in laughter. One added, "They're prettier than my mum's."

"Silence," commanded my brother as he approached. The new white robe my wife had stitched him for the occasion shone with its own heat. By now our stranger had begun to hump her back into the terrible growth, weary with its weight or with shame. "I am Mandrik le

Chouchou," he said, inclining his head of clean, soft curls toward her. "Who are you?"

"Ruth Blum," she said, her voice drawn in small. She was only a bit taller than he was, but had to turn her worried face modestly down to look him in the eye. If I looked strange to her, imagine what a sight was he—his hair as long as hers, his blue eyes glimmering with the light of divine knowledge, his white robe bright as the sun.

"And the city of your birth?"

"Boston, Massachusetts. Cambridge, actually, if you know Cambridge. Across the river. Your brother said you had traveled."

In the murmuring that followed after her voice died down, my brother bowed three times, then stood with his hands in prayer, eyes closed. All the village waited for his words. "I have heard," he whispered finally, "of your city. I am most pleased to meet you."

Had night fallen in a rush right then, mid-afternoon, no greater silence could have damped the festive air. The darkness spread her fingers into our throats and hearts.

Even the stranger shivered at his pronouncement. "I'm glad to meet you, too. And, well. I'm so glad to be in Mandragora." She looked nervously around. "I had heard a rumor[2] that your village might be here. I was hoping to find you, praying, actually, but I got lost. You're not on the map." She fidgeted back and forth on her feet like a young girl, though by the lines around her eyes I guessed her to be my own age.

"May I see your map?" my brother asked.

---

[2]"I wasn't always your mother," my mother told me in the kitchen, when I was eight, and could not grasp that she had ever been my size. "I was a little girl once, and later a young woman."

"Were you beautiful?" I asked, because that mattered to me. As did blondness, which no member of our clan had ever achieved.

"Beautiful enough. And very free. The summer that I graduated from college, I traveled all over Europe by myself, slept under trees, drank wine at the feet of fountains, you name it. I dreamed of becoming an anthropologist. I was going to spend my whole life sleeping in huts in small villages." She went on with what she was doing to the vegetables.

"Why didn't you?"

She shrugged her shoulders. "I married your father, and then I had Nurit and you and the baby."

I was glad she hadn't become an anthropologist, but the word began to hold its sway over my imagination. "What was your favorite place?"

She sighed as she thought about it—Esther Blum's singular sigh, which never conveyed disappointment or disapprobation, a sweet sigh. "When I went to the Scottish countryside, I never wanted to come home. The hills rolled like the sea, and there were beautiful old forests, huge billowy clouds in the sky, old stone fences around the farms. I never was happier anywhere in my life."

"I'm not sure that's—"

"Beware her trickeries," said Stanislaus, clearing his throat. "They may be vile."

"Stanislaus," Mandrik interjected, "she hasn't done one frightening thing. Why not trust her?"

"Come up out of who knows where, and so strangely clad? I do not know if she means well or ill—only that we should be cautious until we are sure."

"When my grandmother arrived," my brother added, "she, too, was accused of strangeness, yet died a well-respected woman."

Jungfrau snorted. "In your family, any kind of freak can be respected."

"Perhaps you'd best feed her," said Prugne Martin. "She looks a sight too thin."

But already Ruth was working at a strap across her chest, and when it sprung, it released the awful tumor to the ground with a resounding thud. Bartholomew said, "Mercy." The crowd instinctively recoiled, but as a gasp escaped me my heart also rejoiced to see the long, gentle curve of her back reaching over the apparatus. Her black shirt fit snugly, and I saw the sweet bumps of an ordinary, bending spine.

"What do you call this?" Adelaïda asked, leaving my side to point one hesitant finger toward what had, a moment before, seemed too dreadful to name.

"My backpack."

Adelaïda half frowned and sat down at a safe distance from her on

---

"Why?"

She put her work down and came to sit with me at the table. "Something about the landscape, how somber it was in its beauty. I felt at home." Even in the glare of the overhead lamp she looked rosy. "You'll understand someday."

"I feel at home here."

"Then you're lucky." She gathered both my hands into hers. "There were tales, Ruthelah, of people on one of the islands off the coast living a very simple life—people without electricity, without anything modern, simply working the land, as people always have. I chartered a boat for a day—all I could afford back then—and I went looking for the mythical village of Mandragora, tucked like an egg into the middle of a nest of mountains, but perhaps it's no surprise I didn't find it. I've never heard anything else about it, so I guess it was a fairy tale."

"It's too bad," I said.

"Yes, it is."

"I'll find it for you," I told her.

She raised her dark eyebrows at me. I could not wait to be older, and to be taken seriously. "You do that, Ruthelah. You'll make me so happy."

She went back to making dinner, but as you can see, I filed it, more or less, verbatim.

the grass. Anya, from the back of the crowd, called, "Be careful, Adelaïda." What a difference between the figure of my wife and that of the stranger—the one plump, golden, full of sweetness, the other dark and hard, despite her odd beauty, as the Reaper at his grim work.

Ruth worked open a fastener that made a strangely bright sound. Adelaïda startled slightly and drew farther away. Ruth, too, startled, and said, with a shy smile, "It's only a zipper." She worked it open and shut a few times. It sang.

An amazing array of objects left the sack—more slender pants, balls of woolly fabric, and many items wrapped in small parcels with a luminous sheen.

Adelaïda sang:

> *Oh, the stranger came bearing her Backpack,*
> *'Twas the strangest sight I'd ever seen—*

"Silence, sister, I pray you," Mandrik urged her. He bent down reverently to touch a shiny package, his knees creaking though there was no sign of rain.

"That's a Baggie," Ruth said, "with granola."

He leaned closer toward her, a gentle expression upon his lips. "You needn't tell me the names of things."

"Adelaïda," she said, pronouncing it strangely, "asked me what the backpack was."

"I am not Adelaïda."

She colored slightly. "I can see that."

"He's like an anchorite," Ydlbert offered, "only not locked up."

"More like a freak, if you ask me," Jungfrau interjected.

"I wouldn't be wise with the holy man," I warned him.

"What's the difference between a holy man and a freak?"

"If I knock out your teeth, will that help you understand? Oh, but I forget me, you don't have any teeth."

Mandrik clicked his tongue against the roof of his mouth. His cheeks were flushed. "Do you know nothing, Yves?" he called back to me over his shoulder. "As our sainted father would have told you, wasted breath is wasted breath, and a fool's a fool."

Ruth extracted a tightly folded paper and held it a moment in her hands. "I'm not sure I should show you this."

Stanislaus said, "What do you seek to conceal from us?"

"Nothing, I—"

"For nothing is hidden from the eyes of the Lord."

She paused, then opened her paper to an absurd breadth, which revealed blues, greens, and browns as vivid as any in God's creation, and the names of fairy places in an even, minuscule hand. The crowd drew closer, pulled by its beauty as it fluttered in the ripening breeze. "Look. Here's your island." She tapped unceremoniously at the paper's edge. "Here are the mountains, so somewhere in here must be your valley. And nothing."

Mandrik and Stanislaus knelt over the map, drawing it in with their eyes. "This map is beautiful," said Stanislaus, "but it is entirely wrong."

"No," Mandrik said, "not entirely."

"Wrong about everything," he persisted.

"At all events," my brother concluded, "it is incomplete, and must be removed from public sight."

"Is that," I asked, "the sea?"

"And that," Ydlbert said, pointing at a blob ten times greater than the one on which Ruth claimed we lived, "is that Scotland?"

Mandrik pushed us ever so slightly away. "I will not have you worry about these pictures. As I said, they are not complete."

Ruth said, "Should I not have shown you the map? You demanded to see it."

"What is incomplete," said the priest, gathering what little pluck he had, "about a map which shows nothing of what is and a copious lot of what isn't?" How we all missed old Father Icthyus.

"Forgive me, Father," Mandrik said, with a slight bow of the head. "It was not my understanding that you had ever left this village."

Two of Ydlbert's younger sons, Manfred and Jowl, pounced on the map and ran with it crackling in the wind behind them to the Maypole. "Lords of the map!" one cried, pleased to be in possession of the prize. The other children followed to view the wonder. Another of Ydlbert's sons cried, "All hail the Archduke Mappamondo!"[3]

My brother remained at the stranger's feet. "Just as well," he said, watching the fluttering object go.

---

[3] The father of the current Archduke, Urbis of Nnms; an amateur cartographer and legendary rake.

Ruth leaned down toward him, saying, "I'll probably need that back, eventually."

"All things go to their appointed homes, by and by."

Adelaïda, peering into the stranger's eyes, said, "Prugne's right, we should feed her. We are being most inhospitable."

"Do you like oats?" Anya asked. "Because oats is what we're eating."

Ydlbert nudged Anya gently. "Bring her cheese and fruit."

"Bring her meat," Mandrik commanded. "She clearly requires sustenance."

Anya hoisted her smallest child, whose name I also could never recall, in its sling, and went off muttering, "Crank."

"Sheep fucker!" came the shrill voice of Friedl Vox, who had yet avoided the gathering, over the assembly. Her aged, disheveled form lumbered into view, and Ruth took a step back. "You can't hide your sins before God!" Stanislaus blushed past his ears, because it was always him to whom she referred thus.

"Hello, Friedl," he said.

The outlying villagers moved aside to let her stench pass.

"Death is coming to take you all—sooner or later, he comes! And you stand around listening to this cattle molester, listening to his blasphemy and lies. Look what this stranger brings with her—pestilence and death!"

Friedl Dithyramb was the oldest person in our village—past fourscore years if popular memory served—and had, in her time, borne six children to her husband. All but one had been taken by the same influenza that snatched my family from me nearly whole; her one remaining son, Jude, farmed quietly at the outskirts of town, but had never been able to marry because of her madness, and had therefore banished her from his house. Friedl had lived, then, in a dirt hut by the church as long as I could remember. When first my voice began to deepen its pitch, Friedl ceased to care for her widow's weeds, until finally they hung about her, tattered and faded, dark gray. Then did she cease to wash, and her white hair hung about her body in fearsome snarls. Her right eye remained clear and blue, but the left, long since blind, turned upward until it shone like a boiled egg. She began to wander the countryside night and day, screaming maledictions and talking in tongues, and she no longer responded to ordinary gestures of kindness. Our spiritual leader then was Father Icthyus, himself quite aged, and one May he followed her about for two nights and two days, regaling her with questions and heaping prayers upon her. Come the third forenoon he grabbed her by the shoulders and shouted, "Friedl! Do you not remember who you are?" To which she replied, her voice crabbed and choked, "Vox Clamantis in Deserto!" Since that time my countrymen had called her Vox, and though they grumbled at the ever-inventive foulness of her tongue, they put out stale crusts when they heard her sharp cries coming up the lane. Some said her bad eye was the sure sign of the Devil's mark upon her, but my brother spoke differently. "Rather," said he, "has it turned to look inward—a skill the rest of us most sorely lack."

"What is this harlotry?" she shrieked, one bony finger imagining it traced the wild line of Ruth's hair. "Iulia Gansevöort, back from the grave? Do you accept a stranger amongst you?"

"It is a stranger," Mandrik replied, "but not the one you think."

"How could I forget the sea's stench upon her, cursed witch? Banish! Banish! Why do you accept this vileness?"

"Because she's our first visitor," I said. "Our first since my grandmother's time."

"And it seems our duty as Christians," said Stanislaus, "to treat her charitably, at least until she proves her thralldom to Darkness."

"Please," Ruth said. "I wouldn't hurt you." Her face did not remain composed.

Mandrik placed himself between her and Friedl's pointing. "Friedl, haven't you anyone else to curse today?"

"You think it's easy, don't you?"

Jude, as always, gave up hiding behind his neighbors and went forth to claim what once had been his mother. "Come on then, Mum," he said. "I'll give you a pudding if you'll quit it."

"Ever trying to distract me from the work of God with baubles and fruits."

"Aye," he said.

She looked at the ground, then cried:

> *Iulia Gansevöort, come from the sea,*
> *Spare us your tricks, my poor family and me!*

"Stop it, Mum. Iulia Gansevöort's safe under her cairn."

She sighed and followed him off, holding loosely to his sleeve as if it might be diseased.

Mandrik turned back to our visitor. "You'll forgive us, I hope, the peculiarities of some of our neighbors. Particularly Friedl Vox."

Ruth arched her mobile eyebrows, but did not otherwise reply.

"This is a great day for my village," said Mandrik. "On all our behalf, I extend my warm welcome."

"Thank you."

"Provided," Stanislaus interjected, his voice cracking, "you do not prove, as Friedl suggests, demonic in nature."

"And," my Uncle Frith added, his barley ale dripping into his beard, "that someone cover her naked body from sight."

Stanislaus said, "We'll keep our watch upon her, aye."

"I'm not a spirit." She looked down at herself. "And please excuse my clothes. I dressed for the hike; I wasn't really thinking whom I might offend once I got here. I'll try to do something about it. I promise you, though, I'm not naked." No one would be the one to tell her she was wrong, so we scratched our ears, swallowed, and looked around. Stanislaus, against his nature, and as it seemed against his will, recovered enough to bow to her, his Adam's apple bobbing. Ruth bestowed upon him a frank smile such as none of his parishioners ever offered him. He must have been disarmed, for his wan face glowed with pleasure. When she turned to Mandrik, he also bowed, and smiled at her warmly. "It will be," he said, "such a pleasure to talk to you."

She nodded. "And a pleasure to talk to you." When Anya returned with chicken legs and bread, Ruth sat down cross-legged in the grass and ate with her hands as gracefully as another might eat with his spoon at table. Mandrik seemed pleased at her hearty appetite, and sat down with her to discuss whatever were their topics. The crowd dispersed to more frenzied merrymaking; I left my brother and this stranger in peaceful communion over their black bread. As I walked off, fear rose, unbidden, in my throat. I tried to swallow it or shoo it off, but it would not go. Behind me I heard my wife singing:

Oh, our stranger she knows
She looks strange in her clothes—

With that Backpack upon her
And Zippers that gleam—
Yet she seems to be kind
And to own a good mind,
And our menfolk do find her
As fair as new cream.

The sun set upon my drunken compatriots gorging and rollicking in the grove past Desvres's field, but I retired home. Yoshu was waiting out by the road for me, and she barked happily, but I was not anxious to see her flea-bitten face. Vringle, the billy goat, and the lambs Squelcher and Norwald all bleated their hellos when I entered the barn, the one place a man is safe to collect his thoughts. I was lonely. It felt sad to know that Hammadi, without me, was still at the ball in her merriment, but I could smell the sweet, warm comfort of her, and I sat myself down in her clean straw. I heard the soft, lovely suck of the lambs nursing at their mothers, and Sophronia's great, unhurried mouth at work on a parcel of hay. Ragan, our she-pig, snored, as her mate, Mauritius, scratched at the dirt floor. I looked at the writing box Mandrik had long ago given me, which I kept near Hammadi, my other treasure, and wished I knew what to do with it. Little did I know then how soon pen and paper would become my closest companions. When at last the night grew cold—how did the animals stand it without the fire I allowed them only in midwinter?—I retired to my house, built up the fire, and waited in the night's uncustomary silence for my wife, daughter, and horse to return.

My brother belonged to no order, and worshipped—much to the priest's annoyance—beyond the confines of Father Stanislaus's church. He had taken, however, a vow of chastity, daily mortification, and prayer when he reached the flower of his manhood in his seventeenth year. Much had already befallen us—the deaths of our parents, two brothers, and a sister—and while I had taken a wife to ease my misery, he had resolved both to renounce the world and to set off in search of it. His work, he explained—the work of the treatise which soon took him to Indo-China—demanded the full force of his carnal drive. It was what holy men did, after all, and we knew by then that God had touched him, for he saw visions both of the dead and of things to come,[4] and had already begun his most propitious experiments with trees.

"But," I warned him, thinking with fondness of the various wonders of my wife's body (God rest my lovely Elynour's soul), "you don't know what you're missing."

He did not like what he had heard nights by our fire, and would not squander himself on women and their weird fecundity. "Every time you touch one, out comes another mouth to feed. At least in most families." He had an ordinary man's strength of conviction, though he dressed in the robes of a mendicant or a madman.

"How can you say that when so many die, with Clive, Marvin, Eglantine, and both our parents gone off to the other side? It's a good thing they had lots of children."

"If you don't have the mouths to feed, you have heartbreak. I can afford neither."

He had never, to my knowledge, broken any of his vows. Still the community watched him ever to see when his resolve would crack. Wido Jungfrau and our Uncle Frith used him for the butt of every joke; and indeed, none of us knew to what extent his vows emanated from the depths of his soul, and to what extent nothing particularly tempting had happened by to lead him astray. I was only somewhat surprised, therefore, when late that night the dog began barking wildly and my wife came in with the glow of the hops about her and Ruth Blum, too tall to pass through my doorway upright, in tow. My daughter, tagging after her, was half suffocated in her string. Immediately I grabbed the child and freed her arms, though the ale still coursed through my blood.

Adelaïda was watching me closely. "Yves," she said, "it would not have been right for Mandrik to host the stranger in his house, even though they get on so well; he never would have lived it down. And you know, everyone else is more afraid of her than we, so I brought her home. I hope you don't mind. She says she has blankets for sleeping."

"I don't want to impose on you," Ruth said. Obviously she had never been in a house before, for her eyes fixed with uncouth interest on objects I had never bothered to notice—the iron kettle, the well-

---

[4] I can only conclude that Yves was too modest to see that his congress with his dead siblings was every bit as unique as his brother's more general traffic with the Beyond, and that his clearsightedness, though of a different nature, was of the same magnitude as Mandrik's own.

kempt central hearth, a straw hat Mandrik had brought from the Beyond that hung over our bed, some flowered red silk he had also brought back, hanging, our only other decoration, on the long wall by Elizaveta's hammock.

"What are you staring at?" I asked her, perhaps too sharply.

"Excuse me, I didn't mean to."

"No," I said, "I beg your pardon. It's an honor to have you," and trusted, once again, that the sentiment would follow its utterance; an honor, who could say, but if nought else a thing of interest.

"You don't mind my staying? It's not an imposition?"

"We will be pleased to have you among us."

"I'll be happy to help around here, if there's anything I can do."

I nodded—even with the harness, our lives were full, dawn to dusk, with work—but she did not see me, having already turned to settle her backpack in the corner by the upended washtub. Adelaïda sat onto the bed, and Elizaveta pulled her wooden doll from beneath her mother's pillow to show the visitor. Soon Ruth was kneeling on the floor, touching the doll's bald head. "What's her name?"

"Pudge." Elizaveta grinned and galloped out the door into the night.

"Ruth," I said. "Please sit down with me."

She took the bench on the opposite side of the table.

"Tell me why you've come here."

Her black eyes blinked twice, then shone in the light of the fire.

"I have told you already you are welcome in my home and in this village. But I want to know what brought you here."

Her head shook, willing her low voice to speak. "Like I said, Yves, I lost my compass, I lost my way. I was looking for you, but it's dumb luck that I found you."

"And, as you say, Mandragora is quite different from your home."

She nodded her head, but regarded the table.

"Different how?"

She shrugged her sharp, square shoulders. "Every way you can think of, really. I don't know how to begin. How our houses look, how we travel, how we dress. The food we eat, how we cook it, how we talk. Everything."

Her words were vague, but they tantalized like the odor of bread in the oven. "But how?"

Her brows knitted together. They were fantastic, so often did they move. "Yves, you've never left Mandragora?"

"We go to the market in town. I told you, only my brother has left."

"And did he tell you what it was like in the world?"

"Yes, but what he described along the Silk Road—the farms full of cocoons, the rice fields, the steep hats, like that one—seems to bear little relation to you."

"Where did you say he went?"

"To Indo-China."

She raised half of her mouth in a smile, which made a solitary dimple. "Is there a Silk Road in Vietnam?"

"Indo-China." I felt myself growing cross.

"He left here, went directly to Vietnam, and came back again? I don't follow."

"Do you malign my brother? Do you contradict his word?"

"No, I'm not maligning him. He's been really—he seems nice."

"And yet?"

"I'm trying to make sense of what you're telling me."

"As I am trying to make sense," I said, "of what you're telling me."

Elizaveta ran back in, looked about at us all, and went to her mother on the bed.

"Ruth," I said, more gently, "I want to know why you've come here."

Her forehead wrinkled like the waves of the sea drawn on a map. "Because I'm a graduate student in anthropology."

"I beg your pardon?"

"I study people, Yves. I'm here to study you."

Her expression was guilty, but I was uncertain why. "You look as if you were ashamed of study."

"Not at all, no. But I don't want to—I wouldn't want to belittle you, by making you my subjects."

"We're the subjects of the Archduke," Adelaïda gently interjected.

"And subject," I added, "to the will of God. We know our place." Still her forehead remained vexed. "Something yet troubles you."

"Sort of. I'm not sure if it'll make sense to you."

"If what will?" It was difficult work trying to follow all her meaning.

"I feel dumb telling you this, Yves."

"Nay, it seems to go easy enough with your tongue and the words, though they're not always clear to me."

At last her brow relaxed, and the lopsided grin passed again across her mouth—the expression reminded me of my brother's arch humor. "The reason I came here, Yves, instead of going someplace else, is that I felt Mandragora calling to me." I had never known such a feeling, but I remembered the fire in my brother's eyes when the Beyond first beckoned to him. "I'm sorry if that sounds strange."

"Not so strange," I told her. "How long did it call you before you took heed?"

She closed her eyes, and opened them again slowly. "I've been thinking about Mandragora a long time, since I was a child. I always believed it was here, even though there was no empirical proof. No one knew anything about you, really, but I could feel this place in my bones. And lately I began to feel like it was my duty to come. Like, if I didn't do it, nobody ever would."

I felt certain that, if I sat quiet, the whole of her tale would unfold. She worked a fingernail between the boards of the table. "Yves, listen. My mother was in Scotland—on the mainland—once when she was young, and she came looking for you—looking for your parents, I suppose—but she never found the village. She told me story after story, though, about how she thought you did things here, so remote from the world. And nothing ever came of it—she never found you, and she never did what she wanted with her life; she sat around and raised three kids and that was the end of it. She died right before New Year's, and I began to think that I should come here and do it for her, in her honor." She worked the nail deeper into the crack, and I wondered if she would be able to extract it when the time came. "Do you know what I'm talking about?"

Death had visited this hearth so frequently that I was almost ashamed to tell her. "Yes."

She drew out her fingernail and looked down at the table. "I hope you don't think that's silly."

I could not follow her word by word, but I understood the sense of what she was saying. "When my parents died, they left me a farm to tend. If your mother told you to come to Mandragora, I think it right and good that you followed her directive."

"It wasn't a directive, exactly. More an idea she put in my head. But thank you."

I nodded. "And how did you come?"

"I flew to Scotland, and from the mainland I took a boat. There wasn't a harbor anywhere we could see, there's no beach, but he moored to a flat rock and let me off. He must have thought I was crazy."

Adelaïda, sprawled on the bed, repeated, "You flew."

"And then I went on the boat."

My hairs bristled like a barn cat's. "How did you fly?" I asked.

"In an airplane."

Perhaps she was like my grandmother, then—there had always been stories that this one and that one saw her wafting about the parish, her long hair fluttering behind her on the breeze. My mind crackled like sap in the fire. "Tell me, how does it plane the air?"

"Have you really never even seen one?"

I shrugged. Who knew what she meant?

"Yves, even if you didn't know what it was, I know you've seen one. A thing like a bird, silvery gray, crossing the sky. They fly more smoothly than birds do, and they're louder." Her eyes continued to expand until I feared they would devour her face. "They rumble in the air overhead, they roar like thunder, only it's a steady sound. It grows quieter as the airplane gets farther away. You must have heard one."

I had seen such a creature, and heard the sound a thousand times; my mind's ear heard it then. Wido Jungfrau had long since postulated that they were ravenous beasts scanning the countryside for unloved children to eat up, but Wido was fuller of foolish notions than a sated pig was full of slops. When once I asked my brother what kind of bird it might be, he shooed me away, saying, "Call it a bad angel out cruising."

"I have heard that sound." The admission felt grave. "And always wondered about the thing that made it."

Ruth shook her head. "I don't know what I expected, but it wasn't all of this. You don't even have heat."

"Yes, we do," Adelaïda said, waving a sleepy hand toward the fire.

"No electricity, no zippers—tell me, do you lack modern technology, or do you know about it and resist it, like the Amish?"

Adelaïda said, "What are the Amish?"

Rather, I thought, more to the point, I asked, "What is it, exactly, you intend to study?"

"The most basic things about your daily life, your social structure, your agricultural methods. I simply want it all to be documented, preserved."

I was certain I still did not fully comprehend. "We have our priest, Ruth, but he is only a workaday priest—no great scholar of the ways of God. I am this village's inventor, my brother its thinker, and the rest of us are ordinary men, working the soil at the price of our lives."

She shook her head slightly. "I don't understand."

"I mean to say that I, and my brother, and even our middling priest, have all the village's respect for our studies. Surely to have another scholar among us—no matter that her field of study is hardly worth a moment's pondering—will be a great honor. And however odd your ways, we will try to respect them."

She gave a slight, graceful bow with her head. "As I will try to respect yours."

"And if you're interested in matters theological, there's a great deal you can learn from my brother, and I'm sure the priest will want to share his books and his learning with you, once he assures himself you aren't the Devil's minion."

I was beginning to like her sideways smile. "Is he going to try to convert me?"

"Are you a Christian?"

"Ruth Blum? Of course not. I'm a Jew."

Though I had heard tell of them, certainly, in my readings from the Bible, I had never before seen one, and wondered if they were all so tall. It certainly explained her accent. "Then it's quite likely that Stanislaus will try to save your soul."

"You have to excuse me if I'm rude," she said. "Please understand how different everything is where I come from. Until this evening, I could hardly imagine such a life, so pared down. You make do without so much of what my people consider basic amenities."

I looked around at my home, replete with food, tools, good blankets, and a fire. "What amenities am I without?" Then, "Thanks to me and my brother, we harness our horses, and our carts now have two wheels instead of one, and are far more stable, far more efficient. We plow with much larger plows than our ancestors ever dreamed of."

"Two wheels," she said, and whistled through her beautiful teeth. "Next thing you know, it'll be four, and then what."

"Four wheels?"

"Excuse me, I—"

"How do you mean, a cart with four wheels?"

"Excuse me, Yves, I shouldn't have said that."

"But you did, and now you must tell me how such a thing works."

She cast down her eyes, and answered, in a near whisper, "Two axles. Front and rear."

Immediately my mind began to chase after the new cart's design.

"I'm sorry," she said, still not looking at me. "I shouldn't interfere."

"No, it's an excellent idea."

Her face, which had started out a pale and impenetrable mask, was growing prettier as it softened. "But if I'm going to study you, I have to leave things how I found them, not tell you how to fix your carts."

"I appreciate the suggestion—and if you have others, I want to hear them. I am our village's one true inventor by default, but I do not seek to cling to the title like the ivy to the alder."

"We'll see, won't we, how we work with one another?"

"Oh, aye," Adelaïda said, "there's more work than you can dream of. We'd be so grateful for help."

"Excuse if I'm being stupid, but, Yves, none of this"—she waved her arms to indicate the hearth, our village, the liquid black sky— "none of this is for my benefit?"

"My brother would tell you the whole of God's creation is to bring you, and you only, to bliss."

She shook her head. "It's so hard to believe that this is here. I've been imagining it for so long, and then to sit by your fire, talking to you."

"I cannot imagine imagining my life," I told her, seeking to stretch my mind around the new idea. "It is all I know." Never had anyone looked so out of place at my table as she looked, tall and slender, and hunching toward me with interest. "What are your people like, Ruth? Your family, I feel, are not farmers."

She laughed quietly. "University people. We're all in the university."

"Meaning?"

"That we all study something or other—people or books—for our work."

"A whole learned family? A whole family of people like my brother?"

"More or less. It's more common where I come from than it seems to be here to devote one's life to learning."

"Don't you miss your people, here on my farm?"

She nodded, and ceased to look at me.

"Sometimes, when I work my farthest fields, the sun sets in the sky as I am alone with my horse, and I think, what if this were the last time, in all of history, the sun were to set so? Then my family would not be here to see it with me. And though I am but a short journey from my home, I miss my hearth, and I miss their faces, with all the longing a man's heart can know."

"I can't explain it. I miss them dearly—my brother and sister and I all live at home, and I'm close to them both, I love them, I don't think I've ever been away from them so long. But everything has changed. And as long as it's changed, I wanted to find out how things are here."

For the second time that day our hands met, though this time our hands reached forth at the same moment. For praise God, he gave us the gift of understanding, the gift of knowing what lies beyond the things our words can say. I saw how her home had gone barren and strange with her mother's death; the departed surely lingered in furniture and corners both. I had not the facility to imagine her home in her strange land, but my heart knew how she felt there, filled with terror each time she woke herself up at night, confused by seeing everywhere the marks and signs—nay, even catching the scent—of the departed. Little did it matter from how far off she had come, for in that moment I glimpsed her soul, and was made humble by her grief. Her words did not make me like her, or make her seem less strange; but they showed me her humanity, which until that moment had sorely lacked.[5]

She had blankets for sleeping, softer than wool straight off the lamb, and as bright as her backpack in hue. Like the backpack, they fastened shut with a zipper, which Elizaveta worked slowly open and shut, her

---

[5] My house did change after my mother died. I don't mean the old, faded sheets over the mirrors, the wooden boxes for sitting, strange-smelling foods from other people's kitchens in their unfamiliar Pyrex and pans. I mean the house itself. Word of her death trickled down the house like rain, from my sister, Nurit, who had the misfortune to answer the phone on her way out of the shower, to me and my father, preparing what would have been a nice breakfast downstairs, to my younger brother, Eli, still asleep in his twin bed in his basement lair. Nurit's scream, a piercing "No," shook the house to its nails, and while all the rest of our stomachs drew in in terror, the neighbors called the police. My father took off his glasses, which left bean-shaped red spots on the sides of his nose, and held his arms out in front of him. The blank look on his face terrified me. "Ruth?" he whispered, not approaching me, standing with his arms out, waiting for me to fill them. "Ruthie, come here. Mommy's gone." I cried into his chest as I had a thousand times in my life, but that time I was certain of what my arms held—muscle and bone, a layer of fat to soften and protect, a carefully calibrated system of impulses in nerves. I breathed deeply to smell his scent, and realized that though some of it was our family soap, some his shaving cream, there

small face grave with awe. We built up the fire, Ruth combed her wild dark hair, and she bedded down beneath Elizaveta's hammock, across the room from our bed. I hoped my daughter would not inadvertently water her during the night, but there was nowhere else to put her. She thanked us again for allowing her to stay, and though she did not

---

was something in it I would never be able to quantify or keep, something precious: his absolute essence. He was, as we all were, I realized, exactly one breath away from dying, a divide across which my mother, eaten away by cancer and pain and the concomitant fear of death, had so easily slipped.

She had died an hour after dawn, when it must be easiest to leave—in a chill, bright stillness, untroubled by sirens and televisions and daughters hanging on your elbows, begging you not to go. It had also, a few hours earlier according to the weather report, begun to snow; so that when she left, the world behind her was soft and pale. The four of us drove to the hospital in her ratty burgundy station wagon, and it would not hold the road. It used the excuse of the thin coat of snow to wobble and sail, to turn sideways each time Nurit braked. "Easy, easy," our father whispered, but he was looking out the window, and did not respond to Nurit's expressions of panic and vituperation, or to her wheezing cough, which worsened each time he chastised her.

The day before, our mother had retained the wispy shreds of her sense of humor, her personality. That morning, she had become wholly body. Her sparse lashes remained, the arch of her black brows, the firm lines of her elegant, bony nose. She had asked me for a manicure earlier in the week, and the nails on the curling hands were still pearly and pink. Her eyes were closed, but all three of us had inherited them, so I could watch her expression of confusion and unrest as I looked to my brother and sister for guidance. Eli, at twenty, was too young for this, and he slouched and brooded, seemingly on the verge of hysterics. Nurit clearly wanted to take charge of something, but in a room with a peaceful corpse, there is nothing to take charge of. Our slightly plump, blue-eyed father, who had always brought levity into our anxious, serious home, perched on the edge of a chair with his eyebrows raised, his eyes dimmed as if with cataract. We said our goodbyes, but mine, at least, were not those I wanted to say—they seemed forced and trivial, more for the living than the dead, as light as air.

Nurit, as always, took care of everything. As Eli and I sat on the living-room floor fingering the contents of our mother's purse—a few half-shredded Kleenex, a plastic hairbrush, lip balm, baby pictures, fortune-cookie fortunes—Nurit cleaned and made lists. By mid-afternoon the house was spotless for guests, all our piles of papers had been stashed in closets and drawers, food had been ordered, and everyone had been notified. She kept pushing at her hair, although it was pulled back tightly and elongated her narrow face. Her black wire-rimmed glasses made her eyes look bigger, but there was still no sign of tears.

"She's mourning in her own way," my father said, but I didn't understand how.

Eli sat at our mother's vanity table half the afternoon, methodically looking into her many small boxes of hairpins and beads. No one wanted to disturb him there, though I was jealous that he could probably catch the scent of her on the faded needlepoint bench. When he emerged, near dusk, he had replaced the steel studs with which he'd had his ears pierced with a tiny pair of our mother's gold hoops. It warmed my heart to think how she would have pursed her lips in disapproval, but instead of telling him, I buried my face against his itchy black sweater and held him.

Our house had never been big enough to afford privacy. Once we began sitting shiva, the house became like a grand eighteenth-century salon, admitting a steady stream of relatives, friends, and well-wishers to lessen the weight of our cares. All I could think of, though, was the work we would have to do when everyone left. There were clothes to be combed through, most too large for me or my sister to wear. Thousands of papers, those that were important stashed in drawers along with thirty years of canceled checks and grocery receipts. My father looked too bleary-eyed for any of this, and had to prepare to give exams come the New Year. Eli's under-

overtly repent for her odd behavior, the tenor of her voice made her apology clear.

That night as I slept, my brothers and sister came from the place they resided after death, and took up their old, earthly forms, not as they looked when I laid them in the soil, but as they had looked in the flower of their youth and health. Their bodies and clothing were luminous like June clouds, but I recognized the roundness of their cheeks

---

graduate career wouldn't be ruined by waiting till next term for his tests; Nurit had long since passed into the hallowed realm of undisturbed dissertation writers, carrel and all; only I, who still had to finish my Master's and face the impossible task of finding a thesis topic—only I was in danger of spoiling my academic career through overassiduous cleaning.

But I was the one whose blood drew me to the task those dark, bitter January days. I separated the precious scraps of her handwriting from the printed dross. Nurit and Eli cared for their work and took refuge in it; I had been dragged into the academic life by the combined weight of all their interests, and I was in no hurry to go back. I felt awful every time I opened one of my mother's journals, but there they were, and I read them through, almost as slowly, it seemed, as she had written them. I lived through her daily worries, what she read, what we did to pain and delight her. And every now and again I caught a glimpse of her as she remembered herself at twenty, with my broad shoulders and dark hair, tramping around the Scottish countryside, dreaming of spirits in the dells, sure of becoming an anthropologist when she returned. I know that she never regretted marrying my father, or having three children before she was thirty—there would have been evidence somewhere in the scores of notebooks—but I could regret it for her, now that she was gone. I could regret the time she had wasted writing everything down, knowing in retrospect that she would die before her promise came to full flower. I could regret all the things she had invested with usefulness, which had once more become mere things, and useful to no one.

When there were five of us, going about our business, fighting with each other or yelling en masse at the television, the house had possessed its own electricity. My mother had never seemed any more central to it than anyone else. Now, suddenly, there was quiet. As dearly as I loved my father, Eli, and Nurit, none of them passing could ever again make so much difference in my life. Even at Thanksgiving, with my mother in the hospital, it had seemed fine that I should be twenty-eight and living at home—particularly when my thirty-year-old sister was doing the same thing—to save money to finance an education in a field in which I wasn't certain I belonged, and for which I frequently believed I had no real aptitude. I hadn't found my topic yet; hadn't found the thing that drew me. Come the New Year, with its heavy snows, impossible to shovel from our pitted brick walk, it seemed that I had already wasted half my life. All the books I'd read had been a waste of time. I hadn't been on vacation since I'd gone camping with my brother and sister in the White Mountains five years before. I had never left the country.

I began to dream of what my mother had told me, almost as often as I dreamed of her. I began to dream of her remote island in the Hebrides, and reasoned that if I did not have a specialty of my own, at least I could do what she would have wanted to do, if she had had the opportunities I was so willing to squander. Even if it turned out not to please me, it would be enough to do the work in her honor.

So each night as we ate our spaghetti, the only acceptable dish in my father's repertory, or Nurit's concoctions of vegetables and beans, I dreamed of that world. I imagined myself in the places my mother had described to me. I imagined myself her; young and open-eyed, with no idea how much dreariness the future held, how much pain it would cause, and how quickly it would be over.

And then I found this place, stranger than all my imaginings.

and the curls in their fine hair, and my heart thrilled and danced to the sounds of their voices, which my mind was ever forgetting but which my soul never would. They billowed with the motion of a breeze that blew through a chink in the wall. I tried to express my gratitude for their visit, but they would not remain still enough to accept thanks. Instead, Clive and Marvin, tall like our father and slightly stoop-shouldered from years of toil, stood gleaming at the foot of the bed with a flute and a psaltery, and Eglantine, her golden hair in two slender braids, floated, skipped, and tumbled over me, singing. Her words were as quiet and high-pitched as far-off bells, and I trailed after their meaning as a dog trails after table scraps, greedily and with my whole mind intent. I had only begun to make out her refrain—"Beware! Beware!"—when suddenly I woke. No longer was I the being to whom my sister, only moments before, had sung; I sank heavily into my earthly body, all sweat and palpitations, and fear gripped my bowels and heart. For in the far corner our stranger was crying a soft, steady stream of tears, and though I could do nothing to comfort her, and though I had no real liking for her, I felt myself drawn to the burden of her sorrow, and knew in that moment that some of its terrible weight would become my own. I could not tell my wife of my siblings' visitations. She would never have consented to stay in a bed where the dead had not only left this world but to which they so often returned.

In the morning I took a torch into the barn. The women were still sleeping, but Yoshu circled eagerly around my legs, and my sensible horse whinnied to indicate that she had been up, and bored, for hours. "I have work to do—will you forgive me?" I asked, tossing her a wormy apple. She shook her head and blew air through her proud, black lips—an equivocal answer at best. I pushed the yelping dog away.

In the corner of the barn nearest Hammadi's stall, I kept the box Mandrik had brought me from his journeys—finely engraved in dark wood, with a polished stone inlaid in the top. Therein, as he requested me, I kept the pens he had given me, ink he had made me, and a few good chalk rocks. Mandrik gave me the box and the implements in order that I should write with them; but having nothing to say that I could not say aloud, I used them generally to draw on the paper he'd made, no doubt intending it for a somewhat loftier purpose. I took out his hallowed tools, dipped once, then again for good luck, in the ink, and began.

I drew the new cart without a moment's hesitation or doubt, without a single false mark on the paper. The design was so simple I knew it had been God's original plan, of which all previous carts had been but pale imitations. The two-wheeled cart (already a marked improvement over its predecessor) had its wheels squarely in the middle of the load. Though this was simple enough, the cart often tipped when we loaded or unloaded goods. Two axles, one front and one rear, meant a cart bed as steady as a table, whether the horse was attached or no. We would be able to load firewood on the front and flax on the back—it would no longer matter, because stability would inhere in the structure of the thing itself.

I signed my name to the drawing with a flourish, and took off down the road with the ink still shiny and wet. Ydlbert was outside smoking in his underdrawers, recovering from the evening's debauchery, his balding pate bare to the morning sun as I ran past. "Hail, lad. What ails you?" he cried out to my back.

I could not stop running, but called back, "Brothers and sister came to visit."

"What, again? Hope the wife doesn't catch wind."

"I'm building a new cart."

"Godspeed," he said, his voice disappearing into the distance. He was the only one besides my brother I could tell about visits from the dead; the only one who didn't think such an admission stranger than icicles in May.

The sun was up, but the villagers, after a hard day's celebration, were still asleep. My footsteps stormed along the road. Five minutes short of my destination, before a stand of oak all bursting into leaf, my brother appeared, streaking along with his cassock fluttering behind him and a sheaf of papers in his right hand. We both stopped, perplexed but smiling, before the trees. "What happened to you?" he asked.

"A new cart. You?"

"A visitation. What manner of cart?"

"Double axle." I held the drawing out to him. "One front, one rear."

"Ingenious. Though I wish you'd save the paper for writing."

"The stranger's idea. Who visited?"

"Our brothers and sister."

My throat began to close with terror and joy. "No."

"Verily, they came with instruments and singing to help me in my work."

"They came also to me, singing."

"Then let us give praise." He bowed his head, and I bowed mine, and offered my heart's thanks to the world that brought my siblings back to me.

"Did they tell you beware?" I asked.

"Not exactly. They wrote me some verses. I brought them to show you." We sat down in the fragrant soil beneath the trees. "I think it's good."

The first sheet read:

"In the beginning there was the Light, and the Fire, and from the Light and the Fire came forth the Great Mind. In the First Ages it brought forth Darkness, and from the Darkness did it bring forth Man. From Man did it bring forth that which pertains to Man—Greed, Penury, War-Making, Ugliness, Pestilence, Sorrow, and Death. From Death did it bring forth all the other sundry Creatures, for in Death are they all the same Stuff. From Death came this great, mysterious World, and to Death does it ever and anon return. And when the World itself—yea, every Mite hereon—has returned to its final slumber, then Death, too, will die, and be subsumed into the Great Mind, and then also will the Great Mind become part once more of the Light and the Fire. And in that Age will all Creation begin anew."

How did my brother, with whom I had sucked on chunks of sugar, have such thoughts? He was as mortal as I, raised by the same parents, three years my elder. But his mind fixed on the infinite while mine fixed on carts, crops, and weather. I suppose that a family with more than one dreamer would be cursed beyond measure; still did I envy the breadth of his mind.

"I wouldn't," I said, "let Father Stanislaus see it."

"No, no."

"Because he's not big enough to understand it."

"Absolutely not."

Despite that he was in every way my superior, his eyes searched mine for deeper praise.

"It is magnificent work."

The light in his smile would have repaid any earthly debt. "But do you think it true, brother? Does it make sense?"

"How could I know?"

He nudged my leg with a stockinged toe in his sandal. "Oh, come, Yves. What does your gut say?"

"My gut says it's hungry, and anxious to build this new cart. And that I wish I had been you, that I had been thus blessed."

"Nay, Yves. You're the one with the harness."

"A harness is worlds different from a knowledge of first things. Will you help me with the cart, anyway?"

"A knowledge of first things is not all in this world."

"No."

"You could speak to our brothers and sister, and see if they had anything for you to write."

Holy man or no, I gave him a fine shove upon the shoulder. "Like what?"

"Any number of things. A ballad? Or a history?"

"Don't be daft, monkey. Somebody's got to till the fields."

He stood and wiped the dirt from his cassock. "And how did you get on with your stranger last night?"

"Somewhat difficult to understand. Adelaïda seems shy of her."

He nodded. "But she's lovely, isn't she?"

"A bit tart."

"But lovely."

"Not everything is pen and ink, Mandrik."

"I'm aware."

I, too, stood, and we walked at a gentlemanly pace toward my abode, our family home, where he, too, had passed the bumbling days of childhood. We walked in silence a few minutes before he began to mutter, then finally burst into song:

> *Alms! Alms for your Chouchou*
> *Awakened by Visions,*
> *Now helping his brother*
> *Improve the life of the whole town!*[6]

[6] A rare example of a non-rhyming verse.

The housewives were used to his sweet tenor, and began appearing at their doorways with baked apples, cheeses, and hunks of dark bread. They bowed their heads to him as he accepted their offerings into his capacious sleeve. The Widow Tinker, who still cooked as if she had a great family, though her daughters were long since married off, wrapped him a whole leg of lamb in a cloth and bade him Godspeed. When he was sufficiently laden, he held open the cache to me, saying, "Here, have a nosh before we get there." I accepted a hunk of ripe cheese and a heel of black bread from the alms sleeve—grateful for my brother's skills, however odd—and dreamed of my new cart as we walked.

Mandrik dumped his booty on the floor of the barn. When Hammadi blew him a welcome, he gave her an apple and a pat on the nose, but turned immediately to help me in my work. With great effort we turned the cart to rest on its bed, the two great wheels creaking with the force of their own revolution. We pried off the axle with an iron bar, and set to work salvaging the nails.

"Mandrik," I said, "the stranger's account of her homeland doesn't tally with your own."

My brother raised his eyebrows. "And does she hail from Indo-China?"

"No."

"Well, then."

I worked on in silence a moment, but I was not done. "And when twice I said to her, 'Indo-China,' she said back, 'Vietnam.' "

"There's no accounting for the ways of strangers."

"Mandrik, when yesterday she told you where she was from—"

"From Boston."

"Yes. Had you really heard of such a place, or did you dissemble?"

He put down his hammer and separated the good nails from those yet to be tried. "Of course I had heard of it, brother. I see no reason to tell her lies."

"And yet Boston is no place I've ever heard you speak of."

"I heard tell, in my travels, of a thousand thousand places. I will be glad, if it please you, to name you all their names, but it would take a fortnight—"

"Nay—"

"—and a great expenditure of breath. Still, whatever your pleasure."

"Nay, Mandrik, nay. I see that you're right."

Soon our banging and grunting brought both women and my daughter to the barn door, where they stood silhouetted against the bright morning. Ruth was attired in a looser, more modest pair of trousers—a thing that but the day before I could never have imagined remarking about a woman—of a soft, faded blue, and a shirt that covered her with due propriety to the wrists and hips. Dimples of light still shone through her slender legs.

"What happened?" she asked.

"We're rebuilding the cart the way you said."

"With four wheels? I never should have mentioned it."

Mandrik hammered delicately at a nail. "I can hardly believe we didn't think of it sooner."

Ruth said, "I'm eating myself with guilt about this cart."

"Why?" I asked.

She shook her head in a brooding fashion. "I suppose you would eventually have figured it out yourselves."

"Aye," said Adelaïda, "Yves is always at his inventing."

"And," I added, "I am glad for your inspiration."

My brother continued with the nails, three light, expert strokes to each head. "Indeed, in every culture there are stories of foreigners and other fanciful beings with strange knowledge. Surely not all the tales of our grandmother can be true; it was her status as an outsider that made her so fruitful a topic. Every culture does this; you are simply our first opportunity, this generation. And we appreciate your fine idea."

"Are there more cultures," Adelaïda asked, "than hers, ours, and Indo-China?"

Mandrik smiled. "More than you can dream of. But you cannot see them from here."

Elizaveta bolted into the yard, and Adelaïda turned to follow her.

"Where can you see them from, then?" Ruth came to sit near us on the ground.

"From the seas, of course, and the imagination."

"But none of you goes to the sea."

"I have."

She waved her hand. "None of the rest of you."

"Imagination will have to suffice, then, won't it?"

"Besides," I said, searching through wood scraps for possible wheel spokes, "the sea is too far. No one wants to go all the way to the sea."

Ruth said, quietly, "Indo-China."

Mandrik said, "Indeed."

"I'd like very much to talk to you about your journey."

"Perhaps in due time."

Ruth watched his work, and only on occasion glanced upward at his face. "Whenever you think it's right."

"The tale of my travels is longer than Midwinter's Night, and I wouldn't want to bore a stranger."

"Perhaps when I'm no longer a stranger, then."

"Yes. Ruth," my brother said, barely looking up at her, "have you any skills? Can you turn a spoke on the lathe, or work with metal?"

"I could learn—I could be useful. I don't want to be in your way."

"I was only wondering about your line of work, back home."

I tossed a stick at him. "She's my age if she's a day, Mandrik, sure. What would she be besides a wife?"

"Any number of things."

"I'm not married," she said. "I'm not sure I ever will be."

"Is it because you're so tall?"

She grinned. "I think of myself as being medium-sized."

"You must come from a land of giants. Why are you not married?"

"I've had boyfriends."

I'm sure I raised my eyebrows. "More than one?"

"Not at the same time."

"What was wrong with them?" I asked. "Had they no land?"

"To answer your question, Mandrik—I'm still in school. I'm a grad student."

"A student of what?"

"Anthropology. Peoples and civilizations."

He nodded as if she made good sense, his lips pressed tight in concentration. "Well, then. We must be quite a boon."

She said, "Yes," then paused. "I am so anxious to learn everything you're willing to teach me."

"We will do our best to oblige."

She stood and brushed nonexistent particles from her clothes. "If it's no bother, then, I'd like to make notes on your work on the cart. Would you mind?"

I graciously shook my head no.

"Great. Let me get my notebook."

I felt magnanimous as I watched her return to the house for whatever object she required. "It must be because she's so tall," I mused aloud. "Otherwise, what could be wrong with her? She's quick of mind, pretty enough. Neither markedly pleasant nor unpleasant. Speaks peculiarly, but perhaps they all do."

"Don't fret her with questions." Mandrik hammered away. "I think she has work to do. I don't think she wants to be married."

"Who doesn't want to be married?"

"I don't, for one."

"She doesn't seem like what you are."

"You can say 'mystic,'" he said, the corners of his blue eyes wrinkling with amusement. "It doesn't hurt."

"I don't like the sound."

"I think it's the sense you object to."

"I can't believe she's come from the Beyond, and she sits here, talking to us."

"From beyond the Beyond. You're lucky to have her, Yves; lucky that my calling precluded her staying with me, and lucky that none else in the village would accept her."

"Were they asked?"

"No, but I can imagine their response. Have you taken her yet to the cairn?"

"I ran to get you practically as soon as I woke."

"Take her."

Adelaïda sneaked into the barn on silent feet, and squatted down beside us, her eyes bright with worry. "That stranger has done some odd things in your absence," she whispered. "I thought I should tell you."

"Witchery?" I asked.

She gave a wide-eyed shrug. "First thing, when she woke, she went into the yard with the most magnificent, pearliest cake of soap I ever saw, and spent ages at her ablutions—scrubbing that face like it was laundry, then rubbing herself with unguents about. Then she did something to her mouth with a bright green stick that made her foam like a mad horse and reek of peppermint leaves. Then, when she came back in and I offered her a slice of bread, she held it over the fire until its edges were quite black, and ate it as if it were the world's finest delicacy."

Her report seemed cause for alarm, yet my brother kept at his hammering and said, simply, "Toast."

"I beg your pardon?"

"Toast. Burnt bread. There are some peoples, Ruth's among them, I suppose, who like to eat it. For breakfast."

Adelaïda looked disappointed. "What about the other things?"

"None dangerous, I think. You should get back to the house before she finds you here whispering about her."

She stood, sorry, it seemed, to have no cause for alarm, and went out to feed the chickens in the yard.

"You're sure you're right about this?" I asked him. "I have a child to protect."

Mandrik kept unhurriedly at the nails. "She is no danger to Elizaveta."

When Ruth returned, she sat quietly with a block of the finest, fairest paper I had ever beheld on her lap before her, and asked to know about measurements, the lathe, and the slight bow in the shape of the finished wheel, an improvement we had stumbled upon quite by accident, producing perhaps our third two-wheeled cart, and whose efficacy she did not at first understand. She admired our craftsmanship, which made me proud, and addressed my brother with the shy attitude of respect such a holy man deserved. She fingered the engraved box and pronounced it beautiful, but did not ask to look inside—which I took as a sign of good judgment.

We wrighted two new wheels that day, and the next built and attached the second axle. The next Market Day, we drove the new cart into town, to the never-sated astonishment of our brethren and the natives of Nnms. Cheers erupted as we drove, laden with the first fruits of spring, through Mandragora that fine morning; Desvres, Ydlbert, and our neighbors lauded us as if we had personally sprinkled the ground with the morning's dew. But as I watched, from aloft, my brother walking alongside the new invention, beaming with pride and answering the many questions with grace, I began to wonder anxiously what I could invent next. And who knew but that all our neighbors' attention was focused not on our work but on the tall, square-shouldered stranger who rode with her arms stretched along the rear gate and her smiling face pointed toward Heaven.

To attend church Ruth wore her loose trousers and a pale, modest shirt, and wrapped a handkerchief around her throat. She still looked odd, and her legs were still rather too visible, but at least her modified garb might prevent Father Stanislaus from choking. My wife and daughter dressed in their town-bought linen of robin's-egg blue, so fine it made the petals of the blooming wildflowers look coarse. We climbed into the cart, newly strewn with fragrant hay, and drove to town behind our Hammadi, the wind whistling through her black mane. We arrived as the last bell tolled, and tied Hammadi to the post, where she snorted affably at Ydlbert's Thea and received a nose to the cheek from Jepho Martin's gray Gar.

Were I to build a church, I would name as its patron one of the great avenging saints: Michael, I mean, or George. But when our forefathers started a parish, she who drew their hearts was St. Perpetua, no worker of miracles, but a young Roman who, for her faith in the Church, was sentenced to die by a stampede of cows. Since childhood I had puzzled over this choice of patroness, gathering from her story that one should keep quiet about unpopular beliefs and be wary of kine. My brother, however, had a deeper understanding of its import, and wrote a translation of her tale, with an exegesis in which he explained that in Perpetua's story our forebears must surely have seen the image of their own persecution. Ruth, too, must have been surprised to see our patroness's name over the door, for as we entered our sanctuary she whispered, "St. Perpetua? Who's that?"

Elizaveta whispered back, "Someone who died."

The murals, painted by Cedric von Broleau, were the most vibrant and beautiful thing in our village. To me they were specially dear because of the old rumor that Cedric had fallen in love with my grandmother before she married, and, brokenhearted, painted her face again and again on the walls of his parish church. I believed I saw some resemblance between the saint and my daughter, especially about the dark eyes, which were rare in my family; and, as Friedl Vox had remarked, the paintings bore a passing likeness to our Ruth. Whether the rumors were true or no, I took great comfort in these brilliant scenes of martyrdom; that pale face, with great dark eyes and ripples of dark red hair like the waves of the sea, beckoned and held me. Strange indeed these murals must have seemed to a foreigner, strange the ravening kine. The church, as always, was abustle with bodies, full of chatter and laughter, the occasional sick lamb or piglet brought for blessing, and playing in the hay on the floor with the children. As we entered with our stranger, some of the talk fell to whisper, but Ruth held her head high. We took our customary seat on a bench toward the front, while many, whose families had not been able to donate one, sat or stood on the floor in the rear.

"Where's Mandrik?" Ruth whispered beside me.

"He doesn't worship in church."

"Neither do I."

"Shh."

When Stanislaus came in from ringing the bell of which he was so proud, he widened his already wide eyes at the spectacle on our bench, but managed not to make mention of it. For the next hour, he spoke to us of our duties—to obey the Word of God and the Archduke, and wives to obey their men. For the children he gave a sobering tale of a wayward child snatched up by the Dark One's handmaiden and never returned to his mother's hearth more. These middling examples of oratorical prowess (how much of Hellfire he might have learned from my brother!) having been got through, he commenced exhorting us in Latin, which none of us understood. Some passages I recognized because Mandrik had pointed them out to me, but much of their import was lost even upon me, the most educated of Stanislaus's parishioners. The brothers Martin, as always, spoke in low tones of the issues of their various farms; Franz Nethering and his Vashti, still lovely though weathered with age, pretended to hang upon every word; and Dithyramb, despite his best efforts, sat with his head lolled over and snored. Aelfred Laight reeked of the liquor he'd imbibed the night before. Folk leaned against each other and the pillars, that their dozing might be less apparent. I examined the murals. Though I had spent countless hours so engaged since childhood, each Sunday revealed a new fold in a robe or a new glimmer in my grandmother's eye, and thus did I keep myself from sleeping. Many of the less studious villagers were not as fortunate in this regard, and soon followed Dithyramb in his unscholarly pursuit. Elizaveta and Fatoush, one of Ydlbert's youngest, soon found each other and began shoving, until their mothers pulled them apart by their strings. Ruth kept turning to look at the people and the statuary, and each movement of her head brought forth titters and shifting of feet. One piglet began squealing for its absent mother, and another urinated near my bench. Against such odds did Stanislaus preach us the word of the Lord. Come Communion we were glad to have something new to do, as well as to stretch our legs, except for Ruth, who refused to be brought to the railing. Instead, she sat on our bench, her big brown boots occasionally in the pig urine, smiled, and bid hello to all who passed. Part of me wanted to feel offense at this disruption, but even an ordinary Sunday was a circus, and I took pleasure in watching my neighbors respond to this new thing. Dirk and Bartholomew bowed so low their foreheads nearly touched the ground; rosy-cheeked Prugne Martin waved shyly; Tansy Gansevöort, carrying her fat new bairn, let her eyes go round as the moon; and Wido Jungfrau simply looked away. But Ruth acknowledged them all with the quiet happiness of a father greeting the guests at his daughter's wedding, and as they returned from the railing, they all looked at her more warmly. If any man communed with God that Sunday, it is surely a sign of God's never-ending grace.

Ruth was a stranger, but no more than a fortnight passed before she began to seem one of my own, as ordinary as sodden weather, if no more dearly loved. Her clothing, affect, and manner of speech still gave me a start from time to time, for her habits were unlike any I had known. She used as much water in washing herself as we did to cook, each day ministered devotedly to her white teeth, and, as Mandrik said, "toasted" her bread. "Don't you know I already baked that?" Adelaïda asked each morning. These peculiarities began, however, to seem a natural part of her presence; and indeed, her presence began to seem as unremarkable as the fire's. Elizaveta, at her start, had been fragile as a dewdrop on a spider's web, but Ruth was as strong as history. What could daunt her, if a sojourn alone in our wilds had not? She ate at my table, slept on my floor, peeled potatoes with my wife, spread feed to the chickens, and gallantly shared her warm tub with my splashing daughter, who else would not consent to be bathed. Only four days after her arrival, Elizaveta followed me into the yard and declared, "Papa, I wrote a song."

"Really?" I asked. "What kind?" For she had long since been reciting nonsense in imitation of her mother's odd talent.

She stood firmly atop her tiny red shoes, raised her chin, and opened the petals of her mouth to squawk:

> *Roof, Roof,*
> *She tells the troof.*

My heart fell through my stomach—my brother, in his infancy, had begun with such songs, and it seemed quite an accomplishment for a child but two years named, barely as tall as the wash tub. "That's a beautiful song," I said, knowing that my words could not convey the depths of my admiration.

"I did it myself."

"I'm very proud of you."

The two dark moons of her eyes examined me for further praise and deemed it not forthcoming before she ran away.

Ruth Blum, spinster native of Cambridge, a world away, inspired my daughter to song. All the admiration that had once been mine for harnessing the horse was now upon her, both for her double-axle cart, which increased capacity and made the carts easier to drive on the bumpy High Road to Nnms, and for her strange and luminous self. I did not mind the attention my countrymen paid her—the time for my own celebrity, perhaps, had passed—but I wondered who this woman was, this emissary from a place beyond the known world.

While we waited to understand her, my wife hesitantly undertook to teach her the basic tasks of the kitchen, and showed her how to card wool. She was not yet skilled enough with her hands to spin or to weave, but she could wind spun thread into an even ball, and when learning a new task, smiled broadly despite the clumsiness of her fingers. It clearly both irked and amused my wife to have so inexpert and yet so dogged a helper; perhaps when our daughter grew, she would be just such a young woman. The more Ruth learned the tasks of the household, the fonder I grew of her; and as I grew fond, I began to wonder, would she leave, and bring back to her country stories as fanciful as those Mandrik told of the Orient, and trail shreds of our hearts and our imaginations out behind her? Who could say if she would like Mandragora enough to remain; and if she did, what that would mean for our village.

CHAPTER THREE

THE ARCHDUKE

erhaps a week later, as I helped Adelaïda sow a second batch of cucumbers (as the first seedlings had mysteriously withered), a great clattering of hooves and wheels arrived in the yard, followed by a tuneless and impertinent blast on the trumpet. Yoshu went into a frenzy of barking, rolling excitedly from one side of her back to the other in between bouts of her din, and all the naked sheep crowded against one another in the pasture. I stood to wipe my hands, and was shocked to see four liveried servants, wearing tunics and bloomers of red, descending from a cart with the old-fashioned single axle, painted in shocking, swirling patterns of red, blue, and green. Their dapple gray horse shook his fine head. The servants helped the Archduke's attaché, still in his black silk and with beeswax in his mustache, to step lightly on one dusty yellow wheel and down to the ground. He brushed at his fine trousers while the red underlings arranged themselves in pairs. Then the trumpeter, a blond lock falling over one eye, squawked out a second greeting.

"Yves Gundron?" called the attaché.

"Aye, sir—you remember me? I brought the petition about widening the gates."

His imposing stance relaxed. "Oh, hullo. That was such a fabulous idea."

71

"Thank you."

"Yves Gundron, rumors have reached the fortress that you have made inventions which have not been reported to his Urbanity, that you harbor a foreigner in your home, and that since its arrival the village of Mandragora has been beset by strange occurrences. What say you to these accusations?"

Ruth was crouched on the ground, taking down notes about seeds. "Well," said I, feeling that if I were a turkey cock I would bulge out all my feathers and strut, "she's a she, sir, not an it. And I have not noticed any unusual happenings."

The attaché's blue eyes twinkled. "Harboring a *female* alien, is it?"

"Aye, sir, in the house with my family. This is she."

Ruth stood, unceremoniously brushed dirt from her trouser seat, and waved. She dwarfed the attaché, who nervously fingered the narrow tip of his beard. How could she not be tall where she came from? Ruth said, "Hi. Hello."

The musicians all blushed, and the attaché, averting his eyes, said, "Oh, dear. This is strange enough in itself."

Thankfully, Elizaveta bounded forth with Pudge, dressed in a washrag, held out in front of her. "This is Pudge," she said.

Ruth said, "No, Elizaveta."

The attaché nodded me his approval. "You've taught her English."

"I already knew it."

"But her accent is guttural and strange." The attaché watched her with some disdain as she struggled to attain composure. In sympathy I looked away, and saw the four servants, one absently fingering his trumpet, two looking at the ground, and the last, his gaze out at my ripening fields, scratching his bulbous nose.

"What is this stranger's name?"

"Ruth Blum, of Cambridge, Massachusetts," we both answered in more or less the same time.

I watched him turn the awkward syllables over his silent tongue, willing the fallible organ to retain their shape for relaying to the Archduke. "Ruth Blum," he intoned, "the Archduke Urbis of Nnms requests your appearance at the fortress, Market Day forenoon."

"I'm delighted. Where's the fortress?"

"Is she daft?" he asked me.

How I wished I had not been digging like a pig about the garden. "She's a stranger. How would she know?"

"I suppose you're right."

"I would be glad to bring her to the fortress, if you like."

The attaché bowed, and twiddled his shiny mustache. "Perhaps the Archduke could travel abroad to see her."

"Whatever his desire."

His hand retreated from his mustache, and both hands parted the long skirts of his coat to rest on his slender, city hips. "Mind if I look around?" As if in illustration of our terrible rusticity, Sophronia let out an ear-splitting moo, and Hammadi, who could generally be counted on to behave, sent forth a roping, yellow stream of urine.

"Not at all."

He came closer to us, leaned down to finger the budding leaf of a radish, and smiled awkwardly. Then he took rather an aimless walk toward the house, pointed therein, and when I vouchsafed my assent, stooped (though he was well clear of the door) to enter. His four red men relaxed so completely that they were soon upon the ground. Elizaveta tugged at my wife's skirt and said, "Help me make up a song about Pudge."

Adelaïda said, "You start it."

Elizaveta gathered herself to her tallest, reached her mouth toward the sky, and began,

> *Pudge, Pudge,*
> *She—*

Adelaïda watched her with wide eyes, kicked at the dirt, retied her apron strings, and finally said, "Nothing rhymes with Pudge."

"Nothing?"

"Smudge," Ruth said. "Or nudge."

"Use real words."

"Nudge is a good word. I use it all the time. Or what about drudge? Pudge, Pudge, she's such a drudge. Or something."

"What a fascinating home," said the attaché, returning with his face bright.

"I hope its humbleness does not offend you."

"No. I think the Archduke would like to visit a representative farm."

"If you think so."

"But has she any more decent clothes, Gundron?"

"She says she's dressed."

"I'm sorry," she said. "I'm doing the best I can."

He looked her up and down. "I cannot say when it will be his Urbanity's pleasure to journey forth. Soon, though." His men stood up dutifully behind him, and the blond one tootled at his instrument before their strange conveyance drew them away.

"Pudge, Pudge," Ruth said, "she likes to eat fudge."

Elizaveta laughed, though it was nonsense, and Adelaïda cast Ruth a dark look.

Four wheels and two axles meant that we could use our vehicles for a purpose never yet dreamed of: sport. What had been the tool of drudgery could now carry us for pleasure as we steered from behind with the reins. As the cart was easier to maneuver with its weight over four square points, we began actually to *enjoy* the jostling ride in its box, though we still had to be careful how we drove, as there was no sure way to stop the conveyance once it was in motion, except to turn uphill.

Can you imagine the thrill that passed from Hammadi's strong gait through the leather to my fingertips, and from the earth through the boards to my feet? I had so rarely before done a thing purely for its enjoyment, and here a task which once had been frightening and loathsome was become as pleasant as the first spring rains. When I drove the cart, the wind brought the blood into my cheeks and made my heart lively. Even on days besides Market Day, I began to hitch Hammadi to the four-wheel cart and to drive around, visiting my neighbors, my far fields, and the orchards. In my wanderings I found freedom, and a clear, strong voice with which to praise my Maker, despite that I had not, unlike now four generations of my immediate family, been granted the gift of song. Well could I imagine Clive's and Marvin's joy at such an invention—and great was my sorrow that I could not share with them my pleasure.

"Hey, Yves!" Jungfrau called to me one morning as I sped past.

As I could not slow down, I craned my neck to face him.

"Watch out you don't end up mad like your brother!"

"Your mother's a blacksmith's apprentice!" I called back, and sped on my way. For what did his opinion matter? My family had been strange for generations, not only because of my grandmother. My grandfather, Andras Gundron, who had brought the farm to its present size, was beset by visions in his fortieth year, and lived out his days fashioning figurines in wood and clay, some writhing in torment, others merely malnourished. His wife, Iulia, was the one washed up with the tide. She was also the first of us known to sing, though those of her songs my father saw fit to write down seem to have been mostly her sad complaints, or brief ditties about the weather.[1] In her last days she began to pine for the sea and mimic its cries, which no doubt contributed to her being kept out of the churchyard. My father, Zoren, was an ordinary householder, as is his brother Frith still, but a third brother, Childrik, became a hermit in his young manhood and died of exposure soon after. My mother, Iona, grieved for two lost infant children all her days, kept their swaddling rags in full view, and talked about them always as if they still shared our home and our labors. With all his oddities, my brother had at least managed to keep the common touch, and had found his place in our town despite his decision not to participate in most of its ordinary activities. Everyone loved him, at the very least, for his fruit. All the generations of peculiarity had not marred my position. Indeed, though my inventions were sometimes viewed through narrowed lids, I was secure in my rank. What matter if Jungfrau looked askance at me now for enjoying the speed of my horse and cart?

Even in the rain I went out. I loved Hammadi's silky white hooves splashing in the mud, loved the fine spray that sprang from the tracks of the wheels, and loved the sound of us covering ground in what used to seem foul weather.

I invented a new word for what I was doing in the cart: Pass-Time. Our forefathers had no such word, for all they knew of time was that if they were not thrifty with it, they would starve come winter. Except during fierce snow and heavy rain, or for the occasion of a birth or a wedding, they could not devote time to mere pleasure. But with a horse

---

[1] A few of the extant poems resemble haiku: "Deep autumn/New snow buries old snow/Under the dim moon."

who could plow and an ample, stable cart for marketing, I had the greatest luxury of all: the ability to spend a portion of my time pursuing whatever activity, however useless, I desired.

Adelaïda had work of her own to do—I had not yet dreamed an invention to release her from the daily necessities of cooking, cleaning, carding, and spinning—but Ruth could help her now, and sometimes they both accompanied me, their eyes closed with the pleasure of movement, the wind in my wife's ample skirts. Elizaveta huddled into the rear of the cart, her palms outstretched and gripping the floorboards. And our Ruth seemed to love the fast motion, when she was not hunched over her books and writing implements. The four of us faced the wind and surrendered to the all-consuming speed. We did not talk, for each became lost in a private bliss. As I felt the ground beneath me and watched passing objects lose their outlines, giving up their shapes to the softness of the general blur, I began to understand my brother's pursuit of solitude, and began to feel in my own body the benefits he derived therefrom. Whether my wife, daughter, and charge experienced any profound emotion driving I cannot say, but when together we dismounted the cart, their eyes shone with the self-same brightness I felt in my soul. Indeed, one Sabbath after services I approached Father Stanislaus to tell him I had discovered a new sacrament. He twisted his face into a curt grin that pulled his hook nose farther downward and said, "Now, good brother. We keep these thoughts to ourselves in the house of God."

We men are no different from a herd of sheep. Where the flock goes, there go I, caring little what I think so long as my brethren are nearby and I have sufficient grass to chew. So as I drove for pleasure through the town, I watched the germ of a thought take root in my neighbors' minds: *Perhaps,* they began to think, *we should go driving, too.* Ydlbert, of course, tried it first, with three or four sons scuffling in back and throwing one another over the sides. A few days later, some of the solidest householders among us could be seen encouraging their horses to a stately clip, their faces set against the deep frivolity of merely driving *around.* From the ground they looked as stiff as dying trees, but sometimes if I, too, was driving, I managed to catch a friendly eye even in the stern visage of my Uncle Frith, and the sensation buoyed me up as I bumped along the road. Soon the clatter of wheels and the caws of frightened-up birds sounded as common as the Vespers bells, and late at night we grew accustomed to hearing the youths go hollering by, their cart beds full of ale skins and the laughter of such as red-haired Prugne Martin.

The best time for driving was, of course, Sabbath morning after services; we were not supposed to engage in work, so what ought to have been contemplation quite naturally gave way to the newfound pursuit of pleasure. As we had once passed one another walking to and fro, so now did we pass one another driving, and shouted our greetings over the heads of our beasts. Perhaps in years past one lone infidel would have polluted the Sunday calm with the rumbling of his cart; come that summer, fourteen or fifteen men drove along the same stretch of road, pulling their horses to the side to allow one another to pass. Though there had never before been any rules regarding this conduct, the courtesies of pleasure-driving rose up naturally, without any man's complaint. We had as much work to do as ever before, but with horses to draw our carts and plows, and with such stable carts to pull our stuffs to market, it seemed fine to take time to race. Never had I experienced such joy as I did trotting along the road, and I saw it—along with great gratitude—reflected in the faces of my peers.

Ruth was as full of questions as a four years' child—and fuller, for she had so many words at her command, and a working knowledge of a whole world whose ways were all around different from our own. When she arrived, in April, I thought she might simply be stupid, the way she pointed to the drop spindle or the bed warmer, asking, "What's this?" Adelaïda and I would exchange glances, then answer whatever was appropriate. "That's the drop spindle," for example. Mandrik would sit in the corner and beam.

"What's it do?"

Uncertain she wasn't being poked fun at, Adelaïda lifted the spindle in one hand, the hank of fragrant wool in the other, and set the object spinning. Ruth watched as it fell, drawing out a long, thick yarn behind it. "Does it always come out the same thickness?" she asked. "What do you do for summer?"

Adelaïda picked the spindle up to start again. "I spin finer thread, naturally."

"Huh," Ruth said. "And you have to make enough of it to make enough fabric for everything you need?"

"Unless we want to go about with holes in our clothes. Every once in a while we buy something precious and fine. Like that blue linen."

"Amazing." She nodded at all of us in turn. "Wow."

"Ruth," my brother said, "you'll spoil them with so much wonder."

Ruth colored under his admonition, however gentle. "No, I won't spoil them. They're spoiling me. You'll have to teach me to use it, Ade-laïda, if it isn't too much trouble."

"If you're still here when she's old enough to learn it, I'll teach you and Elizaveta together." There was nor eagerness nor resentment in my wife's tone.

Unlike a four-year-old, Ruth retained the answer to each question, and usually scribbled it onto her snow-white paper. And after a time, as I began to grow used to her impertinences, I had no desire to snicker when she asked after something so basic that I could not imagine life without it. In fact, I began to be flattered when she sought out my wisdom about trees and crops, the nests of birds, and the plow.

One early Sunday morning in perhaps the second week of May, Ruth and Elizaveta followed me into the southern fields to check the progress of the rye, which was as sprightly as my daughter herself and already knee-high. It cast its gentle green hue upon the hill leading up to the house and barn, and down the hill toward the fence and my neighbors' land—which, I noted with pride, looked less well grown than my own. In honor of the warm weather, Ruth had begun wearing, about the house at least, a shirt with truncated sleeves that exposed her arms to the elbow. When first I witnessed this attire—of an otherwise pretty pink—I stammered and looked away, for soon enough, I felt sure, she would come to her senses and cover her skin. But the customs of her country must be different, indeed; and by the time we stood in my field together, I had grown accustomed to seeing her thus clad, if not immune to the beauties of her long, sun-freckled arms.

"What's down there?" she asked, pointing over the stone fence.

Elizaveta said, "Plants."

"Franz Nethering, and Ion Gansevöort, Adelaïda's brother, and far to the west, Ydlbert's younger brother, Yorik."

"Which way is west?"

I pointed; Yorik's chicken coop was just visible.

Elizaveta spun in a circle, singing,

Ruth, one fingernail ruminatively between her teeth, said, "They wish they could dance," and my daughter's laughter lit up the fields.

Perhaps it was because only members of my family had ever done it before, but I liked someone who could rhyme. "Someone in your family must be a singer."

She exhaled quickly through her nose—like a horse's substitute for laughter. "Hardly."

"Came from the sea, then?"

Now she began to smile at me over her chewed finger. "Anyone can rhyme, you know."

"Not everyone does."

"Yves—what are they like, down there?" she asked, pointing into Yorik's yard.

"What do you mean, what are they like?"

She worked harder at her fingernail with the strong teeth. My sister, Eglantine, had once thus given herself an infection that bedded her for a week, but Ruth seemed to have no fear. "Do they grow what you grow, and make their own butter and cloth? Do their wives sing?"

"The singing's special," I told her. "Only my brother and wife, in this generation. And the land is only good for certain things, you know. But each farmer chooses what grains to sow, so that if one crop is killed by blight, there are other stores to tide us all through winter. Gansevöort keeps a herd of cows for making cheese. He's a fine cheese maker." How small it all sounded, issuing from my mouth.

"Would they mind if I went and talked to them?"

"What about?"

She shrugged her shoulders and kept her dark eyes fixed on me.

"I don't know that Wido Jungfrau wants to tell you how many chickens he keeps or how many eggs they lay; though Laight might chew your ear off about how he plans to buy his land from the Archduke. If he's not insensible with liquor."

"And Adelaïda's brother?"

"A kind man."

She nodded. "I won't make trouble. I want to talk to them, that's all. I want to find out as much as I can about this village. I need to."

"Ruth, if you're going off about the countryside haranguing people, I'll have to give you gifts to appease them, and you'll have to put on another shirt."

"Are short sleeves bad?" she asked, laying one palm protectively across the opposite elbow. "I mean, I know not for church, but not around the house, either?"

"Among the family, I suppose it's fine." I looked at her.

"I'll go change."

It was impossible to look at her closely, and equally impossible to look away. "You'll have to learn the spells for the crossroads, and what to do when you pass my grandmother's cairn."

She looked surprised. "Okay."

"Else, the spirits will get you, sure. I'll at least have to teach you to spit to ward off danger." She regarded me what seemed a long time, and in her sober gaze I thought I detected mistrust. "What?" I asked, perhaps somewhat snappishly.

"Nothing. It's only I've never done anything like that before."

"Aye, and look at you—mother dead, you farther from home than any among us could imagine. You might learn to take a precaution or two. If you'd spat to the four directions, your life might not be so bleak."

Her eyes widened, but she did not respond.

"Besides which, Ruth, you can't follow people about all day, bothering them with questions."

"Am I bothering you?"

"No," I said, somewhat surprised to realize it. But my family was different—marked out among the village as the one that could read and tell tales; one of the few that could support so idle an extra mouth. "Perhaps at church we can ask about for people who don't mind questioning."

"I'd like that," she said. "I'd really appreciate it if you'd ask for me, if that would be the right thing to do."

Elizaveta said, "No more church," but was mainly objecting, I thought, to being tied to her mother.

I said, "I could do that."

"I'm so interested in all those people," Ruth said. "I can't wait to find out about their lives." The assertion raised a flicker of jealousy; were Adelaïda and I not interesting enough? No such thought had ever before occurred to me, for no one had time for "interesting" when we scraped for sustenance with our fingernails. I was surprised even to care what she thought of me, but I did.

"I'll ask tomorrow at Mass, then. But you'll put on a more modest shirt."

Now she laughed. "Okay, Dad."

I knew not what she meant, so I smiled.

Ruth said, " 'Dad' is short for 'father.' "

I nodded.

"That's a joke, Yves. I'm kidding."

"Yes, very well." The appellation felt strangely pleasant.

Services were, as always, harder labor than dragging the plow had ever been; to stay awake required an effort of will so mighty that none but a saint could expect to achieve it. Father Icthyus, in his day, had at least understood that our farmers' minds were concerned mostly with farms, and spoke to us about our animals; during times of trouble, he hunted down the right Biblical passages to allay our doubts and fears. Ever were his sermons about fields and flocks, flocks and fields, and our minds easily grasped his meaning. He talked about casting pearls before swine, and often as not a sick piglet was in church to be blessed. Stanislaus was the son of Titus Marnt, who had farmed at such a distance from Mandragora that when he died, his house and land were left to rot, so close did they skirt the edges of the known world. Titus's son still knew surprisingly little of what ordinary people did. His talk was of brotherhood, duty, sacrifice—noble and lofty things all, but of little consequence when one had a load of potatoes to haul to market.

Stanislaus also suffered, in my eyes, from a subtler ailment—his inability to match my brother's skill in rhetoric. Mandrik was no priest, but he could spin a tale to raise the hair on a man's arms. When Stanislaus began that morning with, "Brethren, you have the lot of you been lax in your devotions to the Deity," we immediately took to dreaming of our fields. At last, after he'd berated us roundly for attending church but once a week, he was done, and offered, as ever, to let us speak our minds on issues of interest to the community—something Icthyus would never have done, despite which there was no comparison.

Jepho Martin shot up to his full bean-pole height, and announced that the Great North Meadow was well enough grown again for public pasture.

"Aye," his nervous elder brother added, "but be sure this year to keep the sheep from out the graveyard. I can't tell you what a time I had last spring, trying to visit our parents."

"I should think the sheep's, you know, droppings should be good for the grass growing over the dead."

"Aye, but not strewn about where the sheep drop them."

Stanislaus squeaked, "Gentlemen," cleared his throat, and added, "that will do."

Waldo Smith, his shirt black from yesterday's work, arose, nodded, and wiped his nose on his dirty sleeve. "If any man's horse wants shoeing, I'd gladly trade labor for help cutting and fitting a new harness."

A chorus of assent filled the hot sanctuary, for every man's horse needs shoes.

I stood and faced the assembly. I had known most of these people all my life—had known all their families, always—and had never felt so shy of them. It was no ordinary thing to stand before them on a stranger's behalf. "Our guest, Ruth Blum, would like to talk with the various members of our community, that she might learn to know us all and understand us better. To which end she proposes to sit today outside the church awhile after services have ended, that any who would not mind her questioning might tell her so, and she might go visit them at home."

Such a request had never been put forth in our church—or indeed, I suspected, anywhere—and my neighbors regarded me dumbfounded.

"Question us about what?" asked the Widow Tinker.

I shook my head, for I did not want to embarrass Ruth by revealing the simplicity of most of what she asked. "About our lives and opinions."

The brothers Martin nodded, with a look of satisfaction in their eyes, and some around them slowly followed suit. I suppose many of my neighbors had been curious about her all along, but had kept their distance for fear of a hex. In the quiet sounds of assent I also heard, which I had not expected, that some of my brethren were willing to talk about themselves; something I never would have known from our clipped conversations. It suddenly occurred to me that Ruth had a good idea, coming to listen to us.

Stanislaus *benedictus*ed us and *pax vobiscum*ed, and allowed us to sally forth into the warm, fragrant air. On so bright a day, with the fields all agreeing, a man might pass the afternoon in any way he saw fit, and yet would his activity be at heart a hymn of praise. Adelaïda and the rest of the young mothers whisked their small ones off to water the trees, and the middle-sized children set off in pursuit of a leather ball stuffed with hay. Ruth sat down cross-legged in the grass a few yards from the church door. Since I could neither leave her alone there nor fold my legs into so ungainly a position, I stood behind her, close enough that her slatternly hair brushed my leg each time she turned her head. My neighbors hesitated to come near, but in time they gathered like a litter of kittens to a bowl of milk. Half the people of my acquaintance shyly invited her over for nettle tea and biscuits. Even my Uncle Frith, bent nearly double with age and always so dubious of my endeavors, offered to open his door to her. The youngsters were clearly more interested in her garb than in her company, but the adults seemed almost pleased at the prospect of questioning. I saw Mandrik leaning against the church gate, waiting for us to exit, and when I raised my hand to him in greeting, realized that his eyes were looking toward Ruth.

What villager had been honored by a visit from the Archduke, in any man's memory? Just as my brother and I were specially marked out among the living to have traffic with the dead, so did it seem that Ruth was marked out for glory. It lifted the weight of worry and grief from my heart to think of the event. So too, from the look in her eyes, did I think it lifted the weight from Ruth's. The cares that had driven her here clearly paled somewhat in comparison to a nobleman's visit.[2] Adelaïda mended holes in our clothes, embroidered flowers on her and Elizaveta's pale blue dresses, and began to experiment with new ways of pinning up her braids.

In the midst of these preparations, Ruth set off on forays to, as she said, *interview* my neighbors. "Why not plain talk to them?" Adelaïda asked, kneading forcefully at the week's dough.

"That's what I'm doing." I had given her my carrying sling to truck loads smaller than that with which she'd arrived, and she sat on the

---

[2] His nobility held no intrinsic interest for me, but the awe with which the villagers talked about him filled me with curiosity; and I was interested, of course, to see how a nobleman's life differed from the lives of the farmers with whom I was now spending my time.

swept dirt filling it with papers, odd pens that contained their own ink, and hunks of our bread and cheese. "I talk to them, and they talk to me."

Adelaïda licked a bead of sweat from her upper lip. "You should call it talking, then."

She would return each day only a brief span after she'd set out, for she eagerly awaited the Archduke. She was not accustomed to being out in the sun, or she would not have returned so red-cheeked from each day's wandering; but despite the skin peeling from her nose, the stranger returned happy. "Ion Gansevöort introduced me to each of his cows by name, and gave me cheeses from three different years to taste, one of them covered in dark green mold," she reported after one expedition.

"Aye, that's the best one, isn't it?" My wife nodded, her eyes gone wistful.

Another day, "Aelfred Laight is scheming for a way to buy that farm. You should see the ledgers he's drawing up with chalk marks on slates. I never saw such a complicated accounting system."

"And was he drunk?" I asked.

She shrugged. "He didn't smell so great."

One afternoon Mandrik took her to visit the cairn, and she came back subdued in aspect, her color high. "What a remarkable story," she said. Mandrik, in the corner spreading plum jam on bread, beamed. I had no doubt he had told Iulia's story well.[3]

What a pleasure to find that we were interesting! That she desired to know our neighbors' stories, that our lives did not seem small to someone from the outside. So it was no wonder my brother had returned from his wanderings; we were more interesting than whatever

---

[3] "A strange, sharp-spoken, curly-headed thing like you, she was. And being the first, the people were nowise prepared for her oddities."

Her cairn was as tall as I, and rose starkly from the bare dirt surrounding it. Mandrik was strewing daisies around the base, which only made the rocks look more barren by contrast. "And where did you say she came from?"

"From the sea."

"Before that, though."

He crouched down on his haunches to admire his work, then regarded me with his wide, still eyes. "She was the sea's creature, Ruth, as sure as you're the creature of the Beyond. As sure as the light of Heaven burns within us both."

I felt abashed at the frankness of his faith.

"Do I frighten you," he asked gently, "when I speak to you thus?"

I said, "No," but in truth he did frighten me. I had never dreamed of anyone like him, and was flummoxed to find him in what I had thought would be a prosaic farming village.

lay beyond. I felt a great relief that our lives to her seemed worth listening to; and in the glow of such recognition, I neglected my work from time to time.

Once I realized I had been too long away from the land which sustained me, however, I made haste to visit my crops. Though the season had been niggardly with rain, my wheat and rye were coming up hale and green, and the great patch of vegetables sent forth shoots that bore the promise of a comfortable winter. I offered a moment's praise for the bounty of the garden, wishing I had my brother's facility for offering up thanksgiving in verse. How much sweeter it must thus be in the ear of the Creator. I knelt in the dirt to pluck weeds from the burgeoning plants, for they encroached upon them and sought to choke them out. My hands were, as ever, sure in their pruning—I need hardly look to know what is essential and what stands in its way. My father and his father before him pruned thus, and their knowledge lives on in my fingers. Kneeling upon the ground that day, I missed them terribly, and regretted that they would not be with me to witness the reception of an Archduke. While up in my northern fields I flung a pebble upon my grandmother's cairn and said, "Do you know yet, the Archduke's coming to visit?" She did not reply, but in the whistle of the breeze in the wheat I thought I could hear her, or whatever was left of her as she rotted beneath the ground, pricking up her ears, all strung with sea-vegetables, at such good news.

Each day we swept the hearth and the yard, and tied Elizaveta to the table leg to prevent her getting underfoot. Ruth, her hair in one silly short braid, wrote things down with her remarkable pens, stopping occasionally to peel a potato or get water; Adelaïda mended clothes and dusted the tabletop, but her excitement kept drawing her from the work of the house, and soon enough she'd be telling tales to our visitor, her face still wary, but her tongue by degrees more loose. I, imagine! I did not have the concentration to spend long days tending my fields. Tasks that required less time sat easier on my restless mind, so I made spotless the animals' stalls, then brought my sharpening stone into the yard and worked at the blades of the ax, scythes, and Adelaïda's household knives. I smoothed down the handles of splinters, and waited, my stomach awhirl, for the great event to transpire. When after a few such days I had not a tool left to mend, I brought out the churn and began to make butter, though it had always been a woman's chore; if my ancestors looked down on me from Heaven, they laughed. The next Sabbath morning I awoke before dawn to a dream of four ghostly men, dressed in the black garb of death, come to take our stranger away, but when I woke in our great bed, I saw her sleeping peacefully on her pallet on the floor, and tried to calm the unfounded frenzy of my heart. As the sun strained groggily to appear through a thick cover of clouds, the fear gripped me that if we left for church, the Archduke would appear in our absence and be stuck with the terrorized pigs and sheep. I soon recalled, however, that even the greatest of men owes his weekly homage to his Maker, and that if we hurried home from services, we could not fail to meet our visitor.

And so our souls prevailed. We went to pay our worship, Ruth marching up the hay-strewn aisle beside us, though it wasn't, she said, her God. Father Stanislaus, though he had never been much of a speaker, gave an admirable sermon about our tolerance in accepting this stranger into our homes; he had not heard even one report of demonic behavior, and therefore urged the congregation to quit putting so much sugar in her nettle tea, lest all her pretty teeth fall from out her head. What little we knew of the ways of God, he admonished us, who might after all have even greater miracles in store. My neighbors had been somewhat skeptical of Ruth's visits, but had minded them less when she brought them gifts of gooseberries or eggs. We had never been tried before, not since the days of my grandfather, but this, our first trial, wasn't turning out so badly.

Out on the road, Elizaveta played peaceably with Pudge, and I enjoyed the familiar rush of the sweet, fresh wind. All the fields were greening, the work of my neighbors, their beasts, and the great mysteries of Nature. Soon enough, before I could catch my breath or take a full night's sleep, it would be time to harvest all this and take it to market. A stranger among us, what would it matter then, when the real work was to be accomplished and the rewards of my labor to be reaped with the corn? Would that I had been a plain farmer like the rest of my countrymen, not always seeking after things and ideas, content to brood about my soil—for then how much more time would I have had for the work. Or would that my brothers had lived and taken charge of this land, that I had been a younger brother, with no inheritance, and free to wander about, inventing.

"What's that?" Elizaveta asked. When I turned to look, she was grasping out the back of the cart to the open air, her mouth agape.

My wife gathered in Elizaveta's small arms, but the child continued to grasp.

"Leave the wind be," I chided her.

"That's not wind," she said.

Adelaïda said, "I hope she's not like your brother, hearing voices."

But Elizaveta was right—it was something beyond the wind. For out of the distance came the high tinkling of myriad bells, crisp as the voices of angels, and the warbling of a flute. They approached out of the east and hung like dewdrops on the warm spring air.

"More trouble," Adelaïda said, pulling the child farther down into the cart.

"Anyway," Ruth said, "music."

We passed my brother's hut, where I saw him sitting in meditation beneath a plum tree, oblivious. The music was sweet, teasing at the edges of my hearing, fading under the rumble of the wheels and the calls of the birds in the fields, then sailing forth on the next gust of wind.

As we neared the top of the rise at Ydlbert's house, I clicked my tongue to Hammadi, and she slowed her gait without the cart hugging up behind her. (Downhill, of course, it was a more dangerous proposition.) Off in the distance, below the rise and halfway to Nnms, the music approached—five players in red livery, so far away as to seem smaller than Elizaveta's doll. Between them walked eight men more, all of a height and dressed in a yellow so deep and so vibrant of hue that I had never before seen its like. On their shoulders they bore aloft a stretcher with a tent, all red and gold, its silken draperies glinting in the sun. As if it would toss its contents headlong into the ditch, the tent lumbered from side to side as the men walked and the minstrels played. The lot of them were as bright as the brightest field of poppies I had ever beheld—which Mandrik showed me once on a day-long walk, which is quite another story.[4] We remained spellbound until Ham-

---

[4] "I don't know why he's so forthright about some things and so coy about others," said Mandrik when I asked him later about the circumstances of the poppy expedition. "He'll talk about his desire for his wife, and he'll talk about death, but opium poppies will rain the wrath of Heaven down upon him. Who can blame him, I suppose. It's an ugly habit, even among those Eastern peoples with whom it originated.

"When I returned from abroad, we spent a great deal of time together, discussing what had happened in my absence, and where I had been since last he saw me. I had resolved, upon my remadi, her tail aswitch, grew tired of idling and began to draw us home. The sweet refrain of the music was quieter as we drove, but from time to time it gained strength and washed over us. When we arrived at our house, I put the horse to pasture and the cart away, and continued to listen as the unfamiliar sound drew nigh.

"Do you have a song for this, wife?" I asked as nonchalantly as I could, opening our door to the music.

"Nay," she replied, "though you might try me again later."

It drew closer as we ate a quick bite of soup and Ruth washed the bowls. The fear of the Lord came upon me, for what was this, in addition to the arrival of a stranger? Was the world this interesting, this complex, when my grandmother washed up from the sea? What had happened to the years and years of undifferentiated time in which our fathers' fathers had quietly lived out their days? Alongside the fear sprouted the conviction that, whatever this apparition, it was, like all the others, for my own benefit. And the bright litter and its attendants made their stately way into my yard, preceded by a smell so pungent and sweet that it filled my whole skull with desire.

Ruth, sticking her head outdoors, wrinkled her nose and said, "I smell oranges."

The tent listed to one side and the other as its bearers brought it to the ground, and its sides, shot through with gold, quivered like a child's translucent eyelids in sleep. The musicians ceased playing mid-phrase,

---

turn, to tell him all the truth, that he might know the grim details of what I had witnessed. But faced with his dear, sloppy-toothed grin, and with those clear gray eyes (how their expression reminded me of our parents and siblings), I became abashed; my voice caught in my throat, and would not issue forth. Pressed with questions, I gave slippery answers; and tired of my own tale's vagueness, I occasionally made things up."

I suppose I must have looked at him askance, because a nervous smile flickered across his ordinarily serene face.

"When we went to see the poppies that day, I am afraid I ran quite away with myself inventing a tale about poppy fields in distant lands. I described riding a mule down a treacherous slope of the Himalayas, through a cold, thin air that left the sky the palest blue. And there, in the valley below, beneath the craggy shadows of the snow-capped mountains, spread a sea of red, sunward-turned flowers as far as the eye could see. The uses of opium, with its dim, smoke-filled rooms, full of silken carpets, great cushions, and lax bodies, the shining, dirty hookahs with their sinister bubble and suck—all this I had on written authority, so I did not feel altogether untruthful in relaying it."

"And Yves took this all on faith?"

"Yes, I believe he did."

I was desperate to question him further, but found my mind empty when I tried to dredge up a single concrete thing to ask. I felt nauseous in my confusion between my curiosity, my idea of my professional duty, and my dumb awe in Mandrik's presence.

and of a sudden there were no sounds beyond the wind and the grubbing and snorting of the barnyard. Then the dread bugler lifted to his lips his accursed brass, though this time he blurted forth a catchier, syncopated tune. Two of the bearers parted the curtains and bound them up with golden cords. From the tent's interior (which glowed as deep as the night's last embers) emerged the portly figure of a man draped in a fiery cassock not unlike Mandrik's in shape, though quite otherwise in splendor. He wore a broad smile on his broad face, which was otherwise engaged in the eating of the intoxicating fire-colored fruit. All the village children had scampered in the wake of the strange conveyance, but they kept their distance. Only Jowl, his dark hair in his eyes, would venture a comment, and that only a long-drawn-out, utterly amazed "Yo."

"All hail," said the trumpet boy, "our Archduke, Urbis of Nnms."

The barnyard replied with its characteristic snuffling unconcern, but I made a bow, feeling rather shabby.

"Welcome, your—"

"Urbanity," he prompted with a graceful nod. "The same Yves Gundron, I presume, directly responsible for the Di Hammadi and indirectly responsible for the feats of modern road-building which bear my and my esteemed father's names?"

"That is I," said I, wondering that so great a personage took note of my existence, and ready to prostrate myself before the delicate odor emanating from his mouth.

He must have seen the division of my attention, for he snapped his fingers and one of the red boys brought forth a net filled to bursting with the dimpled fruits. "A gift for your family," said the Archduke, and I held his bounty to my face with sheer delight.

"Oranges," Ruth said quietly. "I've been craving them."[5]

With hungry eyes did he regard her slender form in her soft blue trousers. We should have found her a dress. "This must be the stranger rumored to live among you."

"It's no rumor, sir," I told him, bowing once more, "and thank you."

"What great sadness in this life, to have had no oranges. But allow me to make this stranger's acquaintance."

---

[5] Where the Archduke had gotten orange trees in the first place, I never was able to ascertain; but I later learned, to my great delight, that he had cobbled together a primitive greenhouse of leaded glass to protect them from the elements, and that he nursed and watered them daily with his own two hands—the only manual labor he ever performed.

I bowed again, the fruit clasped to my chest.

"I'm Ruth Blum," she said, introducing herself as ever with that fatally peculiar grasp of the hand.

The Archduke recoiled before extending his own stubby palm to her. "Charmed. I presume you know who I am, strange though you be."

"You're the Archduke."

"Urbis, son of Mappamondo, of Nnms," he said, and bowed. "Hail."

Elizaveta, whose eyes had gone wider than eggs, ran to meet him, but her string pulled taut and dragged her to the ground, whereupon she commenced caterwauling.

"Hush!" Adelaïda cried, running to loose the string.

"No no, little one," the Archduke addressed her, squatting down beside her like a wife in her garden, "don't cry." And from out the sleeve of his cassock he produced a chunk of dark sugar as large as the child's fist. "Take this to ease the pain, yes?"

Her eyes lit up like twin stars, and to my delight, she remembered to thank him before retreating to the house with her booty. My home and yard looked dim against the dazzling Orange—for the color was exactly like that of the new fruit—of the Archduke's robe. Even his sandals, much like Mandrik's in design, seemed made of spun gold.

"It's a great honor for you to come visit," Ruth said.

"Yes," he said, nodding curtly. "We have never had a stranger in this lifetime. Tell me, Ruth Blum, of whom are you descended, and of what city are you a native?"

Her grin dimpled her sunburned cheeks. "Daughter of Aaron and Esther Blum, of Cambridge, Massachusetts."

"These are common names in your country?"

"Common enough."

"Perhaps it is only your accent that makes them seem strange. Massachusetts is—"

"On the other side of the Atlantic. But from my conversations with Mandrik, I gather the ocean doesn't figure on your maps."

His brow darkened. "Have you come from the Highlands, or farther overseas like our ancestors?"

"About a hundred times farther, in the other direction—to the west. Some of the boys, Ydlbert's boys, took my map, but if I can get it back, I'll show you."

My mind stirred in its attempt to understand—she had come, quite literally, from the other end of the world, farther, perhaps, than even my brother had traveled. The Archduke's blue eyes—like any other man's, I was surprised to see, if somewhat smaller and heavier-lidded—fixed on her pretty face with rapt interest.

"I have not seen any Massachusetts," he told her, "on any map of the world."

"Despite which, your father must have been a great mapmaker, to earn his name."

He nodded approval. All this, and literate, too.

"I will try to get my map back," she continued, "and if not, perhaps I can draw you a rough approximation of where I'm from."

"Shh," Adelaïda scolded, as if Ruth were our child (and in some ways, she was). "Don't take up his time." Then, because the Archduke was watching her with somewhat less tolerance than he showed to Ruth, she said, "We didn't know quite when you were coming, but we made up a feast anyway. That is, as much of a feast as we could muster."

We had not counted on so many attendants, and could not sit them down around our single, rough table. We were saved from certain embarrassment, however, by the snap of his fingers, which occurred in so complex a rhythm that my feet of their own volition began to dance. "Men," he said, "can you amuse yourselves without disturbance to myself and these fine farm folk while we dine on their representative cuisine?"

The blond trumpeter gave a two-handed, intricately fingered salute, and we led his Urbanity, still redolent of oranges, into our home.

If my father, who loved nothing so much as his farm, could have seen and heard the sparkling, jingling entrance of such nobility into his home, he would have fainted dead away. The furniture he had built—to replace the barrels he grew up sitting on—would now hold up the blessed bottom of an Archduke. And my house, for all my pride in it, looked impossibly shabby and dark, the smoke from the fire thicker than the tissues of the great man's robes.

"A rustic cottage," said he.

"Isn't it beautiful?" Ruth asked.

Adelaïda brought forth a roast of ham—but lately our she-pig, Ragan—fresh cheese, wheat bread, sweet cider, and an apple tart Mandrik had contributed to the festivities.

"Where can a man find beauty," he asked, "when he has lived in such splendor as have I?"

Ruth set wooden bowls around the table. "Anywhere he looks, I imagine."

"Ruth," I whispered, "don't sass the Archduke."

"Nonsense." He sat his weight down upon our creakiest stool. "She may speak as she sees fit, especially if, as at present, she is probably right. I shall commission better maps, that she may show me where she comes from, in the event that I find it beautiful." He smacked his lips together, which Adelaïda took as a sign to cut the ham.

He did not comment upon our delicacies, but grunted in approval, and took great hunks of food upon his spoon. My stomach was so wild with worry that I dared hardly eat, but watched him and his tankard with the utmost care. We heard not a sound from the attendants outside, and Elizaveta hunkered down under the table and noisily sucked her sweet.

"I think," Ruth said, "this is the most beautiful house I've ever been in, certainly the happiest. Yves and Adelaïda have made me feel perfectly at home. Of course, it doesn't have all the conveniences of the house I grew up in—"

"Conveniences?" the Archduke questioned.

Ruth looked toward her lap. "Excuse me."

"What for? I command you to tell me what you mean."

Her voice dropped to a guilty mumble. "Washer and dryer, dishwasher—"

"Servants," he corrected.

Ruth shrugged her shoulders. "I guess you could put it that way. What I meant to say was, none of those things seems to matter. The people here live differently from my own people, but their lives are in most ways the same. I find them kinder and more intelligent than many of the people at home—and that without all the leisure we have to devote to philanthropy."

The Archduke turned to me as if we were the only two people at table. "If it weren't for that damned harsh accent, I'd say she sounded book-learned."

"I think she is," I whispered, as if it were confidential. "I think she's a learner by profession."

"A woman with a profession, and not a wet nurse or scullery maid?" The Archduke opened his eyes wide and wiped his mouth upon his broad sleeve. "You cook as well as any in my own house," he said to Adelaïda, who blushed with pride. "God only knows how you've lived this long without oranges. I must ask you now, however, good farmer, to leave me alone with this stranger, that unobstructed I might learn some of the history of her land."

Adelaïda looked stung—Ruth, after all, had cooked nothing—and Elizaveta shrieked, brown goo dripping from her mouth, when I retrieved her from under the table. Here, at last, was the Archduke in my home, where I might show him my south-pointer, or simply learn who he was, and he dismissed me like a common servant. But, of course, compared to Ruth and her spectacular arrival, and her brilliant teeth, I was as lowly as the soil I tilled. I grabbed a jigger of ale on my way out the door, and deposited my family on a fragrant clump of grass at the edge of the yard, quite near the bearers, who were all napping or cleaning their nails, and the children of the town, whose parents by now had followed them to witness this strange occurrence. Adelaïda, her pale eyes rimmed red, stretched her hands out on the grass behind her, lifted her solid chin toward Heaven, and began, thus, to sing:

> *Oh, the Archduke came calling*
> *One fine summer morning—*

"That doesn't rhyme," I said.

"Shut up and let the lady sing," said the blond murderer of the trumpet, smoking an odd-smelling pipe. "Crikes."

Adelaïda said, "Thank you."

> *Oh, the Archduke came calling*
> *One fine summer morning,*
> *But my husband and daughter*
> *He didn't care see;*
> *He arrived in a litter,*
> *I ne'er saw one fitter*
> *For a man who could not deign*
> *To speak to poor me.*

"I feel certain, wife, that he can hear you—"

"Leave her be, lad," said the trumpet boy, and boxed me playfully on the ear before falling into the grass beside me and offering me the long pipe. "Go on."

Adelaïda colored under the young man's admiring gaze, and composed herself a moment before going on.

> Oh, there seemed a slight danger
> He'd grow sweet on our stranger,
> But how could an Archduke
> Come court a strange Jew?
> She's most certain a heathen
> And to court her is treason,
> Though our stranger is fairer
> Than springtime's first dew.

The pipe bit back when I sucked on it, but it filled my lungs with a delectable pleasure. Two of the musicians whistled their approval, and a third began to beat slow time upon his timbrel. Elizaveta, hearing the music, stood, lifted her arms in the air, and began to bounce, a beatific grin across her face. The musicians cheered her on, and one of the pipers began to whistle Adelaïda's tune.

> The neighbors mistrust us

"No, we don't!" someone shouted, then guffawed.

> And do us scant justice,
> But is it our fault
> That our family sees clear?
> Strange happ'nings befall us
> Each time that God calls us,
> But we pray for God's mercy
> And shed not a tear.
> Lai dai dai dai doh,
> Lai dai dai dai doh,
> Lai dai dai
> Dai dai dai
> Dai dai dai dai doh.

The musicians joined in, one singing counterpoint, and the yard filled with music as it had not since the day of our wedding. The song grew more boisterous when I brought from the storage shed a cask of barley malt, and the louder the singing grew, the more Sophronia, not to be outdone, lifted her huge mouth to the heavens in praise. Hammadi held her peace, and trailed her black tail with dignity around the near pasture. Inside my house, who knew what wonders they discussed,[6] but outside, where my ancestors had done their days' labor and lived out their short, dreary lives, how pleasant was the atmosphere. My wife's song was excellent diversion; the sun in the sky was a great, hot ball of the only light there is that does not smoke or sputter; and all my sorrows, for all their depth and persistence, were nothing compared to the sunny smell of the grass and the clarity of my pleasure in sitting upon it. What little change matters when the real things—the plainest things—remain forever unchanged.

Afternoon waned, and the soft light of the setting sun cast deep shadows across the bodies in my yard, the house and barn, and even our hills; the tart nectar, which had raised everyone's spirits so high, had now left them in various states of slumber on the ground. The Archduke did not leave till past sundown, and when Ruth escorted him out her face was as weary as if she'd done a full day's labor. He wore a broad, regal smile. The bearers and musicians had all long since fallen asleep under the lull of the pipe, and sighed and snorted when they awoke to find their day's work but partway done. I provided flaming torches to the two pipers, that their instruments might be silent and they might lead the way home. And how the Archduke, his glossy hair, his bright gown, and his intricate sandals, did glow in their glare. The most intrepid of my neighbors, mainly the young, still lolled about the periphery of my property, but the rest had gone home to prepare for tomorrow's honest labor. Ruth and the Archduke bowed to and thanked one another so many times I began to fear they'd both gone stark mad; and then finally he approached and placed his arms about her with a

---

[6] Primarily the Archduke's largish ego, and whether or not we had this or that marvelous thing (e.g., harnesses, pavement, crenellation) in Cambridge.

gesture of such shocking familiarity that I began to fear for her honor. He patted her back and said, "I will look forward to our next meeting."

"Oh," she said, "me, too. It's been a real pleasure."

"Gundron," he said, bowing full low, "I can't thank you enough. Keep up the good work, man—and send word by Ruth of any new innovations, hear?"

"I will, sir, though I've got some other—"

"Hut hut!" he called to his men as he entered his litter.

The sotted thirteen began to grumble and raise themselves onto elbows and knees. "Ready to take you home, master," one of the bearers offered valiantly. The eight of them stumbled to the litter, spat in their palms, rolled their shoulders, and otherwise prepared for what was sure to be a dreadful journey. Two of them let the curtains down, all eight lifted the contraption groaning aloft, and with the pipers silently out front to light the way, he left at a stately pace, accompanied by the drums and trumpet. My neighbors, waving us good night, followed off behind, and the procession, as it left my yard, looked like a peculiar funeral.

Before they were even gone, Ruth stumbled back inside and collapsed onto her pallet. "Good God," she said.

We rushed in to question her. "Tell me everything," said my wife.

Ruth covered her eyes with her hands. "There's not much to tell. He wants me to write his biography."

"His what?"

"The story of his life."

"What for?"

"To spread his fame outside his immediate surroundings, I guess. He seems to have a pretty clear idea that Neem—"

"Nnms," I again corrected.

"—isn't all there is. He thinks there are pagan settlements all about, and he wants to bring them to God and under his own dominion. So he wants me to write it all down so he can go out, and, I don't know, conquer new territories, or at least spread his fame. Do you know anything about tribes of heathens, out in the hills or whatever?"

"There are tales," Adelaïda said solemnly, "but no one counts them for much."

"There was at least one fisherman," I said, "to bring my grandmother across the hills."

"Anyway, he wants his story told."

Only the greatest of princes, the most mythic and heroic, had ever, to my knowledge, received such an honor. I had not known our own Archduke was so great, and wondered if indeed he were so. "And did you agree?" I asked, picking at the remains of what had been an excellent ham. Poor Ragan, gone to feed us, her mate, Mauritius, snuffling disconsolate in the barn.

"Not really. I told him I'd think about it."

"You are wise not to decide quickly," I said, snug in the knowledge of her independence of mind, "though certain it would be a great honor."

"I'm sure"—she nodded, closing her eyes—"but it wasn't really what I had in mind."

"You knew not about the Archduke before you came here?"

"I might have guessed you'd have one, but that's not what I'm interested in. I mean, I want to write about you, about your neighbors, about your life here. We have enough rich people at home. Everyone knows what rich people do."

Of such a book, about common men such as myself, I had never heard, and though it made my heart race, I dared not ask. Whatever she meant, it was great reassurance to know that our Ruth's judgment was not clouded by nobility; and that she would not also embark upon the project of memorializing the Archduke—which might well, to be frank, strain the limits of our hospitality—without asking our opinion, our permission, our blessing. I rejoiced in the soundness of her thought.

I wonder now what would have been her decision had the next week's events not befallen us.

CHAPTER FOUR

THE GREAT NORTH MEADOW

he next Sunday there were no more visits to look forward to, so after church we went driving. Adelaïda and Elizaveta wore their frocks of blue linen so fine that the slightest hint of breeze threatened to bear it away. Ruth, in a black shirt in the back of the cart, cut a surly figure. We began by turning toward the Great North Meadow, which Jepho had said was grown fair. Thence we planned to travel to the Great Mountains to the east, from which Ruth had come, and which she had not since visited. At Mandrik's urging we had brought flowers, water, and a stick of fragrant wood to offer at the foot of the mountains, to thank them for her safe deliverance among us.

"I wonder if the Archduke's going to make those maps," she shouted over the clatter of the cart.

"Why do you ask?"

"Because I'm curious what they would look like. He can't have any clear sense of geography beyond this island."

"What need have we of maps? We never venture to the outside world." I grazed my darling's bay quarters with the willow switch, somewhat more forcefully than I might have, alone and without female intrusion. She neighed her complaint and sped up. "Perhaps you should make maps yourself, if you're keen on them."

"It's no fun if I make them. I know what they're supposed to look like."

Hammadi ran like the wind, and the sound of the wheels was soon louder than Ruth's voice. Even when they come from afar, women are women.

Then, in a flash of sunlight, a bird with a wingspan as broad as a house, as smooth as a burnished pewter mug, came hurtling down from the sky. The whistle of its spiraling descent drowned out even the sound of my wheels, and burned like fire through my ears. High above its rumbling wail did I hear the terror in my daughter's shrieking and Hammadi's opening her mouth before God. Foul smoke trailed from the nether parts of the terrible bird as it wound with a stiff and awful grace toward the ground. When at last it hit—half a day later, by my reckoning, though it could only have been a moment—it erupted in a mass of pale flames, throwing the horse back toward us as she bucked, reared, and averted her head from the consuming heat. The cart still desired its forward motion and barreled onward, striking Hammadi square in the neck with such force that her noble head tore from her body with a thick, squelching snap that froze the marrow in my bones. I heard my family screaming behind me, but could see only my own slow progress over the mangled, blood-spitting carcass of my beast. The cart, hitting her squarely, overturned, and as my family wailed at a distance of thousands of miles, my body, freed from the ordinary constraints of motion, traced a long, slow, beautiful path through the smoky, bloody air and toward the beckoning ground.

In that moment, as placid and seamless as any in my life, I felt both the dull weight and the spiritual gravity of my body, and knew in my marrow what it meant to die, and did not regret the separation of my earthly form from my deepest selfhood, bent as it was on returning to so many I had loved. My flight was longer than the centuries, and when at last my flesh met Mandragora's soil, its cold, hard welcome was as inevitable as Death's crook beckoning me to what lay beyond. The ground pressed the last air from my body, and I left myself behind without regret as I wakened into the world of the dead. I lay still and awaited my parents, my first wife, and my brothers and sister, armed with their instruments, singing the songs I had heard only faintly in life.

Soon, however, it became clear that there was no music, and I grew panicked that the world of the dead was so ordinary and quiet. It let out a soft, general hum, which soon enough gave way to Elizaveta's plaintive shrieks and to Adelaïda's and Ruth's voices, shaken and comforting her. Then the dry, bitter smoke entered my mouth and nose in a torrent. When at last I opened my eyes—the same eyes I had closed forever but a moment before—the sky was as gray as the prospects of the damned, and beneath it I saw the body of my horse, entwined with the wood of the cart, which yesterday had seemed a masterpiece. Her life's blood stained the meadow black, and gave forth the stink of misery.

My Hammadi was dead, but since I could realize it, I reasoned, I could not be; therefore did I decide to sit up, loath though my body was to support the weight of my eyes' grief. The great bird had split head from tail and lay crumpled and steaming. My horse had met her end, but her blood pumped as vigorously as if she were atrot. My daughter's cries, though they grieved me, meant she still made her way among the living, and my wife's and the stranger's quiet voices gladdened my paralyzed heart. I turned to face them, and there they were, in their earthly bodies; my wife with one hand on the child and her forehead to the ground, praying, and Ruth reaching across her own leg, which lay at a strange angle, to comfort my wife.

The great bird hissed.

"Did you see it," I asked them, "come out of the sky?"

Adelaïda sat up and gathered the wailing baby to her filthy breast. She did not, I think, hear me speaking to her.

When I stood, the world, already off balance, turned sideways, but I pushed through it to walk to them. They were covered in the season's rich mud—the blue dresses ruined, their pale skin bloodied and exposed through the gashes in their clothes—and their hair stuck to their faces. I knelt to hold my wife and daughter with such force that I knocked them down. When we righted ourselves, I reached out to take our stranger's hand, and looked at her for the first time. Ruth's leg had a bend in the mid-calf, to look at which gave me a wrenching pain in my stomach.

"I think it's okay," she said, her lips pulled tight across her teeth. "I can't feel it."

I said, "If you can't feel it, it's not right."

Adelaïda let go the child long enough to examine the wound, which caused Ruth to draw her breath in across her teeth. "Mandrik will set it, the Father will bless it, and if we pray—"

"I'm not worried about it," she said, her voice gone harsh. "I'm worried about the people in the airplane. I hope they're okay."

"People die of broken limbs," my wife said.

We all regarded the smoking carcass. My throat was raw. "That monster killed my horse," I said, unwilling to look anymore upon the carnage.

"It's terrible, Yves, but we have to check on the people. They need help."

My stomach grew heavy as I understood what she had said. "That thing? That is your airplane?"

"Yves, we talked about it—you said you'd heard it and seen it."

"But never this close. It never came and tried to kill my family."

"That's not the kind I came in—it's too small to be a passenger plane—but anyway, yes—"

I continued to look on its stinking, mangled form. "I thought it would be beautiful."

"Yves, please, we need to help the people."

"You tell me you can fly, but you don't tell me you do it in a death machine."

"It doesn't always end in death," she yelled, then turned to press at her leg with her muddy fingers.

For some time, I suppose, the rumbling of our neighbors' carts had been drawing near, but now the hooves and wheels—equal in number—drew nearer still, though all stopped a good distance from the charmed circle in which we sat, panicked, stinking, and still. I saw Dithyramb and Miller Freund shielding their eyes, but Mandrik and Ydlbert jumped down from the cart and ran to us.

"Does it live?" my neighbor asked. "Does your family live?"

At the sound of his familiar voice, my daughter's wail grew louder.

"It has murdered my horse."

Mandrik, once assured that we all still breathed, turned bravely toward the beast. He approached the mangled form and peered in.

"Be careful, brother," Adelaïda shouted.

He leaned closer, and pulled out, by the arms, the slender, lifeless body of a man, dressed in a strange suit of clothing of a bay leaf's hue, with zippers, like Ruth's, over his breast and at his hip. His loose, sandy hair was matted with blood. A gasp escaped the crowd before Mandrik lay the body down. I ran over the tilting ground to help him, and Father Stanislaus was soon beside us. His face wore an expression of panic, and he swung his piffling censer against the great smoke of the dying machine. Mandrik pulled forth a second corpse, identically clad, but with rich, dark hair, and one arm hanging loose in its sleeve, pumping forth blood as terribly as did my Hammadi.

Ruth held both shaking hands to her mouth. "Oh, my God. Is there anyone else in there?"

Someone among the crowd began to retch, and Father Stanislaus's normal pallor blanched to sickly pale.

"No one," my brother said, looking around. "Nothing but machinery, and two great metal boxes."

Father Stanislaus made the sign of the cross over the corpses, then stopped and leaned into Mandrik's ear. "I have always held, Mandrik, that your private devotions are a detriment to our community, and that you would do better to bring them within the confines of our church."

"This is no time—"

"Let me finish. I hold fast to my opinion still. But you are the only other man of God among us, and I must ask your advice. Do I administer Last Rites over these bodies?"

My mouth dropped open. "You're the priest."

He smiled nervously and half bowed. "This, excuse me, Yves, is a matter for holy men."

"I don't think it takes a holy man to see that with two men dead—not to mention my horse—Last Rites are in order."

"Yes, but see here. They're strangely dressed—who knows what paganism they might have subscribed to? And even should they have been Christians, if these men have been consumed by this beast, will they be rebegot at the Last Reckoning in their own bodies, or will their bodies be brought up as part of the beast's?"

Hammadi was dead and my heart shaken, and I stared at him in disbelief. My brother, thankfully, retorted, "Do you use this occasion to discuss minutiae of theology?"

"I wouldn't call this—"

"Do you suggest that a smoking, belching beast will be resurrected, along with man, at the end of history?"

"Mandrik," I whispered, "it's a machine. Like a grist mill."

"Let me handle this."

"Mandrik, you misunderstand me. What do you think will happen to all the food you've eaten when at last you are called up in Rapture?"

"Do you suggest, Father, that carrots, parsnips, chickens, and cows will be resurrected? That the Christ you so passionately believe in died for the barnyard's sins?"

Father Stanislaus's face went red. "No, Mandrik, but I am asking you, will their flesh be resurrected as part of yours when the Lord God calls you up?"

"Well, I don't think so," he answered, flaring his nostrils. "But I don't believe in your niggling church."

My ears sang with confusion and at last my voice rose, rasping, from my throat. "All of this, excuse me, seems irrelevant."

"When we have never before," said the Father, his pointy chin in the air, "seen such a beast? No, Yves. You're mistaken."

My brother shook his head. "This is an odd occasion for heterodoxy."

"I have asked for your opinion, Mandrik, not a sermon."

"Bury them, if you will, then, as Christians," said my brother. "For whatever your speculations about the last day of history, they were not eaten by this—" Mandrik tapped its skull with his finger, and it rang like a low, sickly bell.

I said, "Airplane," and a smile crossed his face.

"Keep out of this, Yves. They were not eaten."

"Clearly you don't understand the—"

"You're right," Stanislaus said, ignoring me utterly, "belched out whole, like Jonah from the whale, before the actions of the digestion had yet begun to work upon them."

"However you care to think of it, Father."

Father Stanislaus looked hard at my brother before kneeling once more to bless the poor corpses. We left him to his duties and returned to ours. "I will talk to you about this later," Mandrik said, turning his head as we walked so that our neighbors could not catch his meaning. "But, meanwhile, say nothing."

Anya had gathered my wife and child, wiped their soiled faces with her apron, and begun to plait my daughter's wild hair. Ruth had broken into a sweat. Mandrik looked at her leg, which was swelling, changing the shape of her trousers. "Cut me a thong from off the horse, brother," he commanded me, "and pry me a board loose from the cart."

"I cannot—"

"I need your help."

My whole body began to shake with anger and pain. "Is no one aware," I asked him, "of the horror that has befallen my horse, and nearly befell my whole family?"

"Praise God he took the beast and not your wife."

"Beast? She had a *name*."

"A bad omen," one of my neighbors commented, but Desvres's voice hushed him.

"Then rest certain God called her by it when he brought her up. Now go."

"Damn it, man," Dithyramb interjected, "be thankful for all you have left."

The solemn words of the Last Rites rose plaintively over the babbling of my neighbors and the pounding of my heart. I pulled my knife from my boot, where it had, miraculously, remained lodged during the tumble, and approached what had, an hour before, been the strong, supple workings of Hammadi, as well known to me as a member of my family. Even over the smoke of the airplane and the sharp stink of my horse's blood, she—her carcass—smelled like herself. I tried to breathe deep of what I would never smell again. I hacked at the strap, and felt faint to see the bones and innards of what had but moments before been as dear to me as life. Horses had died before—they had died frightful deaths—but none had I known so well; none before had seemed so resolutely to possess a soul. As clear as it had been to me when my brothers and sister passed away that they had left their grosser bodies for a more subtle place, so was it clear to me then that what had made my horse dear had traveled hence. My eyes stung as I cut off the straps, which had not bound her strongly enough to keep her with me. The carcass was yet warm, but it did not sing under my touch as even that morning, impatient and imbued with life, it had done.

"Excuse me, Yves," said the miller, his hat respectfully across his chest.

"Yes?"

"But what do you plan to do with the meat? My wife's been hankering after some good horse, and I'd pay you fair."

"Hammadi is not for sale," I managed to say, though my throat was tight.

"But it's not your horse anymore, lad—it's meat."

"Is there someone else to whom I could bring my grain, come winter?"

"Hang it, Yves, I didn't mean to—"

"Hang it, indeed."

I brought my brother the strap, and with my knife he teased open the leg of Ruth's trousers while I fetched a board. He bared her white, hairless leg, mottled with a clotting mound of a bruise, to the grass and sky, and my neighbors piled shamelessly around to watch. Speaking to her softly, he gave a great tug at her foot, at which she screamed and her head dropped to the ground. Anya and Desvres's wife were immediately patting her face and hands as Mandrik felt along the ugly welt on her leg. "I think it's straight," he said, "if you'll bring me the board."

With the knife he planed the roughest edges from the wood, lifted her leg until the board was flat beneath, and bound her to it with the straps. When the women succeeded in waking her, she looked at the apparatus in terror, her face wet and pale with pain. "For God's sake, Yves, why didn't you step on the fucking brakes?"

"She raves," said Anya, a son picking lazily at the hem of her skirt. "Someone fetch water."

"Why didn't I what?"

"Lift her carefully," Mandrik directed as Ydlbert and Dirk moved her to their hay-strewn cart, "and lay her down with reverence."

"Step on the fucking brakes."

Her vituperation stung me though I knew not what she meant. "Step?"

She made a weak fist and banged on the floor of the cart. "You don't have brakes?"

I said, "What is she talking about?"

"It's true," Mandrik said, climbing into the cart beside her, "but you needn't worry about it now."

"How do you stop the thing?"

"We try not to go too quickly, and when necessary we turn up-hill."

"I can't believe I didn't notice this." She shook her head, her face weary. "We've got work to do, Yves."

Mandrik smoothed her brow and said, "Tomorrow," and lifted his chin to Dirk to signal the cart into motion.

"And don't bury those people without checking their pockets," she called, as Thea, hale as ever, bore her away. "We're going to need their wallets."

Each man carried a small, worn leather case in one of the zippered places on his person. In each such case was a wafer bearing a remarkable likeness alongside a name in perfect lettering—John Boogaerts and Thomas Ulyanov, the strangest appellations I had ever beheld. Also therein were wafers with letters and numbers, papers covered with intricate designs in moss-green ink, and tiny images, no larger than the palm of a child's hand, of people—in the one, a smiling young woman in a rosy chemise, her hair in a halo of curls, and in the other a fat child of indeterminate sex whose cheeks and forehead glistened. Both people sat stiffly before their blue backgrounds like saints, but were depicted with a loving precision no artist's brush could achieve even with the finest paints of gold and lapis lazuli.

"Photographs," Ruth said, waving them away with her hand from her new place in our bed. We would spend the night on her pallet that she might better rest—for when one is to pass into the next world, it is best to do it from a proper bedstead. Mandrik, too, wished to stay, in case the patient needed him during the night, and sat meanwhile on the bed beside her, sponging her brow with a mother's care. "Please, I don't want to see them. It's terrible."

How full she was of words, and how disdainful of wonders.

"Their families?" I asked.

"Yes, of course. Those poor men."

"Father Stanislaus will give them a proper funeral. Their souls will be in peace."

"Sure," Mandrik said. "If they were Christians."

Adelaïda gave her a new bowl of a soporific tea and a pipeful of something sharp-smelling Mandrik had brought to ease the pain.

"I don't think you should bury them yet. Wait a day or two. They'll come looking."

"Who?"

She shrugged her shoulders and closed her eyes. In her homeland, I supposed, people did not always give straight answers.

"If it happens," Mandrik said, "we'll worry about it then. But the reek of decay waits for no man."

"How," I asked, since she was not answering, "do they make such likenesses?"

She opened her eyes again and wrinkled her forehead at me.

"The photographs," Mandrik interpreted.

"With a machine that makes impressions of light. Because we see everything we see as a result of light. The machine records the subtle modulations."

"The two of them," Adelaïda mumbled, pointing bedward. "Not exactly married to plain sense."

"Does everyone have photographs?"

Ruth exhaled the pungent smoke, which made my head dance. "Hundreds of them. Thousands."

"You also, then?"

The fire crackled its reply long before she herself decided to. "In my bag, toward the top, there's a red notebook, if you'll bring it to me."

Her possessions were strange to the touch—the fabrics soft, all sliding from my grasp, and other things as cool and slippery as fish in the summer stream. The book, like all her writing places, was pierced at regular intervals and bound with a neat wire coil—a most practical innovation. One of her ink-filled implements was clipped to the front. "Here," I said, handing it to her, and hoping that my eyes did not convey the intimacy of what my hands had uncovered.

She rubbed her dry hand along its cover before propping it open in her lap. "Okay," she said. Adelaïda brought a tallow candle and perched beside me at the bed's edge. Elizaveta, who had swaddled Pudge in newly carded wool and smelled sweet from the oil, climbed gingerly up next to Ruth, steering clear, by intuition, of her injured leg. Inside the notebook she had stashed a pile of images, all larger than the first I had seen. On top was a picture of two girl children, bright with health and wearing identical red dresses. "Me," she said, "and my sister, Nurit."

"Where's you?" Elizaveta asked.

Ruth pointed to the child on the left, shorter of stature and wider of eye. "When I was little, like you."

"You were little?"

"How, exactly, do they freeze the light?"

She tilted the image back and forth, allowing the candlelight to reflect on the smooth surface. "I'm not sure I can explain it, really." She looked to Mandrik as if he knew the answer, but he shook his head. "It records it on something clear, and you can shine light through it again to print the photograph on special paper." Surely, I surmised, if she had such apparatus with her, she would have shown us how it worked. She placed herself and her sister beside her on the blanket, revealing another image, of three people before a shockingly white house. The figure on the left was clearly her, and on the right, no doubt, this same sister; between them was a tall, serious young man in a black robe and wearing jewels in his ears—perhaps the custom of her country. Neither woman smiled, though neither looked unhappy. They were so slender, as if someone had stretched them out. "That's my brother, Eli. He doesn't usually look so grim, but that was his high school graduation. He's in college, now."

Did she invent these words purely for my pleasure? They coursed through me like the fire of whiskey on a winter's night. As I was about to point to some black lines, thin as spiderwebs, on her sister's narrow face, she said, "Those are eyeglasses, to help her see. Her vision's bad." I wanted to blow the Eyeglasses away and look at the face more closely. Mandrik bent down, lips open in concentration, to examine her family's faces.

Next, all in gray like the house by the light of the embers before sunrise, were a woman in a white dress and a man in gray, both looking past their shoulders at something in the distance. The woman looked like Ruth, but younger, or with less about which to worry. "That's my parents' wedding," she said, and flipped to another image of them, barely clothed such that it made my heart leap, and lying still as the dead on a pale, pocked surface. "Whoops," she said, "my parents at the beach," and promptly turned them face down to the sheet. Ruth a child again, bright as a jewel, with one hand in a large bowl and the mother's bare, splendid arm reaching across her shoulders. All three children sun-dazed in vivid grass. The mother, older now, sitting behind a dark wooden table with her hands folded, her eyes obscured by a sparkling haze. The two young women, bare-shouldered, wrapped in one another's arms, Ruth's grin as wide as the sky and her sister's more hesitant.

"That's exactly how she smiles," Ruth said. "That's her exact face."[1]

Mandrik said, "You look happy together."

She blew a speck of dust from the paper. "She's my best friend."

Mandrik's eyes searched mine, then turned back to the image.

Suddenly, though there were photographs beneath these we had not yet seen, she closed the book over them and placed it beneath her pillow. "That's my family," she said, and began to worry her lower lip between her teeth.

Mandrik said, "Show us the others."

I, too, yearned for the rest of the pile. "I wish I could look at my family, thus. Especially those who are gone now."

"Which I guess is why we do it, take photographs. Which is darker than I used to think."

Elizaveta said, "More."

"No more," Ruth said. Mandrik again mopped her face. "I miss them so much. It breaks my heart to look at them." She did not move them before she retired. Just as my siblings appeared to me dancing and whispering of what was to come, so too, I am certain, did hers whisper beneath her head that evening as she sought peace amid her feverish dreams.

Clive came alone that night, without brother or sister, without even the sweet instruments that usually accompanied their arrival. I would not even have known to wake for his coming had his glow not pierced like sunlight my closed eyes. When I regarded him, he was sprawled casually over the pallet on which we slept, but a few inches above it; beneath him the covers glowed. "Tragic," he said, though his face was too radiant for real solemnity.

"The crash?"

He nodded.

I began to panic. "Their souls—"

---

[1] I had always loved how Nurit smiled—as if she truly meant to do it but were constitutionally unable to feel happy. Looking at her then, with her pale skin and her crooked black glasses, gave me a terrible attack of homesickness, and made everything and everyone around me look gloomy and dull by contrast.

"They don't know up from down, a sudden change like that. They're wandering, sleepless and cold."

"Don't tell me things like that, Clive."

"It's no need to fear. These things always settle down in the end."

"Where are Marvin and Eglantine?"

He shrugged his shoulders. "Busy. So much news."

"News of what?"

"So much changing, hereabouts."

"Tell me what happens to the souls of horses."

He shook his head no. "Keep your eyes open, Yves."

"Open for what?"

"Just open." He began to grow airy and thin.

"Clive, don't leave like this."

"Rather," he whispered, "should you bid me joy on my return to bliss." He left behind a delicious odor, like ripe fruit.

Mandrik, hunched over the table in the light of the dying fire, had watched our whole exchange, and his eyes, doubtless tired from working in the dim light, grew misty.

"You should sleep," I told him.

"He might have said hello."

"Perhaps he had other business."

Mandrik bent his head into his hands and scratched it slowly. "How much business do you really think they have, on the other side?"

"What are you working on?"

"Go back to sleep, Yves, before you wake the women." He dipped his pen, wiped the excess from the nib, and resumed his rhythmic scratching. Late in the night Friedl Vox came up the road, rending the air like a screech owl with her incoherent cries, but Mandrik did not even look up to catch my eye.

Gerald Desvres, who had a steady hand for carving, traced the letters I stenciled onto two blocks of granite: "John Boogaerts—Fell from the Sky" and "Thomas Ulyanov—Also Fell." He leaned them against the alder by the wormy pits to which we planned to consign the bodies. Heinrik and Jepho Martin built caskets of pine and good nails. I myself gave winding sheets, for my wife weaves linen softer than any in the village, and it seemed most likely to provide comfort in the journey to the regions beyond. Dithyramb lent two large shovels. Stanislaus took their strange mangled clothes and promised to commission a great reliquary that we might visit them in church. Ruth could not attend the ceremony for her countrymen—even had she been able to move, Adelaïda had cut her free of the remains of her trousers before we put her to bed—but Mandrik left her with a tankard of water and a basket of fruit. The rest of the village turned out, as well as the Archduke's attaché and a great throng from the city of Nnms, who had heard the airplane's impact and the subsequent tales of our disaster, and had come later to investigate. There was no outright weeping, for none of us had known these men, and all had been frightened by their mode of arrival. Our eyes did, however, grow red with empathy, and I shed a few tears for Hammadi. Mandrik, who usually stood near to assist the soul of the departed in its journey, hung back by the cemetery gate, his hands buried each up the opposite sleeve.

"Brother," I whispered to him as our good neighbors prayed, "does something ail you?"

Mandrik shrugged and retreated farther into his sleeves. "Who knows what they would want? Who knows if they wouldn't rather be dismembered and scattered to the carrion birds?"

He himself had mandated this funeral, as I recalled. "You heard Clive tell me they were wandering."

He gave a somber nod.

The Lord's Prayer cascaded around my uncomprehending ears a moment before I managed again to speak. "Do you think all Ruth's countrymen are Jews?"

"Jews? I'll wager most of them are nothing at all."

"Pardon?"

"Did you look at their faces? Tell me if therein you saw the light of God."

This seemed inappropriate at a funeral, howsobeit of utter strangers. "I don't want to think about it."

Adelaïda backed out of the crowd to see what we were talking about. "Nothing," I told her. Her eyes flared with pique.

"I don't think we should have left Ruth alone," Mandrik said. "She can't fend for herself."

"I'm sure she's fine."

"Or will be," Adelaïda said, "after Lord knows how many months of us waiting upon her."

My ears pricked up like a horse's at her tone. "Is there a problem, wife?"

"Not yet, certainly, no." She made her way nearer the spectacle once again.

Twelve of our ablest-bodied—Ydlbert's elder sons in prominence among them—brought the caskets gently to the ground. My stomach sank, for only by the grace of God were my family and I not thus aslumber. If it had been my wife, this day, beneath the alder, next to my parents, my siblings, my first wife, next to all that I once held dear? My heart would be broken; not one loss more could I bear. As it was, Hammadi's body lay headless and moldering in the meadow, and I could bring myself neither to think about it long nor to go to the spot to move her.

"I hope," my brother continued, with what was surely hardly a pause, "they were believers. Else, for all the comfort we are thus giving ourselves, we have done nothing to help them."

"Will you stop discussing it?" I whispered. "You're spooking me."

Friedl Vox stood docile next to her son, and merely wept over the spectacle with her one good eye.

Desvres and Dithyramb began shoveling, and the earth fell upon the first box with a sickening thud. There would be no ceremony for my Hammadi, and no one with whom to commiserate over her loss. Who had lost a named horse before? In our parents' times, life was so fragile, and survival so delicate an endeavor, that they hardly took time to mourn their human dead. My father would have given his strong right hand for the luxury of grieving for a beast of work. But Hammadi herself had made this so—by releasing me from my labors, she had freed me to contemplation. Now truly and for the first time did I bear the weight of its bitterness.

The next day came the season's first hard rain, so quickly that it pooled in the yard and the burgeoning crops, drowning the frailest shoots and turning all else to glistening mud. Mandrik brought Ruth a board to hold across her lap, that she might continue her writing; and he sat busy working at the table all morning. Adelaïda made a point of sweeping around him, cooking around him, as if he were most especially in the way. On such a day I should have found indoor work to occupy me, but I could think only of Hammadi under the glowering sky, the raindrops pressing at her body, telling it, as it rotted, to make haste, make haste.

"I'm going out to bury the horse," I told them.

"Not in this weather, you're not," my wife chided.

Mandrik, however, saw the fire in my eyes, stood up, and girded himself against the rain. "Come, then." Against my wife's protests and what might at some other time have been my own better judgment, we set out to Ydlbert's, our heads bowed under the onslaught of the weather, my wineskin across my body and its contents providing succor at every third step.

We must have looked a sight when we arrived, for Anya blinked at us, unwilling to open her door farther to the dripping messes we had become. By that time, also, I was well drunk. "It's no matter, Anya," said I. "We have only come to borrow Thea and the cart."

"In this rain?" Ydlbert asked, approaching the door with his youngest slung across his shoulder like a rag.

"I can't rest until I bury her."

"Neither can you dig a hole in the rain, lad. Use your sense."

"I cannot rest," I told him.

Mandrik added, "You cannot argue with a man possessed."

He shook his balding head and patted his dangling son without attention. "Do you need my help, then?"

I shrugged my sopping shoulders. I was too sick and weary to ask.

Mandrik said, "With great thanks, Brother von Iggislau."

"Then come." He sighed, slapping my shoulder. A wet spray cascaded from me and descended into the general fray. "It'll be faster with three."

"The lot of you," said Anya, "have no respect for womankind. No idea how much work you leave us after you've filled our wombs up with bairns."

Ydlbert kissed her thin lips and handed her the squirming child before he set off, head bent grimly, toward the barn.

It was hard work for Thea, pulling us along the soft road, and every few steps she balked and turned to see if we had changed our minds, or come to our senses. Mandrik huddled in the back of the cart with his arms up his sleeves. Ydlbert brought the wet whip down a few times against Thea's black hide, but could not make her pull faster, and soon began to exhort her more kindly with words. Thus he convinced her to draw us across the wet meadow, but he could not make her approach the body of her departed sister. Even in the rain was the carcass covered with flies, her proud, glossy coat already pocked and flecked with decay. Above the stink of wet leather, wet grass, and my own inebriation rose the terrible stench of death. Far overhead we heard the low, mournful cry of another airplane seeking its departed kin. We struggled with all our might to lift Hammadi's lifeless body onto the cart, then retrieved her grimacing head, the eyes wide, dull, and littered with flies. Thea could hardly hold the cart still, no doubt because she knew what her nose smelled and her keen eyes saw. Our shoes sticking tenaciously in the mud, we walked back to my land alongside her, as much for the health of our stomachs as because we could not ask her to cart any more of a load.

We turned northwards and pulled the cart through the fallow field toward the cairn, which glistened black in the rain. I myself was rain, covered with rain, full of rain. "I've brought you company, Iulia," I cried to her. "Brought you another." And we commenced to dig a few paces from Iulia's grave. Never in a lifetime of farming did I perform a labor so difficult as digging in that wet, fertile mud. Ydlbert cursed a string of oaths worthy of Friedl Vox, but I could not laugh as perhaps he wanted me to. Mandrik grunted under the strain of the labor, but said nothing. Twice did I think my back would break in twain, and I lay down with my beloved in the loamy comfort of the earth. But I did not die, nor could I feel myself sweat in the driving rain, and though my eyes and throat were hot, who knew but God if I cried, so washed the salt tears into the tumult that bathed the ground. We built a high mound above the body, and took, each of us, an ugly, craggy rock from the cairn with which to commemorate the death of my friend and beast. We lay down in the mud for a while—for what did it matter, after we'd been in it for hours—looking up at the two cruel heaps, and, filthy beyond recognition, drove home to Ydlbert's. When at last Mandrik and I returned to my farm, it had never looked so dismal or covered in mud, and though Adelaïda had warmed blankets by the fire and baked us potatoes in the coals, I stripped, regardless of our visitor, lay down in her soft pallet, and woke some time the next day, unaware that a whole night's darkness had passed, for the darkness behind my eyes and the pain in my body had eclipsed it like the wandering moon the bright sun.

Mandrik stuffed a new mattress with straw, that my wife and I might have a more comfortable bed while we slept thus on the floor, and he went home later that day, for he could not leave his plants untended. But as long as our patient convalesced, he returned daily with nourishing fruits from the garden, with tales to tell and manuscripts to read. Her face brightened whenever she heard his creaking rope shoes coming up the yard. I could imagine how wearisome would be such a confinement without so caring and interesting a visitor, and was glad for his more frequent company. My wife did not complain, but I thought I caught a tightness in the set of her lips, which had not been there before.

The double axle appealed to intuition; the mind's eye could create it where no such thing had been before. But the accomplishment of brakes was a different task. Ruth, groggy with fever and smoke, nibbling the day long on fruit and her revolting crusts of burnt bread, could not make clear if they were to be pulled, or pushed, or whatnot, and could explain their functioning only by making a quick, startled expression that sent Elizaveta into hysterics. "It makes it stop," she said again and again. "What else can I say? I don't know much about machines. Mandrik?"

"I cannot help you."

"If it is strong enough to stop the cart," I reasoned, "then surely it will run it aground or crack an axle. We don't need it. I won't drive so fast anymore. The Archduke will issue a ban on fast driving."

"No, he won't," she said, her voice rising with impatience, "because everyone likes it. It's fun."

"We never used to think about fun."

"Except," Adelaïda said, "on holidays, or sometimes before we were wed."

"So," Ruth said, "now you've had some fun, not on a holiday. Are you willing to go without it?"

I did not like these questions. "I'd rather not."

"Then brakes are easier than accidents."

"I'm sorry about your leg, Ruth."

Mandrik said, "Be thankful it heals."

"It's not your fault. But brakes. They—it *grips* the wheel slightly, so the friction slows the thing down."

"Can you draw it?"

She shook her perspiring head no.

"How am I to build it and put it on my cart when you, who have seen it, cannot even describe its workings?"[2] The fire we kept stoked to heal her seemed unbearably warm. "Well, hang improving the cart. I have no horse with which to move it."

Adelaïda, watching her soup by the fire, sang:

> *Hammadi was a fine horse,*
> *With a star 'pon her brow.*
> *She was nigh a divine horse*
> *With the cart and the plow.*

"Stop that, will you?" barked I. "I don't want to think about her."

"I was memorializing her."

"Do it some other day."

She turned from me, and stirred the pot with renewed vigor. I regretted my harsh words, though I did not retract them. I sat on the bed with a chalk and a slate, puzzling my way through the new invention.

"On a bicycle," Ruth said, "it's definitely a thing that grips the wheel."

"A bicycle?"

"Ruth," Mandrik admonished. "You must quit mentioning things my people know not of."

She furrowed her brow, then closed her eyes.

Mine had been the work that released us from slavery—mine the harness, mine the sundry improvements to the cart, which had rendered it so efficient as to become dangerous. But the following Market Day,

---

[2] If you think I'm not embarrassed that I couldn't explain the simplest mechanisms of modern technology to him, think again.

mine was the back that bowed beneath what I admitted to be the insignificant weight of a carrying sling full of early lettuces. My eyes smarted with the ignominy, my back cried out in imagined pain, and all my soul yearned for the work and the company of my Hammadi. None of my good neighbors had thought to leave room in his cart for my produce, or to come fetch me before the exodus. I walked the long road alone. Those who lived farther from town—Jude Dithyramb, Yorik von Iggislau, Wido Jungfrau, and my Uncle Frith—passed me along the road and called out greetings, as if I had taken this activity up for a pass-time. Frith even whistled and called back, "That'll show you what good it does, inventing things!" I had rounded the bend by Ydlbert's yard when his cart clattered onto the road behind me and pulled abreast. Thea, somewhat ahead of me, turned back to stare, something between shock and amusement lighting her great brown eyes.

"Hop aboard, brother," said her master, "and we won't be late."

I looked up at my friend, standing blithely amid the lettuces behind his reins, and I choked with rage.

"Yves," said he, "in an hour the market will be abustle."

I resettled my burden on my back. "I'll walk."

"Why so?"

"It is my fate now. Without Hammadi, I must struggle to earn my living."

"Come. We'll visit the horse dealer, and by tomorrow you'll have your new girl trained to the plow."

The mention of a replacement infuriated me, and I looked at him with the cold, appraising eyes of a stranger. Beneath that soft, brown cap, I knew, more and more of his pate was naked to the breezes, and his belly was growing fat. Thinking about it gave me pleasure.

"Yves."

"Go, man. I'll walk, and I'll see you there."

He clicked his tongue at Thea, who hesitated to leave me trudging along with so sour an expression on my face. She strained briefly under the weight before she picked up speed—as my Hammadi would never do again. As soon as they had gone I regretted my folly, for no one else offered to bear me and my lettuces to market.

It was a long walk, and the sun was high in a hazy sky before I reached the Great West Gate of Nnms. Within, the paved streets were bustling with traffic, and workmen were laying stone foundations for new dwellings. Great brass placards had gone up announcing the names of the new streets. The broad thoroughfare to the church was Via Urbis, and its sister, branching off to the fortress to the south and the horse dealer to the north, was Via Mappamondo. My progress along Via Urbis was slowed by the throngs, and when at last I arrived, my countrymen had sold the cream of their produce and were folding up their tarps. I took a place toward the end of the row and set out my lettuces, somewhat battered and warm from jouncing against my body. They sold quickly, for they were large for the season and fair of hue, but it was late enough in the day that the townspeople bargained, and grew surly at my attempts to obtain a good price. One lad, his finger so far up his nose that I feared for his welfare, said, "Ain't you the one with the traveler and the dead horse? My pappy says to stay away from you."

"You'd better, then," I said, clouting him across the head with my open palm.

The child ran shrieking away, his wooden shoes threatening to fall from his feet at every step.

When the afternoon waned and I tossed my last two lettuces into the gutter, I had earned not a quarter of my usual take for a good spring day, which did little to improve my already black mood.

The sun hung low in the gauzy pink cradle of the sky when I returned home. Mandrik had left. Adelaïda greeted me with a heap of mashed turnips. "How was market?" she asked, digging into her own bowl.

"Foul," I answered. "We'll be in the poorhouse yet."

Ruth, her work scattered about her on the bed, said, "Where's the poorhouse?"

"It's an expression."

"Did you find a new horse?" asked Adelaïda.

"I didn't look."

She pursed her lips around the wooden spoon. "How, then, do you expect your lot to improve?"

"Damn it, woman, I don't."

"You might fashion a new harness, for when you change your mind."

"You're not listening. I'm not changing my mind."

"Yves," Ruth said, "it's all going to be fine."

"That's easy for you to say, who might die any moment."

"Excuse me?"

Adelaïda brought more turnips to her invalid. "Now now. Just because my brother Carmichael died of a broken leg doesn't mean you will."

"People don't die of broken bones."

"People don't die," my wife emended, "of broken hearts. Bones, all the time."

"That's ridiculous. You set them and they heal."

Her Cambridge must have been a soft and balmy place, where wounds set cleanly and no one feared infection or the long, slow demise. Until her bone healed, how would she be fed and kept warm? How clean herself or look after the basic tasks necessary to her existence? Her inability to recognize the fragility of her situation raised my dander. "People die of broken bones when they don't have my brother to set them, and neighbors to carry them home in a cart, and people to look after their every need. Left on their own, they die."

Her finger traced a shadow on the sheet. "I had no idea."

"We are taking care of you as best we can."

"Thank you, Yves."

"In the midst of our own tragedy, we are looking after you."

"Thank you, Yves. I'm sorry. I didn't mean to be ungrateful."

Adelaïda sighed and continued eating—she had too much work to allow my sourness to spoil her meal. I would not budge, however, from my admittedly difficult stance. Hammadi was different from other horses, and I could not simply replace her like a worn shoe. If it meant more toil and less earnings until I changed my mind, so be it, thought I. This was the price of the great service she did me. It seemed my duty to pay.

We held our monthly gathering on the new moon; the darkest night, it was the one least possible to use for work, even in the tightest of circumstances. When the new moon came that month, despite all that had happened, I swept my barn floor as ever, brought forth liquor, and eagerly awaited the menfolk, who descended in a clump a short while after they finished their dinners.

"Things should not," Jepho Martin said before he even sat down, "fall thus out of the sky. I'm sorry about your horse, Yves."

"Thank you."

His brother raised his bushy eyebrows. "Things fall all the time—birds and hailstones, if nought else."

"But not great beasts. Only think if it had landed in one of our fields. Someone could have lost his crop in a morning."

"We all," Ydlbert assured him, "would have done our best to make up the loss."

Laight, as it seemed, came mostly for the drink, but though he had settled in against a post with his gourdful, he opened his mouth to speak. "You're right, Jepho, that great things shouldn't rain down like that. I'm worried what might be the cause."

"A terrible accident," Ydlbert said. I added, "Ruth says they come and go all the time, with never such bloody results. She says they land and fly off again like birds, a hundred times a day."

"I think it's the sign of something amiss," Jungfrau said, his voice deep with sobriety. "A sign of witchery."

Ydlbert said, "Not all ill luck is the product of a curse."

"And do me a favor," said Dithyramb, "and leave my mother out of your accusations this time."

"My grandmother, too," I seconded, though Dithyramb's Friedl was, I admitted, easy to suspect.

Jungfrau shook his large head. I think he thought we were all rather stupid. "Nothing fell from the sky before the stranger came."

We looked among ourselves, and my stomach drew tight. "And?"

Wido shrugged. "Has she brought any curses on your household?"

"My household is a hundred times blessed."

"Not in horses," Yorik murmured.

"Cows not giving milk, hens not laying?"

"Nay," I said, "my beasts are hale and well."

"And no one thinks it odd we've seen no sign of any family in the parish having a new bairn since Tansy Gansevöort's, at Advent?"

I looked at my countrymen—most with large families, most in adequate health. "Tansy's bairn was among us four months before Ruth arrived, and in all that time there was no news of a child on the way. So yes, I suppose someone might have witched our women, but I know it wasn't anyone resides in my house."

Ion Gansevöort, the lucky father of the lucky child, said, "I think that stranger's been right kind when she's come around questioning."

"Brought us a basket of gooseberries," Heinrik said, "and listened better than I listen to the priest in church."

"She is soft with my daughter. I have accepted her as my own," said I. Clearly I had said too much, for my countrymen regarded me strangely.

Said Gerald Desvres, "And you have no fear for your family?"

"I live ever in fear of God's wrath, Gerald. But I am not afraid of Ruth."

He looked about at the company, and poured another short round. "Of all of us, Yves knows best of what he speaks. We should take him at his word."

I let my cup sit before me, but around me many were raised. "Hear hear," said Nethering, and the ale was drunk.

Jungfrau shook his head. "If no one heeds my warning, then so be it. But I'll tell you one thing: Beware."

That the echo of my sister's words should issue from Wido's mouth both offended my stomach and tickled my spine. I was glad that I did not see the hair rise on any other man's arms. That, at least, might soothe my restless mind.

I was still bothered by Jungfrau's air of prophecy, and still woozy-headed from the ale, when next morning the Archduke's dappled horse and bright cart clattered up, with two attendants and the attaché. The trumpet boy squawked, and the attaché hopped down with something less than the air of sprightly grace I thought he intended. He approached the sty I was halfheartedly cleaning, but would not venture actually near. "Sorry to interrupt, Gundron."

I leaned on my dung rake. "No trouble. What news?"

"The Archduke sends to know where his immortalizer is. If I may say so, and to put it mildly, he's quite thoroughly steamed."

Mauritius, lonely for his lately-eaten mate, snuffled listlessly at my feet.

"Ruth was injured in that terrible fall from the sky. Her leg is broken, and she lies abed."

His delicate face darkened. "Do you expect her to live?"

"We hope, and pray."

He fingered his mustache. "That won't do."

I moved the rake slightly, by way of a sign—which indeed worked to rouse him.

"I'll bring him the news," he said, "but he won't be pleased."

"Sorry I have none better."

He remounted his cart and drove away. I was annoyed by his visit until, later that afternoon, the Archduke sent the cart back with two sacks of oranges and a note in a spidery hand: "Look forward to your return to the living, that I may tell you all my tales."

Ruth heaved a sigh and let the note fall to the floor.

All the while Ruth had spoken of the brake, she spoke as if it would be a great and intricate invention, but in a flash like the storm fires of Heaven, I realized what she meant: a device to raise its hand against the forward motion of the wheel and cry, "Halt!" I realized this thinning out the radishes in the garden, and ran to the barn, where I took out my pen box immediately. Gone were the days when I might go to visit my horse and sketch an idea, but without her I could still draw this new thing. If it would release me from danger, and from the bondage of my guilt over Hammadi's death—if it would allow me to drive where and how I pleased—then it would be worth any amount of effort.

That day I stopped in the house only to eat, so busy was my mind with the invention; and when I went inside, I had hardly a thought to spare for wife, child, and invalid. In the afternoon I tended the wheat in the northern fields, pursuing all the while the new invention with persistence and vigor. The idea gave me renewed strength in my work; I had before me my crops—my hands in the loamy soil, the sun upon my back, the sweet stalks blowing and brushing against me, the sap of life coursing in them like love in a young man's heart; and ever the great promise of the new invention. This was my destiny—the fate for which I had been born, the reason God placed me down on this green earth. I felt the power of His grace and the earth's great abundance rising in me like a fire poised to consume a house—bedsheets, children, and all.

All that week did I tend the crops, and after lunch each day spent a while in the barn working at the problem of the brakes. One afternoon, feeling it a guilty pleasure, I cut the leather for a new harness, for who-ever the next horse might be; and found myself, much to my surprise, dreaming of her beauty, of her long, black mane. Even this short time idling away from work softened me; at the end of each day my hands stung from the cruel hasps of the tools, and the fierce sun burned the back of my neck as surely as if I were Ruth's bread in the kitchen fire. But I persevered in both my invention and the work of the land, for these were the tasks I was made for. Had my father grown soft as I seemed to be doing, we would never have survived the winters. I would not put my family in peril to chase after ideas—only chase after them furtively in my spare time. One dreamer in a family is more than its due, so I would learn to leave my family's dreaming to my brother.

Come Market Day, Ydlbert drove round early with his cart half full, and helped me load up produce for sale. I climbed in with him among my early peas and radishes and his sweet-smelling hay. Along the route we discoursed of weather and pests, wives and weather, as two farmers ought to do, alone on the road together on a fine June morning. It had been a comfortable while since Anya had borne a son, and Ydlbert hoped she would bear no more; I still dreamed of an heir. My chest filled fuller of the good air than it had since the airplane had come. Except that we now shared a cart instead of each to his own, everything seemed as fine as it ever had been. And though I regretted my horse's loss, I remembered my fresh straps of harness leather in the barn, and began to see how the pall of Hammadi's passing would lift.

"You'll buy a new horse, then?" Ydlbert asked, hardly looking at me.

"Someday."

"Andras Drck has a few good ones."

"I'm certain," I said coldly, though secretly pleased at his concern. My eyes absently read the sky for the next day's weather (a wind so fierce who knew what it might blow in from the north), and beheld what at first I took to be a vision. Soon enough it became some other kind of airplane, moss green in color, and with a bulbous head and a dragonfly's tail. It wore a gray halo above it, and its bleating cut the air.

"Look at that," I told my companion.

Without letting up on Thea's speed, he scanned the sky. When his eyes lit upon it, he shook his head, spat off the side of the cart, and cursed. "I thought we'd had enough trouble for one year."

"As did I."

His head kept shaking. "Perhaps that one will leave us alone. I'm not sure you should have taken that stranger in, Yves."

"She has nothing to do with the airplanes."

He spat again. "Did you ever see one before she arrived?"

"Never so close. But of course I'd seen one."

"I think you're misremembering."

As this new one moved across the sky, she grew louder, and larger, and soon, it became clear, began to descend. Unlike her sister, she did not pitch headlong toward the ground, but came toward it deliberately, like a bee preparing to alight on a flower. The force of her nearness was so strong that it rustled the hairs on my head and the nearby grass. She hovered above us, looming large as a barn, before she disappeared from view into the foothills near the city. I said, "Do you want to go see it?"

"Whatever its business, we'll hear of it soon enough," he said.

"I'm sure," I said, though I was also curious.

"And I hope it hasn't done to someone else what the last one did to your Hammadi."

"No," I said, my throat growing tight. "I wouldn't want that to happen to anyone."

"Though, when the last one came, I heard the sound of trouble four miles distant, and this one doesn't have quite that same disastrous ring."

"I wouldn't know," I said.

The Martin brothers went hollering past in their laden carts, the first of our neighbors to bear witness to whatever had come.

Despite all of which, my mind was full of the world's abundance. It would have been more than enough had we been sent a single machine from the sky; but because His world is plentiful, in darkness as in light, God sent us two. For a reason I could not describe, my body was suffused with ease; I felt I had begun to understand my brother's raptures. Oh, to have been a farmer like my father, my mind concerned wholly with the land; but since I had been cursed with introspection, how glad was I, in that moment, to see to what stillness inside myself it might lead me. Where there had been the airplane's thrum, there was now only the fluid buzz of early summer, followed soon by the shouts of my countrymen, who had not yet seen enough of a bad thing. It had landed, sure, but I did not care to have any further knowledge of its whereabouts.

At last, that evening, I finished the plans for the brakes, full of private exultation. I nailed them like a proclamation to the barn door, though I was not sure what they heralded. One more step in the process my harness had begun, or its crowning glory altogether? I did not regret my harness or any of the changes it had wrought, but my heart sang when it realized that perhaps this invention would be the end of all inventions, the one that would suffice for the rest of history.

I fell asleep that night holding fast to that clarity of mind.

Dawn brought my brother, who was in residence in a spot of sunshine against the side of the barn when I awoke. I had rolled out of bed to loose the animals, and was shocked to see him sitting there smiling, his eyes closed and his face tilted best to accept the first offering of the sun's warmth. When he was thus disposed, it was generally difficult to rouse him, but my curiosity was piqued by the parcel he'd brought with him, four feet by one in dimension, and wrapped in chamois like a sacred book. Therefore, despite that he was likely in communion with the Almighty, I stood at his feet and yelled, "Mandrik!"

He opened his eyes with a look of affront, as if I had slapped him in the face. "Christ, you could be more gentle."

"You don't have to do your sitting right outside my barn, either. What's in the chamois?"

"I've been waiting for you to arise."

"The dawn just broke." Indeed, it still trailed wisps of pink and orange cloud across the horizon, though already the day was unusually hot. "How long have you been sitting there?"

He shrugged his shoulders and smiled sleepily.

"What's in the chamois?"

"I devised a smaller splint for Ruth's leg, and two crutches, that she might hobble out to the sunshine."

"You think of her a great deal."

"I should think you'd be pleased, brother, that she won't be abed all the day."

"I like her," I answered, "where I can watch her. Come have tea."

"Adelaïda, I think, will like her better not underfoot." He cracked his wrists, and followed me in. Adelaïda was boiling nettles for our tea and porridge for our breakfast, though Ruth was still sleeping and the child yet lay in her hammock.

"Good morning, all," Mandrik commanded in a boisterous tone unlike him. The slumberers recoiled at the sound. "Sleep may yet beckon you, but we have important business."

Ruth pulled the coverlet farther over her head.

"I've brought lighter implements to set your leg, and two crutches that you might hop about."

From beneath the blanket she murmured, "Thank you."

"Some of your countrymen are here, and you'd best come to meet them. They won't come calling like gentlemen, not like the Archduke. They talk faster and louder than jays at mating season, and go about everywhere with large, gray, whining devices that they claim record everything they hear or see, the world's most perfect scribes. They're not far. They've set up under a canvas tent at Heinrik Martin's."

She startled fully awake, and pushed the covers from her face. "Excuse me, wait. Start over. Who's here?"

"Two men in search of your countrymen who fell. They say they don't know you."

"Did you tell them you buried them? I told you to wait."

"Rumor has it Stanislaus told them, and railed his displeasure against them—hard to imagine, but that's how the tale goes—and now they're ruffled up like fighting cocks."

Something new to interrupt my timely ministration to my crops.

"Stanislaus, of course, told them that under no circumstances could they exhume what had been commended to the Lord. But when he starts up, they threaten their 'government' will 'intervene,' though they claim that's not their chiefest desire. And now the Archduke has sent his men to demand an audience."

"Wage war?" I asked. It seemed impossible, that after all our placid history we should be besieged because two men fell from the sky.

"They did not mention war."

Ruth scooted so far forward in the bed she nearly fell out. "Of course not. We wouldn't make war against some little island off Scotland."

"Some little island?" I said, affronted.

Mandrik said, "They want the bodies back."

"I don't blame them. I don't know what to do about this." She exhaled through her nose, then pointed to his leg contraption, which, though fashioned of pine and willow, did not look especially kindly. It had more supports and straps than seemed strictly necessary, and the buckles were heavy and cruel. "Is that going to hurt?"

"I don't know. It's a new invention."

My wife held a damp rag over Ruth's forehead as I and my brother, our eyes averted from her abbreviated undergarments, cut loose the old splint and bathed the leg, which had, curiously enough, sprouted hair. We bound the leg into the new bracing with minimal fuss from Ruth.

"Is it all right?" he asked her.

"My leg hurts."

"But is the brace all right?"

She rolled her leg gently from side to side. The marvelous contraption gave off creaks like a harness as she moved. The wrinkles on her brow relaxed. "I think it's good. I think I can get around on it. But the only pants I have left are the stretchy black ones I was wearing when I got here."

Mandrik said, "Something will have to suffice."

"What do people do," Adelaïda asked, "in families with no inventors?" From her tone it was unclear if she admired my brother's handiwork or wished he'd kept it in his own hut.

We fed my brother—who demanded to know of the brakes on the barn door, which, upon explanation, he called ingenious—and dressed the child for the journey toward town. Ruth wasn't so simple. Adelaïda's second, dark blue chemise proved too tight in the shoulders and scandalous in length; but it was no more scandalous than her trousers had been, and it was all we could do to cover her. I drew a stocking onto her one hale leg, thinking the while that I should not perform such ministrations and watching Adelaïda bristle as I performed them, and laced on her thick brown boot. I ran to Ydlbert's, explained him our troubles, and he hitched Thea and drove me back to the house. She hung her pretty black head and grumbled when she saw how much weight we were hoisting aboard. Though Hammadi she was not, she drew us without pause to Heinrik Martin's, where a hubbub was under way, centered on a large, singularly unfestive tent of mossy hue. Two men clad in those strange green zippery suits approached from thereout at a dizzying pace, before Ydlbert could coax Thea to stop.

"Are you Ruth Blum?" one called in an accent like her own— broad, flat, and graceless. The other held a whining gray box on his shoulder, and looked through a dark protuberance over his eye. Both men peered into the cart. Martin's livestock were in a tizzy, and Stanislaus stood amid his parishioners with a pained look in his eyes.

"Yes, who are you?"

He with the box said, in a softer voice, "What's on your leg? Are you all right?"

"Lieutenant Commander Nolan Bradley of the United States Navy. The fellow with the camera is Lieutenant John Fiske. Are you hurt, ma'am?"

"Not badly, no," she said. We struggled to lift her from the cart. "I broke my leg in an accident, but it seems to be healing okay." She leaned heavily into her left crutch so that she could extend her right hand. Her unencumbered countryman extended his as if it were the most natural greeting in the world. "I'm pleased to meet you," she said, "and I hope I can be of help."

Fiske lifted the vision box from his eye, and the two men regarded one another. "Ms. Blum," said Bradley, his hard voice full of portent, "would you mind stepping aside for a moment?"

She looked down at her contraption and said, "If we don't have to walk too far." Bradley smiled curtly. Fiske placed his machine gingerly in the cart. Flanking her, they walked a few paces off. I tried to remain close enough to hear their talk, but they whispered, as all of us whispered to each other, gathering around to try to figure out what this new miracle meant.[3]

---

[3] "Listen," Bradley told me, popping his jaw as if he chewed too much gum. "We've been having some trouble with the authorities in this town, with the priest, Father Stanislaus."

"What kind of trouble?"

"Apparently it's a religious community. They won't budge on returning the bodies."

I said, "I told them to wait before they buried them. What are you going to do with the plane?"

"We've removed the cargo from it—sensitive cargo. As for the machine itself, we need to investigate the cause of the crash, and then we can leave it." Bradley let out a sharp, quick sigh. "Ms. Blum, you'll excuse me for asking this question, but are you being held in this community against your will?"

I tried not to stare—they looked so impossibly clean to me after over a month in the village, and half menacing and half ridiculous in their flight suits. "I'm an anthropologist. I'm here making a study of their way of life. They're completely pre-industrial. It's a special situation."

"You're sure? Because we can help you if you need help."

"Thank you for the offer, but I'm doing very well here. As I said, I'll try to get this matter cleared up for you as soon as possible."

Bradley nodded. "Thank you, Ms. Blum. Any help you can offer in expediting this matter will be much appreciated. I don't think I'm revealing too much when I say that Boogaerts and Ulyanov were transporting some highly sensitive materials, highly sensitive, and that the sooner we can clear this up, and the more quietly, the better."

I said, "Of course. Probably, if it's okay, we should do our talking in front of the villagers. So they don't become suspicious."

"Right," Bradley said, and took a step back toward the crowd. "Good thinking."

When they returned, Fiske once again picked up his box, and trained it on our faces, then again on Ruth's beautiful splint.

"Ms. Blum," Bradley continued, as if there had been no break in their conversation, "do you know where Boogaerts and Ulyanov are buried?"

"Not exactly. I broke my leg in the same accident that killed them. Their plane crashed in front of our horse. So no, I was in bed when they buried them. I presume they're in the graveyard. It's not big."

"In the graveyard do they slumber," said Stanislaus, "and there shall they remain."

She kept leaning into one crutch or the other, smoothing her hair and running one palm across her mouth, as if terrified that they could see her. Bradley, who was a few inches taller, his bristling short hair the color of dried hay, took a long look at her ungainly attire. "And you say you're conducting anthropological research here, Ms. Blum?"

Even the animals, it seemed, hushed to hear her explanation; certainly the neighbors leaned closer in. "Yes. They'd had no intrusions from the modern world until I hiked in, in April."

"What is she doing?" Jepho asked.

Mandrik said, "Not now."

"And, if I may, I'll tell you bluntly," she continued, talking to these strange, skinny men as if they were the most normal thing in the world, "that I'm concerned about what your presence here will mean for my work."

Fiske, whose shoulder sagged slightly under the weight of his contraption, said gently, "We don't mean to interfere."

"Rather," Bradley added with more force, "the sooner we can amend the situation here, the sooner we'll get out. Father Stanislaus"— he nodded to the priest, who could not muster up a retort—"has denied our request for the return of our brothers' bodies. If you'll help us convince him otherwise, we'll be on our way."

Strange though the gesture was upon her crutches, she shrugged her shoulders. "I'll do what I can. When does your backup arrive?"

Bradley stared at her.

"Surely the Navy didn't send a team of two to investigate the disappearance of one of its planes and two of its men?"

Bradley was as fair as she, and though his mouth remained stern, his pale cheeks flushed. "As I mentioned, the nature of their mission—this is a matter of national security, Ms. Blum."

She looked Fiske's machine in the eye. "Is it possible to put the camera away? I think that, until you brought it out, they'd never seen one."

Fiske took the contraption down from his eye to regard her. "I'm sorry, ma'am, but it's regulations."

"I understand."

"And what are you doing," he asked, incredulous, "in the field with no camera?"

She shook her head. "I didn't, I didn't think I should be the ambassador of technology. I'm writing everything down."

"I never heard of such a thing."

"The little worm sure does know how to make friendly," said Wido Jungfrau. "Adelaïda better watch out."

"Philistine," Ydlbert whispered.

"We can help you with equipment, supplies—we can get you better medical attention," Fiske offered.

"Thank you, but I don't need anything. I'm fine."

The gray box stared at her leg for an uncomfortably long time. "Your leg is all right in that thing?"

She did not answer quickly. "This is the best they can do for it. I think it's all right."

The box continued to point at her leg, and I saw how gruesome was my brother's fair contraption in its eye.

"We will, of course," said Bradley, "bring these videotapes back for review."

"Please don't make fun of how they're looking after me. The sooner we get this taken care of, the happier all of us will be."

"Aye," shouted Wido Jungfrau, "she's siding with the enemy already."

"I am not, Wido, siding with anyone. I think it's in all of our best interests to see how we can work this out."

"Over my dead body," Stanislaus said quietly, "will they disturb the soul's rest."

Jepho and Desvres drew him back into the crowd.

"And they'll do nothing," said the nervous attaché, "without his Urbanity's say so."

"Ma'am," Fiske said, "we'll try to work this out as quickly as possible. I have a son in Tallahassee, and I'm anxious to see him."

Tallahassee sounded some fair garden where no ill could befall a man—verdant and full of tumbling children.

"Perhaps," said Bradley, "you'd like to come into the house a moment? If Mr. Martin wouldn't mind."

Heinrik's eyes were so wide the whites shone all the way around his irises. "Whatever we can do for you, sirs, so long as you don't rain the wrath of God down upon us."

Ruth said, "Thank you, Heinrik." She worked her crutches without grace, and hopped toward the house. The two young men fell into step behind her, and my brother and I followed a few paces behind.

"Would it be possible to confer without your"—Bradley asked quietly, glancing round at us—"entourage?"

"My friends, Yves Gundron and Mandrik le Chouchou, are some of the most respected men in this village. They know much more about the Mandragorans than do I."

Jungfrau muttered, "Aye, we worship our madmen here."

The attaché stood before her and pushed back his voluminous coat. "As the Archduke's emissary, I feel it my duty—"

"Please," Ruth said. "I promise I'll act in all of our best interests."

Fiske let the box down from his squinting brown eye and looked at her—despite his Lieutenant Commander, I thought—with admiration. And so we left the attaché behind and went into Heinrik Martin's house, the tall strangers ducking beneath his low door. The man of the house ensconced himself in a corner with his gray-haired, freckle-faced wife; both wore slightly giddy expressions, as if they hadn't slept in days but had ceased to care, and Heinrik had, it seemed, been so much at playing with his whiskers that they hung twisted in two long spikes like a sage's. "Hullo, Martin," I bade him.

"Hullo, Gundron. Make yourselves at home. Prugne?"

His eldest daughter, so rosy with health as to be nearly obscene, offered us mugs of ale. Both of the new arrivals took notice of her bosom. With so many bodies in the small house, it was extremely hot, and I accepted my ration with gratitude, and my brother's as well.

The ambassadors put down the gray device in favor of a smaller one that rested on the table like a loaf of bread, and emitted a gentle whir like a distant mill wheel.

Ruth settled her leg with some difficulty onto the long bench. "I'd like to keep this as brief as possible."

"Our sentiments exactly," said Bradley, still standing. "This is serious business, Ms. Blum. The citizens of this—"

"Subjects, I'd say," she interjected. "Excuse me."

"Thank you. The subjects of this hamlet, then," Bradley continued, "have unlawfully seized the remains of two American pilots who were transporting sensitive cargo. When they turn over the bodies, we can investigate the cause of the crash—which we're assuming was caused by mechanical malfunction—and be done with it." He cleared his throat.

"But as the priest told them," Mandrik said without pause, apparently unconcerned that the man used so many unfamiliar words, "we have given these men burial, and freed their souls to the great Beyond. Do they wish to call them back by removing the bodies from their resting places?"

"Mr. Mandrik—"

"The title is unnecessary."

"—there are two grieving families waiting."

"And how will you manage the souls, Mr. Fiske?"

Fiske looked up from the gray box, and the one who'd been arguing said, "I'm Lieutenant Commander Bradley."

"The soul," Mandrik said quietly, "falls not under your governance."

The two youths, their short hair on end, regarded one another. Bradley turned to Ruth with a show of pride. "You see, Ms. Blum, what we've been up against with the authorities in this town."

Mandrik's face unmistakably brightened that they thought him an authority.

"Perhaps," said Bradley, "I have not made myself a hundred percent clear. The cargo of that plane poses a grave threat to the people of this village. The sooner—"

"A threat of what kind?"

"I am not at liberty to say."

She nodded slowly. "A chemical threat? A biological threat?"

"Ms. Blum—"

"Please," Fiske interjected quietly.

"—the sooner you retrieve us our bodies, the sooner we get our cargo out of your town. It's that simple."

Ruth stared blankly at my brother, but I could not see that his face gave her any sign. After a long, thick silence, she turned to Bradley and said, simply, "I'll see that this is taken care of."

"Ruth," Mandrik said.

"Please."

"Then, for the present, we can adjourn," Bradley said, and walked toward the door.

"Is it too much to ask that while you're here you keep your contact with people to a minimum? I'm afraid of what they'd think of a cell phone."

Fiske said, "We'll do our best."

Ruth nodded. "Then we'll be on our way."

Both of them rose to help her up, and the kind one steadied her crutches. My brother deserved praise for their craftsmanship. Mandrik and I helped Ruth back to the cart, beneath the shade of which Adelaïda and Elizaveta were playing a game with stones. Ydlbert had wandered off to relieve himself.

"Call a meeting," she told Mandrik, "for this evening. In the barn."

"Nay, it's too hot to meet indoors," I said.

Adelaïda said, "They do nothing anymore but sit around and talk. I wonder we won't starve, come winter."

Mandrik took the crutches and settled Ruth gently into the cart. "We'll call it in the grove, where we were feasting when you arrived."

"After sundown, when it'll be cooler."

"It'll take that long to gather everyone anyway," I said.

Mandrik nodded and stepped off the wheel, and dispersed Ydlbert's sons to tell the village of the plan. Ydlbert drove us home under a blazing June sun, both of us standing behind the reins. "Don't you think," Ruth said, before she drifted into a feverish slumber, "you'd be happier if there were a seat there—a board so you could rest your feet on the edge of the cart and not have to stand in here with the cabbages and hay?"

"Hang it with my cart, woman."

"Only a suggestion. I'm sorry."

But like the brakes and the double axle before, it bit into my mind like a hungry dog, and by the time we were home, I had forgotten my lack of need for new inventions, and made me a full-blown image.

There was no second way about it: I needed a horse. Ydlbert was my closest neighbor and dearest friend, but I could not keep asking him to drive me hither and yon; that was my own burden. I took my savings from beneath the bed. "Can you watch our sickling?" I asked my wife, once we had deposited her, slick with sweat, back onto the mattress.

Adelaïda's brow was furrowed. "If you promise she won't die before evening. She doesn't look hale."

Ruth's whole body shone, and her face was drawn in tight as she slept. "She cannot die, she's got a meeting to run." I kissed Adelaïda's cheek and might as well have kissed a fence post.

Ydlbert nudged me in the shoulder as we settled in again behind the reins. "You won't get an heir that way," he said.

"No." I laughed, but truly Adelaïda's unhappiness pained me. She had lasted a great while longer than my first wife, but who knew how long I would keep her? I wanted her time on this earth to be glad; I could not bear to think that I might be the reason otherwise.

In days past, it took half a day to reach Andras Drck's, clear at the north end of Nnms, past innumerable alleyways and two foul creeks. Now we had but to drive the Via Urbis to the church square—a much quieter place than on Market Days—and turn northward onto the Via Mappamondo, which brought us to our destination before the sun could make a moment's move in the sky. The road stopped a few paces shy of Drck's, and his horses, bred heavy for work, frolicked in their enclosure between the last row of houses and the pinkish city wall. The man himself, dark-bearded and with his trousers rolled up to his knees, sat barefoot on his doorstep, eating a hunk of pale bread.

"Gundron," he called out, nodding. "Been wondering when we'd see you, what after the calamity with that last one."

None of the horses, I could see, would ever be the equal of my Hammadi; none was so fine or proud. "She was a good horse," I said.

"Plenty of others hereabouts. I'll show you a good workhorse." He stood and left his bread behind him, where his dirty white dog promptly hunted it down. "How about you, von Iggislau? Perhaps you're thinking about buying a second?"

Ydlbert guffawed. "What would a man do with two horses?"

Drck shook his head. "Twice as much work, for one thing. Or breed."

Ydlbert shook his head. "I don't know, brother. Perhaps in my dotage I'll have money to spare for such as that."

Many of his horses were too expensive for a working man; a few lame of leg or long of tooth; a few I simply disliked. At last he brought forth a two-year-old roan mare, her blond mane and tail slightly kinked, like Ruth's hair, her pink lips drawn back in what almost looked to be a smile. "That's a fine one," I said.

"And strong," added Drck. "She'll be an excellent plow horse. Come greet her."

I walked a circuit around her. Her neck was short, giving her quite the peasant's appearance, but her shoulders seemed strong. She was heartier than Hammadi, sure. Still, when I held my hand out to her sweet-looking mouth, she skittered and ducked her head. "What's her trouble?" I asked. "I never met a horse that didn't like me."

"She's a bit shy of strangers, but she'll show her true colors soon enough. And already trained to the harness. A fine sight of a mare."

She was pretty down to the golden feathering over her hooves, and her eyes were sharp and black—but what did pretty matter against the kindness and intelligence of my Hammadi? I walked around and around her, but could not make her look at me. "This horse won't look me in the eye, man," I told him, my throat tight with dismay.

"She's shy, I tell you. She doesn't know you. But she'll be an excellent beast. You can strap her in the harness as soon as you get her home."

"Take her," Ydlbert counseled. "She's strong as the hills."

"She is not Hammadi."

"No horse ever will be. She's a good horse in her own right."

I parted with a great sum of money for the right to walk this creature back through town with me by her bridle. I would use her to drive my family to the meeting that night, though I was not sure I liked or trusted her, and to bring in the fruits of the harvest. "Are you pleased, man?" Ydlbert called down from the cart beside me as we cleared the city gates.

"She has not Hammadi's spirit." She glared at me for a moment before turning away.

"How could she? She hasn't yet got a name."

I regarded long and close her unhurried gait, her short, yellow tail like a broom behind her. If I had chosen badly, this mistake would, if Heaven be merciful, be with me a long, long time. "I'll call her Enya-datta."

Ydlbert laughed, and Thea blew air to second his opinion. "It'll be a mouthful when you want to call her in."

"Nevertheless, it's her name." I clicked my tongue to her. "Enya-datta?"

She continued to look at the road. But what did it matter, I had my horse. She could not be expected to be so humble or giving as Hammadi; she was too young, and did not remember the old days, in which ordinary labor so often led to a beast's death, and gave her humility before her Maker.

"I'll have to fashion that new harness," I said wearily, though deep down it gave me a feeling of some exultation.

"You can't get it done before tonight."

"I've already cut the leather."

"I can help, if you desire."

"Thank you, Ydlbert. But I won't need help."

Adelaïda and Elizaveta came out to greet the new member of our family, my daughter approaching the horse with the full petting surface of her hands extended, as if she could not get enough of herself on the animal. Enyadatta watched these ministrations, and allowed herself to be subjected to them, but did not ripple with pleasure under them as Hammadi would have done; and Adelaïda did not, therefore, show the same enthusiasm she had shown when I brought the last horse home. Perhaps, too, it was because we were older now, and had more cares, but when I placed Enyadatta into Hammadi's stall, I felt lonely and sick.

CHAPTER FIVE

THE EXHUMATION

uth was ill before night fell, either from her wound or from the day's events. She lay sweating and glassy-eyed abed, despite my wife's ministrations. I was busy stitching the harness, while Ydlbert's sons prepared the outlying neighbors for the night's somber festivities. Mandrik, afoot, made the rounds closer to town, and was later seen by many perched in a tree, in which he prayed aloud for guidance, and composed a hymn of praise.[1] Desvres, by report, scythed out the clearing in the abundant summer grove, and cleared out the roasting pit, to which he brought a cartload of cured wood before the shadows began to grow long. Such a civic-minded individual was Desvres. My wife, who had planned to warp her loom and begin making what would clothe us in winter, could do no such thing with an invalid to tend. Heinrik's fields, and Dithyramb's, and Jungfrau's all looked healthier than mine. Even Yorik von Iggislau, who had long since been accused of trying to plant pole beans in his wife and something else entirely in the ground, had wheat whose abundance put mine to shame. I worked on the harness, and tried to converse with Enyadatta, who would not even look at me when she grunted. A dour, hu-

---

[1] "Thank you, Lord, for Sister Airplane,/Though her flight be erratic and her Ways be strange,/For she brings us our Brethren from the skies."

morless horse she seemed, but perhaps she would be kinder when I ceased comparing her every moment to Hammadi. She had to sense that I thought her second-rate.

My wife bathed Ruth like a babe, with rag, water, and bowl, and dressed her again in the chemise, but to no avail—it was soaked through within the hour. As the sun trailed nightward to the west, Adelaïda plied her with broth, but she only began to shiver. "There's no getting out of this meeting," she told her patient. "You'll have to be well."

"I'm fine," said Ruth, with an affectation of lack of care. "I'll be fine."

But before long we heard the neighbors' carts clattering past, all taking the road at a statelier pace now my Hammadi had served as example. Ruth looked no better than a shade; indeed, my own dead sister had looked more lively when she'd come to visit a few weeks since. We gave Elizaveta a heel of bread with which to amuse herself, and hitched the cart for the ride. As I secured the traces, Enyadatta turned to cast me a malignant look.

"Devil take you, horse," I muttered. "It's but your appointed work."

The evening, praise God, came on cooler than the day, with a breeze blowing mournfully down from the mountains. At Ydlbert's farm none but a lone, dirt-pecking chicken was astir, and from the rise did I see the bonfire, lusty as a bull in springtime, through the verdant leaves. Its light threw the trunks of the trees and the bodies of scores of people, Mandragorans and townsfolk both, into shadow. We drove in silence, listening only to the roar of the wheels against the rutted road and Enyadatta's ceaseless complaint. We heard voices in argument as we approached the grove, but as my cart drew nigh, one by one the voices hushed. At last I stood at the front of my cart, hearing only the wind in the leaves and the meadow grass as it brushed against my wheels, a sea of upturned faces regarding me from the heart of the fire, within the grove.

Ydlbert came forward to help me with the invalid, who fared no better for having been jostled along the road. Not since her arrival had my countrymen regarded her with so thorough an expression of wonder and mistrust. In the light of the fire, I looked at her afresh. In Adelaïda's dress she looked lankier than before, her pale face thinner in the shadows. But where, but a few weeks before, she had seemed to me so strange as almost inhuman, her face had become familiar; and as she leaned heavily into her crutches, I believed I saw both fear and determination in her eyes, and could not help feeling protective of both.

"Father Stanislaus," she said, bowing her head toward him where he sat, wound up tight. She nodded also to the attaché. "People of Mandragora. You know why we're gathered here."

The full moon, like a luminous bowl of milk, began to rise over the tops of the trees.

"The government of my country has sent two emissaries—"

"Emissaries of Hell!" Jungfrau shouted. Jepho Martin, rather more pertinently, cried, "Speak English!"

She drew in a long breath. "My countrymen want you to give back the bodies of John Boogaerts and Thomas Ulyanov. This is a serious matter."

"Aye," yelled Jude Dithyramb, "when the soul's eternal slumber is at stake."

A murmur of agreement rippled through the assembly.

Adelaïda clucked to herself. I did not want her sending Ruth ill wishes, but dared not say so.

"Yes, for the soul's sake. But for more immediately practical reasons as well. Partly because the government of my country is much larger and more powerful than you can likely imagine."

"How big?" Jowl asked, before being slapped across the mouth by his mother.

Ruth pinched her sweaty upper lip with her sweaty hand. "Imagine that there were a hundred cities of Nnms, with so many Archdukes, and someone even greater to keep them all in line. And that's not big enough to convey what I mean."

"He who rules the rulers of the world is He whom we call God," Stanislaus interjected. Thin though his voice was, the force of his convictions carried, and a tentative ripple of applause came forth.

"If they want the bodies back, they'll get them, no matter how much you protest. And I want to argue that you should cease protesting now—that you should give them back the bodies, and send them on their way."

Stanislaus rose slowly in his place, his chin pulled down into his neck for fortitude. His ivory cassock grew bright in the firelight, quite eclipsing his slender and tentative face. "Ruth, the exigencies of this life are many, and many its woes."

"Amen, brother," shouted Dithyramb.

Jepho said, "For Christ's sake, *speak English*! All of you!"

"But on such a topic as this, I cannot give even an inch of way to your opinion. The rulers of earth live and die like ordinary mortals—"

"Bite your tongue," said the attaché.

"—but the Ruler of Heaven, whose ways are eternal, has decreed the sanctity of earthly remains."

"You mean that if they move them," Ruth asked, without a trace of sarcasm, "God won't be able to find them on Judgment Day?" I longed to steer her toward a less volatile argument, but also feared to stand thus against the wishes of my countrymen.

"More or less. That the soul and the body will be unable to find one another at the Rapture, and the soul will then be unable to be brought to bliss."

My brother began to sing, passionately:

> *Heard the trumpet blare,*
> *Ain't no body in sight.*
> *Lord, I heard the trumpet blare,*
> *But my body ain't no-no-nowhere in sight.*

"Mandrik!" I shouted. "This is no time."

"Only an illustration," he snapped back.

"I don't know much about religion," she said modestly. Just don't, I thought, tell them you're a Jew. "Though I do, unlearned though I am, have faith that God is all-powerful, and that He'll know where the bodies are when they're reinterred. And I believe that if the bodies are exhumed with the appropriate respect, there's no sin in moving them back to their home soil."

Stanislaus held his tongue a moment, but Wido Jungfrau, his whiskers quivering, answered for him. "Don't you see it's wrong?"

"You cannot go digging bodies like you would a shrub," added Dithyramb.

"Bugger! Since when have you time for shrubs—pah!" yelled Miller Freund.

"There are larger—"

"This is blasphemy!" screamed Jungfrau to a chorus of "Hear!"s and "You tell it to her, brother!"s, and a single "Piss off, Miller," from Dithyramb.

"Larger issues are at stake." Ruth's voice strained over the general hum. "Please. Hear me out. I am listening to your arguments—please listen to mine."

Stanislaus turned to face the crowd. "As Christians, men, it is our duty to let her speak."

"Thank you," she said. Her whole weight leaned into the crutches, and she swayed slightly back and forth under the effort. "There are larger issues at stake, issues which affect us all. Please. Will you listen?"

In reply, the fire crackled as its logs burned and settled in; the trees shuddered. Perhaps as in my family there are seers, in hers there had been an orator or two—for despite the wretchedness of her appearance and the unpopularity of whatever she was about to say, she held the crowd rapt.

"I did not arrive here by accident. I was looking for you. I wanted to find out how you do things here, because it's so different from how we do things at home. So markedly, unbelievably different."

"Are all your people as strange as you?" Dirk asked, but the usual tone of combat was gone from his voice.

"Yes, if you put it that way, and no. If they could see you, Dirk, they would think you as strange a man as ever walked the planet. They would think that of all of you." She paused briefly, dripping sweat like snow melting in the sun. "I have to tell you that I think it's important to bring the story of Mandragora back home with me. I believe that the differences between your home and mine are fruitful, that they'll explain to all of us what we have in common, and that, more important, your story might show my people what we've strayed from, what we once had and have since lost."

She treated the ensuing silence as a lack of argument rather than, as I believed it to be, an utter lack of understanding, and continued. "I have tried not to be impertinent, or to pry where I wasn't wanted. I have hoped to earn your trust."

"You're not much of a bother," Yorik mumbled.

"If that's so, Yorik, then I hope you will trust me now. The truth is, Lieutenant Commander Bradley and Lieutenant Fiske want to get home as quickly as they can. But they won't leave without those bodies."

Jungfrau said, "I don't care a jot about your lieutenants. Why should I care what they want?" and Stanislaus urged him to hush.

"Because there was something dangerous in the plane."

Again a silence fell over the gathering, as heavy and dark as midwinter. Ruth's crutches creaked under her shifting weight.

Mandrik said, "Explain what you mean, Ruth." He watched her mouth carefully.

Stanislaus said, "Dangerous in what way?"

I felt the crowd's interest pulling toward her.

"They have taken whatever it was and put it in the helicopter, but they won't take it away until we give them the bodies. I don't know what they have, but whatever it is, from what I gather from Lieutenant Commander Bradley, it could be the most terrible curse that has ever been placed on you."

My breath came short in my chest. "Ruth, you're the one who'd never spit to ward off danger. I thought you didn't believe in hexes."

"This is different."

"Aye," called Wido, "because she brought it herself."

"I did not bring it with me. Believe me, I had nothing to do with this."

"Nothing but your compact with the Devil."

"Wido, I don't know what they've taken out of that plane, but it can kill us both without regard for our beliefs. I am trying to protect myself as well as protect you."

Stanislaus's eyes were cloudy. "Ruth, I understand that this is serious," he said, "and I have no doubt that your motives are pure. But these countrymen of yours have come to rob graves, and I cannot see how we could allow that."

"Father Stanislaus," she said gently. "Has anyone ever dug up a grave before? Here, in Mandragora?"

"No," he replied.

"Then you don't know for certain what the consequences are."

His Adam's apple bobbed furiously. "No, exactly as I don't know for certain the consequences if I murdered Jude Dithyramb, because I've never done it. But I know it's a sin."

Jude said, "Why pick me for an example?"

"But committing a sin against two who are already dead could save everyone else in this village."

"You cannot," said Stanislaus, "weigh one sin against another. They are equal in the eyes of God."

"But not to the people of this village." Her eyes pled with Mandrik for support, but though his expression was equally fervent, his lips remained tight shut. "Would it not be a terrible act to allow every person in this valley to die when it's within your power to let them live?"

Stanislaus had no immediate reply.

Ruth looked out over the upturned faces, and beyond to the black trunks of the oaks. "Death is certain," she said softly. "Death is imminent. Do you not believe me? Do you not trust me to tell the truth?"

At the edges of the crowd a sound began like the first whispers of a storm. Before I knew I meant to speak, I said, "I trust you, Ruth," and placed my hand on my wife's shoulder to silence her. She shuddered.

The mumbling ebbed, and Jungfrau said, not looking at me, "Aye, the mad tinker thinks she's all right. She's less strange than his own kin."

"You'll not insult my brother and walk from this meeting."

"Your brother? It's your grandmother witches my crops."

"Really, Yves," Mandrik said, one gentle hand on mine. "Stop arguing with him."

Ruth wiped the sweat from her brow with the heel of her hand. "Please, trust that I know the ways of my own people, and what we can expect of them and their machines."

Uncle Frith had sat quietly by some time now, thoughtfully chewing a piece of hay. Now he rose, bowed his head toward our sweating, frantic-eyed lady, and asked gently, "Tell me, whose side are you on, miss?"

The fireside once again grew silent. Ruth looked to Mandrik as if he might have her answer hidden in the palm of his closed hand. "I don't know," she said at last. "I want them to have what they want, so that they'll leave you, us, alone. Because I've always dreamed of you. Because I love it here."

Mandrik said, "Because she belongs among us."

"Is that what the spirits say?" Jungfrau scoffed.

"I have not consulted the spirits. It's what I say."

The gratitude poured forth from Ruth's eyes and, to my mind, outshone the fire.

Stanislaus's face was red from the heat of his convictions. "I would feel myself a bad shepherd if I allowed ill to befall every member of my flock. And perhaps, gentlemen, Ruth's faith in us is as deep as the faith she now asks us to place in her."

"He has seen it," Mandrik whispered.

"Seen what?"

"Seen the truth of what she says."

"I would not betray you," Ruth said. "I cannot speak for the sanctity of human remains, but please believe that I know what's best."

Stanislaus, his head bowed but his eyes full upon us, said, simply, "Chouchou?"

My brother took his hand from my shoulder, buried each hand up the other sleeve, and approached the fire, where he could better face the crowd. "Father, good neighbors. I have seen the horrors of which she speaks—weapons so fearsome they attack cities with the strength of twenty barbarian hordes, plagues so ghastly and merciless that the people pray for the smiting hand of God. I have seen Death in aspects more various than the mind can number. I have seen visions in this world more terrible than all we imagine of Hell. I have seen the terrors man can wreak against his neighbor. With my own eyes have I witnessed what Ruth describes. Take heed, my brethren. The wrath your Maker may bear against you for disturbing the soul's eternal slumber will be but a candle's pale flicker against the bright beam of destruction, the blinding light of Death, man may unleash against his brother."

For the feelings of the villagers I cannot presume to account, but when my brother opened thus his mouth to speak his truth, a cold feeling lodged deep in my spine, despite the heat of the fire.

"Do not allow them to sojourn any longer among us. Make haste. Send them back whence they came in their airborne death machines."

"Hurrah!" came Dirk's lone, hollow cry. The sound of a single voice in jubilation was infinitely, impossibly sad.

"But they will not return without their quarry. We must give them up the bodies of their dead."

Ydlbert stepped forward from the shadows. "Gentlemen, so much has happened these past few months I hardly know which way to look to see the sky. But I do think this Ruth is a kind lass, and what she and Mandrik describe if we don't do as she asks seems terrible to me."

The clearing once more grew quiet.

"We must pray," Stanislaus said, quietly, "for guidance and forgiveness as they draw the bodies from the ground. We have no choice but to hope that we are committing the lesser of two sins."

Ruth said, "I know it's the right thing to do."

"And it will rid us henceforward of this pestilence you speak of?"

"Yes," said Ruth.

Again there was silence, and Stanislaus turned shyly to look at each of us. "Good people," he began with as much force as his thin voice could muster, "our seer and our stranger provide us a difficult answer to the worst question that has ever plagued our village."

My brethren were long silent. "It's only two bodies," Jepho at last said, "and our future at stake."

His brother, Heinrik, said, "We have no choice. Gentlemen, are you with me?"

A somber chorus of "Aye"s came forth.

"Thy will be done, then," Stanislaus said, his hands over his eyes.

"Thank you," Ruth said, and slouched so heavily into her crutches that her hair fell forward and obscured her exhausted face.

"But oh, my sister, what a reckoning there will be if you are wrong."

My brother and I removed Ruth to my cart, before which Enyadatta switched her impatient tail. Adelaïda and Elizaveta climbed up with a cool rag and a peach they had snatched from the smith's garden, and offered both to her.

"You've done your work," said my brother. "I'll finish up our business here. We can talk tomorrow."

My wife clicked her tongue over Ruth as though she were a fretful infant. As Stanislaus stood before the assembled company, discussing the course of the next day's actions, Friedl Vox appeared, stomping in from the high grass, shouting, "Plague and destruction! High are the wages of sin, you cock-sucking, sheep-fucking swine! Hot are the fires of Hell!"

Jude stood up behind the dread spectacle that was his mother, and pushed her roughly back into the moonlit field. Her arms continued to flail as her stream of epithets escaped her, but before long she was past our earshot as surely as she was past our ken. We drove off with our patient before the night's dealings were through, but all the way home did I pray they concluded peaceably, and that Friedl Vox had returned, despite her madness, safely home to bed.

By morning Ruth's fever had subsided, but the dark patches beneath her eyes frightened me. Again and again she expressed her gratitude for the events of the evening before. My land sorely needed my husbandry, yet when the sun was nearly at his peak, I hitched the wrathful Enyadatta once again, that she might take me to witness, for the first time in our history, an unburial of the dead. While I was in the barn, Adelaïda came into the yard with three bolts of cloth of varying hue. When I brought the horse and cart forth, she was squatting in the dirt, examining two blue and a pale yellow stuff with a critical eye.

"What ails you, wife?" asked I.

"Nothing ails," she said, running the flat of her hand across her magnificent handiwork. "But if Ruth is to remain among us, she'll need clothing like a respectable woman."

"Also for Pudge," said Elizaveta.

"It's kind of you to think so."

"Not kindness," she said, coolly. "Only what wants doing."

Our daughter was, praise be, growing past the point where her hem could be let down, and with what had been lost in the accident, and the winding sheets we had given, we were short of cloth to see us through next winter. Only my wife, however, knew how much she could produce, and the selflessness of her gesture pleased me. With the image of her goodness lighting my heart did I set out for town.

My neighbors, too, were out upon the road. Jungfrau pulled up alongside me in his gap-toothed cart, and clicked at his Bodo to slow. "Sure to be a fine day's spectacle," said he, smiling, the previous evening's wrath vanished like its dew.

"Does no one in Mandragora perform an honest day's labor anymore?"

Jungfrau grinned broadly, showing me his two sideways teeth. "There's always been work, Gundron. Roaring machines from the sky, and priests allowing the dead to be dug up like beets and snatched bodily into the heavens—that, my friend, deserves a look-see."

"But my wheat."

"All the care in the world can't keep it from withering, rotting, or being flattened down by hail, if that's what's bound to happen. So do you think that by leaving it for a morning's entertainment you can force it to die?"

I had no answer.

"You and your brother, with all your words, have you not yet unraveled the mystery of death and of life?" Though the question sounded serious, he broke into a laugh, and Bodo blithely relieved himself upon the road.

"No, I have not."

"It's a jest, lad, don't look so dark."

I whipped Enyadatta, and she grunted but picked up her pace.

"Now I've set him off again, old Yves Gundron, mad as his fathers before him, but a right good farmer, too."

"When I am able to figure out—"

"Mind you don't go too fast there, Gundron—you know the consequences—and save me a place close by," he shouted after me.

I drove around my other neighbors with only a wave for acknowledgment; I could not stand their eager grins. Life would be immeasurably better when the cart had brakes and a seat on which to sit; with those provisions I could go as fast as I pleased and stay alone at my driving all day.

A great crowd had already gathered in the graveyard by the time I arrived—everyone in the village, half of Nnms, and twelve of the Archduke's red-clad men—all standing, waiting for the grim events to unfold. Some of the women wore their bright Sunday clothes. Even the men had parted their hair and chased the dust from their trousers, and Heinrik Martin had untwisted his beard. The faces of the assembled wore a disturbing expression, somber, yet jumping with anticipation— all but my brother, who appeared perfectly content, sitting as he was away from the throng on the weathering grave of our mother.

"Mandrik."

He raised one stout finger to his lips.

"Please, I need to speak to you."

Her gravestone, of black granite polished smooth as the still surface of a lake, read simply, "IONA."

"I am having misgivings," I said, "about all this."

"I am busy with the dead." He took a deep breath and opened his eyes to regard me. "Who knew we would have so much traffic with them."

"Not I."

"Or that you would be head of our family?"

"I never wanted to be."

"I am sorry I made you."

"The fault isn't yours."

He waved his hand and let it rest again on the grass.

"Mandrik," I said, "I am full up with questions."

"Ask."

How at home he looked on our mother's patch of ground. "The terrors that you spoke of, the pestilence and death—"

"I do not wish to fill your mind with darkness, Yves."

"But did you see it with the bodily eyes, or with the spirit's?"

His gaze was as clear a reflection of Heaven as any I had ever beheld. "I do not recognize your distinction."

"It makes a difference."

"What difference?"

I felt close to tears. "A difference in my understanding."

"I will ask you, Yves, to look about you and see what happens, rather than to dream up worry."

"You do not answer me."

"Yes, my brother, I do. Without your faith, you are nothing but a dry stone in God's garden, which is all around you full of the most succulent fruit. Now be quiet, and leave me to my work."

The breeze picked up and carried forth Stanislaus's voice saying benediction. Close by the graves stood our two visitors, changed into tight-fitting suits of somber hue, the one's vision box emitting its infernal hiss. Our priest had never cut much of a figure—he was both too thin and too shy to stand proud among men—but on that June morning he seemed fragile as a dandelion gone to seed. What prayers was he to offer, in this unnatural sacrament? He spoke but briefly, in the vernacular, before making the sign of the cross over the yet heaping graves. Though the youths of the village were gathered about, and though a few had warily brought shovels to assist in the dark work, none of us volunteered to begin. A sickly stillness settled in the air about.

Lieutenant Commander Bradley at last said, "Well?"

The birds twittered as if it were an ordinary day.

"I can't dig two graves without assistance."

Able-bodied though we were, we men of the village stared at him.

"Fiske," he said brusquely. Fiske put down his machine, and they picked up two shovels to begin their foul work. No one spoke. As they dug, the two foreigners shoveled the earth into a heap on the remains of poor Jedediah Dithyramb. Friedl Vox had stood at a distance, watching the proceedings with what wit she could muster, but when she saw them thus desecrating the tomb of him dearest to her afflicted heart, she let out a wail like the murdered come back to haunt a guilty house. Fiske shuddered, but both men continued to dig, even as her cry rose in pitch and volume, so high and loud that no other sound could be heard in the graveyard. Her voice grew so loud my ears began to ring with the sound, and she threw herself onto the mound of dirt and frantically began brushing it away. They stopped shoveling, in panic; Fiske looked away. Father Stanislaus, calling her sweet names, attempted to coax, then to drag Friedl off. Anya whispered, "Witch." At last Stanislaus grabbed hold of Friedl's filthy ankles and pulled her howling to the edge of the crowd, where people immediately made room for her terrible stench. The tears flowed from her good eye. "Tend to your mother, Jude," someone whispered, not quite nicely, behind us, and loath though he was to own her, he went up beside her and smoothed her grizzled locks. Stanislaus was exhausted by the labor and stood panting, his hands on his thighs.

Iona, however mad you might one day have gone, how glad would I have been for your guidance then. How glad would I be for it now.

The men shed their jackets and resumed their labor, and at long last, when the sun had traveled a goodly distance in the sky, came the thud of a spade against the first coffin, which flipped my stomach end over end. The soil continued to come up, broken with pebbles, worms, and black ants that scuttled about, intent on their own work. At last the pine coffins, damp and dark from the loam without and the putrefaction that no doubt had already begun within, lay uncovered. Bradley and Fiske bent down in the stinking pits to feed ropes beneath the boxes. Bradley, his face mottled with anger and sweat, glanced about, but none would offer to help him in his labor. One at a time, straining against the terrible weight, they hoisted the ungainly loads back up, and grabbed onto the handles to drag them to firmer ground. Fiske wiped his brow on his filthy sleeve. Bradley, who had clamped his lips so tight shut they'd gone white, said, "Open them."

The crowd moved forward and put out a great shout. Someone made a hushing sound, to which another countered, "Sacrilege!"

"Is it not enough that we allow you to move them," Stanislaus said, still bent, winded, over Vox and dirty with her grime, "from what ought to have been their last resting place? Can you not leave them this much in peace?"

Bradley picked up a crowbar and handed it to Fiske. To Stanislaus he replied, "We have to identify the bodies."

Fiske was sweating visibly, wetting his hair and the crooks of his arms. He pried with all his weight against the good, strong nails. The lid popped open all at once, and sent forth a clinging odor like a bouquet of dying violets, but a hundred times darker and more sweet. I had no desire to see the contents, and yet was drawn forward to the offending stink. There within lay Boogaerts's body, wrapped neatly in my wife's fine linen. Bradley said, "Unwind the shroud." Fiske regarded him, his eyes full of the unfairness of what he had to do, but he took his knife to the neck of the shroud, and gently tore it open. Inside, Boogaerts's skin was thick and waxy like a relic's, his chest sunk in like an empty bladder. Bradley checked him against an image he cradled in his palm, found the resemblance sufficient (though no man I had ever seen looked less like a man), and, his mouth grim, gestured Fiske to shut the lid. They repeated the dread procedure for Ulyanov, who was turned nearly sideways in his hard bed, his eyes, when revealed to the daylight, sunken and black. Already the dirt and her denizens had begun to creep in, and an ant traced a wavering path across his face. Immediately did my imagination fly forth to all the other bodies all around, and imagined them in their neat rows, lying still below ground as their flesh melted into their winding sheets. I saw the shrouds growing threadbare, becoming dirt. I saw my sister's golden hair, dulled by the dank darkness, and my first wife and child, what had been her lithe arms now twisted around the infant in what came more and more to be an embrace of the bones. All around me lay the dead in the slow, purposeful business of casting off the bodies they had sojourned in. They were not here. And when these bodies came up at the end of time, surely they would return in all their softness and splendor, their hair rippling behind them as they flew, the first bloom of youth in their fingers, toes, and cheeks. They would drop their rotting grave clothes behind them like veils. This slow tragedy around me, this squalor I had not meant to witness, would not be the end of us all.

"Very good, then," Bradley said.

Fiske stepped to the side, knelt down, and vomited.

"If you'll at least help us move them to the helicopter," said Bradley, "we'll be on our way."

We looked about at one another, none willing to step forward, until at last Jepho Martin said, "You may load them into my cart, if you must. But I'll not help you else."

Jepho held his gray Gar close by the bridle as he brought him round, but the horse skittered, for he knew ought was amiss. The two lieutenants struggled painfully under the burden of lifting the coffins, but no man among us would help. Jepho held Gar by the headstall and whispered encouragement to the beast as he led him away. My eyes were drawn to the empty holes, already crumbling and seeming somewhat startled to have been opened so unceremoniously to the day. Stanislaus's lips, and my brother's, moved in prayer, while we villagers remained rooted to this earth, to which all of us still, by God's grace, belonged. Then Desvres, slowly rubbing his head, bowed to the empty graves and said, "We should see them off."

We drove our carts around the churchyard, through its unmown grass, to the Great North Meadow, where the living and dead machines had communed this week with each other and the vast blue sky. Though each beast had flattened the grass and flowers as it settled down, the bounty of nature was now once more in full force, and the poppies again faced sunward on their crooked stems. Our horses kept their distance from the scene, perhaps still sensing Hammadi's demise, though the stains of her blood were no longer visible to human eyes. With some difficulty Fiske and Bradley pressed the coffins through the open door of the squat, healthy airplane. After Bradley closed the door with a tinny thump, Fiske once more took up his machine and pointed it into each of our faces, its red eye blinking to remind us that it could see. At last he took the box from his shoulder and stowed it in the airplane. It had branded his right eye with a frightful pink circle.

His white shirt dripped with sweat and was dark with the dirt of graves.

Bradley began to speak, but hard though my ears strained to listen, I could hear nothing of his words—instead, my eyes were taken with the structures of the airplanes, one whole and one desecrated by the unforgiving earth. How they moved, on the ground or in the air, was a mystery, for their bulk was great. What seized my attention, however, were the wheels on the ruined plane, small as a man's hand, black, puffed like a full cheesecloth. How so small an object could bear so heavy a load, when our own wheels creaked under the weight upon them—

"Mr. Gundron?" Bradley said, and my neighbors regarded me as if I had been in a trance. Ydlbert gave me a slight push forward, and with my hands dangling beside me like two cured hams, I stood facing the tall, disheveled man. "Mr. Gundron, may I ask you to convey our thanks to Ms. Blum?"

I bowed my head. "Indeed."

He wiped his hand, then held it out, and I took it. It was cold as All Saints' Eve.

"You'll all stand away from the field so we'll be clear for takeoff?"

"Yes," I said, and we started back, though I wasn't certain what he meant.

In they climbed, and shut their miniature doors behind them. The machine rumbled, then began to purr like an infernal cat. Even the children pulled back. The noise grew louder and fiercer, and all at once the machine lifted from the ground. Its dim halo rained down an uncanny wind that stung the eyes, frightened the horses, and chilled me to my marrow. The machine bounced and wavered upon the air, but it remained aloft, and as it climbed higher it veered toward the south, where eventually it disappeared from sight and hearing both.

"Lord have mercy," Stanislaus said. When I turned I saw him kneeling, his head bowed. Our neighbors stood about and looked at the flowers and bugs, all of which were returning to normal in what was now an ordinary summer breeze. My eyes could not resist the wrecked machine, which Nature sought to prettify, but whose ragged edges and ruined lines spoke all too eloquently of death. Behind us, in the churchyard, lay the empty graves, whose loss we could not make up, though we would bury the shovels cursed by the sacrilege, fill the holes as if they still held their charges. The maws of Hell had not yet opened to swallow us, nor had Heaven yet bid us repent. Stanislaus prayed as if he wished some terrible sign to come. But the June air was thick with the songs of the birds.

Desvres, his eyes baggy and slack, said, "It won't be long till the Day of Judgment comes."

"And yet this is better," said Jepho Martin, "than certain death. Is it not?"

"We will try," my brother quietly interjected, "to have faith, and to hope that God understands why we've done what we've done."

"To save our skins?" Desvres asked.

Mandrik drew his lips in over his teeth, then released them with a sigh. "Not only. Perhaps for a higher purpose, as well."

The night passed, and the next day, with no sign of retribution. Though at all moments I listened warily for the trumpet of Justice, none sounded. On the second night a soft, warm shower gave way without warning to a gale whose wind swept thatch from our roofs and hatchlings from their nests. Yet though my mind warned me that this was the calamity—and only the beginning of the calamity—whose appearance we all had feared, my heart knew how we needed rain, even when it came down thus angrily. It became possible, as time passed, to walk, or tend crops, or fix one's ruffled thatch without worrying that the world would end at any moment. If a punishment was coming, God had something subtle in mind.

Indeed, as the summer grew hotter and the long days dry, I began to wonder if the strangers had ever come—if they had not been a mere fancy of the mind. Our life had settled down as quiet as it had been before; the weather was capricious and we had lost some time to idleness and speculation, but that state of affairs we had never known to call Peace settled once more over Mandragora like a sheet set to dry on a hedge. Ruth was among us, recovering quickly, and seemed markedly less odd in the butter-yellow chemise and blue skirt Adelaïda sewed for her. Mandrik returned to tending his orchard and writing his treatise, and my wife, once assured that her house would not be swallowed by an avenging angel, returned to more ordinary spirits. The sun kept rising. Nothing we could do would change that.

The faith of my youth waned after tragedy upon tragedy—the epidemic which took my parents and siblings, the birthing bed that snatched my first wife in a torrent of blood and stole the breath of the son within her before he could be wrenched from her lifeless body. As I grew to take into my own hands the management of this farm, I relied less upon prayer; and as my brother went out on his wanderings, and came back to preach his own strange gospel, even less did I need of religion, for he had a whole clan's share. Then came the cares of my family to distract me from piety, and as my own inventions, the work of my own two hands, began to change the shape of the very world we live in, only on Sundays and on the rarest of occasions did I give up thanks to God.

Now, with the strangers behind us, and with my crops nearly ready for harvest, I began to reflect upon my position and my life, and realized how much I owed the Lord for my prosperity, and how little thanks I had offered. My land was plagued neither by flooding, drought, nor pests, and gave forth bountifully year after year. My mind was fertile with imaginings, and though my wife had not yet produced a second child, our first was thriving, growing lovelier by the day. Ruth had come to me for succor and guidance, and I was able to give it to her as surely as I reaped the rewards of her presence—her earnest questioning, her strange resemblance to my grandmother, her company. My brother, with whom I would otherwise need have divided the land, making two far less productive farms, brought blessings down on our family and this town by his devotion. I could not, as he did, work the greater part of my labor in composing songs of praise, but I might learn to express it all the same.

With that in mind, then, did I begin, after the airplane left, to attend services at Prime once or twice between Sabbaths. The sun was new and unsure in the sky as I left home with the chiming of the first bell; no one was out driving, and all the eyes upon me were those of kine left pasturing overnight. When first he saw me early in his dim, candlelit sanctuary, Stanislaus's weak eyes near popped out of his head.

"Yves, your family is well, I trust?"

I removed my hat and made my way hunched over to my bench, as if by making my body smaller I might attract less of his attention. "All hale. I've had the fear of God in me, and I think more church might do me good."

"Oh, but that's excellent." He nodded so vigorously that his crucifix and other trinkets tinkled. "I have long wished to see you here more. And your brother? Any—"

"He won't set foot, I'm afraid."

"Ah, well. Glad to have you, Yves. These services between Sabbath Masses have never been well attended. Most of your brethren pay their Maker no heed until it's too late. Since the"—he cleared his throat—"incident with the graves, I think even fewer of our countrymen have been coming on the Lord's Day."

"That's a fancy, Stanislaus," I said, though I, too, had noticed in the intervening weeks some slight thinning in the ranks. "I have seen no such thing."

"I wish I believed you." Stanislaus rang his piercing bell one last time, and brought in Martin's wife and the wanton daughter, Prugne, fresh as a blossom despite the hour. Elaine, the Widow Tinker, hobbled in, leading a lamb by a length of twine.

"Yves," she said, bobbing and smiling when she saw me. "You won't mind my Urs, will you? He gets so lonely if I leave him home."

"Not at all," said I.

Young Urs followed her to where she squatted on the bare floor, and stood rubbing his woolly head against her leg. Beneath her breath did I hear her mutter,

> *Lungworm, ringworm, heartworm, too,*
> *Leave this beast, whose worth be true,*

and I took pity both upon the sick beast and upon Elaine, for having opened her heart to a creature that would most likely not long make its way among the living.

I had never seen the church so empty. On the Lord's Day one can count on the church to be full of gossip and noteworthy behavior; but that July morning I was alone with the word of God, three women, and an oddly quiet lamb. Stanislaus delivered no sermon, but read in a soft voice from the texts for the day, officiating with water and incense over the morning. When he read the psalm *"Levavi oculos meos in montes unde veniet auxilium mihi,"*[2] my eyes were lifted up unto the meadows in which St. Perpetua, her deep auburn hair in a mad tangle all about her, calmly met her end. There were two cows, behind the nearer one a dark angel; beyond the split-rail fence were the ill-clad Romans and their fierce soldiers, all looking down upon her and the congregation. It could have been our own town—indeed, as Cedric von Broleau had lived and died among us, it no doubt was—and to look at the terrible scene about to be enacted rankled me to my bones. Still did I hear the words of the great psalm behind me as the fresco began to grow brighter and nearer, the saint's halo all of light and not mere earthly gold. It could as easily have been me, I realized; easier still it could have been our Ruth, and my anxious mind trailed off after the notion. Soon enough I was back with Stanislaus, his voice once again merely human, the morning light shining through the magnificent glass window and falling in shapes on the floor at his feet. But I knew then I had been wrong to worship so infrequently, and with a mind so full of earthly cares, and I resolved that when the disposition of my crops was not dire, I would visit in the mornings the house of the Lord.

In this time were the days so long as to seem infinite, and the crops coming to full flower. The fruits of the earth were not so plentiful nor so plump as they had been in years past, but they grew strong and without blight. Along the road the air was full of the scent of wheat, luxurious and green. I began to prepare my mind for the hard labor of the weeks ahead, and meanwhile, in the few weeks left to me of relative freedom, began to potter with my newest and, I was certain, best inventions.

---

[2]"I will lift up mine eyes unto the hills, from whence cometh my help."

INTERMEZZO

REFLECTION

t is no small thing for a man of my station to be lettered. My grandfather, Andras Gundron, was among the more prosperous farmers in the village, but was by no means specially marked out for his wealth, and had no pretensions of attaining status in this world beyond that of a land-owning farmer and lover of God. Nevertheless, with the Holy Scripture as his guide, my grandfather taught himself to read, and with a stick in the dirt he learned to form the letters we use to mark out the Word of the Lord. He brought his knowledge to Father Icthyus, who immediately set at him with fire, oil, incense, and chants to exorcise whatever had possessed him. Since, however, the possessor had been nought but the Love of Knowledge, it could not be got out, and Father Icthyus proclaimed his learning a miracle. Andras taught what he had learned to all his children—daughters as well as sons, though only my father, Uncle Frith, and a sister, Una, grew to the full flower of adulthood, their other siblings, Childrik and Dane, having passed beforetimes into the Beyond. Una, despite her high color and thick brown hair, proved impossible to marry because of this mark he had placed upon her; Frith renounced learning and cultivated the habit of dozing in church; and my father, Zoren, needed marry among the Gansevöorts, who had generations since been marked by song-singing, high spirits, and other slight peculiarities of mind. (None of which seems to have affected my Adelaïda for the worse.)

Mandrik, Marvin, Clive, and I learned the ruggedness of the soil and the vagaries of the weather by following our father out in springtime and in snow, by listening to him with half our minds as we lazily assisted in the work and invented games of our own. At midday did our mother send Eglantine forth with a yoke across her sweet, plump shoulders, cow's milk warm in one pail, and porridge, soup, or bread and cheese in the other. Oft, too, did she tie a chalk and slate up in her apron or carry forth our precious Bible, that we might have a lesson while we rested. Thus it was in my own fields, amid the wheat and the flax, that I learned to make sense of the shapes that make up our mother tongue. Evenings, as our mother scrubbed the pots and Eglantine knitted furiously—as many stockings, hats, mittens, and mufflers as four growing boys could ruin—my father read to us from the Bible or spun tales of the fabled Indies and the sea, from which Mandrik learned his yearning to wander. From his earliest childhood Mandrik made up songs (though, until he was nigh manhood, most of them were of no consequence), with which he beguiled the evenings while the rest of us laughed and listened, grinding spices, churning butter, or swatting flies at the request of our mother.

So naturally did our reading and contemplation occur, so seamlessly did they mesh into the fabric of our day, I had no understanding that they were not part of all our neighbors' lives. Ydlbert's parents, God rest their souls, were as kind and quick-witted as any, but they could not read, and did not wish their sons to, lest they fritter away in idleness time that might better be spent on the land. Each Sunday in church, Father Icthyus read from the great Scripture atop the lectern as the assembled spat and admired the frescoes on the walls. There in colors bright as midday, applied ages ago by the gifted hand of Cedric von Broleau, were the scenes that were the one book of which my countrymen read copiously and with skill. Our souls learned equally to cringe and to rejoice at the stories our Father relayed, but only I and my brothers and sister learned to check up on his sources.

Such scholar work might have been supposed to infuse us with doubt, uncovering, as it sometimes did, vast chasms between the words our Lord spoke and the meanings Icthyus gave out on Sundays. But rather did the eerie availability of those words, their sonorous nearness, open our eyes to the mysteries of Earth and of Heaven. Mornings did my young heart tremble at each day's appearance of the dew, and evenings did I rejoice to see the hearth fire burning, the stars in the vast sky beyond. From some of his early readings did Mandrik claim to have learned all he knew about trees, which subject infected him with wonder.

This, then, was our childhood; in addition to which I must here recount what should have been told long before: of how I won Adelaïda after a long spate of tragedies, and of my brother's journey abroad, and of his eventual return therefrom.

My first wife, Elynour, was Franz Nethering's daughter, and all my life I had loved her. When we were three, barely out of swaddling clothes and tethered to our mothers, I looked at her nut-brown curls as she sat before me in church, and wanted to eat them. Elynour was the eldest of four, and the only to live long enough to marry. Her brothers did not die in nameless infancy, but after they had grown characters and second teeth. Elynour, all the time we were growing up together, had always around her a bevy of youngerlings, whom she ordered about and doted upon with a grin upon her thin lips. She was, I have been told, no great beauty, being short of stature with enough curly hair for two, but I adored her dark coloring and the seriousness it lent her most frivolous gestures. Elynour did not sing or play the timbrels, and the cloth that she wove and her needlework were only passable, yet did I love her.

I was fourteen when the Great Scourge swept through Mandragora, carrying off half of what everyone loved, and more besides. In two days I watched Clive and Marvin, who had been out with me picking peas, sicken and weaken to the brink of death. Their lips grew dry and their eyes bright as the stars, and they trembled and gasped for breath. I nursed them, and wept over them, and exhorted them to stay among the living, and Eglantine, with her braids caught up beneath a scarf, mopped their brows and brought mint tea they would not allow past their lips. My parents—both parents—stood away from the big bed where they'd lain the boys down, and sobbed and prayed. Their work and their house fell to a shambles about them, and when they could cease weeping ten minutes at a time, they leaned over Clive and Marvin, pleading with them, or sat at the end of the bed holding the patients' burning feet. The influenza was fierce, and once my strapping brothers had succumbed, they could fight no more; they rattled with chills and grew hollow in the cheeks, and without opening their eyes or saying another word (except the innocent ravings of the fever, to which none of us could listen) they passed into the grave. Clive died early one June night, and Marvin hung on till near morning. When the sun came up, those two we had loved most dearly lay still, blue, and cold, looking exactly like themselves except that their hands had closed like claws, and that they would nevermore speak, and no more be where once they had made their home.

In the middle of the night we heard Friedl roaming the parish, wailing over her and our and everyone's dead, but we were all too afraid to put out an offering for her.

My stomach gripped with fear as my mother and sister bathed the bodies. I had hardly ever seen my father without his hat, and now he wept the day long. Mandrik prostrated himself, his nose to the ground, and cajoled and prayed, but it was too late for intercession. In the morning I ran for Father Icthyus, and it took me half the day to find him, so busy was he saying offices over the dead and those soon to follow. I had never seen the rims of his great blue eyes so fiery, yet he did not weep over his duties. By the time he wearily approached my house, my father was red in the cheeks and curled up on a pallet on the floor. Mandrik, now heir to it all, still had his nose to the ground, and my mother and sister shrieked with worry and care. The bodies were blessed, and my mother gave Icthyus money to send for coffins, but so many were dying that they were in short supply. Two days later, my father succumbed in a rage to his malady. There was no subduing my mother and sister, so mad were they with grief. Mandrik quit his prayer—"Because you can see," he said bitterly, "how much good it's doing"—and we went out to this very barn to saw boards for coffins. The house by now reeked of decay, but my mother and sister would not leave to attend to any business. When we finished the three coffins— plainer than my love for my family would have dictated, but the best we could do—they helped us carry the bodies outside, seal them away, and hoist them into the cart, which Mandrik and I dragged to the cemetery, as was the custom. No gravediggers could be had because they, too, were dying, so with my father's own shovels and spades did we lay them to rest.

Eglantine opened the great door to the air and took the linen out for washing, but the odor of death held tight to our home. My mother, her usually sleek brown hair spread wild around her, walked about nights, weeping. Mandrik huddled into a corner with paper and pen, writing the first chapters of his Apocalypse. And before we could venture to church on Sunday to seek revenge on the terrible God who would take our father and brothers, Eglantine developed the spots on her cheeks. She tried to be cheerful and banish the truth with the same click of her tongue she used to call her chickens. By the Lord's Day, her breath came rasping in her throat, and it became clear that my mother's grief was not something from which she would soon recover. Within a fortnight we buried them both, and Mandrik and I stared dazedly at one another, to see who would be the abandoner, and who, if either, left behind to tend the farm.

Though at fourteen I felt I had the strength and demeanor of a man, I was not ready for the burden Fate had yoked across my shoulders. Mandrik, now the elder of our clan, was angrier than I had ever seen him; sometimes if I interrupted his work he would literally snarl. How could I live in this house that smelled like death and see to my father's crops? How could I, a boy alone, bring in all that he had sowed? Father Icthyus was no help, heartbroken as he was from burying more than half his parishioners, including some of his lifelong friends. Ydlbert and Anya were married then, and Dirk was a four years' lad; and though my friend brought over loaves of bread and bowls of new cheese, he always stopped with them outside our door, as if our very lintel were cursed.

We burned the mattress on which everyone we loved had died, stitched another of burlap, and filled it with straw. We boiled the sheets, the rags, and all their clothes, and left our door open night and day that the cleanly breeze might draw out all traces of infection. Mandrik would not spend the night on the accursed bedstead, and took to rambling about in the darkness. Some mornings I would find him in the barn or up a tree, others lying on his back in the meadow or between the untended rows of wheat. One morning when midday did not bring him home, I called myself hoarse in search of him, and began to fear the worst. By the time I set out upon the High Road I was mad with fear and grief, and choked so that I could barely call his name. I cannot express how fiercely my heart leapt with joy when, at Ydlbert's rise, I heard a person weeping in the high grass. I trudged through to find my brother curled up into a ball, his hands wrapped so firmly around his knees that his knuckles were white.

I fell onto the ground beside him and held him as tight as my strength allowed. His body was hot, and I feared he had caught fever out among the mists. "What happened?" I asked him, but he only cried.

I do not know how long we sat before finally he quieted, wiped his face upon his sleeve, and blew his nose into the grass. He pulled away enough to look at me with his swollen eyes. "I have seen the Angel of Death," he said quietly, "ablaze with light, and full of beauty."

I touched his hot shoulder and arm.

"As I walked this way late last night, trusting to the dim light of the moon, I saw a glow, a terrible radiance over the rise. My heart trembled with fear as my steps brought me to this spot. And as I looked out over the good land, a form became clear to my vision. It stood in the grave-yard, tall as the mountains and made all of light, as if it had no body but spun gold and heat. Its golden hair cascaded down like rivers, and its white robe burned my eyes. Its arms were crossed before it, and in each hand burned a sword of fire whose heat I could feel even here. It did not regard me, for its eyes were like two suns and would surely have burned me had they looked my way."

I touched his soft hair and his shirt, soaked through with terror. "You saw this?"

"As surely as I see you now. It burned all through the night, Yves. It did not move or speak though I called out, though I begged it tell me what it desired. When the first rays of the dawn broke over the city, it vanished. But I am frightened it is here now, gliding among us, unseen, and waiting to consume me with its eyes of flame."

My body trembled with fear. If this were a sickness, he would follow the others soon enough, and if it were fancy, the weight of all our troubles had driven him mad. That my brother in his fervor could see through to the inner workings of things was not yet clear to me, so I held him and rocked him as our mother would have done. When he had cooled down I stood him gingerly up, and with my arm close about him, walked him home to bed.

"I will be leaving you, Yves," he said, once he had hunkered well down beneath the blankets.

"Shh," I told him, unable to keep my hands from off his arms, his face. He no longer burned with fever. "Think not of it."

"Nay, I go not off to join the dead, but to join the living."

"Sleep, Mandrik. Perhaps when you wake, the vision will be gone."

He slept for two whole days—not in the delirium which had taken our brothers, but in a deep, peaceful slumber. I made a pot of vegetable broth and kept it simmering against his wakening, and took it also for my own sustenance. I prayed for him more fervently than I had for the rest of my family combined, so dearly did I need him now. When at last he awoke on the third day, he sat up and said, "I'm hungry, and I think it's time you were married."

I laughed and brought him his soup, pleased that he thought me so much a man. Ydlbert had married at my age, but somehow he had seemed more adult than I.

"Yves," he said between sips from his bowl, "you see how many times Death has visited this very hearth. Hurry now, before you, too, are taken."

I wanted to find his advice funny, but could not. "You need to marry first."

"Not I, Yves—I won't marry, and I won't work this land. I cede it all to you."

"I don't want it."

He shrugged his stooped shoulders. "I have other work to do. I can't tend this soil."

"What other work?"

"The work of a treatise. The work to which the angel beckoned me."

His eyes were afire, but he had not gone mad. Still, my stomach grew tight at his saying.

"I will travel abroad."

"Oh, aye." I laughed, refilling his bowl and then my own. "Mandragora's produced a lot of explorers in her time. You'll be in august company."

"There's always a first, of everything," said Mandrik.

"We're not near the sea. Where will you go overland?"

"As far as I can go till I reach the sea. And thence to the great East, where I will seek out those masters and sages whose knowledge of the

Beyond will succor me." His aspect wore not the slightest air of concern.

"Mandrik," I said, "you'll die."

"God protects those who seek him out."

I had fields full of grain, and provender enough from the previous winter to keep me—but what did it matter? At last I said what was foremost. "Don't leave me."

He shook his dear head. "Not till I find you a wife, but once—"

"I can find a wife on my own."

"Good, then. Make haste, that I might prepare my departure. You will call God's blessings down upon this land. I know it."

I had never imagined myself, the youngest son, master of so great a farm. "Are you sure you don't want it?"

"I won't change my mind, Yves. You must hurry."

I left him that afternoon to feed the animals, gather provisions from the garden, and bring fresh water from the creek. The idea of his departure pained me—bad enough it was to be this alone in the world; I could not lose my last companion and friend. Yet I did not believe that he would go. No one had ever left before, not even to become a tradesman in Nnms. No one since the fisherman who brought my grandmother had seen the sea; how was my brother to find it? When he began leaving, mornings, to make what he called "preparations," it got my dander up, but I could think little of it, though I soon noticed a stash of dried meat in a corner of the house.

Elynour, too, was only fourteen—if she had lived through the plague. If I trudged through the fields to her father's land, who knew what misery might await me there. Though my heart raced whenever I saw her, I had never much considered taking a wife. Clive would have been my father's heir, and the northern piece might have been carved off for Marvin; but as for Mandrik and me, we would only have received some parcel our father could buy, or would have labored—without regret, I think—for our brothers all our days. My prospects were changed. Elynour was as lovely to me as the church's frescoes of St. Perpetua, and she might now be mine.

While I was out laboring, Mandrik did work of his own, in addition to his work of gathering what he needed for his journey. He washed Clive's best shirt and new blue trousers in a bath of lavender, that they perfumed the air when they lay upon the hedges to dry. He blacked his

Sunday boots. He sharpened my father's razor, that I might remove the eight hairs that then sprouted upon my chin. My heart grew light when I saw the fruits of his labors. I believed that my suit would not be in vain, and prepared to go argue my case on the morrow.

I hardly slept all night, and was not helped by Mandrik's fire-lit scratchings the night through. By morning we were both as weary as if a whole day's work had been done. Yet with his prayers, a song of good cheer, and some eggs and cheese behind me, I set out upon my journey.

When I look back upon the events of that day, I chuckle to think that such a sapling could have embarked upon such an errand. Franz Nethering was out slopping his pigs in their sty, and stopped to smile broadly at me when he saw the care of my dress. "How fares your family?" he asked.

The morning's preparations vanished as the memory of my loss rose up before my inward eyes. "All perished, but Mandrik and myself."

Nethering wiped his brow. "I am sorry."

I nodded. "Your family?"

"All well as yet." It was only a matter of days, though, before his sons took ill.

His lovely, dark wife, Vashti, came out upon the stoop to watch us.

"I have come, then," I said, fearful of any further delay, "to ask Elynour's hand in marriage. I am now my father's heir, and can give her the greatest farm in the demesne."

Nethering looked back toward his wife, but no word was said. When he turned again to me, his face was serious, though by no means displeased. "Not Mandrik?"

"Mandrik says he doesn't want the farm."

"Doesn't want the farm?"

"I can't explain it, sir. Please—Elynour?"

Franz Nethering nodded solemnly. "Shall we ask the girl?"

I nodded, and Vashti brought her forth from the house, wiping her small hands upon a brown apron. "Hullo, Yves," she said. "Nice weather, God be praised."

"Elynour," Nethering said, coming forth from the sty. "Yves Gundron has come to ask for your hand. What do you say?"

Elynour laughed, and smoothed her skirt. "And where shall we live, in your barn?"

"His family has all passed on and left him heir. You would be mistress of his father's house."

Each time I looked at Elynour, her eyes darted away. It was absurd that I should stand in Franz Nethering's yard with this as my purpose. "All right," she said. "After the harvest comes in."

I had imagined some more emotional response, but this would suffice. We all shook hands, and Vashti offered us fruitcake, over which Elynour and I watched one another shyly. She took my arm to walk with me to the edge of my father's fields, and as we spoke of the terror which had befallen my family, I watched the roses bloom in her smooth dark cheeks. When we reached the stone fence, I bent to kiss those cheeks, but instead found the flower of her mouth raised to me. To my surprise, she tasted of fruitcake. My mind spun as I probed the recesses of what had, until now, been a mouth purely for speaking; and before long we were down in the sweet grass, and I lay her rough dress over the rougher ground to shield her fragile body from its caresses. Though I had often dreamed of her, I had never imagined that she might come to me so easily, like my father's land. As I touched and kissed the sweet, dark expanse of her skin, I wanted to ask her if it was all right thus to sin against Father Icthyus's teachings, yet all I could do was stammer, so great was my desire.

"I think it's fine," she said, stroking my face, "since we're to be married."

To have known such sweetness in the midst of such desolation seemed the kindest gift of all. It was a hard summer, in which I did the work of four men as best I was able—and much of the crop, over which my father had so labored, withered in the field. But I managed to put up enough for the winter, and in the evenings I met my love in between our land and, weeping, thanked Heaven for her bounty. We were married in the autumn in the church, and Elynour came home with me, all her possessions strapped to the back of the chestnut horse which was her dowry, and which she led to my house by a length of rope. It died in the next summer's carting.

At fourteen, what more could a boy want than to marry a beautiful wife and be master of his household? It was my decision when to rake and hoe, and when to turn in for the night; and it was my pleasure to enjoy my young wife's body. Mandrik stopped sleeping in the big bed with us after our wedding night, returning to his childhood hammock instead. Even that did not sufficiently remove him from our nocturnal goings-on, and he soon made his bed with the goats and sheep.

"Are you angry?" I asked one morning as together we cleaned the animals' stalls.

He raked his hay about and did not regard me. "Not angry. I simply didn't realize that was what it would mean for you to take a wife."

"But Father and Mother—" I blushed, caught between shame and pride. "How else do you expect me to get us an heir?"

He shrugged, and redoubled his efforts. "Perhaps I'll like it better when you show me the bonny babe, that I might bounce him on my knee."

"Mandrik—"

"Don't worry for me. I don't mind sleeping among the beasts. And I'll be off to Indo-China before the first frost."

Still I did not believe that he would go, but before autumn had waned, Mandrik's preparations were complete, and with a sack of supplies slung across his back, he set out for the great world.

"If I don't see you again—" I started.

He would not put his sack down to hug me goodbye. "Don't tell yourself tales, Yves. I'll be back anon."

My bride and I followed him to the top of the rise, and there watched him until he disappeared among the eastern mountains. I thought I should never see him more, and wept bitterly as we returned to the farm.

"God will return him safe—you'll see," she said, stroking my upper arm like a cat.

"It's not but that." How the beauty of the turning leaves and the sharp scent of wood smoke mocked me! "This farm seems so small, when I know he's to set sail for the rest of the world."

"Much greater than my father's farm, by far."

"By a few acres, at most."

"Even so, what more do we need, you and I? We've brought in a good crop, and we've eight good laying hens, and I'll work at making us warm new clothes all winter."

She dangled from my elbow like a toddler from her mother's apron strings. Her dark eyes faced clearly into the midday sun; her cheeks were red in the chill breeze. As we walked home, my eyes blinded by my own tears to the beauty all around me, I realized that, wherever fate might take my brother, it would have to suffice to work this land, now that I had my Elynour.

Though Elynour and I were at our work daily, in fair weather and foul, each day of the next three years, no child came to us. I had heard of such cases—Miller Freund was one such, though all attributed his childlessness to his hoarding of pennies and his wife's shrewish ways— but could not imagine how such misery could befall us after all we had suffered. Mornings I prayed, and wished I had Mandrik's voice, which was so much dearer to God. And as the seasons turned, and as Elynour and I grew better able to manage the business of the farm, I grew accustomed to this curtailed happiness, and thankful to have been granted it despite my life's large measure of grief.

It was high summer of that third year of his absence when Mandrik returned—high summer, a stifling haze, and days so long one was hardly over before the next began. Mandragora had never in memory known a season so dry, and the crops suffered. My heart went out to them—not only because without their bounty my wife and I would starve, but because they looked so weary and sick. A stalk of wheat can have no feelings, sure, but if they had, what misery those stalks would have spoken. Each day I prayed for rain, each day trudged to the cairn and begged my grandmother for rain, and each new day dawned parching and bright. My heart tickled constantly behind my breast-bone, and I could think of nothing but the drear winter ahead. My wife and I labored to bring in our crops, sure, but it was not labor as in other years. There is little to do when nothing has grown. The work was mostly insufferable because of the heat.

I thought of my brother as often as I drew breath, but I had ceased to expect his return two years since. I knew nothing of journeys—no one had ever taken one before—so I could not say how long he would be in returning from his destination; but I knew in my bones how long he had been gone. The seasons turned round upon his absence exactly as if they turned round upon his grave, except that he did not come re-splendent in visions to tell me things, and there was nowhere I could visit him. He had simply, my last true companion, vanished from the earth, and though the grass might grow and the leaves sprout on the trees, the world held a strange, unholy silence.

I was loading sheaves onto the waiting cart—then but a one-wheeled toy tied round the neck of a nameless beast—when he returned. I saw his figure approaching over Ydlbert's rise, and my stomach sank in fear, for though I had grown used to apparitions of the dead at evening, none had ever yet been so bold as to appear in the broad light of day. He bore a heavy burden upon his shoulder, and I shuddered to think what he was bringing me from the other side. The horse flattened her ears to her head. The wind whistled in the trees.

"Yves!" he called lustily, and his voice was nothing like Clive's and Marvin's whispers.

I pinched the bridge of my nose and waited for this to be over.

"Yves Gundron!" He began to run, the great weight bouncing against his back. "Great God, how I've missed you! I've gone all the way to Indo-China and returned, hale and well, bearing gifts. Are you not glad to see your brother after three years of silence?"

He could not be an apparition. I ran to meet him in the road, and was overwhelmed when he cast down his possessions and threw his arms around me—his odor was still the same, and it was his familiar shape, grown somewhat bulkier, which held me, not a wisp like my other brothers had become. "I thought you were dead."

"And leave you alone in this world?"

"After three years' absence, what else was I to think?"

"And how should I have contacted you from the other end of the world, to tell you I was fine?"

I shook my head; my hair rustled against his coarse cassock.

"Your Elynour lives?"

"And thrives, though we have yet no child."

"Soon enough. Take me home and let her feed me, and I will tell you of my travels."

I hoisted his sack, which was heavy as a man, and walked home beside him, delirious with joy and unwilling to believe that it was truly mine. Elynour, at her butter churn in the sunshine, stared in disbelief as we stumbled up the drive. "Wife," I called to her. "Look."

Her sweet face filled with joy. "Why, Mandrik. I can hardly believe it's you," she said.

Sweating and smiling, he reached out for her. "How you've grown. A fine woman, Yves."

"Soup's boiling," she said. "It's not been the best harvest, but it's good enough for broth."

Mandrik said, "Thank you, sister," and my wife went in to prepare our meal.

We followed, and I set down my brother's sack inside the door. "What makes it so heavy?"

"Paper." I must have stared at it a moment too long, because he said, "The volumes of the treatise I am writing, as well as books brought back from abroad." He ducked to release himself from a small carrying sling. With the care of a mother tending her newborn, he retrieved two young plants, their roots wrapped in burlap. "Perhaps by the time you have children, Yves, these will bear fruit." Each, a twig with a half dozen leaves, would have been a mere snack for a billy goat, yet he wiped the leaves with care. "And I brought presents, naturally."

Elynour left her kettle at the mention of gifts, and knelt down beside us. I brought her ribbons and spices from market whenever I could, but in truth it was not often. He lifted a large basket from his sack, in which many parcels were stowed. "For my good sister," he said, and handed her a bolt of red fabric, covered all through with flowers in yellow and pink, and so slippery to the touch that she giggled when it cascaded to the floor. "The silk of ten thousand worms," he told her, broadening her grin, "which I will tell you about the manufacture of over dinner." When she held the magnificent, shining thing up, a string of milky green beads slipped out. "Jades, for your throat," he said, and her dark eyes grew wide. "Shall I fasten them on you?"

"Please," she said, and leaned toward him, one hand to her breast in wonder. He fastened the beads with grace; thus accustomed were his hands to delicate labor. Her fingers reached for her throat, and passed time after time across the necklace's remarkable smoothness.

The house was stifling with the heat of the cooking fire, and Mandrik glowed with sweat as if it were dew. He had changed in his years abroad—grown fuller and stronger, gained wrinkles at the corners of his eyes, allowed his hair to grow into long curls like a heathen's. The earth held no one who could ever be more dear.

"Nor did I forget my brother." He turned the basket upside down, revealing it to be pointy, and placed it on his head. Elynour and I laughed heartily. "You'll wear it out plowing, harrowing, slopping the pigs—it keeps the sun off your neck as well as out of your eyes." He held the ridiculous thing out to me. "Come on, try it."

I shied from its strange circumference. "I'm not wearing that."

"Why not?"

"Because I never saw such a thing. It's ridiculous."

Mandrik looked hurt. "All new things seem ridiculous until you see how well they work. Then they seem indispensable."

This was a lifetime before the harness, and I had no idea what he spoke of. "Can't we use it for carrying fruit?"

He took his hat basket back and placed it on the floor. "It's yours; you may do with it as you please. One more gift, and I've exhausted my whole supply."

"I do not mean to hurt your feelings."

"Of course not." He handed me a light, rectangular parcel, three hands in length and wrapped in pale blue silk. "Perhaps this will suit better."

Beneath the silk was my precious dark box, all carved with the vines and flowers of the forest, another milky jade gleaming on the top, its clasp and hinges shining. I opened it and ran my fingers along its slippery blue interior. "A most beautiful object," I told him, abashed by its delicacy, "but what shall I do with it?"

"You shall keep your pens and ink in there, and write."

"Then it should be your box, for you're far likelier to engage in such activity."

He smiled. "I have a box of my own. I will make you an ink vial and some good new pens. Will you use them?"

"When I have something to use them for."

"Good enough."

I did admire the box. Having it would be like having a puppy to coddle.

Of course we had hardly sat down to eat before Ydlbert arrived, his wife (not yet so sour) and three rambunctious sons in tow. She held the dozing infant Jowl, not yet named, in her arms. We had left the door open to admit air, and Ydlbert stuck his great head in and let out a whoop. "Mandrik Gundron, returned from the dead!" he called out, and they hugged and patted one another with manly glee.

"Not from the dead, from Indo-China," said my brother. "Won't you join us at table?"

For Ydlbert, however boisterous his young sons, there was always room by my hearth. Bartholomew, but four years named, seized the hat, donned it, and ran out with Dirk at his heels. Young Manfred was still tied to his mother's apron, and sniveled in unhappiness. The baby suckled in his sleep. "All the way to Indo-China?" Ydlbert asked, his eyes glued to my brother.

Mandrik nodded sheepishly. "In a paper boat."

"You must have tales to tell, then."

Elynour replenished the bowls. Her necklace glowed against her dusky skin. "He had tales to tell before he'd ever done anything."

"The things you must have seen!"

"More than I could tell you of over dinner."

I was wild with wonder about my brother's journey, but did not want to importune him with questions; I wanted him to eat, and sleep, and then I wanted to trim his hair.

"Boys!" Ydlbert called out into the still-bright evening, then turned back. The two children came panting to the door. "You could begin?"

When Mandrik smiled, the hoods came down over his eyes, giving him a wise and glad expression. "But where to start?"

"With the sea," I blurted, then looked away lest he witness my excitement.

"Oh, but such a great, wild, lonely sea it was. I, and my paper boat, the salt water and the sky, and nothing as far as I could see. This not for days, but for weeks, perhaps months on end, and nothing to eat but dried meat, moldy bread, and the fish I caught by singing their siren songs."

Ydlbert puzzled a bit of gristle out of his teeth. "How did you light a fire, on the paper boat?"

"A fire, lad? I ate the fish raw, aye, and was wet as a fish whenever it rained. I burned under the rays of the sun from the moment he rose to the moment he set; and glad was I when at last I descried the shores of India beckoning to me."

"India?" I asked.

"The debarkation point for Indo-China, for one must travel overland, across the great Himalayas and through much of China, to reach that blessed destination."

And all the time that we had grown together, I had never even wondered what went on in Nnms. Over my mind the doings of people besides my family held no sway.

"As I drew nigh land, the hundreds of people who had been bathing, fishing, and doing their laundry along shore plunged into the water and began ululating in their strange accents, beckoning to me with raised arms. Their raiment was of bright jewel hues, the women draped in articles called Saris, which hung over their shoulders like veils. Into the water they plunged, drawing my craft in with friendly shouts as the fierce southern sun beat down. Their skin and hair were dark, and some of the women wore jewels in their noses."

Elynour said, "Mercy. I'm surprised you didn't die of fright."

"No, I was filled with relief, thrilled to have persons to talk with, whatever their native tongue, to be safe upon land. The inhabitants of that village treated me to a feast that night of vegetables and myriad spices—some of which I have brought back with me—and promised me the next day visits to the shrines of their various gods."

Elynour said, "More than one?" and Ydlbert, "Heathens."

"Hindus. If you think that strange, good man, you won't like to hear the stories of the tribes we met in the mountains, or of the vagabonds, gypsies, and marauders upon the Silk Road. You won't want to hear any of it."

The boys, for the first time in history, sat as if nailed to the floor. Dirk said, quietly, "Gypsies?"

"Singing mournful songs, and stealing their brides."

Dirk nodded as if he had long known much of these things.

Mandrik held forth until late into the night, as more and more of our countrymen came to wish him kindness on his safe return. He told tales until the sun rose, and followed me out into the fields to tell me tales the long, work-dreary day. My brain teemed with the people and places he described, but no stories could displace my joy, my wild, ineffable joy, at having my brother back home. I would build him a house. Now he was returned from the Beyond, I would see that he stayed forever.

Less than a fortnight later, it became clear that Elynour had at last conceived a child. When she told me, I whooped in exultation, and could not quit dreaming of our future life. How much a man would I be with a child of my own! But Elynour did not fare well, did not glow and smile meekly like the Blessed Virgin in church. Throughout the summer and into the autumn she was bodily sick, voiding by mid-morning whatever she had eaten at breakfast, and often, her narrow lips parched, she lay down for half the day. As the winter drew nigh, her belly grew taut with the burgeoning life within her, but her arms and her face grew thin and tired. Mandrik scoured the countryside for herbs and flowers to soothe her and the babe inside, all of which she accepted with a dutiful smile.

In the dead of winter her time came. In a driving snow Mandrik ran off for the midwife and the blacksmith, who arrived with implements I could not bear to behold. The long night through I held Elynour's hand and mopped her steaming brow, but the baby, despite all our coaxing and prayers, would not come. Mandrik's face was pale in the firelight, the drawn, worried face of an old man; though I looked to him for reassurance, his visage only filled me with fear. When the next day dawned and nearly waned, my wife was so weak with her labor that she could not sit up to take water. A steady stream of rich, warm blood flowed out from her nether regions, and her hand began to grow cold within mine. I could not weep, so panicked was I to observe this spectacle; and then the smith brought forth his great calipers, which he had plunged into the boiling kettle then cooled in the drifting snow, and forced them within her body to bring the infant forth. With her last strength Elynour screamed and sobbed and begged him not, but with a grim face he persevered. My wife died with the instrument inside her. The infant, when the smith brought him forth in a torrent of black blood, was a deep, uncanny blue, and wore the black snake of his umbilicus around his neck like the wreath of a terrible honor. Blood continued to gush from Elynour's lifeless body, and when I looked at the sickening grimace into which her beautiful face had contorted, I ran out into the snow and hollered until my throat all but bled. Mandrik could not bring me in to the hearth, so he brought me out a blanket. Under the cold, starry sky I shouted curses until my whole head rang, until they echoed from the mountains on every side. When at last I could scream no more, I could hear nought but the fire within, and my brother, his voice broken, reciting the Office of the Dead.

My nearest neighbors, Ydlbert and Nethering, no doubt heard my screams, for they arrived soon after with baked potatoes in their pockets for warmth. The midwife had by then bathed down the bodies, tucked them like sleepers beneath a clean sheet, and coaxed the expression of pain off Elynour's face. Yet when Nethering saw her, his lone remaining child, lying still on the foul-smelling bed, he broke down, and knelt on the floor weeping. The midwife and the smith left in the morning, promising to send Icthyus when they reached town.

"The world contains nothing more terrible than this," my brother whispered to me as I knelt beside the gruesome, stinking bed. "We have drunk of darkness to the lees."

The pale body was but a shadow of my wife. The infant—who could tell whom he would have resembled? Who could know what wonders he might have accomplished?

"I have, Mandrik. I have drunk it down."

"I, too, brother."

Again the rage rose in my throat. "What do you know of misery? She was not your wife."

Mandrik, like a child at his prayers, placed his head on his hands on the mattress. His back heaved silently for what seemed a lifetime. "I have lost a sister, Yves," he said finally, "and the heir to my father's name. I beseeched our God to save her, and my prayers changed nothing."

"And my prayers?"

"I have begun to think that there is nought but leads to death and misery. But surely that cannot be so. Surely there is some comfort in this world, and not merely in the world beyond?"

I did not think so. All that had ever comforted me had died in the place we now sat—all but him, and I began to understand the full weight of the truth that he, too, would one day be taken from me. That, or I, like all I had loved, would be snatched from this world in pain.

Mandrik would not accompany me anywhere; he brooded about the house, writing whenever he was not racked with sobs. I sought solace in the church, but in truth it provided hardly any comfort. The sweet faces of the saints and martyrs, even the fair countenance of God, mocked me each time I sat in St. Perpetua. My grandmother looked down in pity. At seventeen to have lost a wife and son as well as my whole family was a hard lot, even in hard times. For weeks, each morning we awoke to find the bounty left by our neighbors—stewed chickens, icy to the touch, piles of root vegetables dusted with the morning's snow. But nothing could assuage my misery, and though I kept abreast of the firewood, lest we die of cold, I more or less let my crop go to rot in the barn.

And Mandrik was no farmer. He was up late nights, or up early in the mornings, having visions or writing about them, and so was of little use to me. Days, as I worked, or when I stopped for midday repast, he relayed to me what he was learning of the world beyond, until I grew too frightened to sleep. So did we live our lives in the darkest part of that winter.

Yet God is merciful, and sadness, like any other foul weather, eventually passes off. I missed my Elynour each day, and Mandrik wore a stricken face each time he spoke of her, but as the ground began to thaw, so too did our hearts. I was by no means mirthful, but as I prepared the soil that spring, I found a measure of joy in the work. The long-absent glimmer returned to Mandrik's eye; as I sowed my crops, I realized he was harboring a secret. One June day he came skipping home in such triumph that one of his shoes was lost along the way. "I've found you a new wife!" he cried, galloping across the north field, where I was watering, in the shadow of the cairn.

"Mandrik, please."

"I did, I found her."

I knew full well the name of every marriageable woman in the parish, and that I cared for none of them, so I kept at my work. "Your left shoe, brother."

"God will provide another. Don't you want to know whom you're to marry?"

"Let me see." His excitement itched me like a rash; with the magnitude of his grief, how could he forget our Elynour so quickly? "Ah, yes. The Widow Tinker."

He slapped my arm. "Be serious. A beautiful girl, and as strong as any in the valley."

"This is sacrilege."

At once his aspect grew more sober. "When Elynour lay upon her final bed, I thought I could save her, I thought I could intercede with the Almighty. But I could not, brother. And now I will make you amends. I will stop the gap of your sorrow."

"I don't want it stopped. My wife is dead. I have good reason."

"Don't you even want to guess to whom I've betrothed you?"

"I can't think who."

"Adelaïda Gansevöort."

I set down my water skin and let it fall into a puddle. "Who?"

"Ion Gansevöort's youngest sister—and our mother's cousin, besides."

When I pictured Ion, an affable fellow who lived too far from town for socializing, it was surrounded by a cluster of yellow-haired sisters. "But the youngest is a child."

"Not a babe-in-arms: she's eleven."

"Eleven!"

Mandrik smiled his one-side-higher-than-the-other, usually infectious grin. "She's a good girl, with a kind heart. And she's young enough we can train her to do what you like."

"And to make clothes for her dollies. Why didn't you get one more my age, if you had to get one at all?"

"Because the older ones can't sing."

He was quite serious. I was lucky not to be such a lunatic myself. "Can't sing?"

> Oh, the Gansevöort sisters are lovely and fair
> From their plump little toes to their thick flaxen hair,
> But small Adelaïda's by far the most rare—
> For she is the one who can sing. Hey hey!

"Aye, but does she know her way around the back end of a cow?"

"Aye, and can card, spin, and weave cloth finer than women twice her age. And knows how to cook all manner of stews. But, Yves, you're not listening: she can sing."

"So can you. So could our mother. It doesn't bring meat to the table."

"Our mother got it from her Gansevöort grandmother, and I from her and from Grandmother Iulia. Only one family in this whole village can express itself in rhyme. And I tell you, she's better at it than I was at her age."

I laughed, though the remembrance of my mother's sweet songs left me sick at heart. "Yes, but you used to sing, 'Toad, toad, why do you lie in the road?' "

He smiled; he never minded a joke at his own expense. "And 'Cow, cow, next to the sow.' Aye, I recall. She rhymes better than that, and in a low, sweet voice. And think, Yves: When I leave you for a place of my own, to work on my treatise, how else will you keep from getting lonely at night?"

It was true—only during his absence, and during the most tragic evenings of my life, had I been without a song from my mother or brother to cheer me and make sense of the stuff of the day. "But eleven years old—she'll cry at night for her mother."

"Her mother is four years dead. Ion's crazy to get all those sisters out from under his roof; and you can treat her like a sister, if that'll make you feel better, till she's old enough."

Though I still could not picture to which of the Gansevöorts my brother had promised me, I began to like the idea. I dreamt of the blond, smiling lot of them that night, and in the morning acquiesced to marry, though Elynour was hardly six months in the soil. We dressed carefully—Mandrik having retrieved his shoe—picked all the cherries and greengages off our trees, and set out with hearts more hopeful than light to greet my new bride.

By the roads it would have been half a day's walk to Gansevöort's, so we cut through the fields, west through Nethering's land, and finally to Ion's sloping dairy farm. His cows were out to pasture, lazily ringing their heavy bells or sleeping under the shade trees. As we wove through them, barely even exciting their notice, the strains of a song in a low voice touched our ears:

> Lord done gimme these cows
> To watch over all day.
> Lord, why you gimme so many cows,
> Make me watch 'em all day?
> The brightest damn one among 'em
> Cain't understand a word I say.

A smile broke over my whole being like the sun after a rain shower: they'd be sassier songs than Mandrik's, then.

"Is that Adelaïda?" Mandrik ventured, though we knew who it was.

"Who's afield?" asked the voice, without any tenor of concern to mar it.

"The Gundrons," said he.

"Mercy, then." She rose up from the grass: still a child in the softness of her cheek and nose, but nearly as tall and broad as I, with a head of yellow hair streaming out behind her and collecting clover and grass. "Good day."

"Good day," I answered. At once I noticed the gap in her teeth. Though my heart still yearned for Elynour, there was no denying the beauty of this child.

"Adelaïda, I am pleased to introduce you to your future lord and master, my brother, Yves."

"Not lord and master," I said. "Your friend."

She curtsied, lifting the soiled hem of her skirt above her solid ankles. "I know you from church. I can't wait till we're married and my sisters quit bossing me around."

I said, "I would never order you to do anything."

"No, of course not. Mandrik says you're sweet as a Michaelmas apple, and soft as a duckling's down."

The back of my neck prickled, and Mandrik clearly saw it. But it hardly mattered what he had said if he'd gotten me this fine, strong girl for a wife.

When we brought Adelaïda home after the harvest, Mandrik did not give up his place beside me in the bed; we strung her up in a hammock like the bairn she was. She took over our cooking and the baking of bread—a delicacy we had lacked since Elynour's passing. She swept, tidied, and washed about the house, and kept herself busy from dawn to dusk in giving us a proper home. And in time, as the seasons passed, I grew to love her as dearly as ever I had loved Elynour; she did not erase the memory of my first wife, but daily she worked her miracles of compassion, which slowly eased my sorrow. When at last she was old enough to perform all the duties of a wife, we built Mandrik a hut of his own close by the church, and began to live like an ordinary family.

God sent me Adelaïda to allay my grief; she and my daughter are the rewards for all I have suffered. If they should be taken from me, after all that has passed and all that I have already lost, I do not know how I could continue to make my way among the living. I pray fervently, morning and night, for their well-being. I know that God's will is not susceptible to my intercession; but it is my hope that if he knows how dearly I love them, how dearly they are needed on this earth, he will let them sojourn among the living a short while longer yet.

PART II

CHAPTER SIX

THE HARVEST

s the summer grew fierce, Ruth's leg grew sound once more, and before long we removed Mandrik's contraption and she hobbled about the house and yard. She seemed much less strange now she looked more an ordinary woman, and she helped as best she could, picking vegetables and cleaning and preparing them. She could still not be taught to spin or weave, but she carded as ever with my daughter, and wound the wool from my wife's distaff into neat, even balls. All these tasks she performed with quiet pride, as if she had long doubted her ability to be useful; and each day that she walked about, the color returned somewhat more to her face. Mandrik proclaimed her recovery miraculous. The stranger and my brother were always about our house, and though I enjoyed their company, my wife and I rarely spent time alone together anymore. One hot afternoon we found ourselves with no one else around in the barn, taking the last hay down from the loft that we might place the new hay up.

"I'm not sure how I feel about her helping with everything," Adelaïda grumbled.

"You didn't like her lying about, and now you complain she lies about no longer. Which is it?"

Adelaïda raked hay onto my head below. "Both and neither. I suppose I'd like a home like other people's, with children about. Not so many grown people with their own pursuits."

I grabbed her ankle, pulled her playfully down the ladder, and kissed her broad, fair brow. "Do you really mind this strange windfall nature has blown us?"

Her lips smiled, but her eyes followed halfheartedly. "It depends when you ask me."

"I'm sure our neighbors' farms run more smoothly, but think, Adelaïda: ours is the one with the great unanswered question within its four strong walls."

"She can't stay forever. That's all."

"I'm sure she won't."

I pulled her down beside me into the hay, and she allowed me to begin playing such a game as we had known more frequently before we had a child and a guest.

As it grew time to bring the harvest in, Ruth gave up her crutches altogether, and though she limped at each second step, she moved about the farm as freely as I. One morning, drawing with a stick in the yard's dust, she taught Elizaveta the first letters of our alphabet; another morning I took her out with me as I surveyed the fields and the sky, planning the shape and speed of my harvest. We started out north, in the wheat field nearest the fallows by the cairn, which she greeted with a friendly wave.

"How do you know," she asked, "when it's time?"

"The rye comes ready a week before the wheat."

"But why not always wait a day longer for whatever it is to grow a day bigger?"

Such would have been my lot, this questioning, had my son lived; he would have been ten years old, nearly as tall and hale as Jowl, with the knowledge of my land in his bones. My stomach sank at the memory of his stunted form, but lest I grow melancholy before the stranger, I reminded myself how much trouble and strife a rambunctious son could be. Elizaveta never gave us a moment's worry; and so I remembered to be thankful for my prattling daughter. "If one waited ever, it would all rot in the fields."

"But how do you know specifically? Why haven't you started yet?"

From where we stood, I could see the house and yard in the distance, our sheep in the hilly far field, my wife and daughter, both in red aprons, weeding the vegetable garden. Around us, obscuring us past the waist, the wheat bent and rippled to the modulations of a breeze I could barely feel. Dared I tell her that over generations the land grew accustomed to our rhythms as we grew accustomed to its? That though I knew the general season for bringing in the harvest, I and all my brethren would feel it in the bones when the right morning came? None of this had ever seemed the least bit strange—for the world is as it is, and Nature offers no apologies for her ways. Now, hearing the question honestly put by someone who honestly did not know, I felt self-conscious. "Because it isn't yet time."

Her eyes were most pleasant when she squinted into the sun—dark as the darkest night, and turned up in half-moons with friendly wrinkles. "I should have asked them for a tape recorder."

"Pardon?"

"The Navy guys. They offered me equipment, and I should have taken them up on it, so I could record your voice, listen to you time and again. When I'm not here anymore."

"Do not speak of them, Ruth. I would rather forget." I picked a stalk and released the fair seeds into my hand. "I wonder what it will be like, when you are gone."

"Like it was before I came, I guess."

"But not exactly. No." Adelaïda had changed already; and who could say if the stranger's departure would return her to her old ways.

Ruth looked about her. "You know, where I'm from, nobody farms. I think most of the food comes from factories."

"Factories?"

"Man-made. Like pottery or cloth."

Sometimes I did not understand her tales of the Beyond—as if artifice bore any relation to porridge or bread.

"You ought to take a lesson from my brother. When he talks of the far world, he says things that make sense."

She regarded the fields as if she were their archduchess. "Do you think it would bother your brother, if I questioned him the way I question you?"

"He's the last person it would bother. He's the one who understands."

"I tried when I first got here, but he seemed reluctant to talk to me. And I'm worried he'd think I was trying to usurp his place."

"Nay, he has no mind for worldly position."

She opened and shut her mouth without speaking.

"What?" I asked her.

"I'm shy of him. I never met a holy man before. I never met anyone like him."

"Nor I, either, but you'll agree he's got a kindly soul."

"Absolutely, but—" She sighed quietly through her nose. "Somehow I'm frightened of him, of that stillness in his gaze."

"But a reflection of the heavens."

She nodded. "I know you're right. And I know he likes me. And I'm so anxious to know more about his journeys."

"I'm sure he'd be pleased if you asked him. He knows you better now, which might unloose his tongue."

We started again uphill. I had ignored the crops—treated them, indeed, with flagrant disrespect—but they strained upward toward the sun as mightily as a farmer could hope. At each step I felt a wave of gratitude that despite my poor husbandry this year's produce would not disappoint. When I looked at Ruth, she was biting at her fingernails. I gave a slight tug at her apron string; and when she refused to look up, I realized something was amiss.

"What ails you, Ruth?" I asked.

The sun on his westward course beamed behind her, lighting auburn the edges of her hair. "What if my work here takes a long time?"

"It takes time to grow the flax, and time to spin and weave it. I wouldn't be ashamed."

"I'm worried I'll outstay my welcome."

I hoped she did not know how warily Adelaïda regarded her presence. "You'll worry about that when the time comes."

"Sometimes I feel awful, eating your food, wearing your clothes—"

"We have to spare," said I. "Through God's grace and my ingenuity, we have more than enough. It's an honor to use it thus."

"I don't know how long this will take, Yves. If it takes another six months? A year? I don't want you to grow to hate me."[1]

I stopped walking. "Have you nothing better to think about? In two days' time I'll start bringing in this harvest, and that will cost every

---

[1] Adelaïda made her displeasure with me abundantly clear, but as often as not I confused her real unhappiness with my sister's low-grade fault-finding. Nurit had a negative turn of mind, but her disapproval never amounted to much; whereas I had to keep reminding myself that Adelaïda, according to Yves's reports, had a sunny disposition when I wasn't around. I wanted badly to earn her trust.

hour of labor, from the time the sun rises till after he sets, for the re-
mainder of the season. If you are well enough to assist, in any way you
see fit, I will greatly appreciate another set of hands, however inexpert.
You have a great work ahead of you, yet you spend your time worrying
against the possibility that I might grow tired of your presence. Why
would I? Have you tired of me?"

"No."

I shook my head. "Then what are you thinking?"

"I'm sorry," she said.

"Think about your last end. It might arrive tomorrow."

"I don't—"

"I have crops to bring in. Will you sit idly by in speculation?"

"No." Her hair hung forward like her visage. "I'll help you."

"And I'll help you in your work, when the time is right."

She regarded me, but did not speak.

"If the harvest is good, and the winter safe and sure, I'll help you in
this endeavor to the best of my ability." I had not given a moment's con-
sideration to her project, so why had these words issued forth? What
did I care, the outcome of her poking about, when I had a farm and a
family and a cart to attend? Nevertheless, the statement, when I made
it, felt true to my marrow.[2]

She said, quietly, "Thank you."

Adelaïda, in the yard below, sang one clear, plain note out into the
westering breeze that we might return home for porridge and vegetables. I closed my eyes briefly to allow the sound to wash over me. Her
pitch rose, trilled, and fell, and the evening silence was as rich and full
as all Heaven's bounty. We turned to heed the call, and pushed at the
wheat stalks that brushed against our chests. All this, all around, was
mine to reap. As we walked toward the house in silence, I contem-
plated the work I was about to begin, and thanked the Lord for my
harness, that at least the grain would be easier to cart away.

Harvest is the most difficult work of the year—for though plowing requires as much sweat, the product of the labor is not so near to hand,

---

[2] I am amazed that in that moment I could not see how little my own work would amount to in
comparison to Yves's own.

and one fears less any possible mistake. At harvest one is precious near the goal, yet the rain can, at any moment, wash the fruits of one's labor away; or fires, sparked by the anger of the sun, can tear through the stores, taking in a trice what might have lasted through spring. Most of the rest of the year we divide up our labor husband from wife, and we let children with milk teeth drift in and out of work, learning as they go. At harvest, however, each man's wife follows in the next row, wielding her scythe as expertly as he wields his own, and any child old enough to concentrate moment by moment is pressed into labor, gathering behind what the adults cut.

Market Day I bought a third scythe, the largest I could find, for Ruth, and when I returned home sharpened the other two once more against the singing stone until I feared to press my thumb against their blades. Adelaïda worked up to her elbows in a tub of dough, that we might carry bread with us into the fields at dawn and not return home until sundown. The night before we began, the whole house sweet with the scent of baking, we retired well before the sun, and lay in the gray dusk wild with anticipation for the morrow.

Adelaïda had already set the kettle to boil when I woke to hear my brother's song echoing up the road:

> *Let me reap what I have sowed,*
> *Lord! Let me reap what I have sowed,*
> *Help me to bring the crops in.*
> *Let me pay all that I've owed,*
> *Lord! Let me pay all that I've owed,*
> *But don't make me pay no wages of sin.*

I stuck my sleep-addled head out the door and saw him coming with the sun's great glory behind him, and with Manfred and Jowl, Ydlbert's boisterous middle sons, gamboling out before him on the road.

"He sends you these two for the day," my brother called, "and wishes you Godspeed." He had a parcel of fruit tucked under one arm and a sheaf of papers under the other—a good sign.

We ate heartily, and the boys ate enough for ten Elizavetas. The child's brown eyes were wide and roving, and she set her doll to dance over the tabletop, upsetting the salt, so great was her excitement about this event she was too young to remember from the year before. Ruth was already in the way, but beaming, so I forgave her, though certain my wife would not. Adelaïda packed three great loaves of bread, both wheat and rye, into her carrying sling, and a tub of butter, and two drinking gourds; then she filled two buckets with rainwater and gave them to the boys to carry splashing to the barn. As they went shouting out the door, my brother closed his eyes while his lips moved in prayer. I could not hear his words, but trusted in their efficacy.

I hitched Enyadatta. She could not be asked to draw so many of us (though her foot-stamping and head-wagging might also have been for show), so Mandrik and I walked alongside her, patting occasionally her lovely, reddish face. The water buckets, jostled by the movements of the cart, soon spilled most of their contents over Ydlbert's yelling sons, my shrieking, laughing daughter, and the women, who in truth did not seem greatly to mind.

"We'll have to send the boys back for more," said Adelaïda.

"Later," I said, turning to regard her. She stood wringing her red apron and blue skirt over the side of the cart, and laughing. The sun lit the side of her broad face, shining his rays into one perfect blue eye, and lighting up the gold in her hair. All the years of marriage and the hard labor of running a household had only increased her robust beauty. I caught her eye, and her grin widened to reveal her second set of dimples. Lest my mind wander utterly from the task at hand, I scanned the horizon, saw none of my fellow farmers as yet, and said, "Ruth, do you know a way to prevent the cart bouncing so?"

"Sure, but I'm not going to tell you."

The boys hollered, always ready for a confrontation, and she, too, began to laugh. Mandrik walked with his hand on Enyadatta's neck and basked in the sun.

"I'm serious. I'm learning to keep my mouth shut."

"You don't want to impinge upon our purity?" Mandrik asked.

"How can I, and then write about how you've always done things? Besides, with my big mouth I've told your brother all kinds of ways to improve this cart, and has he done anything to fix it?"

"Oooh," exclaimed Jowl. "Trouble."

"I have drawn up plans for braking this machine," I countered. "But only after harvest is there time for tinkering."

"My, how he changes as he grows older," said Mandrik.

"Those of us who don't have the freedom to wander off to Indo-China must do our inventing when we can."

"Anyone," my brother said, his eyes happily closed to the warming rays, "may travel anywhere he wishes at any time. May he not, Ruth?"

"Within reason, sure."

"It is only a matter of desire, of a deep longing to go."

"I have a deep longing for my family not to starve come winter."

"Then your course of action is clear, isn't it?"

The water had ceased to splash, so Manfred and Jowl took the drinking gourds and threw more of it upon one another. Elizaveta, who doubtless knew nothing but the general mood, expressed her glee. As we neared the boundaries of the property, I saw both Yorik von Iggislau and Franz Nethering hitching their beasts.

"Hail, my brothers!" I called, uncertain that they could see one another from their low-lying positions.

"Hail," Nethering called back. Yorik waved, and cried, "Godspeed!"

When we reached my great-grandfather's meandering stone fence, we turned westward and followed it out to the very edge of the land. At the corner which divided me from Yorik on the one side and the deep woods on the other, I unloaded my wet charges and our tools, then paused to look around me. The birds and the crickets were already happily chirping in the woods, and Yorik's Maundering Stream babbled in the distance. The dusky rye stretched uphill and eastward as far as I could see in that direction, and it perfumed the air. It would be a good crop; and by the time it was in, the wheat in the north fields would be ripe. "Shall we, then?" I asked.

Adelaïda spat to the four directions, and sang out:

Bless this harvest,
Make it good,
Let us reap
A lot of food.

Then she rubbed her hands together, and took up her scythe. Ruth smoothed down her apron, and said, "What do I do?"

"Watch for a moment, you'll understand."

She looked skeptical, her eyebrows reaching up toward the top of her head.

I cornered myself into the row that ran closest to the forest, and began to mow. Though I had spent countless hours at this activity throughout my life, it had been a long, eventful year since last I had held the tool. Its weight at first swung unevenly, counter to mine, and the scythe chopped through the plants at various heights. But the body remembers past labor more clearly than does the mind, and within a few minutes the swing was loping and even, balanced right over my center, and the blade began to sing as it sheared the stalks from the ground, leaving only a stubble behind like four days' beard. Adelaïda fell into step a few swings behind me and in the next row, and so auspiciously began the first of many long days' labor.

I looked over my shoulder a short distance up the row to see if Ruth had yet the hang of the work. She stood at the end of her row with her scythe held far out from her body, practicing her swing and driving the blade each second or third time into the dirt. "Be careful with that," I said. "That's a good tool."

"I don't get it."

I continued up my row. "In what way?"

"I don't know. Mine isn't doing what yours is doing."

"Well, that's hardly a good omen," said Adelaïda.

"What's not to understand? You swing it," I called. "Get Mandrik to show you how it works."

"With pleasure," said he.

"Who's going to sing to us," Adelaïda asked, "if he's busy teaching the stranger to mow?"

"For now you're welcome to fill the duty yourself," he offered, "and she'll learn anon."

The boys were already following behind us, binding the rye into sheaves, as Jowl whistled something tuneless. In tones I could but barely discern over the whistling and the brisk cut of the scythes, Mandrik instructed her in the use of the implement as he had been instructed long ago, when it had seemed that he, like all his brothers, would work the land. What a different world it was then, when Mandrik, six years old, might have been supposed to lead an ordinary life. When I turned to glance at their progress he was standing behind her, his arms around her, his hands on hers on the scythe, teaching her to rock it before her without imperiling her body or the ground, teaching her its own forward-driving momentum. She smiled broadly as her arms began to understand. He stayed with her, his arms tight girding her, as she mowed the first of her row. "That's it," he said.

She watched her blade. "It still doesn't feel right."

"But it will." He remained with her until the scythe cut smooth, and then let her go. She was a good ways behind us, but she kept forward at a steady pace; and though her blade did not move quick enough to sing, when later I inspected her rows, she had managed to cut only a few inches farther from the ground than I had myself. Mandrik, keeping pace at a safe distance, gave instructions and encouragement in equal measure, and each time I looked back both sage and pupil were smiling despite the labor and the heavy heat.

When we stopped to lunch in a fragrant clearing under the pines, Jowl and Manfred had tired themselves out binding the rye and standing it up into shocks, and Ruth was sunburned, her hands torn open by labor, her bad leg lagging behind. Mandrik wet his handkerchief and bathed her sores. "Perhaps the body is not yet ready for such work," he said gently.

"I'm fine. This is fun." But her eyes looked weary, and the sores were deep and raw.

Mandrik sat beside her and broke her bread that her hands might rest. Adelaïda wore a look of envy as she watched Ruth thus be served. The children were asleep before we could feed them.

"What sermonizing have you brought us, brother?" I asked, lying down among the prickling needles and knowing no finer feeling.

"No sermonizing, but a reflection. I am trying something new."

"A reflection upon what?"

He took the rolled sheaf out from his belt behind him. "Upon language."

"Words, you mean?" Adelaïda said, drowsing back to nestle in the crook of my arm.

"None other."

"That seems a far cry," said I, "from the matters of life and death, and of first and last things, which have occupied you until now. And has nothing to do with Indo-China."

"It seems no great difference to me, if all things are one in the eyes of God. Though, if you prefer, tomorrow I can read to you of matters more strictly theological."

"I express no preference," said I. "I only remarked the change."

Ruth said, "Could I have that rag back?"

Mandrik poured clean water over it once again, wrapped it around her two palms, so they were bound together, and leaned her back against a large rock. "You'd do better to sleep than to listen."

She shook her head. "How could I?"

He placed his papers on the ground and lay down upon his stomach, propped up on his elbows, to read. "For only the second time in our long and peaceable History," he began, "strangers have come among the people of Mandragora."

"Hey," she said, her teeth showing behind her wide grin. "Don't write about me."

"What makes you think I am?"

"The word 'strangers.'"

He nodded, though his head was drawn somewhat between his shoulders. "Why should I not write about you, if you write about us?"

She reached her bound hands up to scratch her nose.

I said, "Don't interrupt him, Ruth. Let him read."

"Sorry."

"Though their ways seem peculiar," he continued, "their presence, more than exposing us to Novelty, has startled us awake, and has forced us to turn the bright Beam of our intellectual Attention upon ourselves. I am not certain we have all been pleased to see ourselves and our rusticity so clearly in this uncustomary Brightness.

"Nevertheless, the search for Self-Knowledge, as has elsewhere been proven, is man's highest Aim; and in order to achieve that knowledge, in order to look inward with the full force of his beliefs, he must first direct his attention to the outside world, that he might know it completely. With this aim in mind do I seek now to explore the Language and Speech of our strangers, that through them we may come better to understand our own words, and ultimately the Word of God."

"Hang on, Mandrik," Ruth said. "I'm the—"

"You write your treatise and I'll write mine. And, Yves, if I have my way about it, will write one of his own."

"Mandrik—" I said.

"How's this, Yves?" Adelaïda asked, pulling away that she might roll over to see me.

"Idle fancy, that's how."

"If you'd rather not have me read, I'd be glad to bore you all to sleep with hymns."

"No, go on."

"In beginning this Exploration will I start with that which has struck me most forcefully: certain peculiar Differences between the strangers' speech and our own.

"Though in Mandragora we speak only one Language, we know that in the Great World others are spoken. God's Word has come down to us, along with the words of many of his chief Disciples, in Greek, Hebrew, and Latin; and as I have reported in my account of my journey to the Beyond, the world has proven itself fuller of Languages and Alphabets than one man can master. All three strangers who have recently appeared among us have, by a miracle, spoken our Mother Tongue. Their accents, however, are rough, broad, and somewhat unseemly—"

"Do you mind?"

"—which prevents our understanding their Speech as plainly as we do our own."

Ruth said, "I'm sure you realize that you sound as strange to me as I do to you?"

Adelaïda said, "Use your sense, lass."

"The harsh Tone of the strangers' speech is not due merely to the way they shape their Sounds. Rather, the Words and Phrases they employ give also the savor of Uncouthness. Where the beauties of language trickle like a Rill from the tongue of the Mandragoran, words emerge from the mouths of our strangers in sharp bursts, uttered with the profoundest Economy. Where our speech is balmy as the first Days of Harvest, theirs calls to mind Winter's cruelest Chill.

"Therefore do I conclude that the strangers' homeland is more brutal and barren than any Land we have heretofore imagined. Misery and Want must have plagued the people untold Generations for the language of Privation thus to have burrowed so deeply into their hearts that they can express themselves no other, more beautiful way.

"Despite, then, that we and the strangers can be said to speak the same language, there are many Points of Divergence which I believe it would benefit to explore. Take, for example, the repeated utterance of the sound 'Um' in their speech. This should not be confused with 'Om,' a devotional sound used by the Mystics of the East, and documented elsewhere in this treatise. 'Om' is the first sound of the Universe, the beginning of the Word, while 'Um' has no meaning that can be divined. The strangers, however, seem wont to interject it between many—nay, even most—of their utterances. The people of Mandragora do not utter this sound; when the strangers do, it is clear as midday that they wish to avoid any more meaningful or specific utterance. I conclude that the repetition of 'Um' by our visitors indicates a deep aversion to speaking Truth."

Ruth said, half laughing, half annoyed, "I don't say 'um' all the time."

"Yes, you do."

She turned to me for assistance, but what could I say? "Your speech is strange, Ruth. I don't always notice in what specific ways."

She said, "You're kidding me."

" 'Kidding,' " my brother said. "Another of your habits of speech."

Adelaïda said, "What treatise are you writing, Yves?" and I wished that she might fall asleep.

"No treatise, love."

"Aye," she said drowsily, "one treatise ought more than to suffice for a family."

"It will be necessary to turn our attention to all of the strangers' myriad peculiarities of dialect, each in its own time, that through each Particle of Knowledge we might acquire more particular knowledge of ourselves. I feel it my duty, however, to warn the gentle Reader and Listener now, that my Understanding of the strangers' speech, after having examined those Aspects to which I have thus far devoted my Attention, bodes ill for our Future. The Strangers have shown us many Wonders and divers Inventions, but they have not shown us any surpassing Insight into the human Spirit. If it is possible for man to learn so deeply in one field of Inquiry, all the while ignoring Another, then I must urge you, my Brethren, to take heed, for the worst of our sorrows is surely yet to come."

My wife's breath was deepening, but Ruth's pique had given way to solemn attention. "I hope you're wrong," she said quietly.

"Naturally, my observances are based as much upon the others as upon you. I think you bode better for us, if there's any boding to be done."

"That was good, though," Ruth said. "That's good."

"Thank you. That's hardly the end."

"Mandrik," I said, "this is not the same treatise. Where's all the stuff about the end of the world? Where's your journey to Indo-China?"

"It is, I admit, a bit of a digression, but you see I was beginning to tie it in to last things toward the end."

Ruth said, "Are you going to go through everything we say?"

"It's no longer a we, is it? Only you." Mandrik again made his small, lying-down shrug. "It depends how much time you'll allow me to study you."

"I'm not sure I want to be studied."

"But the very fact of your presence makes it so."

"Please keep reading."

"With your kind permission."

"Please. I'm interested to hear it."

"Very well, then."

The talk of language bored me. I left them to their follies and drifted off to sleep, but was pleased to hear the glad tenor of their voices in the sweet, piney air.[3]

Harvest had never before seemed such labor, perhaps because in all other years I had worked steadily, whereas so much of this spring and summer had gone to idle fancy. That first night, my hands also hurt from scything, though I dared not admit it. Adelaïda could hardly stay

---

[3] It was later that week, after a long day in the fields, that Mandrik first let me see his manuscripts. His home was clean-swept and bare: a single bowl and cup on the shelf his only possessions, besides his meager furniture, a collection of books wrapped in protective pieces of leather and cloth, and thousands upon thousands of pages of writing in his neat, narrow hand. He had filled every inch of each piece of paper, which I suppose is necessary when you make the paper yourself. He was my age, slightly older, but had already produced more than I could write in a lifetime. I confess that my admiration of the subjects he tackled was tinged with jealousy of his productivity. And I confess, too, that the pleasure of his company more than equaled the pleasure I took in his work.

awake to cook, so we ate our luncheon's bread and butter as Mandrik walked the sleepy boys home. Ruth's hands were worn quite raw, and I feared that though the break in her leg had not killed her, an infection in her hands might well. On the next day, then, we made her stay home and watch the child, that we might work in peace. Mandrik came again to sing to us and to read from his strange new work, but mid-afternoon decided to return to the house to check on Ruth's hands and on Eliza-veta, and to gather more fodder for his treatise on language. "I'll make her say words at me and what they mean, until you come home. That'll teach her what it's like, all her questions about bed warmers and eggs." We let him go; his contribution to the harvest had never been more than to cheer us, and just then it cheered me to be alone with my wife.

"I like the mowing better," she said, "when it's but our family, as ever it was before."

"Tut," I told her, for I could think of nothing more profound to say.

From where we stood, still far west in our southern fields, we could see none of our neighbors, though earlier in the day I had seen Friedl Vox out gleaning her winter's meager sustenance from Yorik's mown rows. I lay Adelaïda's scythe gently down on the ground, and led her to the shelter of our uncut stalks, that we might enjoy the pleasures of matrimony we could lately steal but upon occasion. Still she seemed subdued; though she allowed my caresses, she did not encourage them.

We were blessed with a first week without rain, so the stalks bore no extra weight and were easy to shock; the sun shone brightly and dried the grain thoroughly in the field. Ruth's hands quickly scabbed over, after which she joined us again, scything for a while at a time, then gathering sheaves behind us like a child and awkwardly standing them up together to dry. Mandrik's new work proved tedious to Adelaïda's ears, so he brought forth something older and grislier about the end of the world, which satisfied her better. Some mornings he simply sang to us, accompanying himself with the harmonious sweetness of the psaltery.

> *Oh, the crops they grow tall,*
> *And the grass it grows green,*
> *But many is the time*
> *That elsewise I've seen.*
> *Wild have been the storms*

That washed the crops away;
How thankful I am
For this bounty today.

Oh, my lover is true,
But her eye, it lacks faith,
Each morning anew
Does it dance like a wraith.
Many's the man
Destroyed by such a life,
Yet how thankful I am
To call her my wife.

"What would you know about wives?" Adelaïda asked.

"It's a ballad," my brother said, shaking his head. "One's allowed to say things that aren't strictly true."

"Nay," said Adelaïda, "you might pay dear for that, someday."

Ruth began to write down his songs. "If I had a tape recorder," she said, scribbling. "I'm an idiot not to have taken one of their tape recorders." As it was, when she caught up to us in the sheaving (as sometimes, despite her inexperience, she did, because she was tall and hale) she was full of questions: How long would it take? Would we plant the same crops to the same plot of ground next year? Who had invented the scythe? (And who, I demanded in return, had invented her impertinence?) Where did we get oats if we weren't growing them? (Clearly, she had never encountered a system of crop rotation so sophisticated as our own.) I had lived with my brother's fierce questioning all my life, but it was easier to understand someone who wanted to know where the soul went after death than to understand someone who wanted to know if one grows winter wheat in the summer wheat's field. It is man's nature to seek after that which he does not—perhaps cannot—know; but to seek after that which is but ordinary knowledge? Certain I could spend half the days for the rest of my life asking Ruth how things are done in her homeland, but I do not see what would be the profit of such inquisition.

We finished our southern fields late one afternoon, and decided, rather than cross the High Road to the northern fields, to leave off laboring for a few hours. I felt tired to my marrow, and glad of a few hours' respite. Out came my pipe, the ale, and the psaltery, and it had never felt more a pleasure to lie down in our dirt yard, the barn looming to one side with the shorn fields behind, and across the road our still-untouched wheat fields, resplendent. Mandrik's labors, which consisted mostly of giving lessons and bringing in some occasional sheaves, had been far less tiring, but he, too, collapsed out in the yard, his instrument standing by untouched. Elizaveta, God bless her, had spent some of the earlier days of the harvest with Ruth in learning to sew, and from her mother's scrap basket had fashioned a whole crooked wardrobe for Pudge. She sat in the barn's long shade, pulling first one misshapen dress and then the next over the doll's scarred wooden head, and showing us each of the fruits of her newfound talent. Adelaïda began to hum as if she meant to sing, but never got around to the idea's execution. And Ruth, who had hitherto shown no particular gift for the affairs of the kitchen, brought forth a vegetable soup that tasted nearly as good as my wife's own cooking, and served it out with the modesty and pride of an ordinary wife. In short, my belly was full, my crop more than half in, and I felt the right to be satisfied.

When she brought our emptied bowls back to the house, Ruth returned thence with a writing tablet and a pen. I could not help the feeling of despair that rose in my breast at the sight of them. "Oh, Ruth, must you use those now?"

She looked uncertain if I were in jest. "You don't want me to?"

Adelaïda drew nearer to me. "If only you weren't always asking so many questions, and about the strangest things."

"I'm sorry. I'm trying to learn what I can."

"Then look about you," my wife said sleepily. "What's to know that you can't see with your own two eyes?"

I propped one arm under my head that I might better watch them both.

"I don't know," she said.

"Ruth," said Adelaïda, "you've been after us since springtime. When will you run out of things to ask?"

She tucked a loose strand of her wild hair behind her ear, a gesture of humility. "I don't know."

My brother reached lazily to pluck the strings of his psaltery.

"Perhaps, since it's bothering you, Adelaïda, I should begin asking my questions of Mandrik. Would you mind?" She was either blushing or too much in the sunlight.

"I know far less of the things of this world than Yves does."

"Less about farming, but you could tell me about your journeys. If you think it's time."

Mandrik sat up and crossed and recrossed his legs. "It would take too long."

"I'm not going anywhere."

Adelaïda woke up enough to cast her a dark glance.

"Tell her about the silk boats," I coaxed, "and the men in dresses."

"I cannot tell you of my journeys now. Not with this audience."[4]

"But later. In addition to reading the manuscript. If you no longer think me too much a stranger."

"Nay, as time passes, you come to seem more our own."

"Thank you."

Mandrik nodded to her. "I will like immensely to speak with you of the far world."

Adelaïda said, "You always tell tales of Indo-China."

"But never the whole tale. Never."

---

[4] "Why wouldn't you talk in front of Yves and Adelaïda?" I asked him, sitting that night at his neat table.

"Because I have not told them all of my journeys."

"Of course you haven't."

He shook his head. "But I have not even begun to tell them what I have seen."

"It would have been a good opportunity, then."

So that I could drink from his cup, he made his own tea in the wooden bowl. His hands were angry, however, as they crushed the nettles. "Do you not listen to me? I have seen things about which I cannot tell them."

Just then his oratory struck me as overly dramatic. Still, I liked him, and liked watching him be flustered. "Such as?"

He slammed the two vessels down before me. "Would you believe me if I told you I had sojourned a fortnight in your city?"

"Boston," I said quietly, "is not Vietnam."

"It certainly isn't." He offered me a chunk of honeycomb, which I declined. "I didn't go to Vietnam."

"What'd you think, of Boston?" I asked, to still the other questions that were bubbling up in me.

"A grim little suburb of New York." His smile was lopsided, extremely inviting.

"Don't get me started," I said.

He replied, "No, Ruth. Don't get me started," and set one hand on the table, bent over me, and kissed me. Had I not been sitting, I would have lost my balance. His mouth was gentle, his hand on my hair shaking—who knew if he had ever kissed anyone before? I knew I shouldn't mess with my data set, and I could imagine my sister, Nurit, the crack student, railing at me for thus spoiling my research; and yet despite my misgivings, I drew him closer, coaxed him down onto the bench beside me. I had never before kissed anyone who smelled not of shampoo and shaving cream but of human sweat, and the midday sun, and the nettles for tea. All my misgivings paled against the splendor of his nearness.

Despite that she was lying prone, Adelaïda ventured the following snippet of verse:

> Oh brother, oh brother, oh brother of mine,
> Why must you go off to Indo-Chine?
> I'm going in search of knowledge divah-hine—
> And that's why I'm going to Indo-Chine.
> That's why I'm going to Indo-Chine,
> That's why I'm going to Indo-Chine,
> I'm going in search of knowledge divine,
> And that's why I'm going to Indo-Chine.

Ruth kept tucking at her hair, though by now it was well behind her ears. "I have to go talk to the Archduke, too. He wants me to write that story."

"Then you'd best," Adelaïda said. "He won't let you go back on your word."

"I don't want to, though. I'm not interested."

Adelaïda said, "He'd feed you better than we ever could."

"You could go to the Archduke's in the morning," I told her, "and visit with Mandrik when he's finished sermonizing us, in the late afternoon."

"Do you think?" she asked. She clipped her implement to the front of the tablet—always a good sign—and set it back behind her.

"Else I wouldn't say it."

She turned to Mandrik. "I look forward to it so much. It would make it much easier to go talk to the Archduke, to know that I could also talk to you."

"I, too, look greatly forward," he said. My brother's blue eyes were gone nearly black in the fading light, and were wide open, regarding her. Even in childhood, Mandrik had been tranquil—though he was our family's seeker, his hunger was ever for the soul's knowledge. Now his eyes had, ever so slightly, changed. In their expression, in their fervent desire to tell and to be heard, I recognized that something had long gone unsaid. Why had he not told me all of his adventures? Why this burning need, this pleasure so otherwise unlike him, to talk to her? I watched him in silence, and tried to reconcile myself to this new idea. But I could not; Mandrik had always been my closest confidant, and look what had passed unsaid between us, and would pass into the greedy ears of one I barely knew. Months of fellowship were nothing compared to a lifetime of relation, but look, now, to whom he turned.

The next morning, Ruth set off, her implements and a hunk of bread in my carrying sling. "You're quite certain," I asked her, "you remember the traveling spells? Who knows what might befall you if you forgot them."

"Yves, I'm fine."

Adelaïda spat to the west. "So they all say, until the wrath of God rains down upon them."

As we worked the northern fields, I could see Ruth trudging down the High Road, her gait still uneven, toward the city. So pleasant an occupation she had, I thought, to write things down while the rest of the village sweat. All that week she gathered words, and returned home at nightfall with pages covered in her large hand. Had it not been harvest, I would have trained her in the setting of traps, that her long day's labor might also have brought home something to roast.

She was home before our work was through, her stride slower and her back bowed under the weight of her papers. One would think, at least from my brother's clear brow, that the work of the mind was less taxing than the work of the body. Ruth, however, would find us in the fields come evening, drop her burden to the ground, follow behind us gathering for perhaps half a row, and collapse exhausted to the earth.[5]

---

[5] No university politicking was ever more difficult than those six long days I spent interviewing Archduke Urbis of Nnms. He talked incessantly with his hands; they were stained yellow, and smelled foul from all the oranges he ate. We sat together on silk cushions on the floor, fanned by the red servants and looking through the windows at his remarkable greenhouse, which sheltered his precious orange trees so brilliantly. I tried to write everything down, but it was hot, and we were half reclining, and the temptation to sleep lured me like nothing I had ever known. The warm breezes blew through the windows, and the birds sang in the branches. I was so bored, and so uncomfortable in the itchy clothes Adelaïda had made me, that I wondered if I had made a mistake, coming to Mandragora. Urbis had stories about everything—from his father, who had exercised the *droit de seigneur* with every woman (including Friedl Vox) in the parish, to his own, more modest exploits (which had not yet resulted in his taking a wife), to his plans to extend his great paving project out onto the High Road and the Low Road (which seemed a fine idea, if it would make the cart rides less bumpy), to his further, and secret, plans to raise an army and conquer all the territory in these mountains, thus bringing the heathens he believed to be all around under the gentle dictatorship of fruit-rich Nnms. By mid-afternoon I longed for Mandrik's company: for his plain speech; for the simplicity of his hut and what he offered me to eat there; for the tantalizing bits of his story he had held out before me; for the intelligence which sparkled in his large blue eyes; and not least for his kisses and the tentative way he traced the lines of my collarbones with his fingers. Urbis was a good interview, but none of his ideas was incandescent.

"Fie on you!" I teased her when I had only three rows left to bring in.

"You don't know the half of it."

"My brother tires you?"

She remained on the ground. I moved to a different row and scythed there. "Your brother is a delight, always. The Archduke."

Adelaïda shook her tired blond head. "The only person in the village with the opportunity to talk to the nobility, and she complains about it."

"He's boring, Adelaïda."

"What could be boring about the man who rules us all?"

"His mind, for one thing. His interests."

"You should be ashamed of yourself. Preferring the company of farmers and mystics to the company of the Archduke? Think, woman. You stand to make an excellent match."

"Oh, please."

"So you say now, but you'll cast a cold eye my way when you're the Archduchess."

Ruth's face darkened, but she kept her peace, and eventually, as she did now each day, fell asleep to the rhythmic cutting of the scythes. Elizaveta had napped half the day in the shade, so she was working then, gathering bundles as thin as spiderwebs. As her hands grew, so would what she saw fit to carry. Adelaïda's cut was every bit as quick and strong as mine. "Do you really think the Archduke intends to marry her?" I asked her.

"I don't know. It was clear he was smitten, the day he was here."

"Smitten and married are such different things."

She reaped faster than I did. "Far better for a woman to marry an Archduke, who'll take care of her properly, than a farmer who wastes half his time dreaming."

I stood still, caught my breath, listened to her scythe sing. "Adelaïda."

"Well, it's true."

"But you wound me."

"I'd have nothing to worry about if you'd invent less and work the fields more."

I wanted to apologize, to offer to give up my idleness, but my heart rebelled. My life was for tinkering, for making new things, for examining what we had and making it better. What great profit could come from year after year of plowing, sowing, and reaping? There were scores in our village who did that, and nothing changed for them, year in, year out. The grain would disappear—baked, made into porridge, or gone to rot—by this time next year, but Manfred's and Jowl's sons would continue to drive in four-wheeled carts, perhaps even with brakes. And who knew what next I would invent to make our lives better? There was no comparison between the two activities. Still, I did not want to argue with my wife. Instead, I thought with pleasure as I mowed how I was killing the delicate stalks—killing them outright, that they would never, without my intervention and care, grow again.

"Why must you always think of things, Yves? We haven't time for ideas."

"Adelaïda, please. Let's put down our tools. We'll finish tomorrow. I don't want to talk about it."

My brother, now, was lodged in my mind. Despite my better nature, I kept imagining him standing down the row before me, that when I passed, my instrument might tear the hem of his robe or cut his ankle. I had always known him, fought with him, trusted him, turned to him for advice. Now he followed his inclinations and I followed mine; but his were lauded, respectable in their way, while mine were a mere fancy that drew me from my work. And I thought about him, telling stories to the stranger in the afternoons. I had always assumed that he told me all that he knew and thought; as I had confessed my youthful escapades, so had he confessed his. Why had this stranger come among us to cast me into doubt? I finished my day's work with fierce intensity. Let her sleep while I toiled. Let both of them rot in my fields.

Ydlbert, with four of his sons fully capable of labor, finished reaping before I did. As I was scything my last row the next morning, I saw Jungfrau and a few others who farmed small plots go whooping past in their carts, and Ydlbert brought Dirk and Bartholomew to help me cut the last of my crop. As I had but one row left, Dirk did the work himself, scything like a house afire, and Bartholomew sheaved the grain. Ydlbert and I hung back to admire their work.

"We're not so young anymore," Ydlbert said, wiping his brow.

"You're not so young," I said.

Ydlbert toyed with the sunburned, hairless spot at the top of his head, and I felt a pang of guilt for what I had said.

"Thanks to your fine sons, this crop will be in before the sun is high," I said, perhaps changing the subject without too much grace. Ydlbert nodded. He kept fingering his head, looking out at the neat rows of stubble striping my rich black earth, the leaning shocks of pale brown wheat, the fallow land above the cairn gone to flower. "Thank you, brother," I told him.

"I wish there was more I could have done."

It was I, though, who truly so wished—for I wished the harvest could be more than a mere harvest, more than so much sweet-smelling wheat being dried for the threshing floor. "Now I'll have time to work on my new inventions," I told him, for I could not speak aloud of the sadness I was feeling, nor of my misgivings about my brother.

"What have you got for us now?" he asked, bending down to work a clod of my soil between his forefinger and thumb.

"More to do with the cart."

Dirk returned with the scythe slung over his shoulder in a precarious fashion, Bartholomew wiping his hands on his trousers behind. "There's a party down in the grove. Will you be heading down there?" Dirk asked.

"In a bit," Ydlbert said, nodding approval at his son's attempt at politeness. "You go ahead."

"Thanks, Father." Dirk set the tool down and they sauntered off.

Ydlbert said, "You've had the cart on your brain for years now. Don't you want to go back to farming?"

"Every time I fix what I set out to, I realize something else is wrong."

"Any special reason?"

I shrugged my shoulders. They were sore. "So complex a thing always, I suppose, admits of improvements."

"No, I'm asking why you brood over the cart."

"I hadn't really looked for a reason."

"Yves, there's nowhere to go." He turned to look around him. Mountains to all sides, the cairn to the northeast, and the broad, blue sky. "To market and back, and lately to town however many times a week. And where else? One can drive about, but there's no need to go any faster or farther. You've done us a great service by inventing all that you have."

"I am glad you think so."

"But, Yves, there's nothing more we require. You can stop now. Or move on to something else—try your hand at improving the mill, or turning lead into gold."

"You mock me."

"No."

"I have no interest in the mill. I have work to do on the cart."

Ydlbert shook his head. "We've got a whole crop to thresh, winnow, and grind, and the fields to glean and plow under. You'll need to rethatch before the frost. I've looked in your woodshed, man—you need to split a good dozen trees before winter, never mind shivering your kindling. Why not make these your tasks and your projects, as ever you did before?"

I picked up the scythe Dirk had left on the ground and stepped on the blade, working it sideways into the dirt. "I'll do everything this farm requires of me, but it no longer draws my heart."

"You won't be my friend, will you, when you're busy inventing all the time."

I looked at him, expecting him to crack a smile, but he did not.

"You've tried the life that I lead, and found it dull. It was good enough for your ancestors—"

"Not dull. It's not that I don't want to farm." Although, at that moment, it was. "But my mind is restless. It seeks after things to fix, things to grapple with. It isn't enough anymore, this looking after my land."

"It's not good enough for your brother or for you." He wasn't angry, but an expression of regret lodged around his great gray eyes. "It isn't only your brother, is it?"

"How's that?"

"Who's marked."

I drove the blade deeper into the ground with my heel. "Don't say such things."

He pushed my foot away and gruffly extricated the tool. "No use spoiling a good scythe, Yves. I didn't mean to offend you."

I shook my head. I had nothing to say.

"Come on, then, the whole town'll be drunk before we arrive."

We walked toward the house. "I am renouncing nothing."

"But the madness is calling you."

"It is not madness."

"Hush, lad. I didn't mean anything by it."

Work was calling me. Why were brakes so different from a field in want of harrowing or a horse that needed to be shod?

We gathered our women from our homes and, with our jubilation quieted by our disagreement, set out for town. The bonfire was blazing again in the grove, despite the heat of the sun, and from the rise we could see the rest of the stragglers, on High Road and Low, converging. What caught my eye, however, was not the familiar sight of my neighbors gathered to quaff ale, but farther out—practically to Nnms—a cluster of men blocking and crouching over the road. "What'll that be?" I asked.

Ydlbert squinted. "It's been years since they smoothed the ruts out."

Ruth stood up to stick her head out between us. "You're right, Ydlbert. That's a road crew." Anything she said would have annoyed me, and the words' strange sound burbled in my ear. "The Archduke said he was planning to pave the High Road and the Low Road, but I didn't think he meant to do it so soon."

Suddenly the bonfire and its concomitant merriment held nothing for me; my mind was fixed on the Road Crew. As if she were similarly held in its thrall, Enyadatta trotted past the assembled farmers, who whistled after us in what did not quite seem a friendly manner, and continued onward toward the strange sight. We drove down past where the roads joined, past the church and the graveyard and the wreckage of the airplane, and perhaps five minutes' drive from the Great West Gate we were stopped by the shouts of the workmen.

"Halt!" shouted he closest to my horse.

Enyadatta walked onto the grass, and the cart turned and eased to a stop behind her. Now we were turned broadside, we all flocked to the long edge of the cart and peered at the men in wonder. They were dressed identically, in raiment of deepest blue, on which the road dust floated like the clouds in the sky. Their loose trousers were tucked into thick laced boots, and their shirts were rolled up above their elbows, revealing their sun-darkened, muscular arms. One of the fairest wore a kerchief around his head like a woman. And all of them—six or seven in all—chewed, spat, and worked the ground with shovels, spades, and pikes.

"There'll be no thoroughfare," said the man with the woman's hair scarf. He was red with exertion and sunlight.

"What are you doing?" Ydlbert asked.

A tall, dark one gave a crooked grin, pointed down at his feet, and said, very clearly, "Roadwork."

"We're paving under orders from the Archduke," said the kerchief wearer.

Ruth said, "This is amazing."

The dark one looked her over and spat. "If it isn't that creature of his Lordship's, all skulking about with the farmer folk."

Ruth said, "Excuse me?"

"I think you heard me clear."

"And where, exactly, are you paving?" I asked.

Said the dark one, "On the road."

A third one cuffed him across the head, and he grumbled and quieted down.

"Paving," said the cuffer, who looked like a cousin long since passed on, "from the West Gate, out the High Road, to four miles past Mandragora. We're to double back along the Low Road to the village church. And we're to make the road a cart's width wider as we pass."

Ydlbert said, "What a lot of road."

"On whose authority," I asked, "will you cut a cart's-width swath from the length of my land?"

The affable cuffer shrugged. "The Archduke's, naturally. Most of it's his land anyway."

"Land, schmand," said the dark one. "Give me a fortnight's pay and a jigger of ale and I don't ask no questions."

"Will the work be done by Market Day?" asked Ydlbert, who was clearly already imagining himself driving in style along those paving stones.

The dark one looked behind him at five or six cart's lengths they'd already smoothed. "That's a day's work there, so I'd say no." Then he laughed.

"Give us perhaps a month to get to the point where the roads join," said the cuffer. "After that, we'll go, as I told you, around, so wherever we're not paving, you good folk can drive."

It was a lovely plan—how the road would glitter, paved!—but we had brought in our grain, and in the next month would have our largest market crops of the year. I could not imagine how we would bring them to Nnms with no road. And how long had Ruth known of this project and said nothing? Her brow looked clear enough. She was digging around in her sling. "What are you doing?" I asked.

"Looking for a pen. I'll stay and talk to them."

"You'll do no such thing."

Their ears pricked up as they admired her lithe form, bending over and fidgeting.

"Not what you think, lads," I said, pushing her roughly into the cart.

"Yves, I have work to do, do you mind?"

"Work!" One of them chuckled. "I'll be glad to work her." Another said, "I hope it's the same kind of work she does for the Archduke."

Ydlbert said, "Gentlemen, please."

"Yves," Ruth said, "what's your problem?"

My throat grew tight. My mouth would not form the words to tell her of my misgivings.

"You think I've never been catcalled by construction workers before? I'm fine. Besides, I'm bigger than they are."

Ydlbert said, "I'll stay and watch her."

When our eyes met I thought for certain he could divine my thoughts, but his expression did not change. "Very well, then."

"Thank you, Ydlbert, but I don't need to be chaperoned."

Ydlbert said, "You'd be a mite easier to get used to if you spoke English all the time, like the rest of us." They went clambering over the side of the cart. Ydlbert offered me a lazy salute and said, "We'll see you by and by."

The roadworkers waved and spat to their sides as we drove away. Me, my brother, the Archduke, these workers—there wasn't a man in the parish Ruth was afraid of, and I began to wonder if it was a quality of which I approved.

"Is this good news or bad," my wife asked, "that we must now convey to the assembly?"

"Good news, though perhaps a slight difficulty at present. Why?"

"Because I want to know if it's going to make us more reviled, or lift us in the popular estimation."

"I don't believe we're reviled."

She neatened her skirt. "That's because you're the one with the mad family."

"It's our common ancestors have supplied this hamlet its fair share of weirdness."

"Fine, then. The mad brother. You can't argue that my brother's mad."

Driving toward the celebration, I kept thinking of the scene we had left behind us on the road. If digging bodies up from the earth had called forth a subtle and insidious punishment, perhaps with such strange events did it begin.

The peas and beans on their poles twisted about wildly, sprouting leaves everywhere, sending forth myriad flowers, and growing so many lovely fruits that we could not pick them all before some, hidden as they were amid the vegetation, grew too large to be of use and festered. Yet harvesting vegetables is as child's play compared to harvesting grain—to do it requires no songs for encouragement, and even Elizaveta could tromp about the garden with a basket in tow, pulling off whatever edibles she could reach. The fruits of the garden do not come ripe all at once—the result, my brother says, of their gentle nature, their desire not to make us too much labor—so gathering them feels more pleasure than work, a daily opportunity to dream as the rich, sweet odors from the vines cling to one's nose and fingers. Bringing in the garden plot of flax was a pass-time compared to the labor of reaping. Mornings, too, we gathered the apples from Mandrik's orchard—perhaps the most pleasant work of the year, climbing trees, breathing in the ripe perfume, and plucking the sweets as they blushed and bloomed. Though I was still full of misgivings, a day in the orchard was like a day in Paradise—and led to long, soft afternoons, peeling and coring the fragrant fruit, that it might be boiled down into applesauce, or pressed into cider soft and then hard, or strung up on sticks to dry over the fire.

These lesser harvests left me some leisure—which in former years I had used to mow hay for the animals' winter fodder, or to begin threshing. This year, however, the farm's duties did not beckon, and at each spare moment I retired to the shade of the barn, there to pursue my inventions. The seat on the cart came easy, though it took two tries before I figured the exact distance at which my feet could either hang into the bed of the cart or rest upon its front. The execution of brakes required more thought, though their caliper shape, which I had drawn from the blacksmith's dread instrument, had been easy enough to arrive at. They did not desire, on their own, to grip the wheel with just and equal pressure, and each new experiment sent the cart spinning and Enyadatta off in a snit.

I had installed perhaps the fourth set of brakes when Adelaïda took to the yard to dye the first of her wool for winter. On the ground she had built three fires, each with its iron pot, and in each she brewed a decoction of flowers and leaves, into which she mashed her yarn and thread with wooden poles. Her sleeves were rolled up and the sweat beaded on her brow. Elizaveta, beside her, mashed doll clothes around a bowl with a kitchen spoon. Ruth occasionally stabbed at one of the pots, stirring the foul-smelling wool, then retreated to examining the materials—rubbing the petals of the flowers between her fingers, asking my wife where and when she'd gathered this and that. She didn't have her notebook—paper is vulnerable to a stirred pot—but I saw well enough the furrows in her brow, and I knew what she was doing. So did Adelaïda, whose scant patience had perhaps at last reached its limit, and who answered the questions with as few words as possible.

I drove Enyadatta in a broad circle about the yard, careful not to excite her, but pleased that the women would witness firsthand the results of my genius. When the horse had gathered sufficient speed, I yanked upon the brake rope, which broke from the pressure as the caliper pinched shut. Enyadatta jerked forward as the cart rumbled off to the side, and I pitched sideways along the seat. When I recovered enough to look round at my audience, my daughter was laughing, praise God, with abundant glee, and Adelaïda was driving her stick into a vat with all her might.

"That's pretty good. But next time," Ruth called, "you don't want it to grip so tight."

I hopped down from the cart to inspect the damage, which was but slight. "Well noted," I said, my dander up. "And you, wife, have you any observations to help your old man in his work?"

"I think you'd get more of it done if you'd quit fooling around."

I was used to this tart tongue Adelaïda had developed of late—and grateful it was not so bitter as her friend Anya's. Yet on this occasion she wounded me. "There's nothing so pressing," I ventured in reply to her charge, "that I can't fiddle with the cart a day or two before we bring the last of the shocks into the barn and gather the hay."

"Nothing but that one day's foul weather might ruin. And nothing wrong with the cart that it wants so much fiddling."

"When it was the harness, you were as happy as all get-out to watch me make it."

She gave her vat a last stir and stood with her hands on her hips, regarding me. "That was two years ago, when I had no idea how hard it would be to have an inventor for a husband."

Ruth looked between us, her eyes guilty.

"When I've brought fame and honor to this household—when even the Archduke comes to see us and no other farmer in the parish?"

"The Archduke came to see Ruth, not you—because she's a curiosity. Wasn't the man I married proud to work his father's land, proud to bear his honorable name, destined to become a pillar of this community?"

I walked closer to her half-circle of boiling vats. I felt I could not bear the sadness and rage my wife's accusations raised in my breast, yet there was Ruth, kneeling on the ground with her head bowed, and before her I could not lose my temper outright. "Am I not," I asked, "a pillar of this community? If not I, then who?"

"Desvres. Ydlbert. Even Heinrik Martin with his startled eyes and his half-dozen rocky acres. They don't make spectacles of themselves and their families. They don't have mad brothers who—"

"Mandrik is not mad!"

"—moon about defying the church and lolling in the orchards; and if they do, they don't follow their brother's lead. Look how respectable Jude Dithyramb has made himself, all because he's had to strive so for respectability. Other men don't leave their wives with the work of the house and run off to dream."

"Adelaïda," I said. Her beautiful face was so flushed that I feared an attack of apoplexy. "Everyone knows—I am certain every one of our neighbors believes—that I do what I do for the betterment of us all."

"And so does your brother, and I still say he's mad."

I felt myself, body and soul, near to breaking apart. What would it matter, this great work of mine, if my own family would not understand it? I unhitched Enyadatta, led her back into the barn, and let the cart lie where it was, untended, in the middle of the yard. The horse burred gently when I offered her oats, and allowed me to pat the regal side of her face. As I stood there, looking at the previous failed sets of calipers, my eyes began to water. For it was not worth this. I would not lose the love of my wife over an object; and yet I could not chase the object from my mind. The next day I began taking in the hay with all my strength and vigor, and allowed myself only a few hours of what my heart most desired, time in the barn with my cart.

Before a fortnight had passed, the brakes were perfect. Though they resembled the tool that had dragged my first child lifeless from his lifeless mother, when pulled they sang against the right front wheel and brought the cart to a halt. Enyadatta turned her golden ears backward each time they shrieked, and shot me cross looks when the weight of her burden behind her forced her to stop. But I had built a cart with brakes.

The women were not sufficiently impressed with my work. "It's great," Ruth said with the same overeager smile my mother had given to Eglantine's first attempt at baking, which had produced nought but a flat, burnt patty of a loaf. Adelaïda said, "Praise be. Now you can get back to work." And Elizaveta merely covered her ears with her hands at the sound.

I drove straight to Ydlbert's to show him my success. I hurtled down his path, pulling hard on the brakes just before Enyadatta charged into the sty where my neighbor was slopping his pigs. The pigs broke out running and squeaking, and Ydlbert dropped the whole slop bucket into the trough. "Goddamn!" he screamed. When he realized I was laughing as I jumped down from my cart, he tried to rearrange his face for merriment, but still looked somewhat mistrustful. He climbed over his low split-rail fence. "What news have you brought me now?"

"Brakes—that as fast as a horse can gallop, we can still stop the cart."

He stood by the front wheel and tugged at the rope. "I'll be damned."

"Adelaïda's ready to kill me."

"No, you'll be done your inventing now."

I said yes; what else could I do?

"It's a good thing, Yves. Will you help me do it for my cart? Think what a ruckus we'll cause on Market Day."

Then I remembered the paving. "But they're at work upon the roads this week."

"Road or no road, a fine cart's a fine cart." Ydlbert pulled and pulled at the rope. "I'll be damned. What more could a man want than a cart that stops itself?"

"Tires, for one thing."

He kicked at the wheel's thin iron shoe. "We've got tires."

"Soft tires, like on the ruined airplane."

"A great lot of good they did."

The pigs returned to their food and resumed snorting happily.

"I suppose you're right."

"Now you're chasing after fancies, Yves."

"Nay."

"Anya gets rancid as week-old milk when I so much as take wild-flowers to market."

"Adelaïda's no malcontent."

"Easy, man, whom you call names." He kicked at the wheel again, as if to see what it would feel like, soft. "Don't get carried away with all this. Help me move the cows, and let's get started building."

I was not the only one who wandered forth every second day to see how the roadwork progressed; and Manfred, Jowl, and sundry other neighborhood boys were conscripted into searching for paving stones. Every day till sundown we heard roving bands of them whooping in the fields and forests. When they found one good enough, there was a solemn procession to bring the great thing in. Widening the road meant, of course, a narrowing of all our fields, but after a brief dissent from Martin the Elder, we all kept quiet. It would be worth losing some land to have such grand access to the city.

The road could, however, hold only so much of our interest, so busy were we bringing in hay, threshing the grain, and driving around the roadwork to get to market with the fruits of our gardens. Though the weather had been fair, none of us had had a spectacular yield; the arrival of our strangers had affected me more than most, but it had kept the whole village more or less from its labor. The slight possibility of want danced like a wanton spirit before our minds, and we were anxious to bring our goods to market as soon as we could, that if the winter proved harsh, we could afford to buy back what we needed.

The next Market Day, when most of my hay was in and I loaded some of it along with sundry vegetables, Ydlbert and I drove in style in our braking carts; the road crew was a trouble to drive around, but it did not dampen our pride in our new machines. Thea and Enyadatta also seemed proud of what they dragged about, and pranced with their feet held high. Near town, once we had reached the place where the road was already paved, we could drive abreast of one another. With our vain beasts giving one another the eye, Ydlbert and I could now talk as we drove, sitting tall and proud above our carts. Heinrik Martin soon pulled up alongside me on the grass, his whiskers in a tizzy, and did not even bid me good day before he began his talk.

"Strange news, Yves," he shouted over the ruckus of the wheels.

"What, my brakes?"

"What?"

"No one's poorly in your family, I hope?"

"Not in mine. But it's to do with your brother."

I pulled off the road and applied my new brakes. Ydlbert slowed, but I waved him on as Heinrik came to a clumsy stop a few lengths down the road. Enyadatta ambled up to him and exchanged scents with his horse.

"Mighty fine stopping thing you've got there, Yves. And what's that you're sitting on?"

"I'll help you fix your cart up the same. My brother, is he ill? I've not seen him these three days."

"He's not ill, no."

"What, then?"

Heinrik scratched at his beard. "He's taking up with a woman, looks to me."

I did not like this confirmation of my fears. Nevertheless, I leaned over to pat his strong shoulder. "Heinrik, in all our lives, you've never told me a joke."

He scratched the more fiercely. "I wouldn't have stopped you if I didn't think it true, and perhaps a bad omen."

I held my breath for a moment and let it out in a puff like a gust of wind. I could not yet read his expression; he might yet have been jesting. "I appreciate your concern, but that simply can't be."

"I've seen your brother sporting about with that stranger. I thought I should tell you what I saw."

"He's telling her about Indo-China, for what she writes about us."

"Day in and day out?"

"It's a long story, his travels. And I think he's writing a chapter on her for his treatise." Convincing Heinrik was a lesser part of my work than convincing myself, but I spoke the argument with authority.

He stroked at his beard and watched our neighbors clamber past. "I'm sure you know your brother best."

"What did you see?"

He worked his lips together before answering. "I've seen them up a tree together, and out walking the fields. And they've gone in his hut together at midday and not been out again till dusk."

"But they're writing—she's getting stories from him, and he from her."

"As I said, Yves—you know best." He lifted his reins with a worried look on his wrinkled brow. "I'll see you at market, then."

"Thank you, Heinrik."

"Aye."

As I drove alone the rest of the way to the gate, I tried to dispel Heinrik's tale from my thoughts. Though my mind had, of late, turned somewhat against Ruth, she did not seem corrupt; and my brother I knew to be better than myself. The world's pleasures had ever been nought to him. With my own hands I had helped him build his hut, and at each juncture he had asked to have it smaller and plainer than I would have built. I had offered him warm clothes, heavy boots, livestock, and thatch for his roof, and he had ever declined all but food, which he ate as sparely as a grown man could. We had plentiful women of beauty and wit right here in our village, if women were any temptation; but they never had been. Heinrik was neither gossip nor liar, and what he said confirmed my deepest fears, but his report had to be stuff and nonsense, the idle speculation of an ill-informed mind. By the time I drove, at the rear of the line, into Nnms, I had convinced myself once again of my brother's purity. The townspeople were about—picking rags, hanging laundry, trudging to and from market with various bundles—and paid me no mind as I brought up the rear of the provisionary caravan. They were ordinary burghers and tradesmen, householders and servants, and sure they had little enough to dandle about in their minds. Presented with such a spectacle as a mystic traipsing about, followed by a long-legged stranger, they, too, would bound to conclusions. At market I found that Ydlbert had kept me my usual space, and I lost no time in arranging my fruits to their best advantage.

As I drove home, clear into the grass to avoid the workmen, I spied my brother and my charge walking toward his hut through the abundant orchard. They were unencumbered by ought but something Ruth held aloft in her apron, and turned smiling my way when I called out to them.

"Good market?" Mandrik asked as I brought my cart to a stop alongside him. They both blushed fiercely, but it might have been the heat.

"A fine market." I patted my bulging pocket. "Good day?"

Ruth held her outstretched apron toward me. "Look at these blueberries."

"No telling of tales today?"[6]

"Not," Mandrik said, "when the berries have come ripe all at once."

"At the bounds of the North Meadow?"

"And a bumper crop," he said. "We didn't even pick one bush clean."

They looked flustered, but not specifically as if they'd been to mischief. Indeed, my chief concern was that the berries would ruin the apron.

"She's never put up preserves, so I'm going to teach her this afternoon."

"Adelaïda tried to show her about pickles, to no avail."

---

[6] The expression on Yves's face nearly broke my heart with shame. I knew that he suspected the worst. Had he known how deep a bond was springing up between his brother and myself, he might have looked on us more kindly, but I saw that he thought I was corrupting his nearest kin. I would have given anything to tell him the truth right then, but Mandrik had asked me to keep silent until he could think of the correct way to convey the news. After all Yves had given me, this did not seem the way to repay him; and yet what I was doing seemed so exactly right, so miraculously the first thing in my life that had ever made me happy, that I couldn't feel very guilty about it.

"Ah"—Mandrik laughed—"but as our father would have told you, pickles is pickles, and jam is jam."

How I missed our father's clearheadedness. How dearly we could have used it then.

"And since she knows nought about pastry, I thought we might bring a berry tart to your house for dinner."

I said, "That would be lovely," as my wife with her work had no time for sweets.

They continued to smile at me, and I continued to smile back, sick with the feeling that I was looking forward to their fruit tart, touched by their innocence, and mistrusting them entirely, all in the same breath.

"Well, then, I suppose I'll head home."

"We'll see you at sundown," Mandrik said, and took her arm above the elbow to lead her away.

I drove home in a frenzy of anger and self-hatred. I had seen nothing, but something I had most certainly seen. It only increased my ire to find Adelaïda weaving a fine checked cloth, our daughter on the floor beside her drawing what looked remarkably like the letter "E" over and over on my slate. Adelaïda's loom faced away from the door and the fire, and she did not turn to look at me when I walked in. "Good market?" she asked.

"Very good."

"I should have thought you'd be the rest of the day dreaming with your brother."

Elizaveta clicked her small tongue.

"My brother and Ruth are putting up berries. They'll bring us a tart this evening."

"She doesn't help me with my preserving."

"Mandrik says pickles are different from jam."

"I suppose that both of them want to be fed?" The shuttle sang through the varicolored warp.

"Certainly you don't begrudge my brother dinner? Without his generosity, this house would not be ours."

"I begrudge your brother nothing. It's only that it rankles me sometimes, how that stranger eats and eats, and can't even do housework."

"Ruth helps a good deal. And as I recall, it was you brought her home."

"I might decide otherwise, now."

"Do not speak ill," I commanded her, "of those I love," though love was not the word that first sprang to my thoughts.

She kept sailing her weft through, and tamping it expertly down. "I once thought it was our family you loved. But I'm glad, at least, to know if it's otherwise."

"Adelaïda."

"Two lazy peas in a pod, is all I think of them."

The image of my brother and Ruth lying together in a pod was more than my mind could bear at that moment, and I had the prickly feeling that my wife had meant it as just such a barb. "What do you mean by that?"

"I mean what I said."

"Perhaps you already know, then, of the rumors abroad that my brother makes merry with our guest?"

"What's that?"

"Rumors that, you know, he's been untrue to his vows."

She paused to unwind a twist in her wool. "That's some news, if it's true."

"You hadn't heard it, though?"

"Nay, but it makes its own, strange kind of sense."

"It can't be true," I said, "or one of them would have told us." I watched her weave, three limbs working in harmony, the remaining foot keeping time. "He's my brother."

She shrugged without slowing her movement. "All the more reason he might not want to debase himself in your eyes." There was, if I did not mistake her, a faint note of pleasure in her voice. "Not that I believe it's true."

"If you don't believe it, why does it fill you with glee?"

"Yves, when did you last hear me utter a gleeful word?"

She had, in truth, been dour a good while. "You don't believe the rumors, then?"

"Not until I see it with my own eyes."

"Making preserves and fruit tarts is no sign of impropriety."

"Absolutely not."

I moved Pudge from one side of the table to the other. "Can you say nothing to convince me of their innocence?"

"I thought you believed they'd done no wrong."

"Aye, but I suppose you could bolster my confidence." I wanted her to take me in her arms. The house was empty but for the child; she could have. "Adelaïda, must you work right now?"

She turned to me, bored with my interruption. "Why?"

I gently touched her worn, soft dress, and felt her firm shoulders bracing against my touch. "It doesn't matter, I suppose."

"Have you a reason, Yves?"

"No."

I retreated to the barn. All the animals were out. I cleaned their dung and, when the task was complete, stood sweating and leaning against the rake. There was nothing to do. I took out paper and removed my pens from their box and arranged them, useless, on the floor. Damn everything and everyone I loved—including the miraculous new cart. I stared at the paper a long while, knowing I needed to do something with it, but not knowing what.

CHAPTER SEVEN

THE DARK DAY

he roads in Nnms were beautiful, but had always been thick with people and beasts. Though we had admired them, we had never enjoyed them fully. As the road crew finished paving past the far ends of our village that autumn, however, the uses and pleasures of roads seized the popular fancy. We sent songs of praise to the Archduke—Ruth, who still had access to the fortress, brought Mandrik along with her to sing his and Adelaïda's compositions, apparently much to his Urbanity's delight. Before All Saints' we had outfitted every last village cart with a sitting board and brakes, and all of us could sit regally atop our vehicles, flying down the new, beautiful road in utter safety. How pleasant was the chill of the harvest moon's wind against the hands and cheeks! How the glory of such speed seemed a slice of Heaven! The paved road was harder than dirt upon the beasts' hooves and louder beneath them and the iron tires, but I cannot describe the purity of its pleasure. I was glad to have given some of my land to this great development, and would gladly have given more.

Rather more surprising proved the pleasure of walking barefoot along the road. My brother had advocated the practice ever since his return, but the villagers, myself included, thought it another of his fancies and an invitation to ringworm. The roads at that time were full of sharp stones, all ready to reduce a man to tatters with infection, and the plentiful horse leavings made the prospect even less attractive. The new road was smooth as winter's first snow, however, and it was worth the trouble of avoiding the fragrant droppings to feel that coolness against the bare skin. So while, each day, some of us went tearing along, whipping our horses into a frenzy, others ambled arm in arm a short ways from their homes. As if none of the past two and a half years had ever happened, a part of our lives returned to its native slowness. It was good to regain the pleasure of seeing Ydlbert, or even Yorik or Dithyramb, out with his trousers rolled up, his feet rather blue, but willing nonetheless to stop and talk awhile, without the noisy encumbrances of horses, carts, and brakes.

In the mid-autumn Adelaïda grew queasy and quiet, and soon announced that she sensed a new life taking root within her belly. This discovery gave me such a shock of joy that I could almost forget all the difficulty that had beset us in the last few months, all her unpleasantness, all my doubts. If my brother had broken his vows, so be it; if I had turned back upon my duties by spending so much time inventing, then this was a reward in spite of my misdeed. My wife beamed when she told me, and I could not contain my shouting, my happiness, for a moment. "This is the best thing that could possibly happen," I said.

"I, too, am pleased," she said. Her eyes shone with the mystery of what went on inside her.

Ruth was out at my brother's as she always seemed to be anymore, and the child napped in her hammock, so for the first time in months my wife and I disrobed in complete joy—though it was midday and there was work, as ever, to do—to enjoy the sweetness of our conjugal bed. What pleasure to touch her strong, fair body and know that it nourished a human soul; and what delight to feel once more her delight at my touch.

Mandrik, arriving with Ruth for the dinner they'd come to expect at sundown, was overwhelmed with happiness—much more than when we told him of Elizaveta's imminent arrival—and bent down to kiss what was still the workaday softness of Adelaïda's belly. My wife giggled, and he reached around to hug her middle. "An heir," he told her, his cheek pressed into her. "A whole, miraculous new life."

"Something bad might come of it yet," she said. "I wouldn't hope."

"No. It's a good sign. There hasn't been a child born in the parish since Tansy Gansevöort's at Advent."

"The Devil's work, sure."

"Which makes this new life even more a miracle."

So said all the neighbors. Even Father Stanislaus threw his arms around me in church the next morning. "A most excellent sign, my brother!" he cried.

"That's what Mandrik said." I was flabbergasted at the priest's familiarity.

"At last," he said, "the spell is broken."

"But it's only a baby. We don't know that it'll live."

He shook his narrow head. "Far more than that, after all we've been through. It is the mark of God's love, Yves, for the people of this land."

Walking home through the crisp morning to my farm—for once again had I discovered the pleasures of ambling to church—I began to wonder if he and my brother were right. The dearth of new bairns could not mean that my fellows did not fulfill their conjugal duties. Our crops were less than abundant, a subtle decrease in productivity of which no one knew the cause, but of which everyone, I am sure, suspected our stranger; and it was my family that would lift us out. I turned briefly off the road with a white rock for the cairn, and I bid good day to Hammadi and thanked my grandmother for whatever had been her influence.

There was praise to be given, and I would give it. I might yet be able to expand our house with the money from the past few years' abundance; build a second room onto the side—not, as had been the last addition, for keeping our stores, but to allow us more freedom to move. Adelaïda and I might have our bed in our own nook; and our children would have more room to play in the winter. I resolved to begin cutting lumber that afternoon, that by spring it would be cured and ready for building. While I was cutting, I would set some aside for a second bed, that Ruth and Elizaveta might have a more comfortable place to sleep for now, and the two children, daughter and son, after the stranger left. And in the darkest weeks of winter, when the snow piled up so that I could barely keep a path open to the barn, I would keep myself warm building me a table and stool, that I might have, as my brother did, a spot to sit and copy down all that teemed in my mind.

A few weeks after I announced our good news to the priest, however, a strange event befell us. For the first time in memory, Ydlbert had found himself with a house full of sons and no work on whose accomplishment their survival depended. He had struck a bargain, then, with the four eldest: if they would be patient, and not fight one another for their turns, each could take Thea and the cart out on his own, and drive about like a householder for an entire day. The boys were, by report, delighted at this unforeseen change in their routine, and agreed to draw straws for the order of their privilege. Dirk drew the longest, and set out with the cart, a skin of water, and a heel of bread the next morning.

By nightfall he had not returned; but Ydlbert knew of his son's dalliance with Prugne Martin, and wished him Godspeed in that endeavor. When, however, Dirk did not return after dawn, Ydlbert began to fear for his welfare. He came by as I was up on the roof, weighting the new thatch with stones. He climbed up the ladder to sit beside me.

"Hail," said I, "what news, brother?"

"Dirk's not back yet."

One of the rocks slipped free of its tether, and I anxiously eyed the ground to make certain my wife and daughter were not nearby. Below, however, there was nothing but the dirt yard, and in the distance the animals going about their sleepy lives in the pasture. "Remember, he's a lad yet. He may have wandered off on an adventure."

"Aye, a lad he is, and my son. I'm worried for him."

"If he's not back by sundown, we'll set off in search of him at dawn."

Ydlbert nodded grimly, and helped me tie the last few rocks.

I fully expected Dirk's return, and felt no misgivings thus advising my friend. But the evening came and went without word of the missing boy, and long before the sun was up my neighbor was knocking on my door, his face a mere mask of its usual, jovial self. Adelaïda made up our provisions as we hitched Enyadatta to the cart, and she gave us a blessing as we left.

We drove first to the city, where I imagined we might find Dirk stone drunk in a tavern, but no one in Nnms had caught sight of him. We followed the Via Urbis out the East Gate, where neither of us had ever gone before; but the road came to a halt before we reached the Eastern Mountains, and there was not a soul about whom we could question. We doubled back through town, then, this time receiving the sympathetic cheers of the townspeople, who no doubt thought our quarry perished by the roadside. None of our good neighbors had seen the lad since he'd headed west two days since, and at last, toward the wane of the day, and miles west of Mandragora, we reached the place where the High Road met the Low, with nary a word of the boy. We dismounted the cart and waded through the meadow, all the while shouting Dirk's name, but our voices rebounded against the Great Mountains to the west, and when the sun set we returned to the cart, our heads hanging heavy with defeat.

"It's your brother's fault," Ydlbert said, his elbows resting on his knees and his head tucked down as we rode.

"Mandrik's?"

"Aye. All those tales of the Beyond Dirk imbibed with his mother's milk. Now he's gone off to seek it, and kidnapped my horse as well."

I was affronted on my brother's behalf, but understood my friend's terror. "It's only been two days, Ydlbert. He's sure to come back."

"Between your brother and the strangers, it's a wonder all the children of the village haven't wandered off, looking for the great world."

"I promise he'll come back," I said, though I knew how futile were such promises.

The next day dawned and set without news of Dirk, and in my heart I began to fear him dead. The day after that, I rose with a heavy feeling in my chest, as if I were full of my friend's grief; early that afternoon I set out for a barefoot walk along the road, to mortify my senses and to give me the opportunity for quiet reflection. It did not seem fair that I should expect a new child while he lost one he had reared from infancy to manhood. So engrossed was I in these musings that I did not see Jude Dithyramb approaching in his cart until his dappled Wicket was nearly upon me. The horse neighed and slowed. His master pulled on the singing brakes, and called out good-naturedly, "Walking in your sleep, Gundron?"

"Dreaming, aye. Thinking about Ydlbert's lost son."

"You needn't look so downcast about it."

"When my closest friend has lost his child? I cannot but grieve."

"Aye, but only a moment since I saw Dirk von Iggislau—that same one you seek and have feared dead—driving, neither fast, nor whooping, nor with Prugne Martin alongside him." Wicket swung his gray, speckled head back and forth before me, and I patted his broad nose. "He simply sat on the seat with the reins slack, and let Thea walk at her will. I waved hello as I passed him, but he didn't even notice."

"That's not like him," I said. "He's usually high enough of spirits. But then, who knows where he's been this half week?"

"Aye, well, he looked a sight. I'll say that. He looked like he'd been through something or other."

Jude was beginning to gray about the temples, and surely would never marry now. In that moment I prayed silently that he be spared the fate that afflicted his mother. "Did you see him go home?"

"Nay, not home. The horse was set on turning into your yard, and your wife and stranger ran out to greet him. I'm sure he's still there. Perhaps you can knock some sense into him—or at least find out what's wrong."

"Will you drive me home? And then go to Ydlbert's, to tell him the news?"

"Of course, lad. Come aboard."

I climbed up, and he clicked to his horse, and we made haste home. He left me off at the edge of my property; and there, sure enough, was black Thea, still hitched to her cart, and dragging it in an idle circle about the yard. I stopped to bring her some of Enyadatta's hay, at which my horse piteously complained.

My family did not hear me approach, and I was well within the door before they noticed me. Dirk was bent over double on the bench, his eyes resting in his palms, and Adelaïda daubed at his neck and temples with a damp rag.

"Has he taken ill?" I asked.

"No," Ruth said.

"Madder'n Christmas in March," Adelaïda said. "The poor darling."

Ruth busily shook her head no. But if I were to believe one of them, my wife, with our heir inside her, it would be.

"It was Thea brought him here," my wife said. "He sat senseless as a doorpost behind her, and she came up the yard to whinny hello. We had a sight of it, trying to coax him down. But finally he came in, and drank some broth, and hasn't opened his lips else but to rave."

I knelt at his feet. His sharp, youthful knees poked out through filthy brown trousers, and his leather shoes were caked with mud. There were cuts along his arms, and a dark bruise blossomed along one sharp cheekbone. He rocked himself slightly to and fro, or perhaps it was the pressure of Adelaïda's hand upon his nape.

"Dirk?" I asked. His leg, beneath my hand, burned like midsummer. "It's Gundron. Will you tell me what happened?"

He shook his head slowly, side to side.

"I cannot tell," Adelaïda said, "if we should send for the priest or your brother. I think he wants blessing."

Ruth said, "I don't think Stanislaus should be involved. I'll go get Mandrik."

"Thea's hitched in the yard," I told her, "if you can drive her. I sent Dithyramb already to tell Ydlbert the boy was home."

Ruth's lips were tucked up over her teeth and pinched white. "I'll be back."

Elizaveta ran out after her, and I don't think my wife even noticed Ruth swiping her up to take along for the ride.

The house seemed dark and hot. "Dirk," I began again. "Please. You must tell me what's happened. I won't be angry. I'll help you if I can." For at the very worst, I reasoned, Prugne was with child; and Ydlbert and I together could certainly carve out a living for him. I was ashamed never to have thought of such a solution before—after all our years of friendship, it was little to offer.

"I have seen a terrible place."

"A vision," Adelaïda cooed.

He shook his bowed head violently. "As real as you. I saw the great, wide sea."

I continued to pat his leg as one pats the back of a colicky babe. "Tell me, if you are able."

He crossed his long arms over his curly head. "There is nothing to do at my father's farm, Yves. Bartholomew is as big as I, and Manfred and Jowl can both do nearly a man's labor. It's boring as Purgatory there, don't tell my father I said so. So we all agreed that I might go out for a wander in the cart, and that the next day someone else might go. I went westward out the High Road, for the rumor was they'd paved way out to where it joins the Low, and I hadn't wandered that far since I was a lad."

"You're a lad still."

"Is it true," Adelaïda asked, "about the road?"

"Aye, and a beautiful sight. As I traveled that way, my Uncle Yorik and your Uncle Frith both called out to see if anything was the matter, so little did they expect to see anyone there. Jungfrau shouted a curse upon Thea for making too much noise."

I said, "Typical."

"May I have some more broth?"

Adelaïda brought him a saucerful. His strong hands shaking, he lifted his bruised head to sip it. His face flushed crimson, and his eyes, ordinarily a pleasant walnut hue, of a sudden glimmered black. He gave Adelaïda back the bowl, and wiped his brow on his sleeve.

"Out I went, then, along the High Road, to its end. Thea is a good runner, and for days she had done nought but stand at pasture, so she was glad of the exercise. I passed even the derelict farm of Titus Marnt, and the ruins of the von Broleau place. Finally there it was, the juncture of the roads, both as smooth and lovely as anyone could imagine. Past them the grass grew tall, and rippled, full of the last autumn flowers, in the breeze. The mountains rose up all around to enclose me, and but for Thea's impatient stamp and the breath in her nostrils, all was silent.

"I ought, then, to have turned down the Low Road and back to town, but the meadows were beckoning. The stalks of the flowers grew twice as high as any near town, and I thought what a delight it would be to bring them back for my mother and for Prugne, even if the blossoms were past their prime. Thea was all too happy to romp in the grass, and she pulled me slowly through it, letting it tickle her flanks and the flanks of the cart, giving me ample time to reach over the sides and take flowers.

"Before I knew what was what, Thea had taken me so far into the meadow I could not see back to the roads. On such a fine, clear day, though, I knew I could gauge my way back by the sun in the sky, and I feared not. It was much farther to those mountains than I had at first supposed, but at last, in the late afternoon, we attained their feet, and there did I give Thea her oats. The great peaks rose up to enclose me, all along their sides the leaves of the trees gone to red, gold, and brown, and I lay down amid the grasses for a nap, dreaming of fairies and the abandoned farms.

"When I awoke, it was dark. Thea was restored by her repast, and stomping her forefeet to remind me of duty. But it was too late to turn back, and I was not yet done my day of freedom—my first, Yves, in as long as I can remember—so, walking carefully in the dim light of the waning moon, I led her along the foot of the Western Mountains. We passed a frothing stream, from whose waters we were both glad to drink. And at last I lay down in the cart to sleep.

"The next morning, I saw that we had stopped near a path such as that cut by the waters of the spring rains—not half so wide as a road, but reasonably straight. I tethered Thea to an oak, and began to climb uphill in anticipation of a fine view back to the village and to town.

"Soon enough I grew tired of the ascent, but the mountain continued to rise up before me. I could no longer see down to Thea in the valley; I had no choice but to continue upward. I climbed until the sun was high in the sky, and continued to climb as he began his descent, and still had not reached the summit. As I made my way higher into the hills, a strange, unpleasant smell began to reach my nostrils, like filthy laundry before Mum takes it out in the yard to boil. And my ears were assaulted with a noise like thunder, though the skies were clear. Near sundown, after what seemed an eternity, I at last came upon my view. A clearing opened up in the trees, and though mine was not the highest mountain, I could see what lay below.

"What I saw, however, made no sense to me. Mandragora was nowhere in sight, nor the steeple of St. Perpetua, nor the fortifications of Nnms. My eyes roved far in search of the familiar sights, yet did not light upon them. In their stead, I looked down upon a gray emptiness, mottled with blacks and whites, but stretching more or less uniformly out to the horizon, where it joined the sky. I feared that I would lose my balance in contemplation of this sight. Slowly did I realize that this was what Mandrik had told me of—I had come upon the sea, and the grayness that stretched everywhere was the water no man can drink. There were two white things, shaped like ash leaves, bobbing up and down upon the water, and in each of them sat a man. Boats, I thought; I had heard the word. Three more boats were tied with strings to the rocks at the bottom of the mountain. In the tiny sliver of barren land between the foot of the mountain and the waves, I saw a cluster, tight as a flock of sheep, of four small houses, each exactly like the next, and painted whiter than winter's first snow. There were no animals in sight. From the sooty roof of each house rose the frightful skeleton of a scarecrow, on which the rooks of this village nevertheless brazenly perched. All around the village were great leafless trees tethered to one another by strings. I stared at the village long, for I still could not imagine myself so turned around that I could not see Mandragora, and my eyes would not accept the ugliness of what lay before them."

Here he paused for a moment, and blinked as if to clear his vision. "I could not turn away, Yves. Having seen this apparition of strangeness, could I make my way back to Mandragora, with only half a story to tell?" His tone, and the fervor in his eyes, reminded me of my brother's—and I realized that what we took in my brother for divine inspiration might in fact be simply the physical manifestation of the desire to talk of what the eyes had seen. It occurred to me that I had been mistaken about my brother, and his calling, all along.

"I walked down the treacherous slope toward the sea. As I drew nearer, the sound and the smell of the water grew ever more vivid. The sweet scent of dung was nowhere around, and I could not discern anything like the scent of fire except a stench like the airplane let off when it died. I thought I heard people talking, but saw no one but the men in the boats and one lone housewife, in a skirt so short it revealed her very kneecaps, pinning the brightest clothes imaginable to a string between two barren trees. She retreated into the farthest house without having seen me. There were strange noises—rumblings and hums, whose origins I could not name, but which made me uneasy.

"I came nearer and nearer down the hillside to this peculiar village, yet no one stirred, no one came to hail me or bid me state my business. Were it not for the woman in the tiny skirt, and for the vague voices, I might have thought the town gone over to the dead. My heart beat so quickly it fluttered in my chest. As I descended, the houses came more clearly into view, and seemed strangely tall. They had no gardens about them, and looked nude without them.

"And as I came close to the house that was highest up the mountain, I smelled cooking meat, and my gut yearned with hunger. I had not eaten since the day before, and what reached my nose was more tantalizing than any dish I had ever yet imagined. I approached the door of the cottage—a strange door, painted greener than the grass—and knocked upon it, but none answered. I knocked again, but heard nothing. At last I pressed against it with my hand, and it swung open into a room unlike any I had ever seen before. The floor was covered with boards like the bottom of a cart, but polished to such a sheen that I could see my own reflection. There were great windows, and every surface was smooth, bright, and clean. On top of a gleaming white box a pot was simmering, beneath the pot a pitiful blue flame. I dipped the wooden spoon into the pot, and brought forth a mouthful of a delicious beef stew. It burned my tongue, but I cared not, so ill was I with hunger. I ate and ate of the delicacy, hoping to fortify myself for the long walk back to Thea, and our long drive home to my father.

"As I enjoyed my repast, a woman entered from another room, which had been hidden to me, and she opened her mouth wide in a scream. I dropped the spoon clattering to the floor, certain I had done no wrong, but uncertain why she was so frightened. 'Please,' I said, 'excuse me for taking this liberty, I was hungry, and no one seemed to be at home.' 'Who are you?' she said, her mouth trembling in fear. Her red hair was in a frenzy of short curls, as if the fire had frizzled it off, and her skirt was so short it made Ruth's old trousers look demure by comparison. 'I'm Dirk von Iggislau, from Mandragora, the village across the hills.' Still she shook. 'Across the hills? There's nothing but wilderness. What are you doing in my house? Get out of my house!' She raised an empty skillet in warning, and I backed up toward the door. 'Nay,' said I, 'it's not a wilderness. It's my village, and the city of Nnms. I am only the second of my countrymen ever to venture forth to the sea. That is the sea, isn't it? Outside?' The skillet shook with the energy of her hands. 'Are you mad? Are you a madman come to invade my house?' 'Nay, ma'am,' I told her, 'just a hungry stranger seeking sustenance.' But she would not listen. A scream burst forth from her twice as loud as before. It brought two neighbor women, their hair and skirts as short, their faces as tight, to the door of her home; and when they saw me, and saw her holding a skillet against me, they hollered for their menfolk.

"Immediately I backed out the door, and began scrambling up the hill, the shouts of two men gaining ground behind me. One fellow wielded a short bat. Though I ran as fast as I could, I was still weak from hunger, and before long I fell, then felt his instrument wallop me on the shoulder. He struck me across the face, and I cried, 'Mercy!' my hands shielding my mouth and eyes. Those two men looked as normal as you or I, but their faces, their expressions, were unnaturally hard and cruel. 'Mercy, What did I do?'

" 'What did you do?' asked the bat wielder from behind a grizzled yellow beard. 'You molest our women, and then you play innocent, you tramp.' 'I molested no one,' I said. 'I went into the house seeking food.' The other punched my mouth with his fist. 'For food?' he said. 'And where'd you come from, smelling like the Devil and frightening our women like that?' 'From the village of Mandragora, across the hills.'

"The men fell silent.

" 'A likely story,' the bearded one grumbled, and kicked me, but the other grabbed him by the arm, and hushed him, and said, 'What did you say, lad? Where'd you say you were from?' 'From Mandragora,' I said. 'Two days' journey inland.' His eyes lit up as he whispered to his compatriot. 'Two days? All my lifetime I've believed it a fairy tale, and two days inland?' 'He's a madman, Murray,' said the fellow with the beard. 'Nay,' said Murray, 'he doesn't talk like a madman. Are you right in the head, lad?' 'Quite right,' I answered them. Said the believer, 'We'll have to go investigate that, then, won't we? If it's true, we'll be famous, we'll be on the national telly.' Even the bat wielder agreed: 'If he'd come in off the sea, we'd have seen him sure; and there's been rumors up and down the coast of dark-haired strangers come seeking that very village.' 'Please, sirs,' I told them, 'let me go. I can bring others from my village here, or you can come across the hills to us, if you don't believe me. Only please, let me go home.' They looked back and forth between them, and the fellow with the bat kicked me a bit uphill. 'Send your neighbors, aye,' he told me, 'or we'll follow you home inland and thrash you good.'

"I stumbled up the hill despite the evening's approaching darkness, my eyes blinded with fear, and felt their malignant curses my whole journey upwards. I was frightened, and still hungry, and tired, and in the darkest part of the night, I could not make any progress at all. I reached the bottom of the mountain yesterday at midmorning, and found that Thea was nibbling the ivy by the roots of her tree; though she was surrounded by a pile of her own excrement, she looked at me with trust and joy. I took hold around her brave black neck and nuzzled into her cheek. I could not believe my luck at escaping the madness behind me, and did not even know for certain that the men were not chasing behind. I drove Thea across the meadow at lightning speed. Only when we approached the road, and she slowed to her natural pace, did I realize how truly, truly frightened I had been. Don't tell Father. I must have fallen asleep sometime in my journey, or we'd have been home last night. I'm worried, Yves, about that other village. I am afraid of those people, and afraid of the sea. And I don't know what I'm going to tell my parents."

"Such visions," Adelaïda said. "I hope they won't continue to plague you, Dirk—Lord knows there are too many sightings of the other world happening here already."

She said that without even knowing of mine.

"It wasn't a vision. I saw what I saw."

"That's what they all say," said my wife, "but what it always comes down to is the people who see visions are simply the strange folk. You're young still—you can clear your mind of this nonsense, before it's too late and you become a laughingstock."

It was best, then, that I did not tell my wife when the dead came to dance and sing about our bed. I did not think Dirk had seen a vision. When the Beyond came to visit me, it brought nothing stranger than music and dead relatives, yet certainly my brother had seen its sights. What Dirk related did not sound impossible—indeed, it sounded exactly right. No man had ever the time or the inclination to wander out to those mountains, and who knew what lay past them? Another village, at the edge of the sea—the simplest, most likely answer.

Thea clattered back into the yard and the brakes screeched behind her as she neighed. Ydlbert ran through the door, followed by Mandrik with Ruth behind him, the child napping in her arms. I was struck by the concern on my brother's usually blithe face; and struck more that those two people, considered so odd by all of our village, could look so much like a family with a sleeping child between them. Through the open door, the sky was as gentle and blue as a hyacinth flower.

Ydlbert ran to his son and held him. "Dirk, I am so glad you've returned from the dead."

"You needn't make a drama of it, Father. I only got lost."

"Dirk," Mandrik said, "this is grave news."

"Adelaïda keeps saying it's visions, but you have to believe me."

"What's visions?" said Ydlbert.

Ruth placed the child in her hammock, pulled the thumb from the mouth, and covered her with a woolen wrap. I was angry at her still, and full of questions, yet was I thankful for the tender care she showed my bairn.

"We shall see yet," said Mandrik.

"People are not visions—they're people. We can go back, Mandrik. I can show you the place."

My brother's color was uncharacteristically high. "I am not sure it's advisable."

"You doubt me it's there?"

Mandrik shook his head no, but did not look happy at this admission.

Ydlbert said, "What are we talking about? What have you seen?"

"A lonely village at the edge of the sea. With houses and boats."

Mandrik and Ruth both fidgeted with their clothes. "Ydlbert," Mandrik said, "will you permit your son to sojourn with me this day, perhaps well into the night? I believe we must talk for many hours, and I do not wish, my good neighbor, to importune you."

His glance toward me was shyer than it needed be, more apologetic. His mind was turning faster than mine, and it bothered me that I could not keep up.

Ydlbert said, "That will be fine. If you return him to me speedily."

"By all means."

Mandrik and Ruth nodded to one another as if they were dancing. Winter's first chill was coming on, and blowing through the cracks in the door. He led the boy out with his head bowed like a prisoner, and nodded again, a slow, noble nod, as he left the house. Ydlbert clapped my shoulder. "Thank you for finding my son."

"He came of his own volition. I am glad we found him safe."

He went out and mounted his cart.

Adelaïda bolted the door against the wind, and Elizaveta twisted in her midday sleep. "Is this your doing, Ruth?"

Ruth opened her eyes wide and paused, as if waiting to spring upon the next question.

"This strange village past the hills."

"It's none of my doing, Adelaïda. Be reasonable."

"If it's reason you want, wouldn't it stand to reason that Mandrik would have passed such a village on his way to the sea? Or perhaps," Adelaïda said, throwing a heap of quartered turnips into the boiling pot, "so much else happened in his wanderings that he neglected to tell us the lesser wonders. Like a village across our own hills."

Ruth began to walk a circuit around the hearth, and trailed her dusty blue hem behind her on the floor.

"Perhaps," I offered, without the fire of conviction, "there are many places from which he might have set off."

"Ruth," my wife said, "you've been writing down Mandrik's tales. Has he spoken of people nearby?"

"I can't remember if he specifically, you know, if he said anything about a town over that part of the western ridge, on the coastline."

"Answer me plain."

Ruth stopped walking, gathered her hair roughly to the back of her head, and said, "He said nothing."[1]

"Then you must have brought a hex upon us when you made us open those tombs."

"Adelaïda," I said, for that thought was too much to bear.

She turned back to her pot.

Adelaïda was surely mistaken, and Ruth surely lying, and in all my years, with every terror that had befallen me, nothing in my memory had raised such a fire in my breast. If my brother had seen such wonders even in our own land and kept them secret, it was too much. But there was no authority I could consult—Ruth would say nothing, and I could hardly call on my siblings from beyond the grave to harry them with such questions. My mind raced, but there was nothing I could do. I had no choice but to know nothing.

My wife walked into the bright yard and vomited forth her breakfast. "It's nought but the child within," she said, grimly wiping her chin on her sleeve. She returned with a brisk step and kept on with her cooking.

By sunset the whole village had heard of Dirk's adventure, though I, for one, had resolved not to tell the tale before hearing my brother's verdict. Naturally, all the questioners congregated at my door, since

---

[1] Now, of course, I can't help thinking that I should simply have told them—yes, of course there is a village—but at the time I could not dream of betraying Mandrik's confidence. It seemed that circumstances would uncover the truth soon enough. Adelaïda's distrust pained me, but I felt somehow less culpable if I didn't interfere.

none would dare disturb Mandrik in his hermit's cell. Gerald Desvres knocked impatiently as soon as we sat down to supper. He had, at least, brought a pudding from his wife.

"Sorry to interrupt, Yves, but, of course, the news."

Elizaveta ran to greet the sweets.

"There's no news yet," said I.

"Either way, it's news. If Dirk von Iggislau found us new neighbors or his own strange path to God—why, either way, that's an event."

Ruth looked ill.

Adelaïda placed another bowl on the table. "Until they come back we know nothing, so you might as well eat."

It was all I could do to keep from running to my brother's, to question him or to beat him, I knew not. Pudding seemed hardly more inviting than gruel, and I did not like Ruth's wan look.

"Dirk," Gerald said, looking eagerly about at us, "always seemed the most normal boy you could imagine. Not a strange bone in his body."

Before he could finish speaking, I heard another carriage, and in came Jude with a bucket of cream. "Sorry to bother you—hello, Gerald—but I wanted to know what happened to the lad? Reports are abroad, you know."

"Abroad how? Who's been out spreading rumors?"

"The little ones—I never can keep them straight. One of the middle-sized ones."

"Jowl?"

"Been running about the township, doing cartwheels, saying his eldest brother figured out the route to Indo-China."

Miller Freund came with a neat bundle of kindling. "Strange news, Yves," he said when I opened the door.

"Lord knows," Gerald said, "how it spreads so quickly."

"Yves," Ruth said, "everybody's coming, it's only a matter of time. You ought to get the fire going in the barn."

"Do you order me about in my own house?"

Her eyes were red as embers. "I'll help you get a cask of cider."

As we rose I realized I did not feel well at all—my eyes burned in my head, and my back, which had rarely been so blessedly relieved of labor, ached. I heard the horses thundering along the road.

"Come," Ruth said. "Is there bread to spare?"

"In the kneading trough," Adelaïda said, gesturing behind her. "Four new loaves in the kneading trough."

Gerald and Jude watched this scene with some interest. I hated Ruth with all the force of my convictions, and yet, as she directed, I went out and prepared my threshing floor for the evening's somber gathering.

Before the stars had time to rise in the sky, the whole village had gathered—including Stanislaus in his most humble winter cassock, dun in hue—around the great fire in my barn, where, in calmer days, we had gathered to drink whiskey and show one another tricky new kinds of knots. Adelaïda brought the bread and all our cups and gourds in her apron, and deposited them on the floor. Ydlbert remained apart, sober of aspect, and sipping at a nipper of spirits more likely to succor him than the still-young cider. Sophronia, perhaps sensible of his distress, kept up a low moan of complaint.

"Gentlemen," I began, then cleared my throat. "The life of Ydlbert von Iggislau's eldest hangs now in the balance, and with his fate will all our fates be decided."

"How so?" asked Anya. "My husband tells me our son fares well."

"If what Dirk tells us, of a land beyond the hills, is true, then it will change our lives in Mandragora forever. And if it be but the work of his fertile imaginings—"

"Then I should have been called first," said Stanislaus, his tone quiet, yet full of conviction. "If it be a demon in him, then none but a priest can get it out."

Mandrik opened the barn door and stood in the light of the fire, in sharp contrast to the deepening night. It was clear from the faraway look in his mild eyes how difficult a day he had passed. "My brothers," he said simply, entering the barn, and with a single will my countrymen rose to hail him.

Ydlbert said, "Where is my son?"

"Asleep by a well-stoked fire, with a pear tart by for when he wakes." He coughed hollowly. His voice, usually rich as church song, wavered thin as a flute.

"Sakes, man," Ydlbert whispered, a shiver more of fear, it seemed, than of bodily chill coursing through his frame, "you might shut the door."

He allowed it to creak shut on its hinges, and stood in the glow of the fire and regarded us all.

"Have you gone to see?" Jepho asked.

"If it took Dirk four days to get there and back, how should I have journeyed thither in an afternoon? I have not gone. I have no need to." He was studiously not looking at me, his hands each up the opposite sleeve. "Gentlemen."

The sheep were snuffling, but all the assembly was quiet.

"I have suffered to arrive at an explanation for you—for if Dirk is found mad, the rest of his young life is ruined, and if a strange village is found but a stone's throw hence, our life as we know it changes forever."

"Not mad, but possessed," Stanislaus offered. "If this be not the truth, it is the Devil's work, sure."

"You're right, Father." Mandrik breathed in deeply, and closed his eyes—speaking inwardly, I imagined, to Marvin and Clive—and when he opened them again they were clear and blank as the wide autumn sky, empty, I was certain, as the day he was born. "I come to tell you that Dirk von Iggislau, though a fine young man, is no visionary."

Bodies shifted, leather boots creaked. Jude said, simply, "What, then?"

Ydlbert said, "I'll thank you to know that my son is not mad. Or possessed."

"Not mad, no. Nor yet, good Father, in the Devil's thrall." Mandrik closed his eyes against the tears which threatened to cloud them. "We are not alone on this island. The world is greater than you who have never left this village can possibly imagine—and so near, only a hair's breadth separates us from it. There are people more numerous than the stalks of wheat in the summer field, places more various, wonders the mind cannot contain."

The chill in the air was not that which lingered from the harvest moon. Ydlbert wrapped his arms around his shoulders as if holding himself back from a fight. "I don't know what you're driving at. In the Orient, sure—"

"Here, Ydlbert. Across the mountains to the west, the north, the south, the east. Past Nnms and the farthest boundaries of your own fields. It is everywhere, so close we can touch it. Our island is far from populous, but the world is nearby."

"Did I not say so?" Adelaïda whispered.

"How can that be?" Jude asked.

Said Stanislaus, "How can it be if I know nothing of it?"

"Why was it my son who discovered this?"

"Sooner or later someone would have found out, but Dirk it managed to be." Ydlbert was still rocking, so my brother placed a hand on his shoulder to still him. Ydlbert regarded him, but said nothing.

Said Dithyramb, "Our first adventurer."

"Aye," said Jepho solemnly. "The first, no doubt, of many."

My brother said, "If the people of this village decide to venture forth, then yes. Dirk reports that our far neighbors are anxious to meet you."

"Why," asked Dithyramb, "would we decide to do anything else?"

"Because we do not know," said Stanislaus, "if our neighbors are men of God." He and my brother regarded one another, their blue eyes equally weary, their brown cassocks each the reflection of the other.

"Nay," said my brother. "I am certain they are not. Think you all upon those who have visited us from beyond. Did they seem to bear the mark of God's grace upon them?"

"But these are different," said Ion Gansevöort. "These are our neighbors. We should set out tomorrow, all laden with gifts, to bid them welcome to our valley. Our Archduke should lead us forth as the army of peace."

"Don't," I said, before I could stop my mouth.

Ydlbert turned toward me. "What do you say, Yves?"

I steadied myself. "I don't think you should go. Let Dirk's report lie, and get back to your farms. Winter is coming."

"Yves," Ion said, "of all the men in this village, you're the last I'd expect—"

"I think we should keep our distance from our neighbors as fiercely as we did, however unwittingly, before. We should stockpile for winter, and see how we like our prospects come spring."

Ruth paced about the edges of the gathering like a shade.

Ion shook his head. "After all you've done for us—after you alone looked forward when all of us clung like moss to the past—how can you say that?"

I could not dredge up an answer.

Ydlbert said, "He's right, brother. Tell me, what ails you?"

"I would," I said, "give Dirk a parcel of my land, if he would still consent to farm it. I would carve off a good living for him, that he might marry Martin's daughter and settle down to the soil like all his ancestors before him."

Ydlbert shook his wide head. "Perhaps Bartholomew may yet work the land, but after such an adventure, Dirk will want to go among the new folk, sure. My God, man, they have the sea."

"Would you let Dirk go, across the hills?" asked Yorik.

Ydlbert's brow wrinkled with care. "I would pine for him each day of my life—"

Anya said, "My heart would break open."

"—but with six other sons to provide for, it might not be the worst thing for one to strike off on his own. I do appreciate your offer, Yves. A kind offer, indeed."

"He'll die," I said, the surety as certain as the walls of the barn were solid.

"What do you mean, lad?"

"Among the new folk. Their ways will be so different from his own."

"I am afraid," Mandrik said, "that my brother speaks truth."

Gerald meted out more cider, and the congregation settled against the posts and one another to listen. Ruth sat down by Enyadatta's stall.

"Good farmers, recall the pestilence that came to us from the sky, your terror and despair that such a dark end could befall us." Except for the crackling of the fire and the sighing of the beasts as they settled down to sleep, the barn grew still. "Our neighbors to the west are not likely to set upon us with the weapons of death. But that they will destroy us is nonetheless sure."

"But," said Gerald, "Dirk reports that they wish to meet us."

"Aye," Mandrik continued, "they do wish to meet you. As curiosities, as creatures from another world. They want to gawk at you. I ask you to imagine people coming and going, day in and day out, carrying equipment—like the machine Mr. Fiske bore upon his shoulder—and pointing it everywhere, shining lights in your eyes and asking you questions upon questions. They'll want it to be bright everywhere, all the time; wherever you go, there will be no peace or darkness. Do you understand me? You will literally be deluged with attention—not with help or with friendship, but with the relentless pursuit of information. You will have no time to farm, only to answer questions.

"Brothers, you must protect yourselves from this plague of interest."

Stanislaus shook his head. "Mandrik, rarely in our lives have we concurred upon a topic so completely as we do in our desire to keep our fellows from going across the hills. But what you describe sounds more a nuisance than a peril to the soul."

Mandrik passed his hand across his face. "What I have described is but the beginning. Because I have not yet begun to speak of how badly you will, all of you, desire their intervention."

Ydlbert said, "Nay—"

"Let me finish, Brother von Iggislau. Those people possess wonders you will crave as a child craves sweets. They have mechanical vehicles that drive without horses, five times faster. Lights that turn on by a switch on the wall and produce no smoke nor danger of conflagration. Windows as large as a barn door to let in the light, and covered in sparkling glass to hold out the drafts. Filmy screens in the windows to keep out the summer bugs. Cold chests in their kitchens where their food stays fresh forever. Others make all their clothes and grow all their food for them, that they simply go to market, any day of the week, and buy."

"That's ridiculous," said Yorik.

I said, "Ruth has spoken of such things."

Mandrik said, "Ruth?"

"It's all true," she said quietly.

The images of the world to come settled over us like a film of fairy dust. Anya said, "To me it sounds like Heaven."

"Exactly like Heaven," added Ion.

"That is as I have feared," said Mandrik.

"My research," Ruth whispered.

I crouched down beside her and peered into her black eyes. "May it rot, Ruth. May it fester in your sight."

Her eyes, fixed on mine, wore a pleading expression.

Stanislaus stood up to face my brother. "It is a life of ease, across the hills?"

"They do not scrape their life from the soil as we do."

The priest's face clouded. "Why, then, it sounds an earthly Paradise."

"But it is not. Ruth?"

Ruth leaned her face into her lap.

"Stanislaus," said my brother, "I thought we agreed with one another."

"I did, I mean, I do think we must be wary. But think you not, Mandrik, that by going across the hills—with all due caution—our brethren might be freed to contemplation of the infinite?"

"If they think not of their Maker now, why should they then?"

Stanislaus's Adam's apple bobbed. "Do you seek to deprive your brothers of the bounty of God?"

"I think we should form a delegation," said good Franz Nethering, "to go across the hills to greet them. We should not judge them before making their acquaintance. We should see with our own eyes if these wonders Mandrik speaks of be true."

"Hear, hear," said several, raising wooden cups.

"They are not wonders," Ruth said, her words muffled by her skirt.

Mandrik said, "Wait a few days at least. Gentlemen, I beg you. Consider this carefully."

But what, I realized, did it matter? If what my brother spoke of was true, then two generations hence, there would be nothing left but meadow, and Mandrik's strange trees, unable to propagate more of their invented species, but bearing for the ages their succulent fruit, each the entire of its solitude.

Adelaïda said, "These are fairy favors come from who knows how far off to tempt us, and it all has the savor of iniquity. It must be that Ruth has brought this with her from the Beyond—this, and grave-robbing strangers from who knows where—and we must banish her before she heaps more wickedness upon us. Before she came, did things plummet from the sky, and did we desecrate tombs, and were we beset by strange neighbors?"

Ruth stood up and faced the assembly. "I am not responsible for this. I did not do this to you." She stalked outside, and I heard the door of the house slam shut behind her.

"Adelaïda," Ydlbert said.

My wife swallowed twice, then lurched for the door. I followed her into the bitter, starlit yard, where she stood retching by the sty. I heard Ruth bustling angrily within the house.

"Wife," I said, and held one hand beneath her forehead that she not hit it on the post, "what ails you?"

Her breathing calmed and she stood. "I am but with child, Yves. Go in."

When we returned, the heat of the fire overwhelmed me, and I remained against the door a moment to right myself. Adelaïda leaned into me.

Ion reached back to touch the hem of her skirt, and said, "Fare you well, sister?"

"Nay," she said, swaying slightly. "But I will be better ere the child is born, unless some curse take this village bodily away."

"The bairn within her," said Anya. "God be praised."

A few of my countrymen murmured, "Amen."

"Have you a song for us?" asked Ion. "It is a dark night, and a song would help gladden our hearts."

"I feel poorly, Ion. I feel no calling to sing. I'm sorry."

Ion patted her foot within her sturdy shoe. She yet looked pale.

"Chouchou?" Ion asked.

Mandrik shook his head no. "My heart is too heavy to lift up to God."

"Then something terrible has passed among this company."

Jude Dithyramb let out a long, deep sigh.

"What ails you, man?" Ydlbert asked.

Jude shook his head. "As often as not, when I think of my father, and the sweat he gave to his land, that I and my brothers and sisters might thrive; and I think of them all now, snug in the churchyard; and I think of my mother, madder than the bulls in spring, and reviled by everyone in the village who did not think her the sum of the world's blessings when he was a bairn; and when I think how much has happened since my father's passing, though we still farm the land, eat, dream, sometimes starve and sometimes prosper; when I think on all of this, I don't know who I am sadder for, my father or me. But I do know that I miss him terribly, and that all this change is for nothing—nothing—if it can't bring him back."

Adelaïda sat down upon the floor. I crouched down beside her and reached for her hand, and felt the warm jump of her pulse like a hatchling shivering in its mother's nest. As her blood coursed through her, so also did I feel it race through me, a shock as one receives from touching wool in the winter, a jolt of life. Here, before my countrymen, I could give no sign of emotion, but I felt fully what Jude had said, and we and the barn seemed suddenly very small, while the cold wind blew from who knew what distance.

"Aye," Ydlbert agreed. "But perhaps Mandrik will yet figure that out."

"There's no raising the dead," I answered, though speaking tore the delicate veil of thought I had begun to weave. "Only in tales. They don't come back. Better carts won't make them, nor strangers with ice chests. Even my brother can't raise the dead."

"It's but," said Jude, "that I wish my father might accompany us, if such wonders are to make themselves known to me."

"Is there nothing," I asked, "that I could say to make you stay?"

"Nothing at all," said Ydlbert. "I wish there were something I could say to make you come with us."

"But there is not."

Ion rose to his feet and held his cap between his hands. "Then we should leave you to your peace, Brother Gundron. A great day dawns tomorrow."

Desvres said, "We must send a messenger to the Archduke, that he might lead us forth."

"Aye," said good Ion, "in all his splendor."

The assembled company rose.

Again I said, "I wish I could make you stay."

Yorik opened the door into the howling night.

"It's too late," Mandrik said. He spoke to me alone. "I, too, would bid them hold—but it would be no use. There is no other way to slake their curiosity. So I send them my blessings, and Godspeed."

Ydlbert said, "And Godspeed to you, Mandrik. And my great gratitude to you for looking after my son."

Adelaïda set out across the yard.

One by one everyone of my acquaintance bade farewell, and I followed to watch them climb aboard the seats of their carts or run off down the road. The wind was bitter as February—no Advent wind at all, no promise of redemption. The horses stamped and grunted at being so rudely and cruelly unblanketed. I stood with the warmth of my barn behind me, the promise of the warmth of my home before me, the neighbors' torches like so many spluttering stars. I could imagine my neighbors this evening, wide-eyed and restless with anticipation. I neither despised nor envied them, but I knew their lives to differ from my own.

At last my yard grew quiet. I felt Mandrik's presence behind me, yet knew that if I turned to regard him, he would not be looking my way. "Imagine that," I said, leaning against the doorframe our grandfather had built.

He remained silent. When I turned, the light of the fire was full upon him, shining into and through the luminous blue of his eyes. At last he said, "You and Adelaïda should not have chided Ruth so harshly."

Her name was the last word under Heaven I desired to hear. Though my temper was hot, I managed to keep it down. "Imagine, a whole village," I said, "so close by."

"You do not answer my accusation." He paced to Enyadatta's stall and back before he lifted those strange eyes to mine. "This is a terrible circumstance, Yves, but why are you so glum? It is my duty to fear for our brethren. What do you know about that village, after all?"

My blood began to simmer. "How did you decide if Dirk had seen a vision?"

"By questioning him."

If only he had not become a holy man, and I could have punched him as I did when we were boys. In the absence of such recourse, my anger rooted deeper inside me. "Mandrik, you knew there was a village there."

He made no reply, and my rage to choke him began to choke me.

"Did you not know there was a village across the hills?"

"I knew."

His quiet gave me a moment's pause, but it did nothing to appease me. "And you told me nothing?"

"Yves," he said.

"You came back after a three-years' absence, during which time I thought you dead, and told me story upon story of what you'd seen, but could not mention a village two days' journey from my home?"

"In those days it was farther—before the harness and the pavement, before the improvements to the cart."

My mind was by now but a distant outgrowth of my roiling guts. "What has that to do with it?"

"I didn't think you, or anyone else, would ever get there."

"And what has that to do with it?"

He sighed. "Nothing, I suppose."

"You're right—nothing. Because you did not tell me the truth, Mandrik."

"I did not—"

"You did not tell the truth." The heat in my belly had burned up to the backs of my eyes, which stung bitterly, though not with tears. "You said nothing of what you saw here at home. Nothing. Everything was Indo-China, praying Hindus, and the great wide sea."

"Because those were the adventures. Those were the best stories to tell."

"Am I such a child that you tell me what's most interesting instead of what's true?"

"I didn't want you to go off looking for our neighbors."

"I am not a child, Mandrik!"

"But look what's happening." He paced again to the horse's stall, and tried to pat her brow, but Enyadatta, as if aware of his perfidy, shied from him. "On the basis of one report—that not even a favorable one—the whole village will go off to investigate. Every last man but you and I—even those who were wise enough to have some fear. Should I have told you, that this could have happened three years ago? You were right, Yves, when you counseled them not to go."

I did not like him steering the conversation from his untruth. "And why's that?"

"Will you sit down with me, brother?"

"No."

He closed his eyes and traced their sockets with his fingers. "Our neighbors will come back, every man of them, hungry. Changed. What Dirk found is an isolated village, a few fishermen on an unfriendly shore; but there are other, more populous islands a stone's throw hence, with scores of other villages, Yves, more villages than there are people in this town."

"That's ridiculous," I told him, but I knew in my bones it was true.

"And once our neighbors see the wonders they possess—"

"Mandrik, why didn't you tell me?"

"Because I didn't want you to go."

"I wouldn't—"

"Yes, you would. Your curiosity—look at them. Look how they ran."

My face burned. "What else have you not told me?"

"Nothing."

"What else?"

"Nothing, Yves, nothing." He held up his hands, beseeching. "What would I keep from you? Why would I keep anything from you?"

The rush of answers which flooded my mind shamed me, chided me, bid me ask, how have you come to mistrust him you hold most dear? Why was I so full of doubt? "I don't know."

He reached out to wrap his arms around me. Though my whole body rebelled, bid me hit him with my fists, I stood still. His sackcloth cassock scratched against my cheek. "With all the wonders of the world about me, brother," he said, "I chose to come back home."

I longed to accept comfort from his embrace. In his strong arms I felt the arms of my father; in the scent of his flesh lived the scent of my brothers' flesh. I felt them all buzzing like bright wasps about us, about the rat-infested rafters of the barn. Beyond the walls of this barn were my daughter, spared me thus far by God's grace, and my wife, a new life burgeoning, also a miracle, within. And past them, a great emptiness—for our family lay beneath their gravestones, our grandmother beneath her cairn, and our neighbors would flee now to the land of plenty, which none of us had known was so nearby. I felt the weight of the mountains, and the broad sky, and the sea, who knew how far away, pressing inward, pressing down upon me. And the arms of a brother who had not offered me all of his truth—who had kept from me half the tales of his wanderings, and was still, I believed, keeping from me the tale of his love—offered now not even the flimsiest barrier, not the least measure of safety. In all the world, there was nothing but me and the cold, dark emptiness around.

I did not sleep that night. I could not wait one day longer to embark on my project of building; I cared nothing for splitting wood or fixing fences, but desired only the task nearest my heart. All night did I keep the animals awake, as with my chalk I traced the outlines of the pieces for my writing desk—a plain top, four slats for bracing, four legs—and began to saw them out. By morning I had fitted them together with nails, and I began work on a stool for sitting. I was not yet certain why I needed this furniture, but I needed it badly. When I looked at the box of pens, sullied now by Mandrik's admission of his human need, his human failure, I knew I had work to accomplish.

CHAPTER EIGHT

THE JOURNEY WESTWARD

efore the dawn had trailed the last wisps of pink across the eastern sky, my neighbors departed on their journey. From my work in the barn I heard numerous carts approaching on their iron-clad wheels, and though it was not yet morning, I heard the beat of the timbrels and the tinkling of bells. When I opened the barn door to peer out, the Archduke's litter had just lumbered past, leading my brethren forth, but it did not look so splendid without the full light of the sun thereupon. As the last of my neighbors clattered by and receded into the distance, I went into the house, and morning came cold and still. Many of the birds had flown away for the winter, and those that remained were too busy pecking the ground to sing. Winter loomed still as death before us. Against her custom, Ruth was out of bed before my wife, her face wan, her clumsy hands working a passable fire. She looked up from burning her bread over the fire. "Would you like some?"

I shook my head no. My anger toward my brother had grown so hot that she, at least, looked an ordinary person again.

"I didn't wake you, Yves?"

"No, no. I was up all night. I was working."

She nodded, and lifted her wire contraption, in which she burned her bread, from the fire.

"I am sorry I yelled at you," I said beneath my breath, "and that I cursed your work."

Her eyes showed the depth of her gratitude, and her lips compressed into the ghost of a smile. "It's fine. I don't blame you."

"But I apologize."

"Is the sun up?" my wife asked, then turned back over toward the wall. I did not recall her lazing thus when Elizaveta grew inside her.

"But a moment ago," I answered, smoothing her yellow braid from out her sleep-sticky mouth.

"I want tose," Elizaveta called from her hammock.

Ruth took her down, changed her wet rag for a dry one, and placed another slice of bread in the wire contraption she'd set over the fire. When Ruth was gone, we would still need to make this strange delicacy for our child. I could smell Elizaveta's sweet breath, unclouded yet by the stench and misery of adulthood, as she padded about the house in bare feet. "Papa, why is Roof sad?"

Ruth said, "I'm not sad. Here. Blow."

Elizaveta blew dutifully on her toast.

"I suppose there's no point in leaving until they all come back. I'll want to say goodbye," Ruth said, struggling under the weight of the kettle.

"You'll leave forever, then?"

"Maybe not forever, but for now. What I wanted to study will be gone."

I didn't care for her defeated tone. "I'll be here. Or am I not interesting enough?"

"You always start with that when you're upset. I'm sure there'll be plenty to study, something new, if I come back a year from now. You'll change, too. Watch."

"Nay, Ruth. You might know me better than that." I turned the bellows on the fire, for what she had built would never come to a boil. I took the slop pot out from under the bed, that I might empty it as I relieved myself of the night's accumulations. My feet near frozen with chill, I hurried into the near pasture, the last brown spikes of grass prickling my soles. The milky-gray sky boded ill for winter. From the east I heard Friedl Vox, perhaps the last person left in Mandragora but me and my kin, calling up over Ydlbert's rise. "Damn your eyes!" she shrieked. "Iulia Gansevöort! Come out from under your cairn. Your brethren from the sea have come forth to claim you at last." I closed the fly of my undergarment, for the wind blew cold. As she topped the rise, I saw that she was not raving utterly, but had two slender strangers behind her, carrying the weight of great backpacks upon their backs, and bunched together as if they feared Friedl's nearness.

"Iulia!" she once again shrieked.

Ruth raised her eyes to me as I stepped inside. "She really does frighten me."

"Come outside, Ruth. Adelaïda, get up."

Ruth said, "What's the matter?" Adelaïda pulled the blanket over her ears.

"She's got people with her. You'd best come see."

Ruth solemnly chewed the rest of her bread and wiped her hands on her apron. Elizaveta caught her air of wonder and stood up slowly, her two hands gripping Pudge.

I leaned over my wife in bed and licked the gap in her teeth. "Get up, Adelaïda. We may need you." She nodded, and my head moved also, in sympathy. "Please, I may need your help." She nodded again, and looked at me with the same eyes with which I'd regarded my dying family, the eyes that could not store enough against approaching absence.

Ruth took Elizaveta's hand, and we walked to the road. Yoshu bounded out from the barn and crouched at the edge of our property, growling at whatever was drawing nigh. When Yoshu began barking fiercely, her cry broke the silence of the morning.

Ruth peered at the figures walking up the road. "This can't be," she said.

"What?"

The paving stones looked unusually pale, as if they anticipated the first wash of snow.

Ruth opened her mouth wide, and in a loud, clear tone, called out, "Nurit?"

All three figures stopped in their descent. The strangers turned their heads toward the sound, which, carried on a visible puff of breath, continued to echo across my fields.

Again Ruth called out, "Nurit? Eli?"

The figures regarded one another, looped their thumbs into their shoulder straps, and began running down the hill, one whooping, and both shouting, "Ruth!" From the tones of their voices, one was a woman and one a man. Both were dressed in blue trousers and heavy short coats.

The moment in which Ruth ran out to greet them lasted an eternity, long enough for me to puzzle through every permutation of what this might be about. Then at once I realized the figures were her siblings, come from her homeland as surely as mine came to me from the land of the dead. They dropped the backpacks by the roadside and ran into one another's arms. "What are you doing here?" she asked them, burrowing her nose into their necks. They were both taller than she. The landscape once again fell quiet.

"Oh, Ruth," said her sister, "I'm so glad to see you."

"How on earth did you get here? My sweet Eli." She kissed the pale side of his throat.

"That woman," her sister said, "is completely terrifying."

"Ruth, we missed you so much."

"Iulia!" Friedl cried, her one blue eye staring at Ruth in fear.

I went out to her in the road and, despite her stench, smoothed down her grizzled locks to calm her. "Shh," I whispered to her. "All's well. Thank you for bringing them hither."

"How did you get here?" Ruth asked again.

"We hiked in over those mountains." He pointed back toward Nnms. He was certainly a man, but a gypsy's jewels dangled from his pink ears.

"The Navy showed us a videotape," her sister said. Her narrow face radiated with winter's first chill, though her smile, however earnest, had a wan and tragic cast. "But this I wasn't prepared for." She ducked her head slightly and pushed the vision apparatus, the eyeglasses, up her nose.

"Friedl?"

"Yeah, her, and like the whole ghost-town thing. It's creepy."

"Is everything okay? Back home?"

"Everything's fine. Dad's worried about you."

"But he's fine," Eli corrected. "You didn't look completely well in that video."

"I broke my leg, but it's good now. As long as it doesn't rain."

"Iulia Gansevöort, they've come at last to bring you back to the Beyond," Friedl said in a quieter tone.

All three of them looked up at her, startled, and I felt as if my mind would explode, watching them—all so slender and so much like one another, with their broad, flat voices, all gesturing forcefully with their hands.

"Friedl, thank you so much for bringing me my brother and sister. Thank you so much."

Friedl was used to no words kinder than invective, and hung her head in confusion.

"And Yves." She reached forth to take my hand. I colored, despite myself. "Yves, meet my brother and sister, Eli and Nurit."

They held out their cold, delicate hands in that peculiar intimate gesture and smiled bashfully, Nurit ducking her head as she bade me hello.

"This is Yves Gundron, who's—I can't tell you how kind he's been to me."

I felt guilty for all the dark thoughts I had so recently harbored against her.

"Yes," said Nurit. "I remember you from the tape. Thank you for taking care of our sister."

"It was but my duty," I mumbled.

"Ruth," Nurit said, "we missed you so much. We were so worried about you."

Ruth, looking back and forth between them, began to weep from the pit of her stomach, racking sobs that bent her double and propelled her into her sister's arms. The brother looked at me with shy dark eyes and bowed his bejeweled head. Abashed, I also bowed mine. Elizaveta said, "Papa, why is Roof crying?"

But I didn't know how to put it into words that some things make people cry from joy and confusion. I could not tell my daughter that remembrance as often as not makes us weep. I had heard Ruth cry the very night of her arrival, sure, but until that moment I had not known she was capable of a deeper emotion. I had thought that because she did not work the land, because she did not know an honest day's labor, she could not know an honest day's pain; and though I recognized from the start the signs of her grief, I thought, how deep could it be, really, if she never spoke of it, and if she had not lost everything at once? How hard could it be for her, in a land of plenty greater than even they across the hills could imagine, when her father and siblings yet lived? Yet there before me stood most of what she had in the world—and there was the proof of how she loved it. All three were ruining their fair, clean complexions with emotion, screwing up their faces like masks of death. I should not, I realized, be watching this, and yet I could not tear my eyes away. Even Yoshu, with her fierce desire to protect our home, stood still, and neither scratched nor bit.

Ruth pulled away from her sister, her head bowed. When she lifted her face to us her mouth was soft, as I had never seen it, and her eyes were bright behind a haze of incomprehension. She looked at us like it was the dawn of the first day of the world. I shivered to see her face so. In a moment, however, her eyes snapped back to life, and she showed us her glorious teeth. "And this," she said, placing her hand on my daughter's round head, "is Elizaveta."

Nurit and Eli bent down to greet the child. Elizaveta turned her face toward Ruth's skirt, but held her doll out before her. "This is Pudge."

"Pudge," Eli said. "Nice to meet you."

Nurit said, "She looks like you, sort of."

"Nay," I said, "they both resemble my grandmother, Iulia Gansevöort, who came from the sea." They both regarded Friedl in some confusion. I added, "Friedl's mad," but it did not unvex their expressions. "Friedl," I said, "thank you for bringing them, but it's time to be off with you, now."

She shook her head at me.

"Come on now, off. Go find your Jude."

"My Jude's gone away with them all." She looked at the strangers, scratched meditatively at the lid of the inward eye, and started back up the road.

"Where is everyone?" Eli asked. "It's disturbing. We didn't see a soul as we passed through town."

The cares of the morning rushed back upon me, and I saw by her expression that they had descended in a similar torrent upon Ruth.

"It's awful. I'll tell you everything. But first come in and put your things down and eat."

Eli regarded me shyly.

"Aye, it's all right," I told him. "Come in."

They thanked me as they once more picked up their packs. Ruth held fast to her sister's hand as we walked up the frost-brittle yard.

How news travels in other locales I haven't any notion, but that day it skipped from my mind to my brother's without even a whisper. Thus did Mandrik arrive with three late pears but a few moments after we sat down to our porridge. He did not look any more surprised to see me with three strangers around my table than I was to have them, though he cast a concerned glance toward Adelaïda, who had sat up to take a bowl of broth in bed.

Mandrik bowed low, with the pears held before him like an offering. Eli stood up from the table, looking for all the world like the Prince of the Arab Hordes.

"Mandrik," Ruth said, "please meet my brother, Eli, and my sister, Nurit."

"I am delighted."

"This is one of my dearest friends in the village, Mandrik Gundron."

"Dit le Chouchou," he added humbly.

Her "dearest" fanned the smoldering embers of confusion in my breast.

"Please have breakfast with us."

Mandrik nodded, and took his seat beside me on the bench.

At least when the Archduke had arrived, it had been spring, my fields at the height of their prosperity. Now the farm looked as barren as death; for winter is a small death as sure as spring is the sign of God's resurrection, and fast did it approach. The last of the leaves on the trees were withered and blew wanly in the breeze. There seemed enough of interest, however, to fill the eyes of these strangers, for they looked as greedily about my home as once had their sib.

Ruth said, "You came by boat?"

"And it took forever to find the island," Eli said, his mouth full of gruel. "But, anyway, now we're here."

"Where are all the people?" Nurit asked.

Mandrik let out a sigh. "Gone away like the wayward moon when a man has a long night's journey ahead."

She shook her head and tucked a stray hair behind her ear, as sometimes I had seen Ruth do when she was uncertain.

"There's another village been found," I told her. "A village like one of your own. And the people of Mandragora are gone off to see the wonders there."

Nurit watched her sister carefully. "A modern village?"

"So it seems," Ruth said.

"What will that mean for your work here? That seems bad."

Eli quietly said, "Gloombox."

Ruth pushed back from the table and fetched the great skillet from over the fire. "Does anybody want some ham?"

Nurit held her hand over her bowl, and colored when I looked at her quizzically. Such volatile complexions they had, as changeable as weather.

Eli said, "My sister doesn't eat meat."

"Doesn't eat meat?" said Adelaïda from the bed.

"It was Ragan," said Elizaveta, "our she-pig."

"She'll starve come winter."

"I'm sorry, I don't mean to be rude," Nurit said. "And of course we won't be staying the winter. We have to get back."

Eli said, "I have exams in six weeks."

Mandrik's smile had quite frozen to his face.

"But you've come from the other end of the world," I said. "Surely you can't turn right around and go back?"

Adelaïda said, "Yves, we've no place to put them." Her eyes looked feverish with joy—these strangers, after all, were her deliverance—but it seemed possible that she was merely ill.

Nurit said, "We missed our sister. We wanted to see if she was okay. I mean, if she wanted to get out of here, she couldn't let anyone know."

"But she's fine, Nurit," Eli said, disordering with his long fingers the hair she'd so carefully tucked. "I'd like to point out that you've been bent out of shape over nothing."

"Cut it out. I have not been bent out of shape."

Ruth said, "I'm fine."

"I can see that, so we have to head back. Eli has to take his tests, and

I need to make excuses to your department about why you left your undergrads stranded."

"I did not—"

"You said you'd be back in the autumn, Ruth. It's past Thanksgiving now."

"I didn't know if I'd find it. I didn't know what I'd find."

Eli said, "She's not blaming you."

Ruth closed her eyes briefly. "I know." When again she opened them she looked between Mandrik and myself, and with a face as clear as rainwater said, "You two don't squabble like Nurit and I do. Do you."

I felt ashamed, for she did not know the depth of our disagreement the night before, or how much I still suspected her.

"It's just as well you need get back," Adelaïda said, placing her bowl on the floor and lying back with a sigh. "Once the snow comes, there'll be no getting out until March, and that in the mud."

She was glad, then.

Nurit turned and cast a pinched smile upon her. "It's sort of too bad, isn't it?" she asked. "I think I might like it here. I'm so glad to be here."

"As we're glad to have you," I said. "But my wife speaks truth about the snow. We'll be tight in within the fortnight."

Mandrik poked with a stick at the perfectly adequate fire.

Nurit coughed delicately into her hand, and said, "Excuse me."

Ruth said, "Oh, no," and when I regarded her in alarm, said, "Nurit has asthma," as if that explained anything.

"I'll be okay."

Eli placed his hand between Nurit's shoulders. "The boat's not coming back to get us for a few more days. If you think you might want to come back with us, Ruth, you've got some time to decide."

"Go back with you?" Mandrik said. "She's working."

Ruth smoothed the surface of her porridge with the back of her spoon. "Working, yes, but who knows how much longer. I've talked to Yves about it, Mandrik. My work here may be done."

Mandrik's eyes fixed upon mine, willing me to speak, but I found nothing to say. His face was not fully composed. Our table produced only the soft scrape of wooden implements on wooden bowls, the clicks of tongues against the roofs of mouths. Elizaveta looked as if she would melt from the visitors' splendor.

"We have liked very much having her among us," I at last broke the silence to say.

Ruth's eyes grew cloudy. "Thank you, Yves."

"If you leave," Mandrik said, "your work is done for certain. But if you stay, who knows how the course of events will unfold? Who knows what you may see?"

"But I don't want to see it. I don't want to see this shrivel into nothing. I know you're right, I know I should stay until the end. That's why I'm still thinking about it."

Eli said, "If you left now, you could always come back in the spring."

"Nobody does research," Nurit concluded, "snowed under." She looked to my wife for affirmation, and Adelaïda nodded on her pillow. Nurit coughed.

Ruth chewed thoughtfully. "If I don't stay, how will I know what they do all winter?"

"You could ask, for one thing."

"It's hardly the same."

"And who knows," I said quietly. "Given all that has happened, this winter may be quite unlike any that came before. We must simply wait for our countrymen to return."

Beneath his breath my brother said, "Lord have mercy."

The room quieted once again. Elizaveta sidled up to Eli. He opened his eyes wide at her, and she laughed.

"It would be a fine day to see the village," I offered, "if you want to take the cart. I would accompany you, but I must cover the garden before the hard frost."

What would it matter, my garden, if the village were abandoned by spring? But in the meanwhile I loved it, and wanted dearly to look after it, to keep it safe against the cold.

"I'll take them out, then," Ruth said, finishing her porridge. "We'll be out of your way."

"A pity," my brother said, "they could not see our village as ever it was—full of life and energy."

"I'm sure it's beautiful anyway," Nurit offered.

They bundled themselves in their fleecy outer garments. Ruth tied the string of her cloak at her throat. "We'll be back before sundown."

Mandrik pressed his three pears into her hands. "Godspeed."

We regarded one another before they stuck their heads out the door and shut it heavily behind them.

My ears buzzed in the sudden quiet. In the stillness, I felt inexplicably tired.

Mandrik rested his head on his arms on the table, as if exemplifying in his body the confusion of my mind.

For the nonce I could not worry about Ruth and her siblings, nor even about what my neighbors were doing up over the western ridge, for there was work to do sowing the winter wheat to the summer's fallows and covering the garden with mulch. Adelaïda had deep red wool upon her loom that we might, come the depths of winter, have a new blanket to replace ours that had gone threadbare despite repeated patching; and she worked on it a while at a time, in between returning to bed to rest. As I scattered seeds in the furrows, I surprised myself to realize that I was angry and sad that Ruth might leave us. In days past my mind had teemed with foul suspicions, but in all I had grown used to her presence and her company, and did not relish losing them. Without her, we might be what we always had been, a family on a prosperous farm in a village of farmers, more and less prosperous—or else what Dirk had brought up from beyond would change everything irrevocably. But that was mere possibility, not something we could count on. We should teach ourselves to be accustomed once again to plowing, harrowing, sowing, reaping—the plain old cycles of the year. There was no shame in this life, no lack of work and entertainments; but it had somehow ceased to be enough. I had come to like being watched by this outsider. Each of my actions and words held significance for her in ways I could never hope to imagine. Her secret life—the life in which my life played a formative role—had woven its spell. Without Ruth, for whom would my life have significance? Wives and daughters died too frequently. I dared not hope they would both outlive me.

Come nightfall, her siblings followed Ruth into the yard, and participated in her strange tooth and washing rituals. When they came back in, the other two were shivering, and Nurit's eyeglasses were shrouded in mist. "Ruth," she said, "you can't stay here all winter. There's no bathroom."

Ruth shook her head and deposited her stockings inside her boots.

Nurit removed her eyeglasses and Eli the rings from his ears, and they placed their glittering jewels on the table. All three foreigners, fully clothed, lay down on Ruth's pallet on the floor, fitting together like three string beans, speaking softly, as if our daughter were not asleep above them nor we across the room.

"I never dreamed," Nurit whispered.

"I did. All those stories Mom told. I always wanted to come."

Their long bodies shifted, causing the mattress to crackle. Nurit's cough drew out like a phrase of a chant, and quieted down again.

"I'm glad one of us believed her."

"I am, too."

Eli said, "How come she didn't write the book?"

Ruth sighed. "She said she could only afford to charter the boat for a day. It wasn't enough time. She couldn't find the island."

"And you?"

"I chartered it for three and, after days of talking with the man, got him to admit he'd heard about this place. But it was folklore, he promised me; I wouldn't find anything."

Nurit said, "That's what the guy told us, too. But here you were."

Past their breathing, past my wife's breathing, I heard the cold, mournful wind.

"The day after tomorrow we should leave to meet the boat."

"Only one more day?"

"Think about coming with us?"

Ruth breathed out through her nose. "Okay. Go to sleep."

"It's early," Eli said.

"It's bedtime."

I saw a faint blue glow over their faces, which was soon gone. "It's eight-thirty, Ruth."

"Is it?"

"Don't you have a watch?"

"We get up when the sun gets up, so you might as well sleep now."

Eli, forgetting his whisper, said, "I can't get up at the crack of dawn," and both sisters hushed him. "Ow," he said. "That's my face."

Ruth giggled. "What, will you sleep while I make breakfast three feet from your head?"

He sighed through his nose, like she did. "No."

"Then go to sleep."

"I like it here," he said.

"I like it here, too."

Their breath became more solemn and childlike as they sank further from this world. All around me were the gentle sounds of sleep, its rich fragrance, the lesser heat from the night's fire. Little was visible in the flickering flames—the mounds of bodies, the hulking table, the occasional glint of implements. Yet my eyes would not close, nor my mind quit racing. I was restless with anticipation, though I knew not of what. When it came, of course, I knew why I had been so caught up in the waiting. For at first it was barely audible, perhaps the highest, softest note of the screaming wind. As it drew my mind farther toward it, however, I began to make out the modulations of a tune fading in and out of hearing upon a high-pitched flute. As the melody rose and fell, counterpoint to the wind, the intoxicating rhythm of the drums made itself manifest behind. My heart danced in anticipation, and I looked eagerly about to see if the music had wakened any other soul. But sleep had cast her shadow over the household. I shut my eyes for the briefest moment, only to blink, and when I opened them again, saw my brothers and sister hovering over the pallet on the floor.

"Look," said Eglantine, passing her shining hand over their faces.

"How good to have a full house again," Marvin said, light cascading from the waves of his hair.

None of them was playing an instrument; I knew not where the music came from. "Eglantine," I whispered. "My brothers, I missed you."

All three turned to me and smiled, then continued examining the strangers.

"Such a blessing," Clive said.

"I've missed you so terribly. I thought you were never coming back."

Eglantine closed her sparkling eyes and leaned her head back to sing:

> *Beyond the Beyond,*
> *To the Beyond beyond.*
> *Beyond the Beyond,*
> *To the Beyond beyond.*

The strains of her music were sad, and frightened me. The drums fell into rhythm behind her; the soft flutes vanished.

"Where have you been? Where are Father and Mother and Elynour? Do they fare well?"

Marvin held a shining finger to his lips.

> *Beyond the Beyond,*
> *To the Beyond beyond.*
> *Beyond the Beyond,*
> *To the Beyond beyond.*

Clive was blessing them with his hands. "Tell Mandrik we were here," he whispered. "Tell him everything's right."

"We love you," Marvin said.

"Why don't Father and Mother come with you? Where are they?" I stood—and though I was barefoot, my nightclothes loose around me, there was no chill upon my skin, so warm was their radiance. "Do not leave me," I begged, stepping nearer to their fantastic heat. But Eglantine continued to sing.

"Tell Mandrik all's right," Clive repeated.

Eglantine finished her song on a single drawn-out note so graceful it split my heart in twain. When her eyes opened, they were brighter and broader than the sky. In her smile was a peace so effortless, so full of love, that her own form could not contain it, and it shone forth, filling the house with its amber glow, and warming the far corners of my heart. My eyes closed briefly, the better to witness this fire within, and when they opened, my siblings, the gods and darlings of my infant heart, stood in a semicircle about me, their luminous feet hovering above the floor, their six pearly hands raised in benediction. The light they shone upon me grew so bright that their forms became like veils, and soon I could see nothing but radiance, before, in, and around me. Nothing but the fire of God. To close my eyes made no difference. The vision was exactly the same.

At once my body knew itself to be in pain, and the sharp sounds of a household awakened to trouble jarred open my ears. I was swaddled. My eyes cast about for a place to rest, and at last found Nurit, remarkably near, her peppermint breath and the shine of her eyeglasses hovering above my nose, her arms tight around the blanket around me.

"Yves," Adelaïda gasped.

"What's this?"

"Yves, you—"

"Are you okay?" Nurit asked. Her thin face was tight with fear, and a deep furrow ran up the center of her brow. "What were you doing?"

The blanket, the sharp tingling in my skin, and the terrible smell all leapt to meaning: I had stepped in the embers. "They were hovering over your bed."

Eli had run out for water from the rain barrel, and now stood with it sloshing gently across the floor. "Is it out? Is everything okay?" he asked.

"That's what they said. That everything's fine."

Eli said, "But I didn't see Ruth."

I looked around; she was absent.

"If you're going to get up in the middle of the night," Adelaïda said, "then wake up before you do it."

"What I saw—" I began, but Nurit was pulling away, pulling back the singed blanket. "Let me see," she said, and leaned close over my legs, inspecting the skin and my toenails. I flinched under her gaze. "It's not so bad, really. A couple of blisters." She coughed as if she might soon spit blood.

Adelaïda dipped a rag in the bucket and wrapped it carefully around my feet. There were heavy black circles around her eyes. "We'll get Mandrik to make you a poultice in the morning. I don't think there's need to fetch him now."

"No, let him rest," I said, though my feet were smarting.

"Eli," Nurit said, "do we have anything in the kit?"

Eli dug through his bag to produce a gleaming white parcel. "Here."

Nurit squeezed something onto her finger, unwrapped my feet, and smoothed the unguent over them. At once the feet began to cool. "Thank you," I said.

Elizaveta peered over the side of her hammock with eyes vast and black as midnight. Nurit stood up next to her and rocked her in her ropes. "Go back to sleep," she said, but Elizaveta continued to stare. "You might really want to move the fireplace, Yves, off to the side of the room, and enclose it, so things—"

Eli said, "Leave him be. You'll ruin Ruth's work."

When my legs were sufficiently tended they all helped me back to bed, and after Adelaïda had fixed up the fire I'd destroyed, she wrapped her sweet body around me to ease the pain. Her flesh was hot. I imagined I could feel the baby pressing against my back, though it was yet surely no more than a wish newly quickened by the breath of God. Eli went out to water the fields, and came back with the cold breath of the night upon him. The mattress responded loudly as he snuggled back under the covers with his warm sister. "They were hovering over you," I told him, despite ʰat I risked sounding mad before two strangers and my wife. "They ga you a blessing."

"I'm glad," he said, as if he, too, could feel the last wisps of their presence clinging to the rafters. "Good night."[1]

Ruth reappeared soon after dawn without a word of explanation, Mandrik a few minutes behind her, having had a premonition that I needed him. He suffered no questions, but inspected my wounds and pro-

---

[1] I left the house the moment everyone fell asleep; I hadn't had a moment since the meeting and my siblings' arrival to talk to Mandrik, and had no idea what he thought of what had happened. It was bitter cold outside, and by the time I reached Mandrik's hut, my extremities were frozen. Nevertheless, I found him sitting on his threshold, his door wide open to the wind. His eyes were closed; when I shouted out his name, he opened them and looked at me crossly. "Don't you know better than to disturb a man in meditation?" he asked. "But of course you wouldn't. You're leaving."

I didn't cry, but I felt as if I might. "I love my brother and sister. I love them as much as you love Yves."

"Then you'll go home with them. Won't you."

"I don't know, Mandrik. I have work to do here."

"Work."

"Can we go inside? It's freezing."

He stood up and led me inside. But he'd left the door open for however long, and the fire had dwindled down to ashes. The cottage was cold. "Doesn't look like I can make you tea," he noted, poking a stick at the embers. "I suppose I'm glad to know it was your work, the only thing keeping you here."

Too much had already happened in the past day, and I was wound up tight. I sat down on the floor, and leaned back into the door to calm myself. The wind blew at me through the cracks. "Don't be this way. I never would have stayed, I never would have kept at this work if I didn't love you, and love Yves, and love the whole village."

"If you love me exactly the same as you love all the townspeople, you'd best be headed home now to pack your things."

His vituperation hurt me, but it pleased me in its way as well. In his anger I saw the truth of the depth of his affection for me; and I could not help basking in that knowledge. I did not know then what would become of us, but I knew that if he had taken me so fully into his heart, I could not be banished from him, banished from this place I loved, by arbitrary turns of events.

nounced them healing well. He applied his own ointment, which smelled more pungent than Nurit's, by way of precaution. Ruth stoked the fire. Whether from its light or from within, she glowed. Elizaveta placed one of Eli's gold earrings on Pudge's head like a halo, but it kept slipping to the floor.

Adelaïda had gotten out of bed and eaten some breakfast with us. She now wound a new ball of red wool onto her shuttle, her back to the room. "We'll have to gather your belongings, Ruth, if you're to be ready to take leave when the time comes."

Ruth lay back across the mattress, a gourdful of peppermint tea on her stomach and her head against the wall. "I haven't come to any decision yet, Adelaïda."

What had looked an ordinary gray sky now breathed forth a drizzle so fine one could only see it in how it veiled the familiar yard beyond the door. Mandrik said, "I need to take a walk."

I looked out upon the dismal weather. "I'll drive you home."

He shook his head. "I don't want to go home, I want to go walking."

"You'll catch your death," Adelaïda said, her back still to us.

"For three years I sailed the world in a paper boat, woman, and now the November mist will kill me?"

"Everyone dies sometime."

Ruth said, "Leave him be."

"Everyone, aye. Yves, leave the cart for your visitors, that they might explore."

"In the rain?"

"Will you walk with me?"

I gestured to my feet.

"The last mud before winter frost is a most beneficial remedy for burns."

Nurit wrinkled her narrow brow, which exactly summed up my feelings on the subject.

Adelaïda said, "I will not have another invalid driving me mad with worry."

My brother's eyes were feverish with urgency. We looked at one another, still as stone, until at last, and despite myself, I said, "I have never yet had reason to doubt your physic," and rose to my tender feet.

"Bundle up about the top, man," he directed, "that the cold on your feet not infect the marrow."

"Madmen," Adelaïda muttered. "Injuring themselves ever, and leaving us to pine."

The household watched me in disbelief as I hobbled about for a knitted vest and my worn hooded cloak. "He fixed her leg, by God— I'm certain he can fix my feet." Even my daughter's eyes looked somewhat less worshipful. My brother's face was still lined with thought. "We'll be back, then."

"Don't be out too long. It sounds like a rotten cure."

"I'll be judge of that," I said, but took my walking stick as a precaution as I hobbled out the door.

Mandrik walked beside me with his gentle hand resting between my shoulder blades, as if I had suddenly gone feeble. I was glad, however, for the gesture of familiar care amid my worries. The mountains all about were shrouded in mist, and even my own barn had lost its sharp outline. The mist had a faint, savory taste when I licked it from my lips, and I lifted my nose to the heavens to divine its origin.

"The sea, of course," Mandrik said. "It's coming in off the sea." I recognized it, that faint, unpleasant odor of salt. As we crossed the road into my loamy northern fields, he said, "The truth is, Yves, it's not a remedy for burns."

"I didn't really believe it was. It doesn't hurt, though, this walking, except for the occasional sharp stone."

His warm hand behind me steered me through the newly seeded rows toward the cairn. "Will the feet hold up until we get there?"

He didn't have to say where we were going. "I imagine so."

Sometimes my land seemed a wilderness—traveling for help in the dead of winter, chasing after a lost sheep one boggy March—but never had it looked more somber and strange. Such weather as this was a warning—to finish sowing, to grind the last of the grain, to stack enough wood for the winter—and demanded that the farmer look past it to what needed to be accomplished. That day, for what felt the first time in my life, I had the luxury of observing the weather simply, not as an impediment to whatever wanted doing, but as itself, as weather. Its somberness astonished me, and wakened fear in my breast, for, in such weather, one could not even see the smoke of one's own chimney a few moments' walk behind. This deadly pallor, I felt certain, was what it would look like at the end of the world.

"To the cairn and back again?" I asked. "Because I don't, in truth, think the feet'll hold longer than that."

"That'll do."

His sandals were so deep in the muck, he, too, might as well have been barefoot. "You wouldn't want exercise if you'd taken the farm."

"Do you chastise me, householder?" His voice broke with a quiet laugh.

"No, no." Each time we fell silent, the mist moved closer in.

"Because I'm glad that you have all this."

"As am I." The landscape before my eyes and the landscape of memory were entirely different from one another, but it did not bother me; it was just, and beautiful, and fine. I raised my face to the salt mist, and closed my eyes, enjoying it on my skin. Strange how, if I were working, such mist would be a hindrance, but with nothing to do but walk and feel it—what beauty, what joy. "Mandrik, when I burned my feet last night, our brothers and sister were there."

"Saying what?"

My throat grew tight to remember. "Beyond the Beyond, she sang, to the Beyond beyond. Over and over."

He nodded. The mist concentrated on the tip of his nose and dripped down into the mud. "And what else?"

"They said to tell you that all was right."

"Why do they send me messages through you?"

"I don't know why. Perhaps you were busy last night in contemplation?"

He closed his eyes briefly. "The dead have their reasons."

"And when I wakened, they and Ruth were both gone." I wished I could feel them hovering about us in that somber air, but there was nothing, nothing.

"I wish I had seen them."

"I wish they had visited you, because I didn't understand what they said. Were you working on your treatise at the time?"

He walked silent, except that his sandals made a sucking sound in the mud. "When I traveled, brother, I know that everyone spoke of my 'wanderings.' But I wasn't wandering. I had my aims."

"I never doubted that," I said, though the Lord knows how bitterly I had doubted his return.

"I don't care for wandering. It implies a want of purpose."

"It is good," I agreed, "to move for a reason."

"Then you know that I have brought you forth today neither for your feet nor for a breath of air."

The mist on my cheeks stung like tears. I licked it, and savored its taste, like tears.

"Ruth will not go home with her brother and sister."

This, then, was what had brought forth the flavor, the secret pain. But I could not grasp his meaning.

"Yves, are you listening?"

"As ever."

"She is not leaving with them."

"Our fondest hopes," I told him, "are not always our due."

He started briefly and examined me, but I had nothing more to say.

At last the cairn reared its tottering head in the distance. Through the mist I felt it beckoning.

"You do not hear me aright. I have asked her not to leave. She is not leaving."

My brow furrowed, each crease chill from the damp. I would hold my tongue until we reached our destination, for pain had begun to rip at my cold feet. Still I felt him straining against the fullness in his breast. I leaned harder into my stick as walking grew more difficult. The pile of stones approached, grew more distinct, showed its colors from leaf brown to deep mottled gray. Some of them—one like an egg, almost rosy in tone, a second for all the world like a shankbone—I could remember placing there in my youth. My wonder never ceased that they did not tumble. Hammadi's smaller mound looked pitiful beside it. The pain in my feet had clearly marked the way I took each step, for there were aches and twinges in my legs the likes of which I had never yet known. Gratefully did I turn my back upon the great somber cairn, sit down upon the wet ground, and lean into the rocks. Below me lay the body of my grandmother, unless she was spirited back to the sea; before me farther than the eye could see, to the edges of eternity, it seemed in such weather, stretched my fecund land, full of seeds to protect it against the coming snow. Mandrik crouched beside me, his joints giving forth cracks at the exertion.

"Yves," he said, "I do not like this silence when I tell you what's in my heart."

Only then did I turn my face full to him. Water ran down his cheeks in rivulets, stuck all but the edges of his curls to his head, turned his cassock darker than the mud. His eyes were full of fire, but mine, I am certain, were blank. "What you're telling me can't be."

He looked out to the rain for answer. "I had no plan ever to—I thought never to relinquish my vows, my life. And yet—"

"There have been rumors about the township, and I have had my doubts, but I chose not to believe them."

"Perhaps you shouldn't have done that."

"Surely you don't—"

"But I love her, Yves." Such words I had never thought to hear issuing from his mouth; they hung on the air like the ringing of distant bells. Had he been a child of sixteen, before his journeys or his visions, how welcome would such words have been; but from a man near thirty, likely close to the end of his natural life, and devoted until then to the pursuits of the spirit, they were unseemly.

"She is a stranger, Mandrik. You know nothing about her but her impertinent questioning. Perhaps they're all like she is. You have no way of knowing."

"Yes, I do." He was not looking at me.

"From the brother and sister?"

"Sure, from them."

I quieted my breath. "And from visions?"

"From visions, yes. And from the world. I have known other people in the world. Her countrymen, her peers."

My heart beat against my breastbone, and all my strength could not restrain it. "But she comes from the west, from the Great Land to the west."

"Yes."

"And you east, in Indo-China—"

"Not exactly. No."

"You—"

"Not to Indo-China, no. To America."

Like a trapped beast did my heart clamor to escape. "You told me of a place you'd never been?"

"I could not—"

"Mandrik," I shouted, then fought to resume control of my voice, "a few days ago I thought you had merely withheld some of the truth, and now it comes to light that you plucked stories from the air? You not only told me nothing of the truth of where you'd been, but made up lies about the world beyond?"

"The stories were better, those that I made up. I told you this, Yves. I've explained this."

"Better than the truth?"

"Yes."

I slapped the ground, raising a muddy splash. "The men in dresses, and the Silk Road paved in brass, and the hookah pipes with their sinister bubble and suck—"

"Based on good authority."

"But none of it seen with your own eyes?" My lungs hardly dared breathe for me; I had to force them along. The sky was opening.

"Nay, brother, none."

Oh, for a loose boulder to crack open his head. "Where were you, then?"

"In America, Yves, in Ruth's country."

"Her city? Did you visit her city?"

"Once, briefly. I did not meet her there."

"In America." My head shook of its own volition. "I cannot believe this."

"And the things I saw there put the Silk Road to shame."

"Then why did you not tell me of them?"

"Had I told you what was true, and how close it was, Yves—I have explained this already—I know you would have gone off, as all the rest are now, after the new life."

"Do you see me running off?"

"Who can say what you—"

"Do you see me running?"

"I had the opportunity to excite your imaginations—all of your imaginations—"

"Mandrik, it's no excuse—"

"Look how you loved the stories. Think how much pleasure they gave you, all mine to bestow."

"You knew of her people. You knew of her world."

"Yes."

"You knew what wonders they possessed—that they could fly in the air."

"I knew this all, Yves. I have flown in the air myself."

"And tell me, brother, can they raise the dead?"

"No, they—"

"Can they bring what has given itself up to God back to the world of the living?"

"They have medicine more advanced than we have, sure. But God's will is God's will ever. Man's desires cannot change that."

"And when Elynour died—"

"Yves, please."

"When Elynour died, you sat by her bedside praying, when all the while you could have run across the hills and brought back someone who might have saved her? Who might have saved my son?"

His mouth opened wide, halfway between a grin and a shout of pain. "No, Yves. No. It was too far. Before the roads were paved, before the new carts, it would have taken four days to get to them, and even then they could have done no more than call to the mainland for assistance."

My head shook back and forth. I could not stop it. "You might have gone before she went into labor."

"No, Yves." He was weeping outright now. "It was God's will. We had no way of knowing how she would suffer. Look you at Adelaïda— she gave birth to Elizaveta without hindrance. How could we have known beforehand what Elynour would suffer?"

"I don't know. You're the one, of any among us, who could have seen the future."

"Yves, stop. I am no medium."

"You killed my wife."

"I did not kill her." He wept bitterly. "I did not kill her. God carried her home. While we wallow in the muck of life and death, she has gone to bliss. Would you deny her that? And think, Yves, had God not called her, you would never have had Adelaïda and Elizaveta. Would you give up that happiness?"

How could I be unfaithful either to the love of my wife or to the memory of her I had lost? "How can I say?"

"Would you give them up?"

My eyes now seeped their own salt, their own deep wound. "No."

His arm reached across me, and for all that I hated him at that moment, hated him more than I hated the darkest demons of Hell, once more I could not resist the draw of him. He knew my weakness, knew how I yearned for the closeness of family. I hid my face in his sleeve, the taste of sweat and dirt and salt rain filling my mouth from the dark fabric.

"My box," I said, surprised that so petty a thought could occur to me at such a moment, "is not from Indo-China?"

"No."

"My brother."

"That hasn't changed."

"It has if I don't know you. It has if you lie to me outright."

"Ruth will be my wife, Yves."

I pulled away. "Oh, Christ, this is too much."

"Why? It's what any other man would do."

"She's not—"

"If Stanislaus won't marry us, then we'll marry ourselves."

I wanted to bite him. "Damn you, Mandrik."

"Why do you turn against me?" I had not heard his voice raised in ages, and I took note. "Is it not hardship enough that in all of the village I shall be outcast and made mock of, that as often as they have ever reviled me they will revile me a hundred times more?"

"They have not reviled you, because you were holy, Mandrik, because you were blessed." My voice scraped against my straining throat. "Do you know what you do?"

"Yes."

"I don't think you do."

"I know full well."

"Your life will not be the same. All of your vows, for nothing. All of your writing, and healing—"

"Why can't I do all of that with a wife?"

"Because no one will trust you any longer."

"The small-minded may turn against me—"

"Everyone will turn against you."

"Even you, my brother?"

As gentle as the rain came my soft answer: "I cannot yet say."

The cairn stretched up to Heaven behind.

"Yves, you are my only brother. If you love me half as dearly as I love you, you love me well. And I know you care for Ruth, that her presence in your home has pleased you. So why do you turn against us if she stays?"

The mist began to thicken into droplets, which trickled down upon us from the rocks. "Because my Elynour is rotting beneath the sod while we sit here amid all the blessings and curses of the living."

He drew a long breath. "I thought you would be glad Ruth wasn't leaving."

I startled myself by making a sound less human than animal, deep back in my throat. "Have you any idea how dearly I loved her?"

"Yes, Yves, I believe I do."

"Mandrik."

"I know you love Ruth. I know you will be happy she stayed."

I scanned his blue eyes, dark against the rain. "I love you both. It murders me to watch what's becoming of you."

"I have not changed. I have only found someone with whom I wish to share my home." He watched me for a reply, but I had none. "Yves, you must understand that. You must have longed for release from your solitude before I brought you Adelaïda."

"Yes, but it's different."

"Why?"

"And how long have you—"

"Since first she came, I suppose. Though I did not know she reciprocated until well into the summer."

Whether from my feet or the general circumstance, I felt certain I'd be ill. "I don't want to know about it."

"I want you to be glad of this, Yves."

"After you have lied to me and to everyone we know. After you allowed my Elynour to die."

"I did not—"

"After you have debased and defiled yourself with an utter stranger."

"Why does it defile me to do what all of you have always done?"

"Why did you reject it in the first place, then?"

"I have had more time for meditation than any man in this village. It has borne its fruit, and led me to this happiness. Do not begrudge me it."

"Tell me how you will look after a wife, man? I've looked after her this half year by the sweat of my brow."

"I can manage her."

"She would have died."

"Brother," he said, looking at the ground, "give me your blessing. For among everyone else I will no doubt be a mockery from now on. If, indeed, anyone is left here at all."

My throat burned despite the chill. I wanted to curl into sleep and wake to find myself a lad, one child among many, restlessly waiting for the winter to be over that we might all run outside. "All my life I have been proud," I began, "to have such a brother as you; I have been proud of what you chose to make of yourself. What have I to be proud of now?"

"That you will have her, still, and all her wit and work? That you'll have nieces and nephews to carry on your name?"

"An ignominy."

"You will be glad when you realize—"

"What about her family? They are too gentle to force, but they have come to ask her to go back among them. What will they think? How will they feel?"

He could not answer right away, for another man's feelings always seem less immediate than one's own. "They will return with her assurances that she and I, together, will go some time later."

"No." I felt that I could not move my limbs, which was only in part a consequence of the cold. "I will not have you leave again."

"Not forever."

"I forbid it."

"Yves, listen to what you're saying."

"For three long years I looked to the heavens each morning, scanning them for a portent, some sign, asking if you made your way among the living. They said nothing. Three long years they held their silence—and how I wept and prayed that I not be left alone, and all along believed that you were drowned."

"You had your wife."

"So shortly to die. And a stranger compared to the one last person I had known all my life. After all our family had left me, I would not have you leave, too." This cairn, the bodies beneath the churchyard, would never have sufficed, despite my siblings' visits. "I will not have you go."

"And exile my wife from her people the rest of her days?"

"She may leave tomorrow if she so desires. They are here to take her back. If she chooses not to go with them, so be it."

"Yves, listen to yourself."

"I have no pity for her."

"Perhaps you will visit the world with us, and we will all return, together."

"I don't know who you've become, Mandrik."

I listened to his breath a few moments, the miracle of his lungs filling and emptying. "No one," he said. "Nothing has changed but my happiness."

And in that I knew how much had changed—how different these fields would be as I walked back than they had been a few moments past. Everything, indeed, had changed, down to the rain and the soil.

"We should go back," he said, each joint in his body cracking again as he stood. "There'll be a great lot of explaining to do."

I did not care to move. Better to remain leaning against the rocks as my father had done before me, dreaming of his beautiful mother, her dark hair rippling like the waves. Better to look out at the land, knowing that the labor it required of me would someday kill me. What awaited me in my house and village I did not care to imagine. If it was my fault, this change, I would have given my teeth to retract it.

"You can't stay here," he said. "It's cold."

I decided to follow him back. I rose up on my haunches and, leaning on my stick, straightened slowly, painfully reassuming the shape of a man. Without turning, I gave a brief pat to the slippery rocks behind me, and silently bade Iulia make note of all that had passed. My feet, near frozen, yet had the sense to pain me. With the sky bleak and gray, we began our journey home.

These fields mattered nothing at all. For my grandfather they had reached to the outmost edges of the world, the boundaries of the wilderness—past them was nought but the imagination, and the blessed sea which had brought him his bride. Perhaps in the winter I would fashion a harness to work two horses as a team, and come spring buy a second horse to relieve some of the burden from foul-tempered Enyadatta. The work of the farm would vanish beneath my gaze. With practice, I could spit to the far edge of what I owned.

"You needn't be so angry at me," he said, his sandals sucking into the mud with a sound that filled me with despair.

"I will give you half this land," I said, and listened in wonder as the words hung in the air between us.

"I expected some other reply."

"Half the land. If between us we cannot make do, we can buy from Frith his portion, if he does not first die from the shock of your actions. And if still we cannot make do, we will have to go westward, with our countrymen."

"Think you, after so many years of meditation, I could once again learn to farm?"

"What's to learn?" I asked him. "You work the land, and she provides." To think of such a stranger bearing a child with my name—a tall, spindly being, whose mother would coo in her native accent—gave me pause, and a strange thrill.

"I have work yet to do, Yves. And I won't take your land."

"They won't let you live on handouts anymore."

"Still and all."

"If what you predict is true, they won't be here anyway. There won't be farms here anymore. So what will your disgrace matter?"

"Don't talk of it."

Every inch of us was sodden when we returned to the house; we let off steam at the fire. It was strange to see my household as ever it was—full now of strangers, but functioning, loom and cooking pots working, child carding on the ground, her brown eyes intent upon her wooden comb. My blessed daughter—how could I ever have thought that I might rather have had some nameless, mysterious son, ten years now in the soil, than this miracle, Elizaveta, now before my eyes?

"Yves," my wife said, dropping the shuttle to the ground and trying to avoid the puddles I made on her clean dirt floor.

"My feet feel better." It was a foul, insinuating rain; I did not like how it smelled in my clothes.

"Off with it all." She held a sheet at the ready while I stripped to the skin. I felt a moment's awkwardness before the strangers, but could not make allowance for their modesty. Adelaïda rubbed me down like a child after a bath. She had completed my new warm shirt, which I accepted gratefully, and provided the patched pants in which I worked in the foulest weather. Mandrik still stood dripping and steaming by the fire. "You're next," Adelaïda said, holding the damp sheet out. He cast his eyes down as he stepped out of the puddling sandals and disrobed. Did Ruth long to dry him? Did she feel it her right and her due? Nurit and Eli busily looked down—only she looked up without shame. I had little else in the way of clothing to offer my brother, so I gave him my good trousers and a sweater knit from the dark wool of Chornaya and Flick, which he accepted gratefully. Adelaïda combed our wet hair back behind our ears. Standing in an ordinary man's gray trousers and warm knit, he looked like an ordinary man—smoother of hand and of skin than a farmer, but elsewise unmarked. It had been a lifetime since I had seen him without the garb of a holy man, and the vision made me nervous. I watched Ruth watch, which made me more nervous still. Adelaïda brought forth last winter's woolen stockings for us. Burns on my feet or no, I was glad of the warmth. "I imagine you're hungry again? I've got breakfast's porridge, and bread. Perhaps you'll kill a hen for supper, Yves, by way of farewell to our guests."

"Please," Nurit said, "don't do it on our account," and tucked at her neat hair thrice.

Ruth, mopping up the floor with a rag, had obviously not told them a thing.

"We don't want you to think we've been feeding your sister on porridge all these months," Adelaïda said. In truth we had been, but I could see her point.

"Let's eat, then," I said. "I've work to do this afternoon."

Ruth cleaned the table of accumulated debris. Adelaïda, whose sourness hung about the room in the smoke, filled motley bowls and handed out spoons, and they all gathered around. But two bites of the slick substance had not been swallowed before Mandrik, his eyes cast down, said, "Do we not have something to discuss?"

Ruth's tongue tried to work the stubborn food down her gullet as she examined her family's faces. Their dark, innocent eyes reminded me of Elynour's, and I shivered.

"You can't be catching cold now," my wife said, "or you'll be in bed all winter."

"I'm not ill," I said.

"You're shivering."

Ruth put her hand on top of her sister's, and with all the subtlety of the day's now drenching rain, said, "I've decided for certain that I'm not going back with you tomorrow."

Nurit smiled St. Perpetua's patient smile. "Is there anything we can say to change your mind?"

"I don't think so. Mandrik asked me to marry him. I said yes."

Adelaïda's jaw nearly dislodged from her face. Nurit and Eli both turned toward the accused, who blushed hot as Hellfire and would not return their gaze. Eli picked at the jewel in his left ear, and Nurit fell into so long and frenzied a fit of coughing that my wife, despite her overall lack of sympathy for the strangers, began to rub her back.

"Does either of you want to congratulate me?"

Eli gave his sister a cup of water, and her cough quieted.

Ruth said, "Are you okay?"

Nurit nodded. Her eyes were red from coughing. She took off her eyeglasses to wipe her face on her sleeve. "Mandrik," she said, "I hope you'll excuse me if in any way I'm being disrespectful, but, Ruth, are you sure you've thought this through?"

"What do you mean?"

"I mean, are you sure you've thought this through."

Ruth shrugged her shoulders. "It's not about thinking."

Eli said, "But you know what she means."

"This is not— Ruth, how will we explain this to our father?"

"From the beginning I told you I might well stay."

"But staying to finish your research is different from staying forever."

Ruth shook her head. "Don't you think Dad will be happy that one of us is finally getting married?"

"I don't think this is what he had in mind." Nurit's face was pinched as if she'd tasted a poisonous plant. "Ruth, this will be a difficult life."

"In what way?"

"In terms of bare survival." Her eyes swung anxiously around my home. "Look around you, Ruth. This is not the lap of luxury."

Eli put out his hand toward me. "Please excuse her if she's—"

"No," I said, "I understand," though in truth it wounded me that in her eyes my life should look so stark.

"Nurit, when did I ever want money, or a big house, or anything?"

"Never, Ruth. But there's a difference between not having a big engagement ring and having to chop your own wood so you don't freeze to death."

Mandrik said, "I will take care of her to the best of my ability."

Nurit, her eyes still red and wet, held one hand up. In the mist the chimney wouldn't draw, and the room was smoky. Her breath wheezed in her chest. "This will not be an easy life. This will not be the life you grew up with."

I had been right, then, in my assumption.

"I know that."

"Ruth," Eli asked gently, "will this make you happy?"

"Yes."

"Are you sure?"

"When was I ever happy? Will you tell me that?"

Her brother and sister watched in a thick silence.

"After Mom died? Was I supposed to be happy after that, when I couldn't swing it before? I never knew why I was doing what I was doing. I never had a passion for anything. And then she died and she sucked my life empty like a vacuum. Now here I am, with a life that means something to me, a purpose, and a person, people, I love. Should I abandon all that?"

All of us, then; she loved us all.

Eli said, "It was only a question."

"It was not only a question, Eli. Because the truth is that until I came here I never took a moment's joy, a moment's pleasure. I was never happy. Because I was doing what everyone wanted me to do and I never checked to see if I meant it."

Mandrik was rapt in her speaking; her brother and sister looked somber. Nurit said, "Mom would want you to be happy."

"Yes," Ruth said. "And she would want me to finish this work before it's too late."

"It may be," Mandrik said quietly, "too late already."

Elizaveta pulled at my woolen sleeve. "Where's Roof going?"

"Eat your lunch," Adelaïda commanded. I whispered, "Nowhere. She's staying here." Her whole tiny body breathed a sigh. What had we done, taking this woman into our home?

"You know how to find me here. If you want to come see me, perhaps next summer, well and good. Maybe I'll go back with you, with Mandrik, so he can meet Dad."

Said Eli, "L'shana haba'a," and I knew not what he meant.

"You tell Dad I'm sorry. Tell him I'll see him as soon as I can."

Nurit muttered, "There's nothing I can say to you. There's no good argument except I want you back."

Ruth put her arm around her sister's neck and ran her fingers through her lovely black hair. "I wish I could be with you and be with Mandrik both. But I can't."

"I don't want to lose you."

"You're not. It's something else."

Despite my confusion, I felt glad that Ruth would still be around to talk to.

"Please don't think," Nurit said, "that I disapprove. I know you must be making the right decision. It's hard to get used to, that's all."

"Nurit, I have work to do; I'm marrying someone I love. There is nothing more I could ask for."

Nothing was settled, in truth, but we ate our lunch without the cold, hard feeling in our stomachs which makes it so difficult to enjoy a repast. Two generations ago, who would have thought of enjoying food? One scraped survival from the hostile land, and nothing more. If it wasn't rotten, one ate it, in whatever way it was most expedient to cook. Now how accustomed were we to bounty that something as intangible as a bad mood could spoil our digestions? We were becoming pansies all, drooping at the slightest adversity of weather.

Come morning, these two intruders would be gone, borne away to a world I could not even truly picture. Until my neighbors returned from their journey, which was also beyond my imaginings, all would be as ever it had been on my farm, and then would come the changes. But I was ready for them, ready to stand my ground against them.

CHAPTER NINE

THE BONE-COLD WINTER

t was new moon that evening. There was no mistaking the blackness. The sun went down like a rock into Maundering Stream, and the night offered not even one star in the dome of the sky. From the house I could hear the cow, Sophronia, nattering to her hay, but I could not see the barn. Ruth had been out with brother, sister, cart and horse since after lunch, and though I knew I could trust her with beast and vehicle, I worried for her. Even with brakes, accidents may befall one, as my feet attested. She had learned but halfheartedly the charms and spells to keep off danger; and now if it came to her, how could she defend herself? Strangers, who don't know the ways of the land and the names of its spirits, must seem succulent prey. No sound, however, came up the road as Adelaïda whisked her shuttle back and forth through the loom and Elizaveta untangled her wool. Elizaveta glowed with the heat of the fire, but my wife looked ill. It would be as long a winter as any in memory if she took sick; and I with the child to care for.

If the village to the west could make the winter shorter, I would be glad Dirk had discovered it.

Adelaïda crossed her arms over the warp, and rested her head upon them. The strings, already pulled taut, bowed down. Her wound braids were golden, but the fire did not afford them their usual sheen. "I suppose it's a son," she said, smiling my way, "because a daughter wouldn't give me so much grief."

"Please don't be sick."

"Daughters do as they're told—marry who they're told to, cook, weave, and bear children all their lives without complaint. Sons are willful."

"Some daughters are, too," said I, thinking of Ruth.

The color began, at last, to rise in her one visible cheek, and to flower like a bruise. "It's not women who leave and yearn."

But I did not know what she meant—surely my wife, as I, had spent the last two days watching our visitor do exactly the thing she described, wreaking disappointment even in her venerable father across the sea. "Adelaïda," I asked, placing what felt a broad and clumsy paw across her shoulder, "would you like some tea? Or a sip of cold water?"

"Water," she said. "Thank you."

Out in the brisk night, blacker than pitch, the water barrel had crusted with ice. I cracked it with the bowl and looked into the yawning darkness. A fine drop of rain fell upon my nose, then another upon my cheek. It was dour weather. I brought Adelaïda the chill rainwater, which steamed near the fire; she raised her head from the loom to accept it, her face now redder than the embers.

"Help me spin," Elizaveta said, dangling a spindle from its thread as it wandered back and forth in its natural arc.

"Later." Adelaïda waved a finger at the useless tool. "Yves, can you show her how?"

"I don't know how."

"Papa doesn't know how?"

My wife nodded, her lips pursed tight. "They pave roads and go racing along them, but they can't make yarn."

Enyadatta's clop came up the road, and quieted as she trod the damp dirt of the yard. Ruth shouted the beast's name as she pulled on the brakes, and her voice boomed out over the empty valley, over the machine's dull screech. Their harsh accents filled the air, as one body jumped off the cart and the other two, less boisterously, climbed.

Within the house, Adelaïda had set the chicken to roast in the embers, then returned to bed. Nurit and Eli began to gather and sort their things—which belonged to whom, and who would carry what, and what would be left behind for their sister's succor. I liked that they thought she could be looked after by things in bright packages.

"Did Stanislaus go with the rest of his parishioners over the mountains?" I asked.

Ruth said, "His cottage looks deserted."

My stomach gripped. "But tomorrow is the Lord's Day."

They all exchanged glances. Eli said, "Maybe they'll be back tonight."

I was coming to like Eli's way, his gentleness, but I did not believe him. "This will be the first Sunday in all my life I have not gone to hear the word of the Lord."

"Nay," said Adelaïda from the bed. "In times of trouble, with plagues and maladies, one never goes."

"The first ordinary Sunday, then."

My wife said, "But it will be no ordinary Sunday."

I stirred the pot of broth that was boiling over the fire. "I should have liked to show the visitors our church. I should have liked them to meet our brethren."

Nurit said, "If we come back again, we'll meet them."

But however things might be if they came back again, things would not be as they were then.

After we ate our quiet supper I stripped to my underdrawers and crawled in beside my wife, whose wonderful body threw as much heat as the blazing fire. I heard them scuffling about the house a while more, removing their shoes and trinkets, then settling in against one another like piglets. Ruth would not leave with them, I reminded myself, yet surely some of her would—some part of her I, and my life on this farm, could never know. Long past the hour when everyone's breathing— even Nurit's—had quieted and evened out, I lay awake, listening to the fire. With all this family about, I expected my sister and brothers to make their appearance; but I watched, to my knowledge, the whole of the night, and heard nothing but the slow shifting of the burning logs, and the brash wind outdoors, which chased every last breath of autumn from our midst.

The morning dawned gray; the air, when I hurried outside for more wood, felt thick. The ordinary sounds of morning were softened by the heavy blanket of cloud. In such dampness the fire took its time to draw, and our visitors, on the threshold of waking, instinctively burrowed deeper under their bright blankets. I thought of Hammadi, beneath the earth, of how even on the coldest mornings she had stamped her forefoot with happiness to see me, and had blown twin streams through her nostrils in anticipation. I thought of my father, who had paid no heed to the cold: "Weather's weather," he often enough told me, "and work is work." I was sour before the sun was full up because my toes smarted with cold. I was neither of their equal. Both of them were rotting, giving themselves up to the ground.

Adelaïda was hot as coals, and could not get out of bed for vomiting in the slop pot. "Don't you remember?" she whispered. "It was like this half the time Elizaveta was inside me. It's no cause for worry."

But in truth, though I could remember a few weeks' indisposition, she had seemed to me then as robust as ever. "Even so," I said, "I'll make breakfast."

"Don't burn Ruth's bread until she wakes. She doesn't like it cold."

I put on the kettle and sliced the bread. Before long, my housework woke them. They huddled around the fire in their blankets, and waited for their broth to grow hot.

Nurit said, "Ruth, I'm worried about you here all winter, snowed in. I'm not sure it's safe."

"Come on," Ruth said, tackling her as one would tackle a lamb to earmark. "It'll be an adventure." Ruth pulled on two pairs of stockings before she laced her boots.

"Promise me you'll come home. You don't have to say when, but sometime."

"I can't promise anything. But I mean to."

Eli began to encase himself in layers of clothing.

"Do you want us to send you anything? Coffee? I'll leave you our toothpaste."

"Send it how?"

Nurit peered up the chimney. "What am I thinking? I wish you had a phone."

"We should go as soon as we can," Eli said. "We should try to get as far as we can by nightfall."

"And you know how to get back?"

"We marked our trail."

I stuffed her bread into her bread burner, ruining the crusts. "I can take you in the cart to the foot of the hills."

"Would you?" asked Eli, and Ruth said, "It would be a great help, but if you have work to do I can see them off myself."

"It would be my pleasure and my duty both."

We all continued to bundle into our clothes. Elizaveta hung over the edge of her hammock, whimpering to be let down. Once I had freed her, I went to hitch Enyadatta, who was furious at having to work in such dank weather. She kept turning her proud head from one side to the next, but I could not grant her wish and release her from labor. "It'll soon enough be spring," I said, but she was not Hammadi; she did not understand the kindly import of human speech.

Within, when I returned, they were all finishing their toast. I could see them out in the great world, a lanky, dark-haired clan, burning their bread before they'd eat it, among their strange neighbors. I could not bring myself to taste the delicacy, but Elizaveta was finishing a slice slathered in Mandrik's plum jam. "Are you coming with us?" I asked her.

She waved her sticky fingers in the air, a private dance. "Is Roof going?"

Ruth squatted facing her, a damp rag in hand. "I'm not going. Nurit and Eli are going."

Elizaveta shied from the cleaning, but could not escape; and her face relaxed, now that she was assured that she would not be left alone with her parents.

Ruth wrapped the child until she could hardly move, then muffled and cloaked herself. Eli, in the meanwhile, had broken a length of red wool from the shuttle. He strung his two gold rings upon it, then tied it round Elizaveta's throat.

"Eli," Ruth said.

"No, she likes them. I want her to have them. Don't lose those, okay? They're special."

Elizaveta gave a solemn nod. The string looked a strange talisman, but there was no mistaking the rapture on the child's face as she stroked her bejeweled breastbone. I said, "Eli, thanks," and was surprised to feel a choking in my throat, that even thus, even in the body, would their presence have marked us.

"Godspeed," Adelaïda said, her eyes still closed, "and a safe journey to the other side."

They waved her farewell. I kissed my wife's warm forehead. Laden with a lifetime's supplies, they mounted the cart.

I turned to look at them. Already their thin faces seemed familiar, and now I would have to store them up for who knew how long. "From where do you depart?"

Eli pointed to the eastern ridge.

Ruth said, "That's how I came, too."

"You must have sent us a sign," he said.

The sun was veiled behind the promise of a thick snow.

As Enyadatta tore, despite her foul mood, along the road, I looked back occasionally to see how they fared, and their dark heads were bowed nearly to the floorboards. Still, when I caught Eli's eye, he looked happy.

Enyadatta slowed as we reached St. Perpetua; who knew if she knew it was Sunday. "Perhaps," I called back to them, "we should pay our respects at the house of the Lord, to bring you a safe journey."

"Do you think it's okay to go in?" Ruth asked. "I mean, if Stanislaus isn't there."

"The church does not belong to Stanislaus."

Eli said, "I would like that."

I hitched Enyadatta to the post nearest the door, and she looked anxiously about her for her kin. But there would be no other horses coming. A fox ran daintily across the road, a sparrow hanging limp in its mouth.

The sanctuary door creaked open on its hinges when Ruth pushed it. Inside there was no fire burning, and no candles were lit. Some of the finest of the frescoes were lost in the gloom. Even so, and despite the chill, Nurit drew in her breath in rapture.

"Can you see at all?" I asked her.

"They're beautiful."

"That's who everyone says I look like," Ruth said, pointing.

"Your sister, too," I said.

Nurit said, "She looks like Aunt Rose," and, at Ruth's wavering assent, turned to me and said, "who Ruth was named for."

Even in the darkness my grandmother watched us—or her eyes watched us, though it was clear from her expression that her heart dwelt on greater things. Her eyes watched the two slender young women who had come from as far off as she, and brought as many wonders. I sat down on our bench, and Ruth sat beside me. A bird's wings tittered against the rafters. "God grant them a safe journey," I whispered, "and grant us all peace."

Ruth's foot traced an arc in the dust, and the church fell silent.

"Shall we send them on their way?" I asked.

She nodded. We closed the door carefully behind us, and re-mounted the cart.

The Great Meadow past the grove was brown as its dust, a pale, windswept brown that did not promise fecundity. Without the thrumming of insects, now, it afforded a profound quiet.

"I guess we should say goodbye now," Nurit said, once we all stood again on the ground, "but I don't want to."

The wind crackled in the dry grass.

Ruth said, "I hope it won't snow."

Eli scanned the sky as a hawk tracks its prey. "We're fine. We brought warm things."

"If you say so."

Nurit nodded, her brow pinched tight.

Ruth grabbed her sister and buried her head in her shoulder. Eli wrapped his arms around them both. I would have given my house and all my lands to have held my siblings thus once more, and my throat grew tight with longing.

"I will miss you so much," Ruth said, her voice thick.

"We'll miss you," Nurit answered, patting down Ruth's loose hair.

Eli said, "We'll try to visit you when the weather breaks."

They pulled apart enough to extend their palms to me. "Thank you," Eli said. "Thank you for looking after our sister."

"It has made my heart glad," I said, and it began to feel true.

They held each other long—for despite their saying, despite their promises for the spring, they surely knew how weak are such promises against the power of God's will.

They hoisted their great sacks up onto their shoulders, and Ruth followed them to the foot of their trail. I crouched behind Elizaveta, one arm across her chest, my hand gripping her tiny left fist, which held fast to the jewel at her throat. They turned to wave farewell, and Ruth blew a kiss on her fingertips. The sound of their boots on the pine needles and leaves was lonely and quiet. Ruth's hair and cloak blew softly back from her body in the gathering breeze. Nurit and Eli were already disappearing into the autumn forest, but Ruth stood with her right arm raised in farewell. "Goodbye," she called. The trees all but swallowed the sound; there was snow coming, sure. From what sounded a great distance came the voices of her siblings in answer, "Goodbye. We love you." As they disappeared from sight, Elizaveta, too, raised her right arm and thrust the heel of her dimpled palm toward their receding figures. She was too young to know the difference between a gesture of farewell and a gesture of pushing away, and her small, fat hand hovered on the borderland in between. Ruth kept shouting goodbye, her tone halfway between elation and grief. I imagined them overlooking our valley as Dirk had meant to, watching our farms and the whole circumference of our world pull away. I could see our dead grass, the snow at the peaks of the mountains all around. I could imagine them looking down upon Ruth's figure, growing smaller as they withdrew, and in contrast, my daughter, with one hand grasping and one hand raised, her gesture to send them off into the world, her hail and farewell.

That night, as the first flurries of snow fell like a baby's breath across the countryside, the people of Mandragora returned home. They had tied the clappers fast within their bells, but I heard the hooves and the iron tires making their slow way along the road. When I could contain my curiosity no longer, I opened the door, and Elizaveta stood shivering beside me, and waved as our neighbors approached. The Archduke's tent, preceded by torches, led the procession and halted at my yard. I walked forth to greet him, and the shining orange draperies were aglow from a candle within. "Gundron," he called, as one of the silent musicians roped back the draperies.

"Your Urbanity."

His body was wrapped in speckled furs. "Gundron, I have seen a land unlike anything I have ever imagined, a place so wonderful that I desire to make it my own. I will bring the far village under the dominion of Nnms. To which end I appoint you to the post of Court Inventor, that you might leave off this dirt-scratching and devote your energies to refining the machinery of war." His face beamed encouragement.

"It is a great honor, but I am a farmer, sir. I cannot leave my land."

"Farm? Nay, none of your brethren will farm any longer. Think it over, will you?"

"Aye."

"Hut, then," he called to his men, who bound him up again in his shining cocoon, and led forth the procession once more.

Ydlbert's cart was among the last, and he turned up my yard and stopped near the door.

"What news?" I asked him, as he, Anya, and three of the smaller boys wearily crossed my doorstep.

"The world," he said, "is full of wonders."

I offered Ydlbert's family some broth. In his hand Fatoush held a white, bulbous thing Ydlbert said made light when twisted into a hole shaped to it. Fatoush commenced digging a place for it in the hard floor, and Elizaveta sat by, entranced but holding tight to her own treasure.

I said, "Tell me."

"It is as Dirk said, and Mandrik. They have machines that wash the clothes and dishes. They eat off plates whiter than the driven snow. Their carts drive about with no horses. Truly they have much that we may envy."

Anya said, "Fares Adelaïda no better?" She took a wet rag to her friend's bedside and mopped down her brow. "Sakes, she's hot as an adulterer's confession."

"Yves," Ydlbert said, "the people of that village are not our lifelong friends but, after our first bewilderment wore off, they seemed kind enough. They seemed ordinary folk like we, but with an easier way of living. You might like them. And you know you were sorely missed."

"That village isn't going anywhere."

"But to make a first impression without Mandragora's finest—we would have been glad for your company, that's all."

I did not like looking at him. I did not like him liking their proximity.

Elizaveta wrested the toy from Fatoush, who took it back with such force that it shattered upon the ground. Both children commenced wailing, and Ruth hurried with the broom to chase the shards outside.

"For some reason, this all makes me sick at heart."

"I can see that," said my oldest friend. "But you've no reason."

Elizaveta, angry at the loss of her friend's toy, lunged forth to grab him by the throat, so that it took both my strength and Ruth's to pry them apart. I handed Fatoush to his father, and Ruth held my daughter.

"Too much is changing, Ydlbert. In the time you've been gone, Ruth's family came to pay a visit from beyond, and our stranger herself is become betrothed to my brother."

Ydlbert's eyebrows raised. "To our Chouchou? Our own man of God?"

"Indeed."

He shook his head. "Then things are changing even faster than I knew."

"Aye."

"Before the Lord's Day next, our brethren across the hills will, if the weather permits, come hither, that they might see how we live, and we might open our doors to them in hospitality. I want you to join with us when we greet them. Will you?"

All this made me want to lie down dead. Ruth, rocking the child in her arms, also wore a furrow in her brow.

"Both of you," Ydlbert said, dandling his son upon his knee, "stop looking like the world is come to its end. Are you worried for the winter?"

I shrugged my shoulders and, when I realized it was a fair enough assessment, said, "I suppose."

"We'll work double time now we're home. Unless you've got some inventing that needs looking after?"

"There's nothing more to invent."

"Not," Anya said, "when they've a machine to do the washing."

He gathered his sniveling son to his breast and stood. "I will try you again, before the day dawns."

Anya said, "If Adelaïda needs my help, run forth to fetch me."

As they left, I felt I had lost him.

The next morning, Adelaïda would not even bid me good morning, so deep was her fever. I drove out to fetch Mandrik, who regarded me shyly, as if I might be wild. "It's no use worrying about anything now," I told him as he climbed up on the seat of the cart. "As our father would have told you, trouble's trouble, and what's done is done."

When the bells rang out for Prime, their sound dull under the malignant sky, we were well ensconced at home. My brother had brought a multitude of herbs for Adelaïda's fever, and some dried plums for her delectation. Ruth gathered eggs and cooked them in a skillet, flavored with herbs from Mandrik's provender. The days were growing palpably shorter as Midwinter's Eve drew nigh.

That day it felt as if the sun began to set before it had risen fully in the sky. As the dusk descended mid-afternoon, the sky at last broke open and thick clumps of snow began to fall. I stuck my head outdoors repeatedly to check it would not impede my progress to the barn, but each flake hovered like a dragonfly above the ground, then melted straight away. "God grant that your brother and sister reach their boat in safety," I said, seeing Ruth's face pinched with worry.

"God grant," she said, and turned to regard the fire.

Mandrik had brought, along with the herbs that cooled my wife, a new portion of his treatise from which to read. Elizaveta paid him no mind, and twisted two strings together by hand, since she had not yet learned to spin. I kept trying to draw my attention to her, to rejoice in her innocent nature, for when I did not I had to see Mandrik straddling the bench and Ruth leaning against him—her back to his heart, his arms around her holding the fresh sheaf—and my stomach performed an intricate, unpleasant dance. Adelaïda, in bed, could hardly have noticed, but I did not like the shape of things to come.

"New work?" I asked him. "Won't you have to give that up, now that you're become ordinary?"

"A wife," Mandrik said, "need not make me a layman."

In my own house he said such things. "I thought your vows and your work were one thing and the same."

Elizaveta looked up expectantly, as if she understood, but I knew she couldn't.

"You were mistaken. Do you want to hear what's new, or should I put you to bed with a pipe?"

Ruth said, "You're not going home in this weather," though the ground was nought worse than damp.

"There's a great lot you have yet to learn about winter," Mandrik said. "Shall I read you what I've brought?"

"Lift my heart to God," I said, and the fire crackled its assent.

Mandrik fingered the papers briefly—the sensual pleasures thereof had always been one of his profession's great draws. He licked his teeth and swallowed.

"Mother Church," he began, "teaches that, after death, the Soul departs the body, which returns to the Dust from which it came. The soul, unfettered, ascends to God in Heaven; or if it did ill in the body, plummets to Hell, or whiles away the millennia in Purgatory, atoning for its poor behavior. On the day of Judgment, at the end of time, the bodies will be called forth from the ground in Rapture, and, all their decrepitude and decay set to right, will become as one again with their respective souls; and Each, body and soul together (as in life, but this time perfect), will come before the Prime Mover one last time, either to be accepted into a Bliss beyond Measure, Time, and History, or to be cast out into Darkness and Misery so deep and so profound that no mere mortal may entertain notion of its Terrors.

"All of this strikes me, not only as a bore, but as a colossal Waste of Time. Compared to Eternity, a human life is a shorter span than it takes to blow the cotton from a Dandelion. Is it not a spectacular squandering of Effort, then, for God to make so many and such intricate human lives, that each might end before the Flower of its possibility might bloom? Far wiser, does it seem to me, the Oriental notion that souls sojourn in the heavens after death, only to be returned, unbeknownst to them, to new and different bodies, that they might, therein, continue to learn the lessons they require. Far more economical, on God's part, to reuse the spirits again and again throughout history, rather than to waste his breath each time two drunken Children, fumbling in the dark, create another child. Far easier to look about the Denizens of Heaven, and condemn one, for whatever reason, to toil, snort, and suffer once more among some group of the living. For each of us, this Doctrine supposes, is Heaven assured—we must simply work the dirt of human life until we are wise enough to attain it.

"Many a time, listening to Father Icthyus, Father Stanislaus, and the countless Clerics I have witnessed on my journeys, I have wondered at this insistence upon the sanctity of flesh. What matters this dust and water, any more than matters the dust in which we seed our crops? We could not grow food without it, so we must praise God for his Providence in giving it to us; yet we give it hardly another thought. Just so must we learn to view these bodies. Just so must we look past the illusion of their solidity to those truths they actually contain."

He looked up to see how we fared. "Do you think it good, Yves?"

I shook my head. "Beautiful as always, but, you know, man—blasphemous."

"But you think it beautiful?"

"As lovely as the first crocus in spring. But hardly the same treatise. You keep changing the treatise."

"On the contrary. The sixty-first chapter."

"I think it's good work," Ruth said.

Because, I thought, you're the instigator, but I said nothing.

"What's the trouble?" he asked.

My heart was once again thumping. "One of these days, Stanislaus will call down the wrath of Heaven upon you."

My brother said, "Perhaps he already has. What little we know, after all, of the infinite. I'm asking you what you think of this."

"It isn't gloomy, like the other parts. I don't like it."

He read to us throughout the evening, until the late night when the valley lay cloaked in silence. When we went out together to tuck away the animals for the night, a fine snow was falling, easing the transition between yard and field, giving bulk to the nude and shivering trees. "What do you suppose our neighbors are thinking?" I asked him, pitchfork in the fragrant hay. I hated that he helped me in this labor; it gave me less excuse to harbor anger against him.

"Of the new life to come. Of the life of splendor and ease."

"I wish I could turn their minds against it."

"Aye. But it's too late now."

I stopped shoveling and leaned against the tool. The bleating sheep arrived at a respectful silence. "We could be wrong. You and I, from stubbornness, could be missing the most miraculous events to befall our people in generations."

"But I don't think we are."

"Nor do I."

The later snows are always the terrible snows, both in their intensity and in the havoc they wreak upon the roads when they melt—though paving stones, I felt certain, would mark this winter out from those before. This first snow of the year was gentle, hesitant as a newborn foal, which must first find its footing before it can gambol about the barnyard. It fell, the first snow, in wet, thick flakes, and slowly worked its soft ministration to the landscape.

When morning dawned, the air was fine and crisp, and the sky bluer than robins' eggs against the general blinding whiteness. My house smelled heavy with sleep, heavy with the warm, mingling breaths of my wife and daughter, my brother and Ruth wrapped in their blankets a seemly distance from one another on the floor. All the world was silent, for even the fire had burnt to its embers. I placed two logs upon it and blew gently into its heat, anxious for it to warm me, yet anxious not to wake the slumberers around me. Elizaveta's sleep, especially, seemed precious beyond words—so pink were her cheeks, so slow her delicate breath, that it seemed a miracle she lived day after day, month after month.

Leave it to the sons of dreamers, the grandsons of a child of the sea, I thought, looking out upon the white ground, to think that the world could end in a day—and such a fine day as this. I knew that I should spend the winter writing all these happenings down, making sure they remained intact for Elizaveta's children, but I also realized that it would serve me to return to work. Neither would work be bad for the progress of Mandrik's soul.

Ruth sat up when I opened the door to fetch water, Mandrik when I heaved the kettle over the fire. "Is it morning?" she whispered.

"Aye." I regarded my brother. "Do you now eat burnt bread at breakfast, like your future wife?"

Adelaïda turned in the bed. "Good morning, wife," I bade her.

She rustled in the blankets, but did not reply.

"No, I still eat my bread like an ordinary man."

"And you, wife? Will you have newfangled burnt bread? Your neighbors have seen the wonders without you, but you needn't be left behind."

She did not even sigh a response.

Mandrik rose from the floor, his knees creaking like a new harness, and pulled the covers back from Adelaïda's face. He touched the side of her neck with the back of his hand, and she started and rolled away. "She's still got this fever," he said, not specifically to anyone.

"No better than yesterday?" Ruth asked.

He stroked Adelaïda's forehead. "A bit worse."

Ruth looked through the things her brother and sister had left her, and retrieved a white object that rattled like a measure of dried beans. "Give her an aspirin," she said, dispensing two white seeds into his hand.

He said, "Okay," and dipped a cup in water to offer it to my wife.

Ruth stood to tuck Elizaveta farther into her hammock, and lingered there a moment, her cheek to the child's face. "Whatever it is, Elizaveta's got it, too."

"Got what?" I asked.

"Whatever. A head cold."

"No, I don't," my daughter said. "I want to get up."

"You're not sick?"

"No."

"Then get out of bed." Ruth hoisted her down. The child's cheeks were fiery, though, and her eyes as bright as glass.

I said, "I don't like this."

Mandrik said, "It's something every winter, isn't it? This year it's early, that's all."

"I feel fine," Elizaveta said. "I want tose."

Ruth smoothed down the child's sleep-ruffled braids. "What ever happened to the toast you were going to make, Yves?"

I looked about at them. "I don't know."

"I'll make it."

"I'm going home for more herbs, and be back by midday," Mandrik said, drawing his stockings on under his cassock.

"And plum jam," Ruth added. "Bring more jam."

"You don't want to go across the hills?" I asked him.

He shook his head.

A cart came quietly up the road and into my yard. I had opened the door before Ydlbert dismounted. "Hail," I said. "I did not expect to see you again so soon."

"Is your brother about? The fire's gone out in his hearth."

"He's here. Can we offer you tea and burnt bread?"

He stamped his boots on the threshold and they shed a thick layer of snow. He looked bashfully from Mandrik to Ruth, then at the floor. "No, thank you. Perhaps a moment by your fire?"

I stepped aside to let him, dripping, pass. "Your family is well, I pray?"

"Not so well as I might hope—Dirk's struck dumb with fever." I tried to gauge the panic in his voice; it did not seem overweening. "He seemed fine last night, perhaps merely to be confined to the house a day or two; but this morning he's stuck between sleep and waking, and hot as a branding iron. I was hoping, Mandrik, you could bring him some herbs? I don't want my other sons to catch it, and I'm at my wit's end. I've already tried the spell."[1]

Mandrik drew his fingers through his hair. "Only so much the spell can work for. Come with me, man; I was headed home to fetch herbs for Adelaïda. I can get more."

"Still with fever?"

"Aye, and the child." He looked back and forth between us, two fathers, aging with so much care. "No need to look so bleak. Everyone gets a fever."

Ydlbert nodded.

"Ydlbert, when your family is better," Ruth said, "I'd like to hear more about your trip over the mountains."

Ydlbert shifted in his boots. "Aye, but for now let's get done with the herbs."

She poured two cups of near-boiling water—without even any peppermint—into cups for them, and bade them drink before they set out upon the road. Mandrik kissed her cheek—turning my stomach, and bringing a flinching smile to Ydlbert's worn face—and they set out into the bright, still morning.

The house's quiet began to seem unnatural. Ruth bundled Elizaveta into bed beside her mother and wiped their two slick foreheads with a cloth. "Would you like me to sing?" she asked.

My eyebrows raised so high I thought they might lift past my hair. "You can sing?"

"Not really," she said. "Not well. But I would if it would cheer you

---

[1] *Spirits of the North,*
Call the Demon forth.
Spirits of the South,
Draw it from the Mouth.
Spirits of the East,
Bring the Soul to Peace.
Spirits of the West,
Give the Soul her Rest.

up. Would it help you to do some work? It'd take your mind off things."

She was, I admitted, coming to know me well. "Aye, we're short of firewood still, and I must mend the chinks in Enyadatta's stall before the worst of the weather sets in. Else she's likely to take her death before spring."

"Then go ahead and work. I can watch them."

She looked as if she knew her business with the cloth.

"Really, Yves. I'll call you if there's trouble."

I lit a torch from the fire and carried it to the barn. The fire had gone out, and the sheep huddled against one another, complaining as if an unforgivable sin had been perpetrated against them. "Quiet," I told them as I cobbled together a fire, but they continued to cry. It set Enyadatta to stomping for emphasis upon the floor of her stall, and Vringle, the billy goat, to chewing at one of the beams. "Stop that," I said, kicking him as I placed the torch in Enyadatta's post. When I picked up the rake, Yoshu came bounding out, covered in hay, and rolled at my feet like a snake trying to escape its own skin. She irked me, but I rubbed her belly anyway. "Stop that," I said. "I have work to do." Still the animals went on with their frolicking commentary while I brought out their dung and gave them fresh hay and clean water. My breath, and their breath, rose in sad, pale clouds. I was consumed with worry for my invalids, but as long as Ruth would tend to them, I would stay here, among my charges, where I also belonged.

I took a chamois from the wall and wiped down the surface of the worktable I had built. It had splinters yet, so I honed it again with a sharp knife, and swept the shavings toward the billy goat's pen that he might eat them.

However dark the winter proved, I resolved to preserve this—all of this—against what I perceive to be the inevitable encroachment of the future. All this time, when we have looked back at how things used to be, we have praised God for showing us how to better ourselves. Now I see that the future—this future we have begun living now—leapt out with its rapacious mouth open to swallow us. What will come up out of the west I cannot say, but I am frightened of its hum and its terrible energy. I knew, as I stood that day in my barn, that I had a winter to spare to keep this story, the story of who we were before the approaching change, alive, in the dim hope that someone, among Ruth's people or my own, would read and understand. I was lucky in my home, my prosperity, my ability to make meaningful marks with pen and ink; and this much would have to suffice. I opened my box, which had not come from Indo-China, and inside were my supplies, as I had placed them: a measure of Mandrik's black ink, two pens I had whittled with my back to the fire. When I touched them, they were full of the barn's autumn chill. But there they had waited for me, and there would they remain.

The desk offered succor, and relief from my cares. I could work until my brother returned with his poultices and tea. I could begin this tale. This work would not wait until the dark days of the New Year, nor even until tomorrow. There is no waiting on such a project, so quickly do things change.

My brother did not return till nightfall. During that time I had gone to the house but once to see that my wife and daughter still made their way among the living. Ruth regarded me then with worried eyes, but we did not speak. My brother had been far longer afield than he'd expected, and there were deep, bruise-like marks beneath his eyes. The cold had chapped the rest of his face like a beet. "What overtook you?" I asked, half angry at having to return to the house, half wild with relief at his return. "Spirits at the crossroads?"

He draped his dripping cloak over the bench and set his sodden shoes by the fire. "Illness throughout the parish. Half the village lies home abed."

"Who's taken ill?"

"Vashti Nethering, Ion Gansevöort, Prugne Martin; Dirk must have given it to her."

"Given what? What has he given?"

"Whatever illness it is."

My heart felt cold. "You have not seen it before?"

"I have seen others like it. It's not a plague, certainly. Some kind of flu."

"Not—"

"I don't know, Yves."

"If you have another chicken to spare," Ruth said, "chicken soup would be good for them."

"Absolutely," my brother agreed.

Adelaïda was curled like a mother cat about our daughter.

"More are ill than you mentioned?" I asked.

"It's winter, man. People take ill. Go kill one of your hens."

"You left them all with remedies?"

"Of course."

"Are they likely—"

"I wish you wouldn't discuss it." He spat into the fire, which sizzled. "Put the pot on, Ruth. We'll see what tomorrow brings."

"I don't want to wait and see."

"You've no choice."

Ruth took the water pail out into the cold night.

"Surely, if this illness has come from the people over the hill—"

"Who said it had?"

"—then they have the remedy? Surely, if their carts drive without horses—"

"There's no cure for the flu," Ruth said, spilling some of the frigid water onto my feet as she poured it into the cauldron. "Though if you're worried, we could take them to the hospital."

"The what?"

She and my brother watched one another. "Do you think we should?" he asked.

She said, "I don't know. I don't know where the nearest hospital is. It'll take two days to get to a phone to find out."

"Let us see what the morning brings."

I slaughtered a chicken in the barn. The other animals smelled first its fear and then its blood, and cried out in indignation. As Ruth boiled the warm carcass for her soup, I lay on the bed, my stomach to the back of my wife, my arm around both her and Elizaveta. Their bodies had begun to smell stale from sweat and lack of washing. This bed had already taken my father, mother, brothers, sister, first wife and child—it could not take one thing more. If need be, we could cart them to the hills and carry them on our backs to the other village. I had no more qualms about it if their lives would be saved.

I could not sleep that night, though Ruth and Mandrik slept well.

Friedl Vox was about the parish, ululating despite the blanket of snow, her shrill cry piercing the fragile silence of my home. The fear of death gripped my bowels, and I waited for the ghosts of the departed to come reassure me, to give me a sign—but they did not come. Neither could I give much succor to the sick, for they slept peacefully, though the fever ate at their flesh. The night expanded, grew so large it filled the weeks and centuries, and when I could no longer stand my home's closeness, I returned to the barn, where the gleaming eyes of my beasts told me they had expected my return, known from the beginning that I could not keep away. I placed my torch in the holder by Enyadatta's stall, and wrote as if the writing would save me, would save my whole family, if not from death, then from the terror of being forgotten.

In the morning, my brother set out around the village to tend to the sick. As he went from house to house ministering to the stricken, he read aloud at each stopping place this proclamation:

"In the midst of Darkness we are in Light, but lo! in the center of the light does there burn a rank and consuming darkness, and it burns with the heat of a thousand Suns, its one desire to consume. This world is in darkness. What, though enlightenment be ours and the breath of God animate every atom of our beings; what if we are his children, his image, and his fondest dreams? We are a vile and sickening lot. With so much Joy and Wonderment all around—hanging ripe for the picking from every tree, as well as lodged deep within the mind and heart—we turn always to our Darkest Selves, our ugliest instincts, and follow them wherever they may lead. Even in my solitude and my renunciation, how oft have I been tempted down the road to eternal ruin by no beckon louder than my own silent thought? If my own mind—my truest Companion since first I rocked in my mother's arms—can turn against me thus, imagine how many and various are the perils offered by the Devil, and by his Body and Spirit, this World. Think each poppy in the field a drop of poison, for who knows where its influence may lead you.

"Our forebears knew little of History. What need had they of facts and dates when they knew when the crops wanted gathering? What changed from father to son but the proper Name, and perhaps the tilt of the nose? We are the first men to have need of what came before; for without it, we cannot divine our destination, or what kind of progress we are making there toward. My own brother has set this deadly rock in motion, and it will continue to roll downhill, past whatever comes into its path, until it comes to rest of its own accord.

"I urge you, my Brethren, to Caution and Reflection in the face of all that is new."

I have been writing these two weeks now, night and day, hardly sleeping, eating what Ruth and my no-longer-holy brother bring me because I feel I must, not because I have any longer an ounce of appetite. The days grow shorter, palpably shorter—though the shortest day fast approaches, it will be months before they feel longer again. We are all of us together in this darkness. My wife and daughter yet lie abed—nor our prayers nor our physic will raise them, but neither have they chosen to walk among the dead. Our neighbors to the west have come twice now, bearing such devices as Ruth's countrymen bore, and with medicines for the sick, and women and men versed in the medicines. They have taken three of Ydlbert's sons across the water to a home for invalids where they may heal more quickly than those who hang in the balance here at home. Our newfound brethren are mad with questions, and everywhere they travel they send beams of light tearing through the countryside and our homes, which brightness strikes terror into my heart.

I am done my inventing. I have done too much already, if this be the result. If I have overstepped my bounds, then I pray that God is as merciful and kind as ever I supposed He must be, and that I will be spared the worst of this punishment. For now, I can hope only that this account, and Ruth's account, and my brother's fair treatise, will leave adequate record, no matter what may come of these individual lives, which are, in the end, as dross. I cannot stop thinking of my daughter's small hand, raised in farewell as Ruth's brother and sister left for the other world. I can only hope that her gesture sent forth, as surely she intended it to, our benedictions. For I have faith in God, and in the rightness of this world He has created. Surely, surely, it could not be any other way.

ACKNOWLEDGMENTS

I wish to thank the Michener-Copernicus Society and the Vogelstein Foundation for their generous financial support.

Many thanks to my editor, Ethan Nosowsky, and my agent, Eric Simonoff, for their insight, wit, patience, and good fellowship; to Laura Harger and Max Curry for helping to translate the primordial ooze into a legible early draft; and to Chris Adrian for being the kindest of readers.

And many, many thanks to my teachers, my family, and my friends.